BREAKING AWAY

BOOK 3 OF THE SEAL TEAM HEARTBREAKERS

TERESA J. REASOR

DEDICATION

To all the families of our men and women at arms, thank you for your many sacrifices. Without you standing firm and keeping the home fires burning, they could not do the job they do. God Bless you.

And to the Lethal Ladies. You are the bomb!

Contact Information: teresareasor@msn.com

Cover Art by Tracy Stewart
Edited by Faith Freewoman

Teresa J. Reasor
PO Box 124
Corbin, KY 40702

Publishing History: First Edition 2013
ISBN 13: 978-09850069-5-2
ISBN 10: 0985006951
Print Edition

Table of Contents

FOREWORD

Breaking Away came to me as two separate stories, and is told in that way for the first third of the book. I wanted you, dear Reader, to know the *whole* story of what had happened to Lieutenant Junior Grade Harold Timothy Carney, better known as *Flash* to his team members, and to the readers of the first two SEAL Team Heartbreakers books, who have patiently waited for his story.

And I felt it important for you to know how Samantha came to be where she needed to be, physically and emotionally, so she could find her way into Flash's arms and heart.

Most books will begin in the middle of the action, or the mid point instead of the beginning. But that would have left many questions about Flash and Samantha's circumstances and meant a great deal of backstory would have cluttered up the story. So, I've broken a *romance* rule and given you Flash and Samantha's *whole* story, in the order it happened, just as it unfolded to me.

I hope you enjoy *Breaking Away.*
Teresa J. Reasor

PART ONE
OF
BREAKING AWAY

GOING IT ALONE

PROLOGUE

Lieutenant Junior Grade Harold 'Flash' Carney sighted, one by one, the four tangos on the adjoining roof through the thermal scope of his MK-11 sniper rifle. Each sentry guarded a corner of the building, making it damn hard for his guys to slip inside. With the suppressor on his rifle to muffle the report, he could take out two, maybe three of the guards, but the fourth might just make it down the stairs to warn the fuckers below of his team's presence. He'd have to wait. *Shit!*

Despite the chill in the Iraqi night air, sweat ran along his spine beneath his body armor. He ignored it. Every breath tasted like dust, as though the sun had scorched the earth earlier in the day and kicked ash into the air. He suppressed the urge to spit and, with a grimace, swallowed.

Hawk's signal on the com system clicked in his ear. He was already inside the building and in position. Good.

A man slithered up to a window on the back side of the structure, cut a hole in the glass, then reached through to unlock and raise the pane. He slid inside soundlessly and signaled. It was Bowie. Another man followed close behind him. Doc. A few minutes later more clicks sounded. Strong Man and Cutter.

And now Flash waited, keeping the four tangos in his sights. The lull gave him too much time to think about the visitors he'd met with back at the base. Cutter was on his ass to tell him what was going on, but he couldn't. They'd ordered him to keep this secret. Their reason—members of his team could be involved in something illegal.

That was bullshit. He knew these guys. He'd place his life in any of their hands without a second thought.

You couldn't find a more stand-up commanding officer than Adam "Hawk" Yazzie.

Zach "Doc" O'Connor was one of the best medics in the teams, and had risked his life more times than Flash could count to recover the wounded and keep them alive. No way would he to even think of doing anything as dishonorable as smuggling.

Other than fishing and women, Dan "Bowie" Rivera didn't spend any money and had no financial woes. So, no reason to smuggle.

Oliver "Greenback" Shaker, the only married member, wouldn't do anything that would take him away from his wife and new baby.

Flash had discovered by accident an assault charge against Derrick "Strong Man" Armstrong had been dropped a few months before their deployment. Could someone be blackmailing him into smuggling for them? Flash couldn't see it. With Strong Man's anger issues, they wouldn't last long enough to compromise him. He'd pound them into the ground.

Brett "Cutter" Weaver was the counselor of the group. If anyone had a problem, they'd be dishing to him. In fact he'd gotten the impression Strong Man had been doing just that on the helo before the drop. He'd talk to Cutter and see if together they could figure out what was going on with Strong Man. Just in case. He'd have to be slick about it. Cutter was a vault when someone confided in him. Which was why the guys used him as a sounding board.

As he maintained a watch on the rooftop tangos and the street below, Flash resisted the urge to wipe the trail of sweat that streaked down his cheek from beneath his Boonie hat. He could understand why NCIS had approached him about this assignment. He knew all the guys in the company well, and he had gambling issues. When he was flush he was flush. And when he was down…

It made sense to choose the one team member with a history of financial ups and downs, with a history of gambling, for this undercover assignment. His apparent addiction left the impression that he could be compromised. The thought twisted his gut with anger and pain. He wasn't addicted to gambling. He used his trips to Vegas to supplement his income, but he wasn't addicted.

Or was he?

Hawk's clicks sounded over the com, jerking Flash out of his reverie. The prearranged signal notified everyone on the team he'd finished placing his charges and exited the building. Strong Man's clicks sounded soon after. Flash's attention jumped briefly to the men on the roof, then dropped again to watch the movement on the street below. He spied Doc and Bowie through the thermal scope, as they crawled out through the same window they'd entered. Their identities were verified by their clicks moments later. Where the hell was Cutter?

Minutes crept by. His muscles tightened with tension. The timers connected to the C-4 were running. They needed to get the fuck out of here. Why hadn't Cutter checked in?

"We have a problem," Derrick "Strong Man" Armstrong said, breaking radio silence.

For a moment those words clanged through Flash's head like alarm bells.

Derrick cut through his reaction with, "C's a no show, over."

How the hell could Strong Man sound so fucking calm?

"Cutter, come in, over." Hawk's voice, holding much the same even tone, was met with silence.

Flash took a deep breath and homed in on one of the sentries. Had Cutter been attacked inside? Captured? No. These terrorist assholes would be going ape shit if they'd discovered him. Something else was going on. Could Cutter's com system have screwed up?

"Last location, over?" Hawk asked.

"Ground floor. I thought he was right behind me," Derrick replied.

"Five minutes," Greenback's voice came over the com.

Why the fuck had they opted to go old school with the explosives?

Because the structure of the buildings made a remote receiver unreliable. And they'd wanted to be far, far away before it went off.

"I'm going back in for him, over," Hawk said.

Shit! Flash mouthed the word. His heartbeat cranked up, pounding in his throat, his temples.

He checked the location of the rooftop sentries.

Minutes ticked by like hours. One of the sentries called down to someone on the street and Flash eased the rifle barrel in that direction. The man on the street answered and slipped inside.

Movement to the right caught Flash's attention and he turned just as a man slithered into the window Bowie and Doc had exited through before. The man's Boonie hat fell off and landed on the ground beneath the window. Who the hell was it? Flash's thermal imager only showed the man in white, without any identifying details.

Shit! Three members of the team were inside a building rigged to explode in three minutes. *Jesus!*

And he was sitting up here, unable to do a damn thing to help.

The sound of an MP-5 submachine gun came from inside the building, and two of the armed sentries ran toward the rooftop door. Flash sighted the lead runner and took him down. The second man paused just long enough for Flash to pick him off, too.

The other sentries took up a position at the front of the building. All hell broke loose down on the street as his team fired, lighting up their positions. The two sentries dropped behind the low brick wall bordering the roof.

Flash looked though his scope at the thermal images. A tango popped up, raised his rifle, took aim. Flash fired. The guy's skull shattered, sending fragments into the air. The other terrorist turned to run, and Flash picked him off, too.

He swung his rifle toward the street. A man emerged from the building carrying a limp body over his shoulder. Oh, shit! It had to be Hawk and Cutter. Hawk had zigzagged only three quarters of the way across the street when the charges they'd set went off. The rumble of the detonation was a rushing train barreling straight at them, and the ground rose beneath Hawk's feet in a wave, throwing him forward. The body he carried flew through the air and landed a few feet ahead of him at an awkward angle. The building they'd bombed leapt at least a foot in the air, then caved in on itself as the lower floors collapsed.

The roof Flash knelt on shuddered and shook as a dust cloud rose with the speed of a sandstorm, blocking his view. Rifle tucked against him, he rolled from his crouched position, grabbed his pack and raced for the stairs.

Cutter was dead. He had to be dead. He hadn't even tried to catch himself. Nausea hit Flash's stomach and he swallowed it back. They had to move out. And the other teammate, the one who'd climbed in through the window, was he buried in the debris? Was he dead?

Flash hit the door, and for a moment the darkness in the stairwell closed in around him. He shouldered his pack and paused to allow his eyes to adjust, his heart thundering in his ears.

He pounded down the rickety, uneven steps, his boots clattering and echoing as he went. Every terrorist within a ten-mile radius would be homing in on their position. *They had to get out of here.* He hit the door running, but pulled up to look out onto the street.

"Flash. What's your position?" Hawk's voice came over the com. He sounded out of breath.

"I'm a hundred feet east from your position."

"Stay where you are, we're on our way."

The dust hadn't yet settled on the street when four men hobbled out of the cloud, gritty sand and concrete debris painting them a ghostly gray-white. Doc supported Hawk on his left side. Strong Man had shouldered Cutter's dead weight in a fireman's carry, and Bowie brought up the rear, his MP-5 submachine gun at the ready. None wore a Boonie hat or helmet. Which one of them had disappeared solo into the building while Hawk searched for Cutter? And how the hell had he gotten out?

"On point, Flash," Hawk said, cradling his MP-5 against his right side his finger hovering above the trigger.

"Movement from the east here," Greenback said through the com from his position directly ahead, where he'd been guarding their back door.

Every nerve in Flash's body went on high alert as they hoofed it down the street toward Greenback.

"Patrol coming at you," Greenback announced. Flash signaled *go for cover*, though the men were already scattering into the dark doorways and alleys along the way.

A truck sped past. A few moments later more tangos followed on foot. Lights came on in some of the buildings surrounding them while shouts sounded from up the block.

Flash stepped out of the alleyway and hugged the shadows as he double-timed to the end of the block to scout out their position. A crowd moved up one of the side streets. He dodged into the open door of an abandoned building and thumbed his com button. "More movement coming from the side streets from the east. Drop back one block west."

He took his own advice and circled around to the next block. A man stepped out onto the cracked sidewalk, a rifle cradled in the bend of his arm. Every muscle tensed, Flash sank back into a doorway and froze. The man jogged past him in the direction of the crowd.

They had to get out of the area *right fucking now*. Flash ran past the last two doorways and, sliding along the edge of the structure, slipped into the alley behind it. He signaled on the com and the team stepped out of hiding and hustled toward him. Derrick was breathing hard from carrying Cutter's two hundred pounds plus his pack, so Bowie gave Strong Man a breather by taking Cutter, while Strong Man moved to the rear.

"We have to get off the street," Flash said quietly. He radioed Greenback with coordinates. Two minutes later Greenback joined them.

"I've scouted a location where we can hole up and triage," Greenback said. He led them through a network of dark alleys into one of the abandoned buildings. A small section of stairs leading to the second floor hung suspended by twisted metal supports, the rest having been blown away. "This way," Greenback motioned them through a hallway to a back staircase that looked somewhat more stable. Flash climbed the stairs on point.

The building was a complex of one bedroom apartments. Flash positioned Greenback on the stairs and took Strong Man with him to do a room-to-room check of the second floor, then returned to the others.

"It's clear," Flash said.

Doc settled the two injured men in one of the rooms at the back of the structure. Hawk lowered himself to the floor while Bowie, with Doc's help, laid Cutter next to him.

Flash stood by, poised to help, as Doc broke open his pack, snapped and shook a glow stick for some light and examined Cutter. "He's got a concussion for sure. I can feel a massive bump on the side of his head, and one of his pupils is sluggish. He may have a fractured skull. He's not going to come round any time soon. We need to make a stretcher."

What the hell had happened to Cutter?

Hawk used his SOG knife to split the seam of his pants and exposed a knee puffed up like a soccer ball. More bad news, as he clearly wasn't going to be able to walk on that leg.

Since Doc and Bowie were helping the wounded, Flash said, "I'll take care of the stretcher." He worked his way through the rooms one by one, looking for any kind of supports he could use. Five apartments down the hall he found an old bed frame. The mattress was long gone, but the bed frame was still nailed together. He jerked the structure up, and using his SOG knife, loosened the nails enough to tear the sides free of the head and footboard. Then he jogged down the hall to the stairwell to hit up Greenback and Strong Man for their t-shirts.

Returning to the room Doc was using as a temporary ER, Flash set aside his rifle and the boards. While Bowie finished wrapping Hawk's knee Flash scrounged the other teammates' t-shirts and created a stretcher for Cutter. Now they needed to get the hell out of here.

"I've positioned Strong Man at the east corner of the building. Bowie, take a position on the west," Flash said.

"Roger," Bowie said and jogged from the room.

Flash reported to Hawk, "Greenback is covering the stairwell, and I'm setting up a defensive position on the roof if I can find a way up there."

In the dull light of the glow stick, he watched Doc insert an IV into Cutter's arm.

"As soon as Doc has Cutter stabilized we'll move out. They'll be expanding their search for us," Hawk said. "And we only have an hour to make it to the extraction point.

"Roger that."

Flash pulled a map from his pack. Now their route was compromised, they'd have to plot an alternate. Using the light of the glow stick, he and Hawk plotted a new course that might get them to the extraction coordinates in time.

Finding no way to get to the roof, Flash took position at the south side of the building. Movement up and down the street, sporadic at first, grew more frequent with every passing moment. His tension escalated.

"We're moving out," Hawks voice came over the com.

Flash's relief was short lived. As he double-timed it down the hall, he had to wonder how the hell they were going to slip through enemy lines with a man on a stretcher.

They'd find a way. *They never left a man behind.*

And if they had to, they'd fight their way across Fallujah.

Bowie and Strong Man took up the stretcher. Doc secured the IV bag between Cutter's legs, then moved to help Hawk keep the weight off his injured knee. That left only Flash and Greenback to cover the team front and back.

Greenback led them to the back entrance of the building while Flash stepped out into the alley and worked his way to the southern end. Seeing the street deserted, he gave the all clear. The rest of the team followed him west across several streets and along alleys littered with refuse and sewage.

Two pickup trucks sped past through the intersection ahead of them, followed by a group of twenty men on foot. He signaled the team to take cover as he pulled up tight against the rough concrete building. The air that had felt clammy before seemed to cling to his skin like mist. The weight of his pack scraped against the building and tugged at his shoulders. His grip on his rifle tightened and sweat trickled between his shoulder blades.

As they waited, Bowie and Strong Man crouched over the stretcher, shielding Cutter from possible attack. The building's back door swung open with a clang and a young boy of perhaps eight darted into the alley. Dim light from the stairwell spilled over Strong Man and he looked up, his blond, close-cropped hair exaggerating his American features. Time slowed to a crawl.

Flash's stomach cramped as he leveled his rifle, the only suppressed weapon in the group, and targeted the boy. His heart lurched. *Dear God, he couldn't kill a kid.*

The child's eyes widened and he staggered back, and would have sprung back up the stairs, had Hawk not shoved the door closed and leaned back against it. The light cut off, Flash blinked and waited for his vision to readjust to the dark, but he was aware of movement as the kid pivoted to flee.

Once his vision cleared, he saw Strong Man had the kid hugged back against his much larger frame, his hand covering his mouth. He reached his free hand inside his TAC vest and the boy froze. Strong Man extended his hand. A candy bar lay in his palm. His softly breathed words didn't reach Flash, but the boy's body relaxed and after a moment he nodded, reached for the candy, then snatched it out of Strong Man's hand.

Strong Man continued to speak close to the boy's ear until the terrorists had passed. Flash watched the men's progress down the street, then gave the all clear.

Strong Man released the kid, patted his shoulder, then took up the stretcher. Flash looked back to see the boy standing at the corner watching their progress down the next alley.

If he alerted his family—

But hurting a kid wasn't an option. He was an innocent bystander.

They had to get the fuck out of Dodge!

They moved west through an area of buildings that had been scarred and damaged by heavy artillery. Rubble clogged the streets, and it was slow going. But the surrounding wreckage also insured there were no civilians to contend with, and no patrolling militia.

The sound of an engine revving in the distance grabbed Flash's attention. The Iraqis seemed to have a never-ending supply of small pickups to transport men and weapons, and every one of them was rolling through the area searching for them right now. And coming damned close.

Flash strained to hear where the closest approaching pickup was located. When the sound dissipated into the distance he relaxed, only to tense again when male voices reached him from only fifty feet or so to the west. Right where they needed to go.

When the team reached the only structure still standing, Flash signaled a halt until the tangos passed.

"We're only about three hundred meters from the pickup point," Hawk muttered.

It might as well be three thousand. How much longer could their luck hold?

The team slipped around the corner and double-timed it silently up the street. The sound of footsteps echoing through the silence reached Flash only an instant before a patrol turned the corner directly in their path. The entire street stretched before them, concrete slabs, sand, and nothing else. The little asphalt remaining on the road was old and crushed by heavy traffic. Only the concrete walls the Iraqis usually built around their houses offered cover. Finding a breach in one of the structures surrounding a business, Flash motioned for the team to take cover behind the barrier. Once they were concealed, he slid in behind Greenback and braced his back against the wall.

Moments later, footsteps crunched the gritty concrete debris on the other side of the wall. With an effort, he kept his breathing slow and easy, but rested his finger on his rifle's trigger. Adrenaline pumped through his system in a rush, warming his cheeks. Every nerve in his body fired. His hearing became hypersensitive to the sounds emanating from the other side of the wall.

The barrel of a rifle, followed by a head and shoulders, thrust through the breach they'd used. Flash tensed, ready to swing his rifle toward the tango.

"Gabir."

The man turned back toward the voice behind him, his AK-47 disappearing from sight.

The voice continued in Arabic, "We will go south and help search the buildings. The Americans have to be hiding there."

The tangos' movements grew fainter as they continued down the street. Flash drew a shaky breath and heard Greenback do the same. He fell in behind the tangos, and, using his rifle's thermal scope, monitored their progress up the street. He turned the scope farther north. Nothing.

"It's clear for now. Move out." At this rate they were going to miss their pickup window, and there were more patrols looking for them every minute. Shouts came from up the street and the sound of a truck accelerating revved from somewhere close by.

The team broke into a trot. Flash glanced over his shoulder and saw the grimace of pain on Hawk's face, but he was keeping up without Doc's aid. It would be really good if they could find transport about now. A truck came around the corner, swinging wide, the vehicle's headlights highlighting every detail of their position. The three men in the truck bed opened fire.

CHAPTER 1

THREE MONTHS LATER
San Diego, California

This would be over in an hour and he'd be back to his old life. He'd go fishing with Doc and Bowie. And hang with Cutter and help him with his physical therapy, if he needed it.

If we don't get called up.

Flash picked up the Babylonian stone seals from the kitchen counter, wrapped them carefully in bubble wrap and shoved them into the gym bag. He'd complete the meet he'd set up, the FBI would move in, and that would be the end of this mess. *Thank you, Jesus!*

He studied the seven-by-five inch stone tablet, the real gem of the FBI sting. Why would anyone want a hunk of stone with cuneiform writing on it? And pay hundreds of thousands of dollars for it? It wasn't like they could hang it in their house and show it off to visitors. And even if they could, who would be interested in it besides other collectors? He wrapped it securely in the protective plastic and placed it in the gym bag as well.

Had anyone but Agent Rick Dobson asked him to do this mission, he'd have told him to fuck off. But he and the team had worked with Dobson on other missions in Iraq. And the guy's Intel had always been solid.

In the five months he'd taken part in this investigation, he'd felt isolated. Working with his SEAL team, hanging with them, had spoiled him to having backup. SEALs were pack animals. They worked together as a unit. Since taking on this assignment, he'd never been more aware of how much he depended on the guys.

Wasn't that just a kick in the balls? For someone who'd been so solitary his whole life, becoming a team player had been...difficult. It had taken him months to adjust to the dynamic of working cooperatively, and to learn to trust. And now he was back flying solo and didn't like it one bit.

After all the work he'd done to turn his life around as a teenager, playing the part of smuggler didn't come easy for him, either.

He picked up the letter from the counter. He'd never written one before. Never felt the need. He'd addressed it to Captain Jackson, to be passed on to Hawk. Hawk would understand why he'd remained mum about the investigation. As his commanding officer, Hawk was the ultimate professional and a trusted friend. He'd back him up with the guys and explain. And he'd know to visit Travis and Juanita to break the news. He slid the letter into his front jacket pocket.

His cell phone vibrated. He thrust his hand into his jeans pocket and dragged it free. "Carney."

"Everything's a go," Dobson's partner, Eric Gilbert said. "Remember this is just like the other two drops you've done for us."

"I still don't like this last-minute change. Why would these guys decide to move their operation onto American soil? They have a lot more control of the situation across the border."

"We've been over this before, Carney. Just do this drop and you're done."

Fuck. He didn't want to do this. "Okay. I'll be there at six."

"Don't be late."

Flash bit back an impatient retort and instead hung up.

He didn't like that guy. But then distrust ran deep for a guy who'd spent most of his early years in foster care. His wariness had led him to pay Gilbert's house a visit. He'd done a little snooping and hacked into the guy's personal computer. The only incriminating thing he'd found on the man's machine was a little porn.

And still that itch niggled between his shoulder blades. Like being in the cross hairs of a rifle's scope and the bullet had his name on it. What had set off this edgy awareness? Something about the last meeting he'd had with Dobson and Gilbert. But he couldn't quite put his finger on it.

Reaching out to anyone on his team wasn't an option. It was already too late.

After a brief moment, Flash picked up his Sig Saur P226 from the counter. Gilbert had instructed him to come unarmed, but he'd be damned if he'd do it. The gun was registered to him and he had a permit to carry. He tucked the gun into his waistband at the hollow of his back and pulled his windbreaker over it.

Flash checked his watch, grasped the handles of the duffle, and walked from the pocket-sized kitchen into the living room. He looked around his barren apartment. Certain the smugglers had someone watching him, he'd rented this place to help make it look like his lucky streak had taken a nosedive, and left the leased Porsche in a parking structure. The car's disappearance would be more telling than the missing electronics. He'd pick up the car and his stuff from the storage unit as soon as this bullshit was over.

One more hour and he'd get back to his life.

He rolled his head in an attempt to relieve the tension building across his shoulders. *Just one more hour.* He shut the door behind him and strode down the hall to the elevator.

Behind the wheel of his Toyota, he pulled into the San Diego traffic, turned onto Euclid Avenue, and looped through a bank parking lot to drop the letter to Hawk into a postal box. If nothing happened, he was gold. If it did, Hawk would know what went down. He pulled through the lot and turned east up a back street behind it.

He had to shake free of all distraction and focus. Just get the job done.

A black SUV swerved into his lane and kept coming at him. Flash jerked the wheel to the right and stomped the gas pedal. His car swept around the larger vehicle with only a gnat's ass worth of space between them. *Prick. What the hell was wrong with him?* He couldn't afford to get into a traffic accident before the buy went down. He floored the gas pedal.

In his rearview mirror, the SUV spun around and followed him. He glanced at the bag in the passenger seat. *Shit!*

The SUV grew large in the mirror. Its bumper crowded close. Adrenaline kicked through Flash's system and his breathing quickened, but he shoved the feelings aside as he strained to see the driver through the tinted windows. Sun glanced off the glass making it impossible, and nearly blinding him.

He whipped into a parking lot, raced through to the other side, and turned a corner. The larger vehicle followed, but he managed to put some space between them. Turning north on Euclid, Flash merged into the line of traffic and kept an eye on the black vehicle, which now lurked three cars back.

Tension ratcheted tighter across his shoulders and up the back of his neck. He turned onto Home Avenue. The SUV continued on Euclid. Some of his tension eased, but he remained hyper-aware of the other vehicles around him.

Ten minutes later he circled the storage facility, checking the tops of the buildings for snipers before pulling his car into the parking lot. He turned the car so it faced the open gate and parked in front of the large metal structure as instructed.

How many high-priority missions had he participated in during the six months he'd been stationed in Iraq? At least sixty. But they'd used him almost continuously as a sniper.

How many times had he felt that contraction between his shoulder blades, as though his body were bracing for a bullet? Only twice. And both times his instincts had been on the mark.

Something wasn't right. But he'd given his word. He had to see this through and help get these guys. And a SEAL never gave up. Not unless he was dead.

A black SUV pulled around the corner and stopped twenty feet in front of him.

Showtime. Sweat ran from his armpits down his sides.

Was it the same SUV that had played chicken with him before? Two men got out of the vehicle. He recognized his contact, Unger—no first name, just Unger. And the other guy, his protection.

Flash grabbed the handles on the gym bag and opened the car door. His heart rate tripped into a jog and his breathing quickened. The hair on the back of his neck stood up. He resisted the urge to turn and look behind him and instead focused on the two men walking toward him. One carried a bag, the other held his hands out, away from his body but close to the bulge of his pistol.

Flash eased out of the car, and swept the area and the rooftops again. *Nothing.*

He straightened and sauntered forward. "Unger." He nodded to the man holding the bag. He'd passed on other small items the FBI had given him without a problem, but those were just warm-ups for this one. Flash set his gym bag on the asphalt at his feet. Unger did the same.

"Go," Unger said.

Flash shoved the bag with his toe, sending it forward at the same time Unger slid his across the space toward him.

Flash's phone vibrated against his hip, but he ignored it and bent to open the container and check the money. It lay in nice neat bundles in the bottom of the bag. *A hundred thousand dollars' worth.* Looping his hand through the handle, he straightened.

His phone vibrated again, and he half reached for it, then hesitated, his head still bent. He almost missed the distinctive sound, like the air itself had been displaced. A wet spray splattered his face.

Instinct kicked in and he hit the asphalt. Unger tumbled to the ground next to him, his face now a crater filled with brains, blood, and splintered bone. In the second it took to register the other man's death, Flash rolled toward the front of his car for cover, hugging the bag full of money to his chest. Unger's sidekick fell to the ground, his chest bloody, his hand clenched on the grip of his holstered sidearm.

The coppery scent of blood blended with the oily smell of asphalt. Bits of bone and gray matter clung to his windbreaker. Flash's stomach turned and he closed his eyes for a moment and fought back sickness. Heart pounding, he drew his Sig with his right hand and reached for his phone to call for backup with the other. Dobson's number flashed across the screen. He hit the receive button and speaker. Rick Dobson's voice came over the line, muffled. "Flash, you have to run. It's a setup. Get the hell out of—" A loud, familiar sound came over the connection and the line went dead.

That was a gunshot. Jesus! What the fuck is going on? He shoved his cell back into his pocket.

Keeping low, he edged to the car's headlight. He bobbed forward, searching for the sniper who'd fired on them. The next second he was on his back, his ears ringing. Darkness threatened to swamp him. He forced his eyes open and rolled to his knees. His fingers brushed the barrel of his Sig and he grabbed it. Blood ran down his cheek and dripped onto the asphalt beside his hand.

Jesus, he was hit!

Get on your feet. Get the hell out of here.

He waited for the earth to stop rocking and braced his shoulder against the car to keep parallel to the ground. He crawled forward. The bag of money lay close by. He shoved it around the side of the car and followed at a snail's pace. Blood trickled down his face and he used his jacket sleeve to wipe it away. Gray static filled his vision. Nausea crept up his throat and settled there.

If he lost consciousness he was a dead man. He dragged air into his lungs and forced his eyes open.

The sound of approaching footsteps reached him. He pushed the slide back on the Sig, checking the chambered round, and leaned back against the front quarter panel, trying to make himself as much a part of the vehicle as possible.

The barrel of a rifle came into view followed by a man dressed in black from head to toe, a ski mask covering his features. He pivoted to take aim and Flash fired, striking the rifle and sending up sparks. The man staggered, and dropped the weapon. Flash fired twice more striking him in the chest. The shooter dropped, his head thumping on the asphalt.

Movement came from the left and Flash was already firing as he turned to face it. A bullet ricocheted off the passenger door inches from his head, making his ears ring again. The second man dressed in black hit the asphalt, bleeding from bullet wounds to each thigh. As he fell, his rifle flew through the air to the right and slid across the asphalt stopping ten feet away.

With both men down, Flash staggered to his feet and kicked the rifles under the car. He bent over the man he'd shot in the chest, ran his hands over him checking for weapons, then jerked his shirt up. Kevlar had kept the bullets from penetrating, but he remained unconscious.

Flash wiped the blood back again as it streamed down the side of his head. He crossed to the man rolling on the ground in pain, bent and jerked the mask from the sniper's face.

A stranger.

"Who the fuck are you?" Flash demanded. His temple pounded with every beat of his heart.

"Fuck you," the man answered.

Not an acceptable answer, since the son of a bitch had shot him. He kicked him in the head and the sniper went still, unconscious.

He flipped back the shooter's jacket, pulled a wallet from the inside pocket, and opened it. A badge glared up at him. His heart seized along with his breath. *FBI. He'd shot an FBI agent.*

These guys had been sent to assassinate him, Unger, and his sidekick. To kill them all.

What the fuck was going on? Who had arranged this? Was it Gilbert?

He reached for his cell phone and hit speed dial. The phone rang and rang, then went to Dobson's voice mail. It *was* a gunshot he'd heard. He was certain of it. *Was Dobson dead? And where the hell was Gilbert*? He ended the call without leaving a message.

The only two agents he'd worked with were Dobson and Gilbert, and Dobson had called to warn him of a setup. Had Gilbert set up this assassination?

When he found the bastard, he was going to take him out—slowly. Very, *very* slowly.

CHAPTER 2

Las Vegas, Nevada

A child's wail reached into the protective darkness and pulled her toward consciousness. It must be Joy, crying. Her child's distress dragged Samantha further toward awareness. She tried to lift her head, but it felt heavy like it was glued to the…It *was* the floor she was lying on. As consciousness returned, pain ricocheted through her body like the recoil of a bungee cord. She groaned. The last thing she remembered was Will's fist coming at her face.

Joy's insistent cries pierced her muddled thoughts. *Have to go to her.* She bunched her knees beneath her and attempted to rise. Her jaw was numb, her vision blurred in one eye, and her arms shook as she pushed her upper body free of the floor. Nausea rolled over her and she gagged. She curled in on herself and pressed her forehead to the floor as dry heaves convulsed her body, intensifying every ache.

Once the sickness passed, she breathed in and out, afraid any further movement might make it return. *Phone. I need the phone.* God, her face hurt. She hurt. *Oh God, the baby!* Fear charged through her. She touched her lower abdomen where an achy cramping had taken root. She looked down her body to her shorts. Her legs were coated with blood. A sharp wail escaped her and blended with Joy's cries. He'd killed their baby. She was miscarrying.

No. No.

She curled on her side and waited for the pain to recede. The sound of a phone ringing broke through her pain. The living room looked like a war zone. Furniture was toppled. The lamps broken. The coffee table had been destroyed by a brutal stomp. It lay beside her, two legs broken off. The muffled ring sounded from beneath it.

She hadn't walked away when she should have. The first time he'd slapped her, she should have left. But he'd threatened to kill her if she did. And now their unborn child was dying because she hadn't had the courage to stand up to him. *Oh, God!*

She'd run for the phone and Will had wrenched it from her hand. And punched her. He'd wanted to kill her. She'd seen it clearly in his eyes, his face.

The ringing stopped.

Joy's cries grew more frantic. And she was beating at her bedroom door.

A knock sounded at the door. Samantha gathered her breath. "Help me." The weakness of her voice shocked her. Why couldn't she shout?

The knock came again. A man's face appeared in the window, dark hair, square jaw. Shock tracked across his features. The door was shoved open and a man and woman stood at the entrance. New neighbors. She'd seen them yesterday moving in. They didn't know to ignore the shouts and cries. The sounds of breaking glass and furniture.

"Dial nine-one-one, Steve," the woman said even as she was coming into the room.

"I'm on it." He was punching numbers.

"Oh, dear God!" She knelt next to Samantha and touched her shoulder.

"Get Joy," Samantha pleaded and pointed down the hall with a movement of one finger. Even that seemed to hurt.

The woman rose, picked her way through the debris, and disappeared down the hall. Joy's cries grew louder and closer.

Her pale blonde hair hung wet with sweat around her face, which was flushed and swollen from crying. "MommaMomma-Momma…." Joy strung her name together in a constant litany, like baby talk, her voice fraught with fear and anguish. She struggled to escape the strange woman's arms and come to her. The woman soothed her by taking a seat on the floor next to Samantha.

Joy's hiccups and sniffles tore at her. This was her fault. This was what she'd forced her child to experience.

"Momma's hurt, but she's going to be just fine," the woman said. She held Joy in her lap, but allowed her to touch Sam's hand. That seemed to sooth her.

Samantha caught her daughter's fingers, and with what little breath she could muster, through the constant painful pressure of her ribs, she shushed her. "Momma's going to be fine, Joy. The doctors will help me."

A siren wailed in the distance.

"Callmygrandmother. Joyneedsher."

The pity she read in the woman's face brought tears to her eyes and shame to her heart. She turned her face into the floor.

"Phone," she croaked, pointing her finger toward the coffee table. "Ellen."

"I'm going to wave the ambulance down," the man said from the door.

With one arm looped around Joy's small body, the woman shoved her hand beneath the coffee table and retrieved the phone, then pushed buttons.

Samantha closed her eyes and listened to the conversation. The words, "she's been beaten" echoed over and over through her brain. How many times had she hidden the bruises, the red marks like burns on her skin, the pain of wrenched muscles and broken bones? How many times had she denied that she was a battered wife? To herself. To her grandmother. She had hidden it until no friends remained to deny it to.

Will had killed their unborn child with his fists, his feet, and she had allowed him to—because she'd stayed. And she'd stayed because of his threats against her, her grandmother, and Joy. If he could kill the child in her womb with his fists and feet, he could kill Joy with one twist, one slap. Her four-year-old body was so small, so fragile.

Samantha clenched her teeth against their chattering. She felt so cold. The blood gushed from her womb. Her thin cotton shorts were sticking to her skin. "Don't let Will have her. He threatened to…kill her."

The woman's lips trembled, and then she pressed them together. "I won't. Your grandmother is on her way."

A siren screamed up to the house, then cut off. Two male EMTs entered the house loaded down with equipment. They set aside their kits, and the woman hurried to her feet at their direction. She hiked Joy on her hip, murmuring reassurances.

Samantha flinched when one of the men reached out to touch her face.

"Easy," he said.

Samantha dragged in as full a breath as she could. "My husband beat me. He threatened to kill my daughter," she muttered as he continued his examination.

"The cops are on their way," he said, shining a light into her eyes.

"His name is Will Cross."

The man's movements stilled. "As in Cross Construction?"

"Yes." A fresh gush of blood erupted between her thighs and pooled beneath her.

The two men glanced at each other.

"If I die, you have to tell them, he killed our baby." The words sounded slurred. It was difficult to speak.

"You're pregnant?"

She couldn't feel her face. The room darkened, as though she were looking through a mesh screen. She ran her hand down over her belly. "Not anymore."

Blackness rolled over her. She welcomed it.

CHAPTER 3

San Diego, California

Flash woke to a headache that pounded against his temples with every heartbeat. Dried blood had hardened on the right side of his face and stiffened his hair into spikes. Head wounds bled like a son of a bitch, and this one had oozed all over the seat.

Where the hell was he?

Finally recognizing the back of his apartment complex, he shoved open the car door and swung his legs out. He groaned as the movement caused the throbbing to ratchet up to jackhammer status. He must have passed out for a while. *What the hell had happened?* One minute he was going along with the plan and the next he was dodging bullets.

And getting shot.

He remembered the drive away from the scene as though it were a fog-enshrouded dream.

How long had he been out? He glanced at his watch. Ten minutes to drive from the storage facility to the apartment complex. Then he'd been out maybe ten minutes.

Gripping the edge of the door, he eased himself up and out of the driver's seat. Dizziness struck and the asphalt rocked beneath him. He swallowed back nausea, and braced a hand on the edge of the open door. He had to get to his apartment and assess how badly he was injured. He should have driven to a hospital. But until he was certain about what the hell was going on, he couldn't risk having a bullet wound reported.

Holding onto the car for balance, he gathered the bag full of money and the gym bag holding the artifacts from the trunk, then staggered forward toward the back entrance of the complex.

What was the key code? If he didn't get it right within three tries, it would lock him out completely for thirty minutes. If anyone was coming after him for shooting the FBI assassins, they'd be here any minute. His vision blurred. He closed his eyes and attempted to visualize the numbers. Opening his eyes again, he punched in the number and a red light flashed.

Wrong code. Damn. *What the fuck was it?* And why wouldn't his eyes work? He closed the left one and the pad grew clearer. He punched in the number again and the light flashed green. *Thank you, Jesus.*

He swung the door open and slipped inside. The back hallway ran from one end of the building to the other, and stairway on the right led up to the other floors. He tugged open the steel fire door and climbed the stairs to the second story. Pain throbbed with every step. His vision blurred and cleared. But at least the nausea was easing. He cracked the door and looked out into the hall. All clear. He hustled down to his door and unlocked it.

Wait. What if they were waiting for him?

Setting the bags aside, he drew his Sig from the small of his back. He pulled back the slide to check the chamber. How many rounds had he fired? Two at the one guy's chest, and three into the other man's legs. Seven remained out of the twelve-bullet magazine, plus one in the chamber.

Standing to one side, he shoved the door open.

Nothing happened and he bobbed around the edge of the door to look inside the apartment.

Silence rushed out and nothing moved. He took a tentative step into the room. Everything was as he'd left it. He retrieved the bags and tossed them into a chair, kicked the door closed, then staggered down the hall to the bathroom. Blood darkened his jacket and had saturated his shirt. He peeled them off and tossed them into the trashcan.

Using a washcloth, he wiped away the dried blood in his hair and attempted to look at the injury. A deep furrow cut across his scalp on the right side of his head to his temple. The coppery scent of blood turned his stomach.

He'd missed being killed by the width of a piece of paper. And there was no doubt he had a concussion because of it.

"Motherfuckers!" he muttered. He had to get dressed and get out of here. Until he knew what was going on, he needed to be wary of everyone who'd been involved in the mission.

He rummaged through the medicine cabinet and found gauze, tape, and antibiotic ointment. He slathered on the ointment, wound the gauze around his head, and, tearing off a piece of tape with his teeth, slapped it on the end of the bandage.

His head throbbed relentlessly. He swallowed two ibuprofen dry, and with a fresh washcloth, wiped away the remnants of blood that tinged his skin pink. He had to get moving. If the FBI had double-crossed him, they'd be coming here any minute to search for him.

He remembered the call he'd received during the buy and jerked his cell phone from his pocket, flipping it open and playing Dobson's first message. Rick Dobson's voice said, "There's something screwy going down, Flash. Don't go to the meet. Hole up somewhere until you hear from me."

The call had come in at O-six hundred. By six-ten he'd called again while he was under fire. The only people Rick would have been with at that time were his team. Had the international cartel they were dealing with somehow learned about them? But how? Had they fallen under attack? It had sounded like it.

The cartel would have known to come after Flash because he was the go-between, but they wouldn't have known about Rick and the team. Unless someone they trusted had burned them.

Rick hadn't told him any names of the players involved. So he had no idea what had been going on behind the scenes.

Flash returned to his bedroom, dragged a shirt from his closet and another jacket. Two minutes later he walked out of his apartment with a backpack hanging over his shoulders that carried a change of clothes, his laptop, medical supplies, and extra ammunition. A baseball cap hid the bandage around his head. The bags from the drop dangled heavily from each hand.

He was going to do just as Rick told him and hole up somewhere until he heard from him… if he was still alive.

Jesus, he felt weak and nauseous. He walked out the back door just as the scream of police car sirens sounded in the distance. Avoiding his car, he walked down the alley and across the busy street at the corner to a nearby park. He dropped the bags at his feet and looked down the alley as two police cars halted in the apartment building parking lot. Four cops leaped from their vehicles and, drawing their guns, descended on his car.

"Jesus," he breathed as shock punched him in the gut, taking his breath.

He was fucked.

CHAPTER 4

Las Vegas, Nevada

Though she had only been given Jell-O and broth, the smell of the chicken they'd served for dinner on the rest of the hospital floor lingered in the room, intensifying Samanth's nausea. The doctor's voice seemed to drone on and on. Wah-wah-wah, like Charlie Brown's teacher.

"We believe you have spontaneously expelled the tissue, so you won't need a D and C. We did give you one unit of blood."

The doctor looked younger than she'd felt in a long, long time. It was hard to pay attention to what he was saying. Expelled the tissue. Is that what they called it when you lost a child? Had he put it like that to keep from breaking her heart even more? Or was he just trying to keep it clinical? She touched the IV that pumped fluid into her arm. The tape holding the tubing in place pulled at her skin.

"You also have a concussion and a fractured cheekbone. I consulted Dr. Nuñez while you were asleep. He believes that the fracture will heal without any treatment. I'll want to keep you under close observation for the next couple of days to make certain the vision in your eye returns to normal."

Sam touched the patch over her eye. At least Will hadn't blinded her.

But what was normal? Her stomach cramped with anxiety. Would she ever feel *normal* again?

"You have two broken ribs on the left side. Those will probably be the most painful during healing."

Was he including her psyche in that?

He paused and seemed to be waiting for some kind of response. "Do you understand everything I've said, Mrs. Cross?"

She flinched inwardly at hearing the name. Every time someone said it, a rush of bitterness and anger welled up inside her. If she were never called Mrs. Cross again it would be too soon. "I understand."

"I can arrange for you to talk to a hospital psychologist while you're here. It will help."

She shook her head. It wouldn't help to relive the last four years of her life. She just wanted to forget everything that had happened, every single moment. Shove it into a closet and close it off forever.

"Is she going to stand between me and my husband so he can't beat me again? Are you?" she asked.

"We have security guards here. He's not going to hurt you while you're in the hospital. You're safe here."

He was so oblivious to the real world. "You don't know him. He'll get in here if he wants to."

And what about Joy? Could he find her and Gran?

"My daughter. She's okay?"

"She's with your grandmother, as you requested. There are two policemen outside who want to speak to you."

She nodded.

"I'll send them in."

Two men came into the room. Both looked younger than the doctor. *Dear God.*

The taller of the two introduced himself as Detective Kipler and his stockier partner as Detective Marshall. Both appeared to be early thirties, dark haired, clean cut. "We've spoken to the emergency personnel who brought you in, Mrs. Cross." Kipler said. "They both said you identified your husband as the man who assaulted you."

"Yes. He killed our baby."

He cleared his throat and focused on the pad he held. "I'm sorry, ma'am."

"The EMTs said you were hemorrhaging and going into shock. Do you remember what you said to them?"

"I told them if I died, that my husband had killed our baby and had threatened to kill our daughter."

"There have been three other reports of domestic issues at your house ma'am. Is that correct?"

"Yes."

"During those issues, did you ever press charges?"

'Yes."

He studied her face, his expression carefully blank. "Why didn't you follow through?"

"I did, but by the time it went to court the charges had been dropped. Once the hearing time was changed and I wasn't notified. The next two times someone had pulled the paperwork."

The cops looked at one another. "That isn't possible, Mrs. Cross."

"It is if your abusive husband's father is best buddies with Judge Henry Moreland." She looked away. "My father-in-law once told me that all I needed to do was be a better wife and Will wouldn't have to keep me in line. He plays golf with Judge Henry Moreland every Sunday."

The two detectives eyed her, their expressions carefully controlled.

Will had almost killed her this time. If he ever succeeded, who would take care of Joy? Will's parents wouldn't allow their granddaughter to be brought up by her grandmother, the only person Samantha trusted.

The cramping low in her abdomen brought on a bout of nausea, and she closed her eyes against it and swallowed.

"He said he was going to kill me. I believed him. After he rammed my head into a wall. That was the first beating. After he broke my wrist during the second, I believed him. He broke my collarbone the third time. And I believed him today when he hit me in the face with his fist and broke my cheekbone, after he punched me in the stomach and killed my baby. After he knocked me to the floor and kicked me in the ribs."

"Your husband is saying someone broke into your house and did this, ma'am."

Was he serious? Fear rocketed through her, stealing her breath. *Did they believe him?*

Sam stared at the young detective with her one good eye until he looked away.

"You don't have him in custody?" her voice rose in pitch with her fear level.

"No, we've only spoken to your husband on the phone to notify him of your condition."

"Oh dear God! You told him where I am?" For a moment she couldn't breathe.

"Are you sure it was your husband?"

"There was no one else in our home this afternoon but the monster I've lived with the last four years. His name is William Jacob Cross. He was born October seventh, 1983. He's thirty years old. He is six foot, three inches tall and weighs two hundred and twenty pounds. He has dark hair and green eyes. He has bruised knuckles from beating me, and he had a blood stain on his shirt when he walked out the door and left me to hemorrhage to death on the floor."

"Do you intend to press charges, Mrs. Cross?"

'Yes, I do."

Detective Marshall snapped his notebook closed and said, "You press the charges. We'll make certain they go through. We'll put out an APB, and he'll be picked up.

"Your neighbors have identified your husband as the man who left the house, Mrs Cross. You've identified him. We'll be picking him up, but it will be up to you to stick to your story," the other detective said, his voice quiet.

"I won't withdraw the charges. But are you going to check each day and make sure the paperwork isn't pulled?"

"We'll be sure to check on your paperwork, Mrs. Cross." Kipler said. "We'll file for an emergency protective order on your behalf, but it will be up to you to file for one with a judge so your husband can't come anywhere near you or your daughter. We can keep him for forty-eight hours, but after that, with his family connections, he'll probably make bail."

"How can I do that if I'm still in here?" Her voice shook as her fear ratcheted up again. How could she do it so she could be certain Moreland wouldn't go right behind her and kick the order out?

"We'll give you the number of an advocate who can help you fill out the paperwork so it can be issued. It's very important for you to get right on this so it will go into effect while your husband is in jail."

A small niggling hope built inside her. "What will you do if the paperwork disappears again?"

"It isn't going to happen, Mrs. Cross."

Yes, it would. Her body started to shake. She gripped the thin blanket that covered her.

The two detectives continued to ask questions, taking her statement and offering her information and advice. The pain in her ribs, despite the medication the nurse had given her, sapped her strength and made it difficult for her to take in everything they were saying.

She needed a lawyer to file for divorce and to see that the police followed through with the protective order. Could her grandmother arrange for that?

"If you have proof he threatened your little girl, that will go a long way to insuring he doesn't get unsupervised visitation with your child while the protective order is in place," the soft-spoken detective—Kipler—said.

A knock came at the door and a nurse came in. "I think she's had enough, fellows."

Detective Kipler left a list of numbers on the bedside table. "We'll do all we can, Mrs. Cross."

Please don't leave. The words screamed through her head. *What if he comes here?*

After they left, the nurse took her temperature and blood pressure. She frowned at the numbers. "You need to rest. Your body has been through a trauma and you've lost a lot of blood."

Sam studied the woman's features. She had a wide round face and a pleasant smile. "I need to call my grandmother and check on my daughter."

Had her grandmother gone back to the house? Had she checked in at a hotel? She had been here earlier with Joy, but Sam had been groggy and weak and couldn't remember much of the visit.

The nurse handed Sam the receiver. "Push the call button when you're through, and I'll be back to hang that up for you. Try not to move around too much, those ribs will be extremely painful. I'll be back with a spirometer to exercise your lungs. We don't want you developing pneumonia."

The nurse wandered out of the room and Sam dialed her Gran's cell phone number. At the sound of her voice some of Sam's worry lifted. "Hey, Gran."

"How are you feeling?" Ellen asked, her tone tentative.

"Better. Where are you staying?"

"We found a hotel close to the hospital."

"Don't tell anyone where you're staying and don't use a credit card. My in-laws might try and come and get Joy."

"They're not taking her anywhere."

It eased her anxiety to hear her grandmother's determination. "The police say they're going to arrest Will."

"Good. That's the least he deserves."

Tears burned Sam's eyes. "I'm sorry, Gran."

"For what, sweetie?"

"For not being able to stand up to him."

"He's over two hundred pounds. You're a hundred and ten. How could you have stood up to him?"

Gran would have. There wasn't anything on earth that Ellen Andrews couldn't stand up against. "I tried to leave. He threatened to kill me if I did. He threatened to kill you and Joy, too."

"We're going to be fine, honey. He's not going to hurt us, or you, ever again. Joy is fine. She's playing with her little people right now."

"She isn't doing the baby babbling anymore, is she?"

"No." Her voice grew more distant, like she had turned away from the phone. "She's talking like a big girl."

"She's been babbling every time she gets scared." Sam closed her eyes against the fresh wave of emotional pain. "That's what set him off today. She was babbling like a baby. He locked her in her room. When I tried to talk to him about her...about why she was doing it..." She swallowed. "He didn't even care what he was doing to her. She didn't want to be near him, and that would make him angry, too. Everything I did made him angry."

"That's on him, Sam. Not on you. You can't live looking back. What's important is what you do from this moment on. You have to do what's important for Joy, too."

"I am. Do you know any good lawyers? A good lawyer who can't be scared off by a sitting judge here in Vegas."

"I do. He doesn't practice in Vegas, but he can. I'll give him a call."

"I won't have any money. The Crosses will lock down the bank account before I even get out of the hospital."

"We'll deal with it."

"The police are putting in an emergency protective order, but I have to file for something more permanent. But if it goes before Judge Moreland, he'll kick it out again."

"Again?" Ellen asked.

Sam clenched a fist against her chest. "I've tried before, Gran."

"He won't be kicking anything out this time. We're not going to allow him to. Tom will file a grievance with the state attorney's office, making sure it doesn't happen. I'm calling him as soon as we hang up."

The emotional weight of fear and depression eased a little. "Can I speak with Joy? I'm getting tired and I just need to hear her voice for a second."

"Sure. Joy, Mommy's on the phone."

"Mommy?" Joy breathed into the phone.

"How's my girl?"

"Grandma El is here."

She sounded excited. "I know. Grandma El is going to take care of you for a few days."

"Are you still bleeding?"

God, what kind of memories would she have after all this? "Mommy's all better, but the doctors want me to stay here for a little while. Grandma El and you are going to have such fun together."

"I'm going swimming tomorrow. I'm taking Fweddy."

He was her favorite little person. God help Gran if Joy lost him. "You may want to just let Freddy swim in the bathtub tonight instead. If you lost him in the pool, you might be sad."

"'Kay."

"You be very good for Grandma El. Okay?"

"'Kay."

"I love you, Joy."

"Love you."

The phone crashed in her ear. Then it was picked up again. "Sam?"

"Yeah, I'm still here."

"Try and rest, honey. We're fine."

Her emotions swung back and forth like a tilt-a-whirl. One moment she was okay, the next anxious. What if Will were to find them? Her heartbeat pummeled her bruised ribs. "No one knows where you are, do they?"

"No, we're good."

"All right." She forced her muscles to relax, the tension making her body ache more.

"I've left my number with the nurses. They know to call if you need me," Ellen said.

"Okay." Exhaustion dragged at her. "I think I'll rest now."

"I'll talk to you later."

"Love you," she murmured.

"You, too."

Sam pushed the call button and held the phone with the button pushed down. She closed her eyes. Dull pain thrummed through her whole body. She sensed someone coming into the room. The nurse would hang up the phone. She just needed to sleep.

The phone was removed from her grasp and hung up. The waiting stillness of the person next to her sent anxious prickles trailing over her skin. She opened her good eye a slit. Her breath seized. She yelped as a large hand clamped over her mouth.

CHAPTER 5

San Diego, California

"Wait for me. I'll only be here a few minutes." Flash shoved money into the driver's hand and exited the cab, then paused to scan the area. The sports bar in the Gas Lamp Quarter was in full swing and packed, as were all the nearby restaurants. Flash hiked his backpack securely over his shoulder, tugged the door open and stood back while four people left the bar. He nodded at their murmured thanks and stepped into the noisy establishment.

Every table was full and the bartenders were doing a brisk business. He wove through the crowd to the restrooms and moved on along the hall to the office. He tapped on the door and after a moment, a man about thirty-five with dark hair graying at the temples opened it.

"Hey, Flash." Ron Anderson, the owner of the bar, stuck out a hand, which Flash grasped with a shake. The team came in on a semi-regular basis to watch ball games and drink beer, and Anderson was a friend to them all. He knew they were military, was ex-military himself. He probably even knew they were SEALs, but he never asked too many questions. "I haven't seen you around in a while."

"I've been busy since I got back." Though every muscle tensed with the need for action, Flash forced himself to appear relaxed.

Anderson frowned and pointed to the bandage around his head. "What happened there?"

"Training accident. I zigged when I should have zagged and damn near got my head knocked off." He knew the side of his head was swollen and misshapen. His eye was starting to blacken as well. He'd taken his quota of ibuprofen and it was still pounding like a toothache.

"Jeez. You might want to think about getting into a different line of work. I heard about Brett Weaver, too. Damn shame."

"Yeah," Flash nodded. Brett had lain in a coma for well over a month but had finally come out of it. "They think he's going to be fine. In fact, I saw him a couple of days ago, and he's out of the hospital and doing great. He'll be full strength in no time at all."

"Good news." Anderson smiled. "What can I do for you?"

"I was hoping to use your telephone to make a private phone call. I need a land line."

Anderson's brows rose.

"I know it's an imposition. But it's business. I need to check in."

"Sure. No problem." Ron stepped aside and made a sweeping motion. "When you're done, stop by the bar and I'll buy you a drink."

"Thanks, I will."

Anderson left, closing the door behind him. Flash fished the digital recorder out of the backpack. He hooked the phone up to the device, then plugged it into the wall. He drew out the prepaid cell phone he'd bought and saved his contacts to. He scrolled down the list until he reached Gilbert's number.

He turned on the recorder and dialed the number on the landline, counting on the fact that the restaurant name would come up on the agent's phone.

"Who is this?" Gilbert snapped.

"This is Carney."

"Flash, what the hell are you doing in the Gas Lamp Quarter? We've been looking for you."

I bet you have, asshole.

"I'm keeping this brief. Your guys tried to fucking kill me."

"There was a mix-up, and the agents were unaware that you weren't one of the smugglers."

"That's a mix-up? Where's Rick?" he asked. "I've been calling."

"Agent Dobson was killed earlier today."

Flash suspected as much but hearing the news...Dobson had been a good guy. Flash shut off the emotional reaction and shook his head. He'd deal with that later—when he had time. "What the hell happened?"

"The smuggling network we're tracking discovered where we had set up surveillance. Two guys burst into the room and shot him and another agent. Both died at the scene."

When Flash remained silent, Gilbert asked, "How badly are you hurt? There was quite a bit of blood at the scene and in your car."

"Your concern is touching, since it was your men who tried to blow my head off." *And then stalked me to try and finish me off. You're in this up to your eyeballs, asshole.*

"Look, I'm sorry Flash. Really. But it's time you came in. You need medical attention, and you need to bring in the artifacts and the money. Once we have those locked down, and you've been debriefed, we'll deal with the investigation into the agents' conduct. And you need to bring their identification back in with you. What the hell were you thinking taking their badges?"

What the hell were they thinking keeping their identification on them when they were assassinating someone? He'd taken their pictures with his phone...with the rifles they'd used when they attempted to kill him. "I didn't want there to be any question about who was responsible for this clusterfuck."

"You fucking shot two federal agents, Carney!"

"Only after they shot me. Two people were trying to blow my head off with sniper rifles. They'd already killed the two men in front of me. They didn't identify themselves as federal officers, so I had every right to protect myself. Your men were lucky I didn't use deadly force."

"We'll discuss that when you come in."

"You'll be coming to me."

"Wait just a minute. That's not how this works."

"I'll choose the place, and I'll call you with the location."

"Wait, Carney—"

"After everything that's gone down, do you really think I'd just waltz into your office? I worked with you guys in good faith. And you damn near killed me."

Gilbert remained silent. "Okay. I know we screwed up."

Yeah. He was still walking around alive. At least he'd gotten the man to admit he'd been working with them. "You'll hear from me when I'm ready to meet." Flash hung up.

Moving fast, he disconnected the recorder and reconnected the phone to the wall jack. He crammed the device into his backpack, zipped it shut, and looked around to make certain he wasn't leaving anything behind. He had to get out quick. They'd be here any moment. The music playing in the club beat against his ears and intensified the throbbing in his head as he strode down the hall.

Ron was circulating through the crowd. Flash approached him. "I have to go."

Though curiosity flickered across the other man's face, he didn't ask any questions.

Flash forced a smile to his lips. "I'll take you up on that beer in a couple of days."

"Sure thing." Ron slapped him on the back.

Flash ducked his head to hide the flinch. *Jesus, he hurt all over.*

He read concern on the guy's face. "Hey, take care of yourself."

"I will."

Flash wove through the crowd and exited the bar. He scanned the street as he approached his cab and studied the driver's face and clothing, making sure it was the same man. Ever since he'd left his apartment and seen the police close in on his car, he'd felt hunted. He'd *been* hunted. Judging from the aggressive stance of the police as they'd converged on his apartment, the FBI had probably put out an armed and dangerous on him.

Once he assured himself it was his original driver, he opened the cab door and climbed in. As the taxi pulled away from the curb, a black SUV pulled up and four men got out. Flash bent as though he were tying his shoe and waited until the cab turned the corner before he asked the cab driver to drop him twelve blocks from his destination. He murmured a brief thanks and waited for the taxi to clear the area and turn down a side street before he started the trek to the marina. With every step his head pounded and his stomach roiled. The briny smell of the ocean blending with the car exhausts intensified his stomach's pitching.

He'd stored the artifacts, the money, and some of his clothes aboard Bowie's boat earlier, leaving room in his backpack for the equipment he'd bought. It was time to break the code of silence and contact someone in his team. But the FBI would be monitoring each of their phones. He was certain of that. He had to think in terms of keeping his teammates safe.

Would they be watching Captain Jackson or monitoring his line? Possibly not, since Flash didn't hang with him like he did the others. He'd already mailed the letter to the Captain. He could mail the recording device to him, with a note asking him to bring NCIS into it. If the Naval Investigative Services got involved, Flash might have a chance at clearing himself.

He'd shot two FBI agents. He hadn't killed them, but he'd wounded them. *Jesus! What kind of fucked up situation was this?*

And even worse, he was AWOL. He'd been texted the code to report immediately while the buy was actually going down. Just before Rick Dobson's message. *What was this shit doing to his career? And what would he do if they busted him? The SEALs were all he had.* His chest grew tight. If Gilbert had fucked up his career, Flash was going make it his calling in life to make the man's life a misery for the rest of his days.

If he lived that long.

He reached the marina and punched in the key code to enter the locked facility. The place was deserted except for a couple of security guards. He waved to one and strolled down to dock eleven, then moseyed on down to slip sixty-eight. He climbed into the stern of the 1988 Carver 3207 cabin cruiser. The boat represented something permanent in *real-life* to Bowie. He'd been making payments on it for a while, but he was generous with the team. He kept an extra set of keys on the vessel should any of them want to fish. All they had to do was call and tell him they were taking the boat out.

If he had to run, Flash would take the boat and head to Mexico. He had a friend there who would help him out until he could figure out what to do.

He hoped that wouldn't be necessary.

Prayed it wouldn't be.

Using the keys he'd retrieved from their hiding spot on the fly bridge, he unlocked the cabin and hustled down the steps into the galley. The salty sea smell of the ocean just outside the bay reached him. He turned on one of the interior lights and dumped the backpack on the narrow built in table in the galley. Exhaustion sapped his strength. He'd been on the move since the mission, and his head still throbbed like someone was hammering their way through his skull. He opened the red naugahyde sofa into a bunk, checked the small refrigerator and found some bottled water, washed down more ibuprofen, pulled his gun from the small of his back, and then stretched out.

Every inch of his body ached. He had to have a concussion. And he probably needed to go to the hospital. He laid his weapon next to him.

How long had it been since he'd eaten? Early morning at least. But the idea of food increased the nausea he'd been fighting most of the day.

He closed his eyes, hoping the pain would ease and he'd be able to rest. The boat rocked. His eyes flew open. A stealthy step landed overhead. Flash rolled to his feet, his hand wrapped around his weapon.

CHAPTER 6

Las Vegas

The hand over Samantha's face trigged such agonizing pain it stole her breath. White lights scattered across her vision, blocking Will's features. Nausea threatened to overwhelm her. If she threw up she'd probably choke to death before he released her.

She breathed in through her nose and closed her eyes, swallowing the saliva that pooled in her mouth. Even that triggered a gag. Her vision cleared, and she stared up at Will with her one good eye. His hazel eyes were narrowed, his jaw taut with anger. *What had happened to turn the handsome man she had married into this—?* He still wore the shirt stained with her blood.

Her hands gripped and pulled at his wrist and she instinctively tried to pull back from the pressure he applied. Her eyes watered from the pain.

"You're going to tell them it was someone else who broke into the house and did this. I'm not going to jail because you fucking wouldn't stay off my back. If you'd just shut your fucking mouth, none of this would have happened. You know how I get when I'm on a big job. Why couldn't you just be a good wife and make things easy for us both?"

It was *her* fault that he beat her. It was *her* fault he killed their baby. At one time she'd believed herself responsible and accepted his pleas and apologies. But when Joy started suffering because of it—*No more!*

She forced herself to release his hand and relax. The pain drove a spike into her temple and eye. She whimpered. She lay her hands palm up on the bed. Seeing her acquiescent posture, Will relaxed his grip and the pain eased.

"You're going to take back everything you've told the police. Or, so help me, I'll make you wish you had." He rested his forehead against hers. "You know I didn't mean to do it, Sam. I love you."

If it would get his hand off her mouth, she'd tell him what he wanted to hear. She nodded.

He eased up on the pressure of his hand a little more, but not entirely. Not enough for her to scream. Her body shook as if she had some kind of palsy. The uncomfortable cramping sensation from the miscarriage made her legs ache.

He was never going to let her go. Never going to stop hitting her, not until he killed her. And as long as he continued to beat and terrorize her, he would traumatize Joy and make her emotional scars worse.

She'd rather be dead than see her child go through life thinking it was okay to be beaten and emotionally abused. She'd rather be dead than see her child live in terror of her father for even one more day. If Will killed her, he'd go to prison and at least Joy would be free of him. Where only fear had resided resolve took root inside her.

"I didn't hurt you all that bad. Just a few bruises and a black eye. I don't understand why they brought you to the hospital." He brushed her hair back from her face.

How could he threaten her one moment and caress her the next?

"You killed your son," she said from beneath the continued pressure of his hand. The words weren't clear enough for him to understand what she said.

He relaxed his grip.

"I was pregnant and you killed the baby," she said as loudly as she could. "It may have been the son you keep harping about, and you killed him."

She watched the shock of it strike.

"You're a lying bitch," he breathed, his face filling her vision as he shoved closer.

He was going to hit her. She could see it in his eyes. Sam gripped his cheeks with her nails and held on as hard as she could. A screech of pure rage and desperation ripped from her as all the pain from the last four years rose up. She jerked forward hitting him in the nose with her forehead.

Will yelped in pain and tore free. Her nails had dug long furrows down each side of his face. Blood ran from his nose. Swearing he drew back his clenched fist to hit her.

Her ribs screamed as she tucked her head down and covered her face with her arms. He hit her in the side of the head instead. The blow jolted her neck and shoved her head into the hospital bed railing.

The door crashed open and the nurse rushed in.

"What are you doing? Get away from her."

Will punched the woman and she dropped as though her legs had been swept out from under her. Her movements sluggish, she rolled onto her knees and crawled toward the door.

Adrenaline pumped through Sam's system. She threw a leg over the railing and bailed out of the bed. Shoving the IV pole out of her way, she dove under the metal bedframe. The pole fell with a crash. The IV line jerked at her arm, so she pulled the tape loose and yanked the plastic needle free.

Will lunged to one side of the bed and she scrambled out the other. The sounds of running feet came from the hall. He caught her shoulder, twisting her around. Her feet tangled, and she fell, landing hard on her hip. Pain streaked down her leg.

His shoes came into view. Fearful of being kicked, she rolled to her knees to crawl away. He grabbed the long hair at the back of her head and dragged her to her feet, nearly ripping the strands from her scalp.

"I'll kill you, you fucking bitch. You'll never raise your hand to me again." Holding her bent at the waist, he shook her by the hair, straining her neck muscles, so she latched onto his arm with both hands.

Sam had been at his mercy so many times. But *no more!*

With a backhanded grab, she latched onto his crotch and squeezed as hard as she could.

Will made a keening sound, as if all the air had been sucked out of his lungs, and fell to his knees, dragging her with him. He started pounding on her with his one free hand, hitting her ribs, her arm, her back, her head. She covered her battered face and, despite the blows, kept the pressure on his balls until her hand ached.

Two security guards rushed into the room. Each grabbed one of Will's arms. While one worked to force Will's fingers to release her hair, the other fought to keep him on his knees until she scrambled out of the way. She crawled under the bed again for cover and curled into a ball on her side.

The two men dragged Will from the room, as he recovered his breath and began screaming obscenities at her.

Her ribs ached so much she could hardly breathe. Pain throbbed at the base of her skull. Knots were already forming on either side of her head. But a small sense of triumph helped make the pain bearable.

She'd fought back for the first time.

A small bubble of pride expanded inside her.

It felt good.

San Diego, California

Flash's heart hammered like it was stuck in hyperdrive. He was trapped inside the ship's cabin. There were no escape hatches, just the one entrance. Why hadn't he realized he needed a back door before? *Goddamn rookie mistake*! As footsteps approached the cabin door, he pressed back against the galley cabinets, where he had the most cover.

At the decisive tapping on the wooden door, he jerked in reaction. "Fuck!" he breathed.

Bad guys did not knock. Most of the time.

He tucked the gun into his waistband against the small of his back, and sidled to the door. Every muscle in his body tensed for action, he paused, and then jerked the door open.

Edward Rice, one of the security guards, stood in the glow of the one dim cabin light, his features barely discernable. Flash recognized his round face and bulky structure.

"Just checking to make sure it was you, Lieutenant. Ensign Rivera would shoot me if something happened to his ship," Rice said with a slight smile.

Flash controlled the sigh of relief with an effort. "Yes, he would. I'm spending the night on board. Plan to fish early in the morning and thought I'd just sleep here."

"That's quite an injury you have there, sir. Are you sure you're okay?"

"Yeah. I had an accident. But the docs say it's mostly just bruising." He touched his face tentatively and felt how far the swelling had traveled. It was getting worse.

"I'd take it easy if I were you, sir. You forgot to sign in when you first arrived. I'll make a note that you're on board. Be sure to sign in the first opportunity you have. We like to keep a record of who's on the premises so we won't keep checking the boats over and over."

Flash nodded. "Roger that. And I'll sign in when I gas her up tomorrow morning, Ed."

"Thanks. Appreciate it. You have a good evening."

"Will do." Flash released a breath as the man turned away.

After closing and locking the cabin door, he slumped onto the bunk and cradled his throbbing head in his hands. Adrenaline spiraled from his system, leaving him jittery. But the pumped, high-alert feeling, as though his body were poised for action at any moment, lingered. It was like being back in Iraq all over again. Except he was in his own back yard and someone he'd trusted had screwed him. *God damn it!*

He had to have an exit strategy in case what he'd planned went south. He had to think this through.

Would Gilbert try to play it straight and turn him in? Somehow Flash doubted it. As long as the cash and artifacts were out of reach, he'd be covering his ass. FBI never admitted mistakes. If Gilbert weren't involved in Dobson's death, he'd be pulling out the stops to find Flash. *And the goods.* Then he'd lay every fuck-up on Flash and try to bury him.

After their conversation on the phone, there was no doubt left in Flash's mind the man was involved. Had they been able to take Flash out along with the others, they'd have the money and the artifacts. And could make up any story they wanted.

After all, they had three suspects down; the lead in the investigation was dead, and the only ones left standing would have been the guys in partnership with Gilbert.

Flash dragged his backpack over and removed the FBI badges from an inner pocket. Why would they be fool enough to carry their ID if they were going to assassinate someone? And that's exactly what they'd done. They'd shot down the smugglers in cold blood.

They hadn't counted on his survival. And they'd been arrogant about their success. Their overconfidence had saved Flash's life at the time. But now it raised the threat level to DEFCON 1.

These two assholes, he glanced down at the names on the ID, Harrison and Ballard, would probably get a fucking commendation for being injured during an operation.

He reached for the prepaid phone, one of several he'd purchased earlier in the day, flipped it open, and keyed in a number. He'd hoped never to have to make a call like this. Especially not to him.

"This better be someone I know," a voice grated in his ear.

"Travis, this is Flash."

"Hey, son." The man's tone changed immediately. "What's happening?"

"I'm in trouble. And I need help."

CHAPTER 7

Las Vegas

Samantha Cross studied Dr. Simons' face. In the last four years, she'd learned to read quick changes of expression to avoid a shove, a slap or a beating. She'd honed her powers of observation to a fine point. Dr. Simons wasn't really sorry for ignoring her concerns and warnings, he was pissed that he had to apologize to her for ignoring them.

"Is the nurse okay?" she asked.

"Nurse Gooding will be off work for about a week."

"I'm sorry. I hope she'll file charges."

"The hospital is going to see to that."

"Until Chaney comes in and offers them a ton of money to build a new wing." There was an edge of bitterness in Sam's voice.

"We have to guarantee our patients' and employees' safety, Mrs. Cross. That includes yours."

"Sure." She looked up at him. "You'll tell the nurse thank you for me. *She* tried to protect me." She allowed a smidgeon of emphasis to color the word "she."

The doctor eyes shifted away. "I'll tell her."

"When can I get out of here? I have to file the paperwork for the restraining order before Will gets out of jail." She eased further onto her left side. Her ribs screamed in protest. She shut her eyes against the pain until it eased.

"The hospital has filed a restraining order. Should he come within five hundred yards of the building, he'll be arrested again." The doctor's eyes trailed over her arms, and face.

"Should you need me to testify on your behalf, Mrs. Cross, I'll be available."

Sam focused on one of the uneven circular bruises that marked her forearm. Last night adrenaline had partially numbed the pain of her injuries. Today she felt each and every one of them. Tears blurred her vision and she touched the patch over her injured eye.

"Now that the hospital has gotten involved, the police have sent a forensic specialist to take pictures of your injuries and gather a copy of your medical files for evidence."

Will had finally taken on someone with more power than he had. If only he could go to jail for a long, long time. Maybe she could stop being afraid. Anxiety raced along her nerve endings and she gripped the thin blanket on the bed and held it against her. Her throat grew tight and her breathing uneven. "They've sent a woman?"

"Yes, of course."

This was just the beginning of the long road to putting her life back on track. She had to suck it up and do whatever it took for Joy's sake—and her own. The shame of having people see her like this turned her stomach. She had to have a moment before facing that humiliation. "When will I get this patch off?"

"Dr. Greenway, one of our ophthalmologists, will be in to do a thorough exam later today. You still seem to have a lot of swelling around the eye socket."

Dr. Simons stepped to the door and motioned for someone to enter.

No! The word rose in her throat and she bit it back. She could do this. It would be proof they could use against Will in court. Maybe.

Her mouth grew dry and she clutched the blanket harder. A small woman of Asian descent, perhaps Japanese or Korean, entered the room, a satchel hanging across her narrow shoulder and a large camera in her hand. Ink-black hair cupped her chin in a soft bob and bangs brushed her brows. Her dark eyes settled on Sam while Doctor Simons introduced her.

"This is Tammi Mai, Mrs. Cross. She's a police department evidence recovery technician."

Sam tipped her head in acknowledgement.

"If there's anything you need, just page the nurse," Simons said. He left and closed the door behind him.

"I'm just here to get some photographs and take your statement about what happened last night, Mrs. Cross," Tami said. "Your earlier statement has already been filed."

Sam nodded.

The woman pulled a straight-backed chair close to the bed and sat down.

Sam studied the young woman's face with her one eye. "Can I see your identification?"

"Sure." Ms. Mai reached into her satchel, pulled a small wallet free and extended it to her.

Sam studied the ID. "I suppose you have to do this a lot." She handed the badge back.

"More than I want to."

Sam remained silent for a moment. Could she trust this woman? Did she have a choice? "What do you want to know?"

"Is it okay if I tape our conversation?"

Sam nodded.

"How long has your husband been doing this? Tammi asked.

"Three and a half years. We'd been married about six months when he slapped me the first time."

"Why did you stay?"

"He was so sorry, he begged me to forgive him. He swore it would never happen again. And, like a fool, I believed him."

"Then?"

"I was seven months pregnant when Will slammed my head into a wall and gave me a concussion. I pressed charges and he was arrested. When I showed up in court, I was told the time of the hearing had been changed and, since I hadn't shown up, Will had been released. He came home that afternoon while I was packing to leave and told me if I ever tried to have him arrested again, he'd kill me. If I tried to leave, he'd kill me. I believed him."

"What triggered his latest attack?"

"He was already upset about something. I have no idea what. The angrier he became, the more our daughter Joy did her babbling baby talk. I could see the violence building, so I got the car keys and was going to take Joy to McDonalds until he either left or calmed down. He grabbed the keys out of my hand and locked Joy in her room, said I was treating her like a baby and that was why she was talking like one."

"How old is she?"

"She's four. But when she senses he's angry, she starts using baby talk. I tried to explain to him when he gets angry he frightens her. He said I blamed him for everything and punched me in the stomach. I went down and curled into a ball. Will has been fixated on having a son lately. I think his father's been harping on wanting a grandson to follow in their footsteps. Will threw away my birth control pills three months ago, but I got a refill and hid it. But the month I missed my pills—" She swallowed against the pain. She should have run away the moment she suspected she was pregnant. The baby would still be alive if she had run.

Sam swallowed and looked away. "I knew I was pregnant. I tried to protect the baby. He kicked me in the ribs and told me to get up. I couldn't. The last thing I remember is his fist coming at my face. When I woke up, I was hemorrhaging, the living room was destroyed and Joy was still locked in her room screaming. The neighbors found me and called 911."

"What happened last night?"

"I had called my grandmother. I wanted to check on her and Joy because I was anxious about Will locating them. He's threatened to kill them both if I talked to the police. I was so tired and my ribs hurt, so I couldn't reach the phone, so the nurse helped me. After I was through talking, I pushed the off button and pressed the call button for the nurse so she could hang it up for me."

"When someone came into the room, I thought it was her. The person hung up the phone, but stood next to the bed and waited. I opened my eyes and it was Will."

The room blurred. Her breathing hitched. Will's hand covered her mouth. She could taste the sweat on his hand as he pushed against her bruised face. Pain shot up through her eye, her temple, and she touched the patch.

Tammi rested her hand on her arm.

Sam jerked. She stared down at the small hand with its perfectly trimmed nails as it rested on her skin. She clung to the reality of it, until the flashback receded.

The woman's chocolate brown eyes held hers for a moment. "Just take it slow. I'm going to ask you some questions."

"Could I have a drink of water?" Her mouth was dry as the Nevada desert.

"Sure." Tammi rose and filled the plastic cup from a small, insulated pitcher and handed it to her.

Sam cupped the container in her hand and allowed the solidity to ground her.

The woman's gentle, unhurried technique pulled every detail of the assault from Sam's memory. After she'd gone over every moment of the attack the night before, every muscle in her body felt weak from the constant tension. Her legs shook beneath the blanket.

"I need to take some photos of your injuries," Tammi said. She turned off the recorder. "Do you think you can stand?"

Though she wasn't sure, Sam nodded.

Tammi lowered the side of the bed. Sam flipped back the covers and slid free of them, her movements careful. Her hand went to her ribs. Her legs felt spongy and weak.

The nurse had given her a sanitary napkin and a belt. Every time she felt the flow between her legs, a fresh wave of regret and guilt engulfed her. She should have run away. She should have left the moment she thought she was pregnant.

"Who is going to see these pictures?" she asked.

"Possibly only the lawyers and the judge. Most assault cases are settled outside a courtroom."

Sam swallowed against the knot of tears in her throat. "If it goes before a jury?"

"They may see them, or the defense may try to suppress them. But before it goes to trial the attorneys have to go before a grand jury. If the defense sees these pictures, they may decide to take a plea. But at least what Will Cross did to you will be on the record, and he'll have to face the consequences of what he did."

Tears clouded Sam's eyes. "He won't care. If he cared, he could never have hurt me like this." She pulled the string at the back of her neck and tugged at the front of the hospital gown to free her arms. She let it go and the gown fell to the tile floor. “The only thing he’ll care about is that someone finally knows what he does in his spare time.”

She knew what she looked like. Old bruises green and yellow, new ones purple, red and black. She’d looked in the mirror and seen them for four long years. She peeled the tape free and jerked the patch off of her eye. Let them see. Let the world see what he did. A scream of pain and rage pushed against her chest. Maybe someone would stop him. *Someone has to stop him!*

The door swung open. Sam covered her breasts with an arm.

“Of course she’ll see me. I’m her mother—”

A security guard gripped Paige Cross’s arm. Both froze at the open door. Paige’s mouth opened and closed as though she couldn’t catch her breath. The security guard turned his face away with a jerk. “Sorry ma’am.” He dragged Paige back out, grabbed the edge of the door and closed it.

“Who is that?” Tammi asked.

Sam fought the urge to crawl back under the bed, as she’d done last night. “That’s my mother-in-law.”

San Diego

Flash wrapped the stone seals and tablet in bubble wrap and shoved them into the cardboard box. Trusting this kind of merchandise to UPS seemed wrong somehow, but he didn’t have much choice. He couldn’t exactly drive up to the Naval Criminal Investigative Service’s building and drop it off in person.

NCIS wouldn’t be brought into the investigation anyway—not yet. FBI guys didn’t admit they needed help or that they’d made a mistake. By sending evidence to NCIS, he might motivate someone to stir the pot a bit, and someone might turn a beady eye on the agents involved in the sting.

But then, Gilbert could tell them anything and they’d buy into it. Cops trusted cops.

But what did he have to lose by doing this?

He wrapped the cell phone he'd used during the mission. NCIS would access the voice mail and hear the message themselves. Thus far the phone and the answering machine audio file were the only proof he had he had been under cover as one of the smugglers.

And he was taking no chances. He'd also copied Dobson's final cell phone message onto his computer's hard drive. Just in case.

Captain Morrow, the commander in Iraq, could vouch for the FBI's visit. And there would be a record of his participation in this sting at headquarters. It had to go through the chain of command. He had the short email message from HQ stating his orders were amended. But it didn't state what the amendment was. *Hell, he'd been in a freaking war zone.* It wasn't as though he could get letters every day. But he'd received the hard copy of his paperwork when he got home, and it was in his safety deposit box.

Why hadn't he demanded more info? *Why hadn't he double-checked with HQ?*

Because his mind had been on other things. Brett had been in a coma, Hawk was injured, Doc was messed up too, and everything was up in the air about whether or not they were going to make it back as a team.

As for the money, he didn't know where the hundred thousand had come from. Dobson hadn't mentioned a name. And he'd been cagy about some details of the mission.

Flash had acted out the scenario as he'd been instructed. Followed orders. There had always been a tracking device in the artifacts bag during each sale. But apparently not this time.

If there had been, the FBI would be in his face right now.

They obviously hadn't thought they'd need to track the artifacts or turn in the money. And now that he had it instead, all they had to do was accuse him of exactly what they'd planned to do themselves. *With his juvie past and his gambling—he was the perfect patsy.*

But why would they risk everything for a little over thirty thousand dollars each? There had to be more to it.

What if they were skimming money from each sale? And Dobson had discovered it?

Jesus! This was driving him crazy. He was sick of going over and over the same scenarios in his head.

He read through the letter he'd written outlining the sting, folded it into a thin strip, then wrapped it around the phone and secured it with a rubber band. He stuffed the phone and the two FBI badges into the box with the artifacts and sealed it. As he wrote the address across the front, his stomach muscles tightened. He was trusting UPS with his future—and NCIS. He'd send the next package in a day or two, once he was clear of the area.

He went to the head, then stared at his reflection in the twelve by twelve piece of glass over the small sink as he washed his hands. The side of his face and head were still swollen from the trauma. Multicolored bruising encompassed his ear, temple and one eye. The trench the bullet had carved though his scalp was crusted with a beginning scab. It looked ugly.

He'd neglected to shave. A beard much darker than his brownish-blond hair shadowed the lower half of his jaw. He'd scare young children if he didn't cover up. *Hell, he scared himself.*

Returning to the galley to retrieve his ball cap, he adjusted the plastic clip at the back to accommodate the swelling and pushed a pair of cheap sunglasses onto his face to cover his eyes. The moment the side stem touched his head it triggered a dull throbbing. *Fuck! Just when it had eased off.* But he had to wear the glasses. People remembered eyes more than any other feature, and he still had no idea what steps Gilbert had taken to find him.

He shoved his arms into the sleeves of his windbreaker, slung the backpack over his shoulder, and picked up the box. Keeping his head down and his face shadowed by the bill of his cap, he strolled the four blocks to the UPS mailing office.

The early morning sunshine reflected harshly off the concrete sidewalk, intensifying his headache, so he moved into the shadows to avoid it. A car rental place came up on the right and he eyed it with longing. Paying for cabs sucked and limited his mobility, but he'd have to use a credit card to rent a vehicle. Had they found the car he'd leased? Would they have it staked out? It wouldn't hurt to check that out.

Only three people were ahead of him in line, and while he waited he called a cab to pick him up outside the store. When he inched up to the counter, the woman looked up, and her gaze traced the bruising he hadn't been able to cover with either the hat or his glasses. "Motorcycle accident?" she asked.

The lie came easy. "Car accident." His car had been involved. It had more holes in it than he did.

She grimaced in sympathy and weighed the package. "Do you want to purchase insurance?"

How much insurance would he need to replace something that was irreplaceable? "No. I trust you to get it where it's going in one piece. But you'll need to stamp it fragile."

She smiled and stamped the box, put a printed tag on the outside and taped both ends. "Just in case," she said with a smile.

Flash forked over the ten-fifty and offered her a grin as she handed him a receipt.

The cab was waiting outside. The driver leaned against the side of the car, his arms crossed "You call a cab?"

"Yeah, that was me." He slid into the back seat and gave the man an address four blocks from the parking structure where he'd left his leased Porsche. The San Diego traffic swallowed them, and he leaned back in the seat and, bending his head, took the glasses off and let the pain recede a little.

"What business do you want me to drop you at?" the driver asked.

"You can drop me at the corner of B Street and Sixth." He shoved the glasses back on his face.

"There's a bunch of lawyers got their offices on that street, isn't there?"

"Yeah. I'm thinking about seeing one."

"Looks like you got a good case. Better take pictures before the damage fades."

"Good idea."

The cabby fell silent and ten minutes later he whipped the car just past the corner.

Flash tucked money for the trip into his hand. "Thanks for the advice and the ride." He slid out of the car and slammed the door. He waited until the cab pulled away before turning down Sixth Street. Then he wandered past the downtown businesses and entered the parking structure.

Instead of heading to the elevator, he took the stairs in the center of the building to the second tier, then jogged up the steep incline to the third level. The rows of parked vehicles stretched silent and shadowed. He scanned the area for anyone sitting in a car and eyed the one van parked close by. Nothing seemed out of place, and the only movement was a guy getting into a Hyundai. Flash waited for him to pull out and head down the incline before approaching his Porsche.

The Porsche's cherry red hood reflected the dim florescent bulbs from overhead. She sat sleek and powerful, just waiting for him to slide behind the wheel. Why hadn't they found the car and confiscated it? Had they found it and put a GPS tracker on it? Were they just waiting for her to move? Or had they forgotten about the lease? Gilbert might have believed he had returned the car to the dealership.

Were these wheels worth the risk?

Flash set his pack down on the concrete next to the front wheel, then circled the car, running his hands inside each wheel well. The Porsche sat close to the ground, so he lay on his back and scanned the undercarriage on first one side, and then the other, then checked out the front and the back. Satisfied the exterior had no tracking device installed, he pulled the key from his pocket and hit the button to unlock the car.

Though it took time, he then searched every inch of the interior and the trunk. Satisfied nothing had been touched, he got behind the wheel and started the car.

He sat for a moment waiting for his heartbeat to slow and the wave of anxiety to ease. If he'd missed a tracker, they'd be on him in a heartbeat. He pumped the gas and listened to the sound of the engine, allowing it to sooth him. *Fuck'em.* He put the car in reverse and backed it out of the space.

He was halfway to Gilbert's apartment before he relaxed enough to enjoy driving the Porsche again. He wasn't going to blend into any neighborhood with a car like this, but what the fuck. He shifted gears and settled further into the seat. It felt good to be mobile.

He studied Gilbert's apartment complex as he approached it. Set within a residential area of condos and homes, the place was a step above his own apartment but not flashy. That wasn't surprising. If you had bundles of cash you weren't supposed to have, you didn't wave your arms around to let everyone know.

He drove past the complex and parked two blocks down in the visitors' slots of another apartment complex. Grabbing his backpack, he climbed out, locked the car and walked toward the apartment directly in front of him, then cut across the well-trimmed grass to the driveway of the complex next door.

Sticking to the trees that lined the parking lot, he followed the fence around the pool. Reaching the complex, he scanned the parking lot to make sure Gilbert's nondescript car was absent before mounting the back steps to the third floor. A woman passed him going down, and Flash nodded but kept climbing. He slowed his pace and waited for her to get into her car and drive away. Then he pulled out the lock picks he'd cobbled together from an old umbrella he'd found in a corner of the boat.

Certain Gilbert wasn't home, he still paused outside the door, braced himself, then knocked. If by some twist of fate the man actually was at home, he'd rush him and take him down fast. When no one came to the door or called out, Flash pushed the improvised picks into the flimsy door mechanism and, with an easy twist of his wrist, opened the lock. The dead bolt took a few more seconds.

He pushed the door open and scanned the living room. *Jeez Gilbert, you ought to have better security.* Pausing briefly to listen to the silence, he finally stepped into the room and closed the door behind him.

CHAPTER 8

Las Vegas

As she stared at her distorted reflection in one of the chrome bars of the hospital bed railing, the openmouthed shock on the security guard's face played through Sam's mind.

Tammi Mai had eased up close with the camera and taken photos of Sam's face from different angles. Then she systematically worked her way down Sam's body, homing in on every mark, even some of the old injuries already fading to green.

Sam tightened her arms over her breasts, bent her head and hugged herself as tightly as possible. She was shaking from nerves more than cold.

"You don't have to speak to your mother-in-law. In fact, she could be charged with tampering with a witness if she did speak to you," Tammi said.

Fat chance anything said would dissuade Paige Cross. "She's here to plead for her baby boy. When you leave, why don't you tell her about the tampering problem? Maybe it will keep her out of my room."

Tammi nodded. "I'll tell the security team you don't want to see her." She bent and drew the hospital gown up over Sam's body and tied the string at the back of her neck.

Sam's throat tightened at the woman's kindness. "Thank you."

"I'm going to give you a list of people you can go to for free legal advice if you need it," Tammi said. "I'm not supposed to do that, so don't tell anyone."

"I won't," Sam's voice came out a husky whisper. "I can keep a secret."

Tammi's lips compressed and she reached into her bag and wrote out several names, then tore off the sheet. "I'm putting it in the top drawer of the nightstand. The first guy on the list is the one I'd call if I had trouble. He's a badass—Well, let's just say he doesn't take any shit."

Sam nodded and gave the woman's arm a squeeze. Exhaustion swamped her and she hitched a hip onto the edge of the mattress. She pressed a hand to her side as Tammi rushed to help her lift her legs up on the bed and lie down.

The pain in her ribs stole her breath and she grimaced. The pain everywhere else made her nauseous.

"Do you need anything before I go?" Tammi asked.

Sam shook her head. "I just need to rest a little while." Her limbs dragged, heavy and weak, when she turned on her side. Every inch of her ached. And a hollow emptiness invaded her chest. Talking about how Will had treated her, what she had endured for the past four years, had reduced some of the pain and shame…for the time being.

The expression on the security guard's face flashed through her mind again. She hadn't had time to be embarrassed by her nudity, but the pity and shock she'd read in his face… And how had Page felt to see her son's brutal handiwork?

Tammi packed her kit and gathered the camera. "You will get through this, Samantha."

"If he gets out and kills me, will you tell them everything I've told you?"

"He isn't going to get out this time."

"Yes, he will."

Tammi's gaze settled on her face. "We'll do everything in our power to keep that from happening."

"I just want my daughter to be safe. I've told my grandmother to stay away from the hospital. If Will's parents find out where they're staying, they'll try to take Joy and use her as leverage to keep me from testifying against Will."

"Call the top number on the sheet of paper I gave you."

"I will. I just need to rest a little while." Exhaustion dragged her eyelids closed.

She woke an hour later when the nurse came in to give her pain medication and take her blood pressure.

"There's a man sitting in the hallway waiting to speak to you. He says he's a lawyer. He asked me to give you his card," the woman said and offered her the card.

Sam studied the business card, but the name meant nothing to her. She swallowed her medication and handed the pill cup and water back to the nurse. She combed her fingers through her sleep-tangled hair. Gran had said she was going to call someone. What had the name been?

The name on the card was Carl Ward.

"Do you want to see the lawyer sitting out there?" the nurse asked.

Every anxious bone in Sam's body vibrated. "My grandmother said she'd be sending someone to speak to me. This might be him."

The nurse left, and almost immediately a knock followed, and the door was pushed open.

"Mrs. Cross, my name is Carl Ward." The man had a slight build, thinning light brown hair, and dirt brown eyes. But the suit he wore looked like it was tailored to his frame. Though Will didn't dress that expensively, his father did. This was not the lawyer Gran would have contacted. "I've been asked to speak to you on the Cross family's behalf."

Sam's heart rushed into a panicked beat and she shook her head. "I thought you were someone else. I'm not interested in talking to you. Please leave."

"Mr. and Mrs. Cross know their son has abused you, ma'am. They want to assure you they will make sure he seeks counseling for his anger management issues."

"Please leave." Sam reached for the call button. The man covered it with his hand to stop her. Sam's heart stuttered, then raced, fear trickling along her nerve endings like ice water. She shrank from him and attempted to swing her legs off the bed. She nearly cried out from pain as the movement tore at her ribs.

"It would be worth your while to listen to what I have to say," Ward said, his eyes cold flat. "They are willing to concede a great deal, Mrs. Cross."

Sam studied his face for a moment. "Look at me, Mr. Ward. *Look* at me."

He focused on her face. His features took on the blankness of control, then he looked away.

"Are they willing for their son to go to jail?"

"I can't say they are."

"Will Cross is a murderer. He killed my baby. He has terrorized my daughter, and me, with his mother and father's blessing, for the last three years. Unless you're going to say that the Crosses will go away, and that neither my daughter or I will ever, *ever* have to see Chaney, Page or Will Cross's faces, or hear their voices, ever again for as long as we both live, I'm not interested in hearing what you have to say."

"No, I can't say that's what they had in mind."

"Then we have nothing to discuss, Mr. Ward."

She slid off the mattress and grabbed the edge of the bedside table to maintain her balance. The pain medication made her woozy and weak, the forced movement tipped her stomach into nausea.

"You could be a rich woman, Mrs. Cross."

Samantha grabbed the tail of her hospital gown and folded it around her to cover her bare behind. "I'd never live to spend it." To walk to the door unaided took every bit of her concentration. She'd never be able to open the door on her own. She knocked on the door and the security guard opened it.

She eased around to lean back against the wall and braced herself. "Would you like to repeat everything you've said in front of this man, Mr. Ward?"

Ward's gaze went from the guard, to her, and back again. He gathered his briefcase. "You're making a mistake," he said, his features tight. "Think of your daughter."

Was that a threat? Would Chaney and Page try to take Joy? Of course they would. Her legs shook and she leaned more heavily against the wall.

Never!

"I am thinking of her. What do you think it's done to her to see how her father has treated me, Mr. Ward? What do you think it's done to her to live in fear of him?"

Ward's thin lips compressed. He stalked past her.

"Are you all right, Ma'am?" the security guard asked.

No, she wasn't. She was shaking and her teeth had the urge to chatter. But she would be okay. One day. She nodded, and after drawing a shallow, cleansing breath, wove unsteadily back to the bed.

She braced her hips on the bed, and reached inside the bedside cabinet, for the slip of paper Tammi Mai had placed there. Edgy desperation settled like a clenched fist in her stomach as she picked up the telephone, hit nine for an outside number, and dialed.

San Diego

Flash spread mayonnaise on a slice of bread, put a thick serving of ham on it, a slice of Swiss cheese, and mashed another piece of bread on top. Since he'd been injured he'd barely touched food, and now the headache had eased, he was starving. *Kind of Gilbert to leave some lunch meat for my sandwich.* Flash's lips twisted in a bitter smile.

He cleaned up any mess that would alert the guy to his presence, then washed the knife and slid it back in the drawer.

He wrapped the sandwich in a paper towel to contain the crumbs and settled in an overstuffed chair close to the window so he could watch for Gilbert's car.

The afternoon wore on. To pass the time, Flash searched the apartment for any paperwork that would tell him about Gilbert. Though he didn't find any telling bank statements or evidence of offshore accounts, the guy certainly had a taste for expensive furnishings and clothes. His closet was divided into middle of the road expensive suits and the really good stuff. A few for work and more for play, Flash assumed. The leather couch and chairs in the living room would cost three grand easy. Which in itself wasn't a smoking gun.

Gilbert had some boss electronics, too, but the desktop Flash had tapped into before was gone, replaced by a state-of-the-art laptop, password-protected, which held him up a whole ten minutes. He looked over the hard drive for anything that set off alarms. He found his own file, given to the FBI, with most of the information redacted. His earlier history, his sealed juvie records, were all there and read like he'd attended Con U and was heading toward a life behind bars. And he would have, had it not been for Travis. He copied down Gilbert's personal account numbers, shut down the computer, and moved on, being careful to wipe his prints from anything he touched.

He set up a small motion-sensor surveillance camera in the corner of the room just over the top of the cabinets. He took the flat screen TV apart and hid another just inside the speaker screen, then put everything back. He set up a computer to capture the signal, installed a program so he could download the feed remotely using Gilbert's internet connection, and hid the small laptop in the crawlspace above his apartment. What happened in the apartment while he was here would be recorded. Flash would send a copy of the files to NCIS.

If he couldn't clear himself with the Navy, he could always do this shit for a living in the *real* world. *After he got out of jail.* The thought did nothing to ease the near-constant edgy alarm that blared in the back of his mind. *He needed to get back to his team. Now!*

The shadows in the lot descended and the streetlights came on. Flash retrieved his suppressor from the backpack and screwed it onto his Sig Sauer P 226. Should he fire the weapon for effect, he didn't want the sound alerting the neighbors. He stuck some zip ties in his back pocket.

Fifteen minutes later Gilbert's nondescript dark blue sedan pulled into one of the parking spaces. "Thank you, Jesus!" Flash murmured beneath his breath and rose to stow his gear. He policed the area to double-check that everything appeared just as it had when he'd arrived, grabbed up his backpack and booked it into the kitchen pantry and out of sight. With the lights out and no window, the kitchen stood in darkness.

Sounds of the locks turning, the door opening, reached him and he sank back against the pantry shelves. A jingling sound followed. Probably change and keys being dropped into the glass bowl on the coffee table. A cell phone rang and Gilbert's voice grew distant as his steps receded down the hall.

Flash eased the door open, took two quick strides out into the kitchen, and scanned the living room. It was empty. He took up a position just inside the doorway, set his backpack down and waited. Gilbert's voice grew louder, closer.

Flash rolled back against the wall and waited for him to pass.

"We'll find him and he'll still have the artifacts and the money. Despite his history, he has too strong a sense of duty to sell them or spend the cash. Then we'll be back in business."

Back in business my ass. He eased forward and caught a glimpse of Gilbert's back and stared a hole through it. Gilbert might have fucked up his SEAL career, but this asshole would *be back in business.*

Heat hit Flash's face like a blast furnace as anger temporarily shot a reddish haze over his vision. *The son of a bitch!* Why hadn't Flash put a camera in his bedroom?

Gilbert kept pacing as he spoke. "If you'd done your job, there wouldn't have been a problem. Dobson should have never been killed. His death has drawn attention to the whole operation."

Was that regret he heard in the man's voice for Dobson, or for the operation? Flash was frustrated by only getting the tail end of the conversation. What else had they talked about? And who the hell was he talking to?

He scanned Gilbert's frame for a weapon. His shoulder harness and weapon lay on the coffee table next to the bowl with his keys. When the man turned, Flash bobbed back against the wall and rested there out of sight.

Gilbert wandered around the living room in restless circles while he spoke, the changing timbre of his voice keeping Flash apprised of his location.

"Yeah, I know. Keep digging. We have to have that contact before we can link the two. Keep me posted." When Gilbert leaned over to toss his phone onto the coffee table he came into view. He brushed his fingers through his hair, stretched, and then turned. His footsteps came closer to the dark kitchen. Flash flattened himself against the wall.

Gilbert hit the light switch, illuminating the room. In a swift, practiced move, Flash rested the suppressor at the base of Gilbert's skull. "Don't. Fucking. Move."

Gilbert jerked, then stiffened. "How long have you been here?"

"Long enough. Why did you try to fucking kill me?"

"I didn't."

"You may not have pulled the trigger, but you were the one calling the shots. What's happened to the assholes who shot me?"

'They're on administrative leave while they recover from their injuries, and the shooting is being investigated."

And I'm the only witness. "Once the first shot was fired, they tried to cover things up by taking me out. Was that their idea or yours?"

His thick dark brows contracted in a frown. "I wasn't involved, Carney."

"I don't believe you."

He shoved Gilbert forward and gripped his shoulder to jerk him down into a chair at the small kitchen table. "Put your hands behind your back."

Gilbert turned his head into the barrel of the gun and looked over his shoulder. "You don't want to do this."

"Yeah, I do." He wanted to lay into the guy and whale on his head. Since he had the advantage of twenty pounds and five inches in height against this asshole, he could do some major damage. The idea was tempting. "You've fucked up my gig with my team, asshole. You fuck with me again and I'll take you out."

Gilbert's mouth tightened and he shoved his hands behind him. Flash set aside the gun long enough to secure Gilbert's hands to the back of the chair, and then secured his ankles to the chair legs.

Flash removed the suppressor from his weapon, shoved it into his pocket and seated the Sig into his waistband at his back. Now that the guy was tied, he shook the tension from his muscles and stepped around to face him.

"What have you done with the artifacts and the cash?" Gilbert demanded.

"They're secure." At least, he hoped the artifacts were.

"You're not making a case for innocence with this behavior, Carney."

"Innocence of what? All I did was go to the meet and follow orders." He jerked off his hat and turned his head. "This is what your guys did, Gilbert." Though he knew it was impossible, he asked anyway. "Are they the same ones who killed Dobson?"

Gilbert mouth tightened. "No. That was someone who tracked our activities. Look, Carney, you don't know everything that's going on."

"Then why don't you explain it to me? Right now I don't feel the love, Gilbert. And I certainly don't feel the trust. Why do you think I'd turn anything over to you with the way things read right now?

"Because I can get you back to your team. I can smooth things over with your command. That's what you want, isn't it?"

That was exactly what he wanted. But once he turned everything over to this asshole, he'd be a sitting duck for being arrested or put down like a rabid dog.

"Start explaining, Gilbert."

"It's complicated."

"I've done complicated before."

"Yeah, I've read your juvie record."

Flash raised a brow. "That was a long time ago and not relevant to this. Quit stalling."

Gilbert pulled against the zip ties, his olive skin flushed with effort. "You're going to regret this."

"Trust me, I already regret ever agreeing to do anything for the FBI. But I'm not regretting one moment of this, asshole. The longer you stall, the more excuses I have for trying something painful to get you to open up."

"I can't talk about the case. We're dealing with national security."

"Yeah? *I am* national security, Gilbert old boy." Flash cocked a brow at him. "Do you *really* want to go there?"

"Fuck!" Gilbert jerked his shoulders then drew several deep breaths. His dark gaze shifted around the room, as though looking for a means of escape. He jerked his head to clear the heavy wave of brown hair falling over his forehead from his eyes. "The artifact smuggling is tied to drug trafficking in Iraq and Afghanistan. The major drug cartels are trafficking in artifacts to create a new pipeline for the drugs. We needed an in with the network to get involved with the drug trade there."

Well, this was going to be good. Flash leaned back against the counter and waited for the man's tell. "I smuggled artifacts into the US for the FBI just so they could be sold and then traded for drugs."

Gilbert shrugged. "Sometimes you have to do bad things for good reasons. There's a guy high up in the Iraqi government we think is behind the whole thing. Instead of taking over through car bombings and acts of terrorism, he's using the drug money to get his own people into key positions. We're trying to create a trail to lead things back to him, so the Iraqi government can take him and his people down."

Flash allowed the information to stew for a moment while he studied the guy's body language. "Why artifacts? Why not just money?"

"This guy is fanatic about his national heritage and about getting us out of his country. He wants us, and our democratic influence, gone. His get-into-business card is a piece of Iraqi history. Think about it. He's sticking it to us two different ways. He's sending drugs over here to be peddled. And he's using the money he makes to fund his own terrorist takeover."

"It's the drug cartels who've set up trade here who are using the artifacts to create a new pipeline for product," Flash repeated.

"Yeah. Most of them have set up shop from other countries, so they owe no loyalty to us. We had no way of infiltrating them so we could get in on the ground floor. So we created our own."

"So you're going to use National Security to take them down for terrorism."

"Which will keep them in prison longer than drug charges seem to."

The scenario he was talking about was complicated enough to be true. Flash studied Gilbert's face. Sweat beaded the guy's forehead and ran down his cheek. He blinked several times. "How are they getting the drugs from Iraq and Afghanistan to here?"

"They're shipping them from West Africa into Cuba, then they're filtering them in through Miami."

Flash had worked in Africa. He knew about the drug cartels there. Drugs were an equal opportunity employer. And big enough money so governments of poor countries ignored their trade to get their hands on some of the cash. But there was something about the scenario Gilbert was outlining…it sounded familiar somehow. "What happened with the two assholes who shot me?"

"They weren't FBI. They were sent to take you out, just like the other squad was sent to take Dobson and me out. Their badges were a thumb-their-nose type of deal." There went Gilbert's quick blinking again.

A fresh wave of anger rolled through Flash. His stomach muscles cramped and he moved around the kitchen. A memory clicked and he drew a deep breath. What now? He stared at the fancy cappuccino machine on the counter. Wonder how much that set his pal *Bert* back? His mind raced. "Why the hell wouldn't you tell me that? You let me believe they were FBI agents and that my career, my life, was probably over."

"I follow orders just like you do, Carney. The powers that be are trying to limit the fallout. Our whole operation was compromised. We lost three agents. But you gave us two contract killers who might be able to lead us back to some key players." Blink, blink, blink.

He didn't doubt that killers were involved. He'd played Dobson's message and heard that going down. "Glad I could help you out, *Bert*." Bitterness laced his voice. If they were hit men and not FBI, their bodies were probably weighted down somewhere at the bottom of the Pacific Ocean.

"It was a competing faction who sent them in. They tapped into our operation and decided to take the whole thing down."

"It sounds as though they did."

"Not quite. We still have some people in place deeper in. But we need the artifacts you have and the cash."

"Well that just may be a problem, *Bert*."

The man's eyes narrowed. "Why is that?"

"They're with some people I trust a lot more than I do you."

Gilbert's eyes widened, his thick brows shot upward. "Who?"

Flash shook his head. “Next time you spin a yarn to a mark, try to control your body language, dude.”

Gilbert face paled, then color shot into his cheeks. He strained against the straps that held his hands and feet and the chair danced on the tile floor. “God damn it, Carney. You have to listen to me. We need those artifacts and the money.”

“I’m sure you do. I don’t know what all this is about. But I know straight up that the bullshit you just spread around in here isn’t it.”

Flash strode across the kitchen, picked up his pack, and sauntered across the living room toward the front door.

“If we don’t deliver those artifacts to the buyer, everything comes apart, Flash.”

“Yeah? Just like you’ve pulled my life apart with this crap.”

“Why do you think I’m not telling the truth?”

“I may have been downrange, but I haven’t been out of touch. The scenario you just outlined happened in South America about two years ago. And let’s just say I’ve had first-hand experience in Africa.”

“You walk out that door and you’re a dead man,” Gilbert threatened.

Flash scooped Gilbert’s car keys out of the bowl on the coffee table and turned to look over his shoulder. “Every time I’ve gone on a mission that’s been a possibility.”

He slammed the door behind him as he left the apartment.

CHAPTER 9

Las Vegas

"Your health insurance has been canceled, Mrs. Cross," the woman said from her seat next to the hospital bed. She had introduced herself as someone from the hospital financial office. "As of this morning you have no insurance. I need you to sign these forms taking financial responsibility for the remainder of your stay."

Samantha stared at the woman. Of course Will and his parents had found a way to put pressure on her. The lawyer had warned her that it would happen. "Was my husband's coverage canceled or just mine?" she asked.

"I don't know. I only spoke to the district manager of the health insurance company about your coverage."

"What did you say your name is?" Sam asked.

"My name is Leigh Gabbard, Mrs. Cross."

"Ms. Gabbard, I'm not signing those forms and I'm not taking financial responsibility for being injured. My husband is responsible for this, and I've paid enough."

"But someone has to accept responsibility in order for you to stay, Mrs. Cross."

Sam drew as deep a breath as she could to fight back the panic. Her stomach knotted with both rage and tears. Without Will's support she had nothing. And obviously his family believed that by cutting her off and making her destitute, they would have the leverage to manipulate her.

Why hadn't she fought harder to have a job of her own, to have her independence? Because Will hadn't wanted her to be independent. He hadn't wanted her to have anything but him. Once again he was abusing her, psychologically. And, like always, he had forgotten his daughter's well-being.

Sam threw the blanket aside and slid her legs free of the bed. She bit back a cry of pain as she rested her weight on her feet. Every muscle in her body seized. Her ribs made it impossible for her to straighten up.

Mrs. Gabbard's eyes widened. "What are you doing?" She got to her feet.

Sam reached for the phone. "I'm calling my grandmother to come pick me up."

"But..." She bit her lip. "You can't leave unless your doctor discharges you."

There was something freeing about the truth. The more she spoke it out loud, the more the weight of all she'd been carrying lifted. "Then I suppose you'd better go out and tell the nurse to call him to come and discharge me. I don't have any money, Ms. Gabbard. I don't have a job. My husband has canceled my insurance to try and pressure me into dropping charges against him. And I can't have thousands of dollars in hospital bills hanging over my head when I'm trying to live without any support. So, I'm leaving." Sam looked through the slit of her injured left eye. Thank God, she could finally see out of it. "I can't pay to stay here. I'll just have to make do."

"But you're too ill to go home."

"That doesn't really matter, does it?" Sam asked. "Otherwise you wouldn't be sitting there with your forms, and I wouldn't be standing here calling for someone to pick me up."

Mrs. Gabbard's eyes looked dazed and a little anxious as she left the room.

Sam dialed her grandmother's number. "Gran, I'm being released a little early. Can you come and pick me up?"

"Certainly. Joy's almost finished with breakfast. I'll get her dressed, and we can be there within the hour."

"Please bring me something to wear. I don't have any clothes here. They cut them off when they brought me in."

"I went to the house yesterday and picked up some of Joy's things and yours."

Dear God, what had she seen? Had the police been there to gather evidence? She pushed the thought away. "Bring me something loose. I can't really bear anything against my skin."

"Okay."

"I'll need some sanitary napkins." Tears glazed her vision but she fought them back. She'd grieve later, when she had time. Right now she needed to put one foot in front of the other and do what needed to be done.

"All right. I'll get them. Why are they releasing you so quickly?" Concern came through in Ellen's tone. "You've only been in the hospital a day and a half."

"They can't really do anything for me, Gran. I just need to heal, and I can do that at home with you and Joy, just as well as I can here."

"I suppose so."

"I'll have to rest a lot at first. I'll need to stay close to the hospital for another twenty-four hours, just in case. Maybe we can go home tomorrow."

"I don't think it's a good idea for you to go back to the house, Sam."

"No. I'm talking about your house, Gran. I know it's an imposition, but as soon as I'm better, I'm going to get a job, and Joy and I can get our own place."

"Only if you want to, Samantha. My home is your home for as long as you want it. You're still my girl."

Tears blurred her vision again and she leaned against the bed for more support. "I know I am, Gran. But I don't want to bring trouble to your door."

"Honey. Do you really believe I could ever go home and leave you and Joy here like this?"

"No." Every shortened telephone conversation, every tension-filled visit they'd had in the last three and a half years came back to torment her. Now that everything was out in the open… "I love you, Gran. I'm so sorry I didn't tell you. I wanted to. I tried to get away from him, and every time—I was too afraid."

"Sam. I know. Do you think I'm blind? I knew you had trouble. I tried several times to talk to you but you shut me down."

"I was ashamed. Ashamed that I'd gotten myself into something I couldn't get out of. Ashamed to tell you that someone I loved was treating me like..." *A punching bag.* "And afraid for you and Joy. He told me he could drive to your house any time and snap your neck, and no one would ever know it was him. I believed him, Gran. I still do. You have to be careful." The panic inside her raced out with the words.

Ellen's voice grew soft. "We're going to be okay, Sam. I promise. He's never going to lay a hand on any of us ever again."

The resolve she heard in her grandmother's voice eased her fear and boosted her confidence. "No, he's not." No matter what she had to do to protect them. There were weapons at Gran's house. And she'd use them, if she had to. They'd be fine.

"I'll be there to pick you up in an hour," Ellen said, breaking into her thoughts.

She hung up the phone and, gripping the mattress, then the foot of the bed, she moved around to sit in the chair Ms. Gabbard had vacated. She had to push on.

As long as she sat very still, the pain wasn't too bad. She braced the heel of her hand on the seat of the chair and tried to shift slightly until she could breathe a little easier.

"What's this I hear about you asking to be discharged?" Dr. Simons said from the door.

Her strength was fading fast. "I'm sure Ms. Gabbard told you about the situation."

"Your health is worth more than the money, Mrs. Cross," he said, his tone stern.

"That's easy for you to say, but I'm living the reality of it all. As long as I'm married to Will Cross, my income is tied to his. This hospital is going to look at his income as mine, though I've never had more than grocery money to spend. I won't qualify for any kind of financial help. So when we split, and we will be doing that, he'll refuse to pay the bill and I'll be left with it. And I can't afford to be saddled with a crippling debt when I have a child to care for, Dr. Simon. Not when I'll be trying to break away from Will, and from his family's control." *She'd need whatever money she could earn to pay lawyer fees and for Joy.* "So, I need you to release me. My grandmother is coming to pick me up."

Dr. Simon's jaw grew taut and frustration flickered across his features. "You'll need to stay close to the hospital for at least another twenty-four hours, in case you start to hemorrhage again. If you have any kind of issue at all, nausea, fever, headache, more pronounced bleeding, you'll need to get back in here immediately, bill or no bill."

Sam nodded "I understand."

He turned away.

"Thank you, Dr. Simons."

He paused at the door. "I'm sorry you've gone through this. But I'm glad you're getting away from…the situation. I'm sorry I didn't take your warnings about your husband more seriously."

So she had gotten an apology after all, but she no longer needed it. "You don't know how devious or determined someone can be unless you've lived with them, lived with…all they can do. How could you have known?"

"I'll listen more carefully next time," he answered and continued out the door.

Sam forced herself to her feet and pushed the call button. She requested a towel and washcloth so she could take a shower. A few minutes later, the nurse walked her down the hall to the shower and helped her inside. "Should you feel faint or ill, push this button." She pointed out the emergency call button. "I'll be watching for it. Okay?"

"Thank you." The nurse left and Sam took her time getting the water the right temperature and setting out her hospital gown. Her strength drained after only a five-minute shower. She rushed to finish, then sat on a bench inside the room to dry off, put on the fresh gown and fit the belt and pad on.

She'd be strong again. She just had to cut off her grief so it wouldn't cripple her. And let her anger feed her determination. She would be free of Will Cross and his family.

She owed it to Joy. She owed it to the child she'd lost. And she owed it to herself. She bundled her dirty gown in the wet towel and wrapped her fresh one around her so the open back wouldn't flash everyone out in the hall. The nurse appeared again and kept a hand on her arm as she helped her back to her room. Lying on the bed again, Sam eyed the phone and asked the nurse to hand her the receiver. Once it was in her hand, she dialed her attorney's number. She gave his secretary her grandmother's cell phone number and told the secretary to tell him about the first volley lobbed at her by Will and his parents.

Less than an hour had passed when Ellen arrived with Joy and a plastic bag. Ellen approached the bed, and taking Sam into her arms, held her carefully. For a moment, Sam was as overwhelmed as her grandmother and they clung to one another.

When Ellen drew back, she wiped her eyes with the sleeve of her cotton shirt and turned to check on Joy.

The fear Sam read in Joy's face as Gran drew her close to the bed gave her heart a squeeze. And when she hid behind Ellen's leg, Sam couldn't catch her breath.

"Momma's okay, baby. I know I look awful, but I just have some bruises, and this is the last time this will happen. We're going to Grandma El's house, and we're going to be just fine."

"I wide on the tractor, old Betsy." Joy eased out from behind Ellen and took a tentative step toward Sam.

"Yes, you will. You and Freddy. And me, too."

Joy approached the bed and Sam raised her gaze to Ellen. She rushed forward to lift Joy onto the bed. Though it hurt to even be touched, Sam gathered her close and held her. "Mama has missed you, so much."

"Daddy's mean."

"Yes, he is sometimes." She smoothed Joy's fine blonde hair, so much like her own. "You're my girl and Grandma El's. Everything's going to be okay."

Joy raised her hand and her favorite little person was stuck on her index finger. "Fweddy missed you, too."

Sam smiled. "Thank you, Freddy, for missing me."

Joy grinned.

The nurse came in with Sam's release papers. She went over the cautions Dr. Simons had already covered with her, then said, "I'll give you a few minutes to change, and I'll be back with a wheelchair to take you to the front exit."

"Momma has to get dressed, baby." Sam said to Joy.

Ellen grasped Joy's hands and helped her slip down off the bed. Sam eased off the edge and leaned against the bed while her Grandmother got her clothes out of the bag. Suppressing any flinch of pain, she took the sweatpants and t-shirt into the bathroom and got dressed.

It was both comforting and strange to wear her own clothing. The scent of the fabric softener she used hadn't changed in the last eighteen hours. The way her tennis shoes felt on her feet hadn't altered, either. But *she* had changed somehow. With that last punch to her face, Will had broken his hold on her. Or had it been the time she'd spent to describe every moment of this last explosion of violence? Or had it been because she had defended herself? She was still afraid, but she wasn't going to take Will's abuse any more. She would protect herself, Joy, and Gran in any way she could.

She opened the door and walked back into the hospital room where they waited for her with the nurse.

Sam was grateful for the wheelchair ride downstairs. She'd have never made it to the main lobby without it. She kept her head down and used her hair to shield her injured face from the other people in the elevator.

"Joy and I will go bring the car around to the entrance," Ellen said, and taking Joy's hand, walked out the side entrance. They disappeared behind a crowd of people standing on the sidewalk.

"Wonder what's going on out there." the nurse said.

Sam shook her head. "I don't know. Maybe someone's family is here to pick them up." Through the crowd she caught a glimpse of her grandmother's car. "That's her car."

The nurse pushed her forward, and as she triggered the door mechanism, Sam bent her head so her hair covered the side of her face. The early morning sun proved to be too bright for her injured eye, and Sam threw up a hand to block it as they emerged from the building.

"That's her," a voice shouted from close by.

The sound of someone running brought her head up and she looked directly into a camera thrust into her face. The click of the picture being taken seemed to reverberate all around her. Surely she couldn't hear that above all the clamoring questions being fired at her, one on top of another.

"Is it true your husband has been arrested for abuse, Mrs. Cross?"

"Is he the one who beat you?"

"How do you know Judge Henry Mooreland?"

"Why are you leaving the hospital so soon after being admitted?"

Sam covered her face with her hands. "Please, stop."

"Stop it." the nurse stepped forward in an attempt to protect her.

"Why is she being discharged?" One man asked.

Who had called the press? And why would they even care about an abused woman?

She gripped the arm of one the men standing next her. "Why are you here?" she asked.

"Judge Henry Mooreland is being investigated by the state attorney's office for misconduct and obstruction. It's come to light that your first case of domestic abuse was mishandled and that Judge Mooreland had a hand in that. Do you have any comment on that?"

Sam drew in a slow, painful breath as her mind raced with possibilities. If she answered that question, she'd be thrown into a firestorm. Chaney Cross and Henry Mooreland had been friends for years.

Then she remembered how long she'd stood outside of Mooreland's office and waited for him to come out so she could beg for his help. He'd threatened to have her arrested if she didn't leave. He'd even had a court officer escort her from the building.

"Yes, I have a comment."

CHAPTER 10

Baja, California

Flash narrowed his eyes against the sun's sharp reflection on the bobbing waves ahead. The boat's engines vibrated beneath his feet. The right side of his head throbbed. He took his hat off, folded it and shoved it into his back pocket. His eyes felt hollow and scratchy from lack of sleep, and the farther he got from San Diego, the harder it was for him to hold it together.

This was much worse than any deployment he'd ever had.

At least he'd made Gilbert pay a little. After driving the guy's blue sedan down the street and parking it next to the Porsche, he'd left it sitting with the keys dangling in the ignition, hoping someone would steal it. Then he drove the Porsche back to the dealership, parked it next to a side door and put the keys in their drop box.

As he walked away, the knowledge that there might not be a way for him to save his career crashed over him. He saw everything he'd worked for, trained for, ending because of Gilbert, and wanted to go back to the apartment and beat the crap out of the asshole. *He should have done it.*

His phone vibrated against his hip. Grateful for the distraction, he pulled it free and pushed the button. "Hold on a minute." He eased the cabin cruiser back to a lower idle speed so the engine noise wouldn't disrupt the call.

"I have coordinates for you," Travis said and rattled off latitude and longitude. "Me and Javier will be waiting on you."

"Thanks, Travis."

"How's the head?"

"A little better."

"I always said you were a hard headed son of a bitch."

Flash smiled, though he didn't feel like it. "I remember."

"How bad are things?"

Flash closed his eyes with a grimace. "I may not be able to get back from this, Trav."

Travis remained silent for a moment. "We'll think of something."

"I'll see you around noon," Flash said.

"Okay. Watch your six."

"Roger that." He closed the phone and shoved it into his pocket. He reached for the nautical GPS and programmed in the latitude and longitude coordinates Travis had given him.

He'd be there before Travis and his son Javier, which would give him time to check out the digital feed from the cameras in Gilbert's apartment. He hoped the son of a bitch had ended up spending the whole night tied up and waiting for someone to come looking for him.

Flash tried to allow the bounce and roll of the boat to ease away his frustration and rage. He had to focus on other things or he'd go crazy. He needed to use his skills to find out what was really going on and then figure out how to get back to his team. But before he could do that, he had to take a step back and create a plan of attack.

Travis was the best strategist he knew. He'd certainly undermined every plan of attack Flash had come up with as a teenager.

The two of them working together would be able to find a way out of this mess. They had to. The thought brought him some comfort.

He glanced at the GPS and adjusted his heading. Twenty minutes later he'd arrived at the coordinates. Flash gazed toward the coast. Mexico was a mile further south. The water was so clear and blue it almost hurt to look at it. He dropped anchor and set up a fishing rod with a lure, cast it, and set it in the support built into the deck chair.

He visited Travis and his foster family in Baja whenever he could, but it had been some time since he'd had enough of a break in training rotations and deployments to do so. And now he was here in the worst possible circumstances. If it looked like he was going to bring trouble to the Gallagher's' door, he'd bug out and go it solo. But where?

If he had a contact in the Naval Criminal Investigative Service it would make things easier. He'd have to develop a contact. But how could he do that and avoid arrest?

He hadn't done anything wrong! Well, technically he had broken into the agent's apartment and bugged it, but only in self-defense.

Flash went downstairs into the cabin to retrieve his laptop. He took a seat on the deck and tapped into the satellite system on board. Reaching the remote unit he'd set up, he typed in the command to check the two cameras he had installed in Gilbert's apartment. The feed was running real time. The living room and kitchen were empty, but things appeared out of place. He frowned.

Accessing the laptop stored in the crawlspace of Gilbert's apartment, Flash downloaded the video he'd recorded in the last eight hours and reset the program to continue recording.

He set up the video and started scanning it while he waited for Travis to arrive. He came to a section where crime scene techs were dusting for fingerprints. *Good luck with that, guys.* He knew he hadn't left any. He'd even wiped down the inside of the television after installing the camera and given the commode handle a going over after he'd used it. Gilbert could say he'd been there, but there'd be no proof...other than this feed. And he'd only be sending out the segments of the video that would help his cause.

The tech guys should have found the camera in the kitchen and disabled it. That would have certainly scared the shit out of ol' *Bert.* He rewound the image back a couple of hours and watched the man struggle against his bonds. Then a door slammed, the sound loud and clear on the camera. Two men entered the room, one tall and slim, the other wide-shouldered and very big. Flash's stomach sank. What if the crime scene techs were there because Gilbert had been killed?

One of the men laughed, the other stood back out of view of the camera. The man within view of the screen looked six feet tall with dark hair and olive skin. He appeared Hispanic.

"How many people have you pissed off today, man?" The large guy out of camera range asked.

"Someone broke in and tied me up. Cut me loose."

"Fuck you. Where's our stuff?"

"I haven't got it. But I will."

"The money's been paid, cabrón. We want it now," the Hispanic man said.

"I'll have it for you soon. I explained to Caesar that someone attacked the couriers and ripped off the merchandise. I have more coming in this week. As soon as it's in hand, I'll deliver it to you myself."

"The boss sent us here to pick it up tonight."

"But I don't have it"

"Then I suppose we will have to give you something to remind you not to be late next time, cabrón."

Gilbert's head tilted back and he tensed. "That isn't necessary. I'm not trying to stiff you, I just need an extension on the time to deliver."

The Hispanic man punched him in the face, hitting his cheekbone.

Gilbert swore and shook his head. "You don't have to do this."

The man aimed more carefully this time, hitting him in the nose and mouth. Blood bloomed from both to run down his face.

"Stop," Gilbert demanded.

The man struck him again and again, and each time, Gilbert's head jerked back. After the sixth blow, Flash regretted having tied him up quite so thoroughly.

"Enough!" The man who had remained off camera stepped forward into the frame. He was shorter than the Hispanic man, but brawny, his skin a duskier hue, and his hands huge. His hair hung down on each side of his face at chin level, partially blocking his features. He threw out a hand to halt the next punch, grabbed Gilbert's hair, and pulled his head back. Gilbert didn't appear conscious. The man tapped his cheeks to bring him around.

"We will be back, Gilbert. The next time you see us, you had better have the shipment," he said.

"Ah…" he answered.

"Cut him loose." The big guy said.

Hispanic guy produced a switchblade from his back pocket and flicked it open. He cut the twist ties, releasing Gilbert's hands and feet. The half-conscious man slid out the chair to the floor and lay still.

The two men left him lying there and exited the apartment.

Flash fast-forwarded the film until he saw Gilbert struggle to his feet. He staggered out of the frame. After five minutes or so he appeared again, holding a wet towel to his face. He stumbled into the living room and out of sight. He returned a few minutes later with his cell phone.

Flash's stomach took a sickening tumble. *The zip ties.* He hadn't wiped down the zip ties. He knew exactly what Gilbert was going to do.

Gilbert connected to someone on the other end of the phone. "Carter, send a forensic team. Carney just broke in here and knocked me around."

Flash hit the escape button and set the computer aside. He paced the deck, every combination of cuss word he could think spewing from him. He grasped the ladder leading up to the fly bridge and pulled against it, wishing it was Gilbert, and he could rip him apart.

The sound of a boat approaching tugged him out of his frustration-induced rage. He recognized the white hull with blue trim, and drew several deep breaths to calm himself. Scooping up the laptop, he took it downstairs and stuck it in his backpack. By the time he was topside again with his gear, Travis had aligned his fishing vessel, the J.G., close to Bowie's cabin cruiser.

Travis stood on the sky bridge, feet braced apart. His six-foot-two frame carried at least a hundred ninety pounds of solid muscle and his features looked like he'd used it all in a boxing ring. His arms were covered with a collection of tattoos, all linked together in a theme of military service, and his gray hair was tied back in a ponytail. Flash raised a hand. "It's good to see you, old man."

"Old! We'll see how old you think I am once you're over here."

Flash laughed. He already felt lighter just seeing Travis's ugly face.

Javier Gallagher, Travis's nineteen-year-old son, launched a small rubber raft over the side and paddled over. Flash accepted the line to tie the raft to a cleat and offered him a hand up over the starboard side of the vessel.

Javier eyed his face and breathed an emotional, "Fuuuuck, bro. They did a number on you, didn't they?"

"Pretty much."

The two of them spent a moment bumping shoulders and pounding each other on the back in greeting.

"Dad said you needed a favor." Javier's gaze, liquid and dark like his mom's, was steady, his expression solemn. "So, I volunteered."

Flash frowned as second thoughts tumbled through his mind and tightened the knots in his stomach.

"It'll be okay, Flash," Javier said.

He shook his head. "I was hoping to avoid involving anyone here. But I can't keep Bowie's boat. It's his baby. And besides, if they start looking for it and it's found here, it'll lead them straight to me."

Javier nodded. "We've got it covered, bro."

Emotion suddenly clamped a hand around Flash's throat. He nodded once. "Look, I just need you to drop the boat back at the marina. When you leave it there, keep your hat on and your head down so none of the cameras catch your face. If they identify you, they'll come here to your mom and dad."

"Have there been any alerts on the news? Anything like that?" Javier asked.

"Nothing. They're keeping this on the down low as far as the public is concerned. But I know they're hunting me. They've frozen my bank accounts and flagged my credit cards." *Like that was going to do any good when he had a hundred thousand dollars of illegal money to spend.* They'd probably found the safety deposit box with all his orders in it as well. "They've searched my apartment and impounded my car. You can't be associated with me, Javier. If anyone stops you and asks, tell them I paid you to sail the boat back to the marina."

"No one's going to ask, Flash. I'm going to drop the boat off, hightail it to Mom and Dad's house, spend the night, pick up your motorcycle and drive it back here. It's going to be fine."

"Don't stay at the house. They'll be tracing my telephone calls and checking on every person I've contacted." His calls to Travis and Juanita were sporadic, but he did call every couple of months to check in.

He drew a deep breath and swallowed back the frustration and rage that careened through his system. "Be careful. I don't want this FBI fucker giving you, or your mom and dad, shit because of me. I don't think anyone knows how close we are and I want to keep it that way. It's been over ten years since Travis and Juanita took me in. And there was never any formal paperwork connecting us."

Javier gave his shoulder a squeeze. "Dad's going to help you figure things out. He always does."

"Yeah." Flash bobbed his head in agreement. If Javier got caught, they'd arrest him.

He'd be helping harbor a fugitive. He'd go to jail.

Jesus, he couldn't ask him to take that chance. He couldn't put Travis's son in harm's way. "There has to be another way."

"Flash, I can do this, man. You're not the only one who can sneak around without being seen. I had my moments when I lived at home. If I can handle Dad, I can slide right by the dudes at the marina."

Flash started to thrust his fingers through his hair, then remembered the injury and jerked his hand back down. Before he could change his mind, he stuck his hand in his front pocket and withdrew two one hundred dollar bills and a piece of paper. "I've written down the berth number. I haven't ridden my Triumph since I got back from Iraq. You may have some trouble with it."

"No, I won't." Javier grinned.

Flash narrowed his eyes. "All right. As long as you don't wreck her, I'm down with you borrowing her now and then."

"I won't put a scratch on her, I promise."

"Good. She'll be my primary mode of transport until all this is settled. Treat her kindly. The registration is in—"

"Dad told me where it is. He said it was in his name. What's up with that?"

Flash shrugged. "If something happens to me, it makes things less complicated. I'll get my gear."

Javier's features blanked. Then he came back with, "I'll hold out for the car."

"I haven't gotten around to that, since I just bought it before my last deployment." And now it was locked up in the impound lot. *And peppered with bullet holes.*

He went below and returned with his backpack and a duffle with a few clothes and the money. He'd debated whether to leave the cash hidden on board Bowie's boat, but worried he might get Bowie in deep water should the FBI discover he'd been on board.

He dropped his duffle and backpack onto the raft. "Leave the key on the sky bridge." He described where the hide-a-key was kept.

"I'll call after I get the bike and bug out, *Mom,*" Javier razzed him.

Flash feinted a punch and Javier danced away with a smirk. They grasped hands and bumped shoulders again.

Aware of the important cargo he had in the craft, Flash went over the side of the boat and eased into the raft. By the time he made it to the J. G., Javier had taken in the anchor and started the engines of cabin cruiser. A fresh wave of anxiety hit Flash. There was no way he could protect his foster brother. He just had to believe he'd be okay.

He tossed his baggage to Travis and climbed up on the metal platform at the back of the fishing vessel. He watched Trident pull away and turned to step up on deck.

"You look like shit, son," Travis said, a fierce frown creasing his face.

Flash laughed. He could always count on Travis to cut straight through the bullshit. The bruising had darkened and the whole side of his head had turned purple down to his jaw.

"Nita is going to throw a fit." Travis enveloped him in a bear hug and pounded his back.

Just being with someone he knew cared eased the tightness in the pit of Flash's stomach. "I have video of the asshole setting me up again," he said as the embrace ended.

"Good. We'll figure out a way to get it to the right people. I've already reached out to a couple of buddies who might be able to help."

His eyes blurred. Flash ducked his head to cover his response. "Thanks, Trav." He manhandled the raft back on deck. By the time he'd done that and taken his backpack and duffle below decks, Travis had secured the raft and pointed the nose of the vessel inland.

Flash joined him on the sky bridge. He dragged in the salt-scented air and tried to relax the tension in his shoulders.

"I'll drop you in one of the inlets, and you can climb up to the coastal road and avoid the police. After I dock the boat at the marina, I'll pick you up."

"I can get to the house under my own steam."

"Not looking like that," Travis said, with a scowl. "Everyone who sees you will remember the guy whose head looks like an eggplant. You could have died from the concussion."

"I thought about that and decided to give it a pass."

Travis shook his head and grinned. "Sometimes I think you're more like me than any of my kids."

"Not so. Javier may look like 'Nita but he's definitely got a streak of you in him. He wouldn't have volunteered to run the boat back into San Diego for me if he didn't." He kept what Javier had said about slipping around the old man to himself. Brothers watched each other's backs. "Javier would enlist in a heartbeat if 'Nita wouldn't bitch about it."

"Over the years she's put up with enough with me being deployed and now you."

Flash could understand that. The life was hard on families. He'd signed up because Travis had shown him a way of life that fed his wild streak and still kept him on the right side of legal. Until Travis and Juanita had come into his life, he'd been on his way to possibly doing something stupid enough to get sent to jail. He'd been damn lucky to avoid it. Ten years later he was using his tech skills and his sniper skills to protect his country. And he got to blow shit up, too.

Flash studied the coastline, with its rugged patches of volcanic rock and clear blue water. Travis pointed toward a gray whale on the starboard side. The huge animal surfaced, sending spray in the air, then dove, its shape a dark shadow moving out to sea.

"This isn't a bad place to be until you get things squared away," Travis said.

It just wasn't where he needed to be. He had to get back to his team.

Travis nodded as though he read the thought. Twenty minutes later he guided the J.G. into a cove close to one of the public beaches. "If you head up past that outcropping of rock, you can follow the property line to the hotel. Walk up to the road and I'll be by to pick you up in about twenty minutes. 'Nita is waiting for me to bring you home."

Flash reached behind him to remove the gun he had tucked into his waistband and handed it to Travis. "There's a hundred thousand reasons why you shouldn't get stopped at the marina," Flash said. "I couldn't leave the money on Bowie's boat, and I couldn't waltz into my bank at home and open an account or rent a safety deposit box. If it looks like things are going to go sideways, dump the duffle over the side."

He climbed down the ladder, swung around to toe himself along the narrow ledge to the bow of the boat. Travis nosed closer to shore. Flash tugged his ball cap from his back pocket and pulled it on. He flipped his sunglasses out of his shirt pocket and eased them on. He waved to Travis, signaling close enough, and leaped into the warm Pacific water.

He trudged through the surf to the large outcropping of rock that Travis had mentioned. He glanced over his shoulder to see Travis backing the boat into deep water and swinging it to port.

The sand clung to his shoes in a crust that weighted them. He waited until he'd reached the sparse grass that met the beach and beat each heel against a rock to knock it off. He was reminded of being soaking wet and rolling in the sand until he was covered like a sugar cookie during BUD/S. It had scraped the skin off in uncomfortable places and gotten in his eyes, but he had survived. He'd worked his ass off to make it through BUD/S and then through sniper training.

He was going to get back to his team, no matter what he had to do to make it happen. He'd just have to find a way to contact NCIS without getting thrown in the brig and turned over to the FBI.

He worked his way around a clump of palms and climbed the hill to the hotel Travis had mentioned. The Spanish-style building was typical of the area, as were the terracotta shingles. Wide, arched doors and windows were set symmetrically across the front of the two-story building and the flowerbeds were sculpted in an artistic plan of color and texture with layered areas of dahlias, ornamental grasses, regional cactus, and agave.

The scent of ocean tinged air, and the perfume of the blossoms blended with the mouth-watering aroma of grilled fish from somewhere in the hotel. His stomach growled, and he had an instant craving for 'Nita's enchiladas and chili verde.

He kept to the shadowed areas of the grounds and strolled past the parking lot toward the road. He settled behind one of the palms, his back to the road.

His pants legs were almost dry by the time he spotted Travis's truck. He hustled to his feet and jogged to the edge of the road, cut in front of the vehicle as soon as it pulled to a stop and got in.

"I can almost smell 'Nita's enchiladas," he said.

"You look as though you could use a week or two of them. The first thing you need to do is get back to fighting form."

He had lost weight just in the last few days. This thing was eating him up inside. "I will."

Twenty minutes later they pulled up in front of a hacienda-style, three-story home. The garage doors were open, and parked inside was a white and blue police car with the Baja city logo on the side. And walking toward them was one of their officers, dressed in a black t-shirt with Baja Police printed on one side of his chest.

Flash's heartbeat shot up to the speed of a cruise missile.

"There's something I meant to tell you, Flash."

His insides twisted as Travis's betrayal became evident.

"What have you done, Trav?"

CHAPTER 11

Las Vegas

Ellen set the newspaper on the bed beside Sam. "Your father-in-law has been dragged into the investigation. He's coming off as an arrogant ass."

"That's no surprise, since he is one." Sam picked up the newspaper and scanned the headline. *Las Vegas Judge Investigated for Obstruction.*

Sam tilted her head back against the pillow, and rested her hand on the paper. Weakness infused every bone and muscle of her body. Her neck felt like it had been wrenched. Muscles screamed at every small move. She thought after the first two days the worst of the bruising would have shown itself, but it continued to darken and creep along her body, forming a map of abuse. Every punch and kick was evident. At least the vision in her left eye had finally cleared.

She'd crept into the bathroom earlier, and, using her phone, had taken a picture of every bruise and mark, just as Tammi Mai had. If the police photos disappeared, she'd have a record of her own. From now on, she also would record every telephone conversation and interaction she had with the Cross family. She was through being their victim.

Just thinking those words sent a shiver of fear and uncertainty through her. She had crumbled before the pressure her in-laws put on her in the past, her fear of losing Joy their biggest weapon. But now that Henry Moreland was no longer in a position to help them, she might have a chance.

"It's almost time to go," Ellen said and touched Sam's hand.

Sam studied her grandmother's features. She seemed a little pale this morning, and stress had marched across her face, leaving deep furrows around her mouth. And she had lost weight since Sam had last seen her. "Are you okay, Gran?"

"I'm fine, honey."

Something in her smile didn't quite convince Sam. But entertaining a four-year-old was exhausting if you weren't used to it. And Gran was sixty-four, though she still looked much younger.

Sam's attention strayed to Joy as she sat on the foot of the bed watching cartoons. Her white-blonde hair hung in soft curls down each side of her face. Her blue eyes were focused on the television, a slight smile curving her lips. She was such a sweet-natured child. She'd stay that way, too, as long as she wasn't influenced by Will and his parents.

Sam had practically slept through the day yesterday. But today was a new beginning, and no matter how bad her pain, it was time to pull things together.

She rolled onto her side and slid her legs off the edge of the bed, then pushed herself up into a sitting position. Though her ribs hurt every time she breathed, she gasped in a breath, and forced herself to her feet. Once vertical, she felt every ache, but focused on straightening her cotton blouse and slacks.

"I'll go brush my hair."

Ellen nodded, then sat down next to Joy.

"Fweddie and Sawah are watching Dora," Joy said her voice high-pitched and appealing. She stuck her index fingers up in the air to show Ellen the two little people stuck on the end of them.

"Is Dora their favorite?" Ellen asked.

"Ah-huh."

"Is she your favorite?" she asked.

"Ah-huh."

Sam listened to them debate whether Dora's hair would look better blonde like Joy's and smiled. There was no stress in her child's voice. She didn't babble like a baby. She was talking in complete sentences and actually laughing. A tightness, one she hadn't even realized she was experiencing, eased.

Even though she had to place every step with care, Sam smiled when she came out of the bathroom. "What are you two going to do while I'm talking to the lawyer?"

"There's a pizza place nearby with games and things. I thought I'd take Joy and let her play."

"She's never been. She'll love it. Won't you, baby?"

"What kind of games?" Joy asked, the question tentative, and her features edged with anxiety.

Sam knelt in front of her. "It's just a place for you to eat pizza and there are video games, but there are other games just for children your age, too. Grandma El will be with you and teach you how to play. As soon as I'm done at the lawyer's office, I'll call and you can come get me. Okay?"

Joy studied her face with anxious eyes. "'Kay."

Sam leaned close to hold her as tears threatened for them both. "Momma and Grandma El will never ever let anything hurt you, Joy. If you don't like it there, she'll take you to McDonald's."

"'Kay."

"Let's get your shoes on."

"I do it, Momma." She slid down off the bed and trotted away to get her tennis shoes.

Sam struggled to her feet.

Ellen gave her arm a squeeze. "She's just like you were at that age. Independent. Despite everything that's happened, she's a strong little girl, Sam. She's going to be just fine."

If she could keep her from becoming a pawn in all this. Joy's protection would be Sam's main focus when she spoke with her lawyer.

Joy tugged the Velcro straps that secured her shoes and scrambled to her feet. "All done!"

"Good job, Tumble Bug," Ellen said and offered her a hand.

The three of them left the motel and strolled across the parking lot to the car. After getting Joy secured and settled, Sam eased into the front seat next to her grandmother. The trip from the room to the car had already depleted Sam's reserves, and she dropped her head back against the headrest. Ellen pulled the car out onto Rainbow Boulevard and turned north to hit West Tropicana to the strip. Sam pretended to concentrate on the passing scenery while the thousand questions she needed to ask the attorney raced through her mind.

The twenty-minute trip passed all too quickly. Her pulse spiked as the car came to a stop in front of the building. She was afraid to dwell on it too long for fear she'd freeze and not be able to get out of the car. "I'll call you as soon as my meeting is over, Gran," Sam managed around the knot in her throat as she got out. She clung to the car door for a few seconds to make sure her balance was steady.

"Are you sure you don't want me to stay with you?" Ellen asked.

"I'm sure. Little miss might get restless. It will be easier if she's distracted."

Ellen nodded.

"Bring me back some pizza."

"We will."

Sam leaned into the car. "Stay with Grandma El, Joy. Have a good time. I'll see you in an hour."

"Bye-bye, Mommy."

"Bye, baby." Sam slammed the door and watched them pull away and turn at the end of the block. Just being separated from her grandmother and Joy made her anxiety spike.

When she turned to face the building, her heart raced as if she'd run a marathon, and for a moment she couldn't catch her breath, so she tried distracting herself with insignificant details.

The structure was seven stories high. All glass and concrete, the façade stretched heavenward, smooth and shiny. Her fingers gripped her shoulder bag strap like a lifeline. Her legs felt weak and rubbery as she shuffled to the main entrance and tugged it open. In the open entrance foyer, modern cream-colored couches and chrome, glass topped tables mirroring the exterior of the building were arranged in groupings.

Sam pulled her long hair forward around her cheek to hide the bruises from the people sitting there, and walked to a check-in desk. The woman who sat behind it eyed her injuries but said nothing. She offered Sam a pen to sign in, told her the office number, and directed her down a wide hallway to the elevators.

The elevator door opened and Sam ducked her head as two people got out. She stepped in before the doors could close and pushed the button for the second floor. The elevator rose, opened, and a wide hall stretched before her with a plaque on the wall designating office numbers. She pulled the scrap of paper from her bag to double-check even though the woman downstairs had told her the number.

Finding it just a few doors down the hall, she leaned against the wall for just a moment. She knew she had to take this step, but it was so hard to know whom she could trust.

The firm's receptionist's desk sat to the right of a suite of offices decorated in dark blue and khaki. The woman there acknowledged her appointment and instructed her to take a seat.

Sand-colored drapes covered a large bank of windows that ran the length of the room, allowing warm light to come into the space without the glare. Dark blue couches and two overstuffed khaki chairs sat at angles before a large solid wood coffee table.

Sam chose one of the chairs, hoping it would be easier and less painful to get out of than the couch, which was lower.

The longer she studied the expensive décor, the more anxious she became. She'd never be able to afford this lawyer's fees. This was a mistake. It was time to get out of here.

"Mrs. Cross?"

Sam glanced up to see an older man approaching her.

"I'm Benjamin Keith, Samantha. You can call me Ben."

He extended his hand and she took it briefly, though she glanced away, embarrassed by the injuries she knew he was seeing.

"Come into my office and we'll talk."

Sam eased forward on the cushion and gripped the arm of the chair to lever herself out of the seat. Benjamin Keith stepped in to gently take her arm and help her rise. When he tucked her hand into the crook of his arm and guided her into his office, the urge to cry rose up and nearly choked her. He urged her into a striped chair of blue, green and beige in front of his desk.

"I won't be able to pay you right away," she managed, her voice hoarse.

"We're not going to worry about that right now." He moved around the large oak desk and sat down.

"I'm concerned about my daughter. My husband and his family will try to take her from me."

"We're going to make sure that doesn't happen."

The deliberate calm in his voice soothed her fear, and she drew as deep a breath as she could in an attempt to calm herself. She ran the strap of her purse through her fingers.

"Tammi Mai contacted me about you. She told me to expect your call."

Sam jerked her head up, then flinched as the sudden move wreaked havoc with her neck. "She gave me your number," she said in acknowledgment.

"Your husband is still in jail at the moment, but he'll probably be released on bail tomorrow morning."

Sam bit her lip. "The police said I'd have to file an order of protection with a judge."

"That will be the first thing we're going to take care of today," the lawyer replied calmly.

"Thank you."

"I'm going to give you a contract to sign. It says that you are giving me the authority to act on your behalf as your attorney." He withdrew a single piece of paper from a file on his desk and handed it to her. "You can read that while I get us something to drink. Water? A soft drink? Tea? What would you like? You look as though you could use some sugar in your system. How 'bout a soft drink?"

A little overwhelmed by him, by everything, Sam simply nodded. She turned to the document and read it. She had expected something with a great deal of legalese, but the contract was straightforward and easily understood. She read over the financial part of the document, a single paragraph, twice. It said she could pay what she could afford, when she could afford it, up to a hundred dollars. Her throat felt tight and her breathing labored. When something was too good to be true, it usually was.

Ben dropped a coaster on the edge of the desk and placed a glass brimming with fizz on it. "Any questions?"

He sat down in the chair next to her. His dark eyes studied every inch of her features with a sweep, and Sam had to fight to keep her gaze steady. “Why are you making this so easy?” Her voice was barely a whisper.

“Because up until this time nothing has been easy for you. Has it?”

Sam shook her head.

“And because twelve years ago my son-in-law, in a fit of rage, beat my daughter to death. And there wasn’t a damn thing I could do about it.”

It took several moments before she could speak. “I’m so sorry.”

“He was arrested, put on trial, and is serving a ten-year sentence. He’s due to be paroled in a few weeks.” Ben looked away toward a strip of blue sky barely visible between the edges of the curtains. His pain was hidden, but Sam recognized it in the lines of grief that cut around his mouth and the look in his dark eyes. She fished in her bag for a pen, signed the contract and handed it to him.

“Do you have a dollar bill?” he asked.

Sam riffled through her bag and opened her billfold. Inside were two tens and five one-dollar bills. All the money she had in the world. She pulled one of the bills free.

He plucked it from her fingers and put it with the contract. “I’m your attorney now.”

She nodded. “I need a restraining order, I want a divorce, I want custody of my daughter, and I want Will Cross and his family permanently out of my life. Can you help me get those things?”

“We’ll work on the first three and then see what we can do about the fourth thing on your list.”

She nodded. “Good.”

“Are you out on your own or are you staying at a shelter?” he asked.

“We’re going to my grandmother’s house after this meeting. I didn’t want to go to a shelter. I thought they might say I couldn’t provide a roof over Joy’s head if we stayed there.”

Ben frowned. “You might be safer at a shelter. The reality is that the protective order is issued to keep the abuser from getting close. But the police can’t really do anything until he’s broken it.”

"I know how much I can depend on the police to protect me." It was impossible to keep the bitterness out of her tone. "I can protect myself at my grandmother's house."

"How do you plan to do that, Samantha?" he asked.

She remained silent for a moment. "I'll do whatever I have to do to, Mr. Keith. Will Cross has had his final chance to raise his hand to me. And he's threatened my daughter and my grandmother for the last time."

"If something happens, be sure to call me right away."

Samantha nodded.

"This won't be easy. We have a lot of work to do."

"After the last four years, the only thing that could be harder would be if I lost my daughter. Chaney Cross has a lot of money and a lot of political pull here in Vegas."

"I'm not going to sugarcoat it, Samantha. This will probably be even harder than you expect. You have to prepare yourself for that."

Her stomach clenched as fear threatened to overwhelm her. She attempted to draw a breath and her hand automatically went to her ribs, pain burning up her side. "Tell me what I have to do."

CHAPTER 12

Baja, California

Flash breathed in the aroma of sizzling butter, fried onions and peppers as he poured himself an orange juice. Juanita stood at the stove folding an omelet filled with cheese, peppers, onions and tomatoes. He paused next to her to brush a kiss against her soft cheek.

She stood a little over five feet, the top of her head was on a level with him mid-chest. From this angle, he noticed the gray threading through her hair. He didn't know why it bothered him that she and Travis were both getting older. He was too.

She reached up and patted his jaw. "Your breakfast will be ready *en un momento*."

"No rush." He gave her shoulder a squeeze.

"This beard you are growing makes you look *muy macho.*"

"I'm thinking of dying it red. What do you think?"

Juanita laughed.

Josh Gallagher sauntered into the kitchen, dressed again in his dark Baja Police t-shirt and pants. "You're not trying to sweet-talk her into giving you my omelet, are you?" He took a seat at the kitchen table.

Flash grinned and glanced over his shoulder. "I wouldn't do something like that, would I?"

Josh's hair and eyes were as dark as his mother's, but he bore a striking resemblance to his father. Seeing him stride toward the truck the first day he'd arrived had caused Flash a major pucker moment. Then Josh had whipped off the mirrored glasses and baseball hat. He'd had to wrestle with himself hard to resist the urge to pound on Travis in reaction.

Later, when he could both breathe and speak, Flash had flipped the design on Josh's t-shirt. "You wear this pretty well."

Josh had grinned. "You serve in your way, bro, and I'll serve in mine."

Flash could understand that.

Having dual citizenship, and being fluent in both English and Spanish, his foster brothers could work effectively in either country. They seemed to fit in anywhere they went. Which was more than he'd done while growing up.

Juanita slid the omelet on a plate and Flash scooped it up, grabbed two slices of toast as the popped up, sauntered over to the table and took a seat next to Josh. At the last moment he shoved the plate in front of his brother. Juanita shot him a grin and pointed the spatula at him. "Yours will be ready next, *querido.*"

"*Gracias, Mamacita.*"

"You forgot to butter my toast," Josh complained, then changed direction, "I've been thinking about what that FBI asshole said on the video. What if part of it was true, but the drugs are being shipped in across the border here? It would make more sense."

Flash toyed with the salt and peppershakers. "You mean, why would they need to ship drugs in from Iraq, with all that's available further south?"

"Aren't FBI guys taught that every time you tell a lie you add a grain of truth, just so the whole thing sounds more believable?"

"I don't know. I've never been an FBI guy. But I've worked with some who can lie double-time and make you believe it. Gilbert is not that skilled."

Josh shoved a bite of egg coated with cheese and peppers into his mouth and chewed. "It's only been a couple of weeks since you sent the phone and artifacts, and one week since you sent a copy of the video feed from the apartment. But you'd think they'd want to get right on something like this."

"The Navy moves at its own pace, which is usually slow and slower. It'll be at least a month before I hear anything, if I hear anything at all. I'm AWOL. They'll probably be more interested in arresting me and throwing me in the brig than dealing with a dirt bag FBI guy."

Josh shook his head. "You've grown cynical, bro.

Had he really hidden that much of himself from his foster brothers? Flash lowered his voice, his gaze on Juanita. "The idea of spending time in a military jail has a way of fucking with your head." *Especially when you were trying to do the right thing.* "I'll be moving on in a few days."

"You can't do that, Flash. If NCIS comes a-courting, they'll need to be able to contact you."

"I'll figure something out. I don't want you guys involved in this."

Juanita slid an omelet in front of him. "We already are. If it affects you, it affects us."

Shit! He should have stayed away. At one time he'd have gone solo and just muddled through. But being a part of Travis's family, being part of a SEAL team, had changed him. He'd learned to depend on other people.

Was he putting these people in danger by being here? Any time drugs were involved, it usually involved guns and danger.

"You are like *un perro* worrying a bone," Juanita complained.

Flash grinned at the comparison.

"Eat," Juanita urged. "Then you can help me with the yard work until Travis returns from his charter."

Yard work beat pacing the floors or sitting in front of the television. With his lighter skin and sun-bleached hair, he'd been wary of being seen coming and going from the Gallaghers' house, in case someone noticed. So that meant going out only at night or sticking around the house, or hanging out around the fenced-in pool out back.

"Don't let Momma work you too hard," Josh said as he rose.

"I got this covered." Juanita pointed a finger at Josh. "You take care of you."

Flash looked at Josh, and, catching his expression of surprise, broke out laughing.

Josh grinned. "I will, Momma. Gotta go." He took his dishes to the sink rinsed them and placed them in the dishwasher. With another grin and wave he was gone.

Flash finished breakfast, cleaned up his dishes and then followed Juanita to the garden. "What do you need done, 'Nita?"

"I need you to find some young woman and get married and settle down and have babies with her and stop this foolishness. I worry about you as much as I do Josh, now that he is *policía."*

Flash stared at her, speechless. *Whoa, where had this come from?*

When she burst into tears, his heart stuttered and he moved to hug her. He said the only thing he could. "It's going to be okay, 'Nita."

"You risk your life. People shoot at you. Your head is hurt."

"It's almost healed now. I'm going to be fine." In the last two weeks the bruising had turned from black and purple to blue and green. And the swelling had receded, so he looked less like a monster. But he was going to have a scar. His hair would eventually cover it, but it would be a reminder for the rest of his life. "I'm going to work this out, 'Nita. I promise."

"You deserve better than this," she said, her voice muffled against his chest.

Did he? Every time something bad happened he wondered if he was paying for all the shit he'd gotten into earlier in life. The stealing, lying, cheating. The scams. Had it not been for 'Nita and Travis, he'd be in jail right now.

His phone buzzed against his side. He tugged the cell free of his belt and looked at the number "I have to take this, 'Nita. It's Josh." Flipping the phone open, he hit the button.

"They're here, asking around. Two agents from NCIS." Josh sounded excited. "I have a number for you."

"Hold on, I have to get something to write with."

Nita pulled away and wiped her face. "I'll get something." She rushed into the house and returned with a pen and pad.

Flash jotted down the number. "Thanks, Josh."

"I'll be on patrol, but I'll have my cell. If you need backup, just call."

He wouldn't call. They both knew that. But the fact that his brother offered meant a lot. "Will do."

"Good luck."

"Thanks." Flash flipped the phone shut, tore the sheet of paper off, and handed her the pad. "I have to get my stuff ready, just in case, 'Nita." He stuffed the number into his pocket.

She nodded, though her eyes clouded again.

"I'm sorry I can't help with the garden."

"Travis and the boys will do this."

Flash hugged her tight for a moment and placed a quick kiss against her forehead. She'd been the closest thing to a mother he'd ever had. "I'll be careful. I promise. But I can't go prison, 'Nita. I haven't done anything wrong." If he went to jail, once someone found out he'd been a SEAL, he'd run one gauntlet after another. He'd have to kill someone to defend himself and he'd end up being in there the rest of his life. *He couldn't go there.* "I can't make the call from here, they'll be monitoring cell phone service."

She nodded. "Come home when you get this settled."

"I will, I promise." He gave her another quick squeeze. He forced himself to turn away from her and hustled to his room. He threw his clothes into his backpack with his computer and phone charger. Next, he dragged the duffle full of money out from under the bed. He picked up his motorcycle helmet, then paused to search the room for anything he might have missed. Reaching beneath the mattress, he extracted his Sig and shoved it into his waistband at the small of his back.

He shrugged into his windbreaker, slung the backpack over his shoulder, and lifted the duffle. When he came back into the kitchen Juanita waited at the kitchen table, composed but unhappy.

"Tell Travis I'll call later and keep you posted on what's happening."

"I will."

With a softball-sized knot in his chest, he set aside his baggage and leaned down to hold her again for a moment. He said the words he'd never said to another living soul but her. "I love you."

"No matter what happens, you can always come home to us, *mijo*."

"I know. I will when I can."

He went out the side door into the garage, where his bike was parked. He dialed Travis's phone, got his voice mail and left him a message, then secured the duffle and backpack to the back of his bike and hit the garage door opener next to the kitchen door. Early morning light spilled into the garage, bringing with it the smell of the sea and the bright red flowers planted along the edge of the driveway.

What if he never saw them again? A wave of pain rolled over him. When someone asked he always said he didn't have a family. Was that because he still felt he didn't deserve one? Whether or not he did, Travis, 'Nita and the boys had made him part of theirs. But if he continued to stay, he might bring more than the law down on their heads. Gilbert was in with some bad people. If only half of what he'd said was true, it was a drug cartel. And no one came back from hooking up with them.

He had to do whatever would protect the Gallaghers. He straddled the Triumph Sprint GT and started the engine. He shoved off the kickstand and paused to listen to the purr of the motor. He needed to find a way back to his life and them. That meant he had to distance himself from them until he found the answer. He released the clutch, pushed on the gas, and cruised out of the garage.

Flash worked his way downhill, weaving through the streets, careful to stick to the speed limit. He hit Highway 1 and followed it along the coast to the Autonomous University of Baja, just as he and Travis had planned. After parking in one of the first lots he came to, he cut off the ignition and took off his helmet. His heart beat like a drum as he set his number to be permanently private and keyed in the agent's digits.

"Special Agent Barnett speaking."

The no-nonsense, military edge to the way he spoke loosened the taut knots in Flash's stomach somewhat, but not entirely. "This is Lieutenant Junior Grade Harold Carney. I heard you were looking for me."

"We received your packages, Lieutenant, and found them very interesting. Are you recovering from your injuries? Do you need medical care?"

"I'm okay, for now."

"We need you to come in so we can talk."

"I'd prefer you come to me. And I'd like proof you are who you say you are."

"You can call the main switchboard at NCIS and ask to speak to Senior Special Agent Isaac Green. He's our supervisor. Give your name and he'll be sure to answer. He can give you a detailed description of us and acknowledge that we're down here because of what you sent us."

"I'll call you back with a meeting location." Flash closed the phone, then opened it again to get the number. It took only a few minutes to dial and be connected to Supervisor Green.

"This is Special Agent Isaac Green. I've sent two agents down to Ensenada to look for you, Lieutenant," Green said by way of introduction.

"I've spoken with them. I'm calling to confirm that they are in the vicinity, and to get a description of the agents before we meet."

"Very good." He proceeded to give Flash a detailed description of his people. A man and a woman.

"We've spoken to Captain Jackson and made him aware of your difficulties, Lieutenant. And he's shared the letter you mailed him the day of the operation. Did something happen to alert you?"

"Just a feeling. Am I still listed as AWOL?"

"For the moment. We don't want to change your status. It might alert Gilbert that you have contacted us."

Flash clenched his jaw against the need to vent. "I'm not a deserter, sir. But I couldn't stick around with him and his men hunting me."

"Understood. Meet with my agents, Lieutenant, for an interview, and we'll get this sorted out."

Sorted out! *Sorted out?* "I've given you proof against him, sir. What part of that needs sorting out?"

"Your part in this, Lieutenant."

"I was approached in Iraq by Agents Dobson and Gilbert to bring artifacts back to the states. I received an email from headquarters saying my orders had been changed to reflect my involvement. If you'd check the record, you'll verify that."

"We'll check your orders, Lieutenant. Meet with my agents so they can debrief you."

Surely they'd already checked his orders. Alarm bells rang in the back of his mind. He hung up the phone and rested his head against the storage hatch over the gas tank. He'd hoped…

He flipped his phone open and dialed Agent Barnett's phone. "Have you checked the orders that were issued at the end of my deployment in Iraq?" he asked as soon as the man answered.

"There were no orders issued, Lieutenant."

Flash absorbed that and shook his head. "Give me your email address."

Barnett spelled it out for him and Flash keyed it into his phone so he wouldn't forget it.

"I'll email you a message that was sent to me in Iraq stating otherwise. You'll need to trace the IP address to find where the message originated. The orders I was given are in a safety deposit box at a bank in San Diego. If the FBI have found it—"

"You need to come in, Lieutenant Carney."

"Sure, I'll jump right on that so you can throw me into the brig and mark this off your to-do list. *I didn't do anything wrong.* I was asked to work with the FBI and I agreed. If I come in now, I'm a dead man. You know who Gilbert is involved with."

"We know who you suspect he's involved with, Lieutenant."

What more did he have to do to clear himself? If NCIS was only interested in throwing him in the brig, they suspected him of being a part of it all. And the way it looked now, they'd bury him. He couldn't turn himself in. Not yet.

He closed the phone.

PART TWO
OF
BREAKING AWAY

A ROAD LESS WEARY

CHAPTER 13

SEVEN MONTHS LATER
Las Vegas, Nevada

Flash struggled to open his eyes. He had to open his eyes. Some psychological trigger alerted him that what he was experiencing was a dream. But knowing it was a dream and breaking away from its hold were two different things.

The sound of the explosion was like dark thunder in his ears. The cloud of dust it kicked up rolled over him. Three of them were dead. They had to be. His heart beat high in his throat. He rolled to his feet and grabbed his gear. The grit in his mouth threatened to choke him. He spit and swallowed to clear the dust scratching his throat. The stairs stretched dark as a tomb beneath him. He breathed in the musty, sour air and rushed down.

On the street, the guys appeared like ghosts from the cloud. Brett hung limp over Strongman's shoulder. Jesus, was he dead?

Then they were running through the streets, looking for cover. The weight of his rifle hung like a bolder over his shoulder. Sweat ran down his neck and between his shoulder blades. Then bullets were tearing into the concrete behind him gouging pieces out of the wall and peppering him. He lowered his weapon and returned fire, piercing the windshield as the truck went by.

The truck ran up on the sidewalk, hit the wall and flipped, scattering the men in the bed onto the pulverized asphalt. Gas from the ruptured gas tank ran along the broken sidewalk, and he thought for a moment about igniting it, but it would draw the enemy down on them.

One of the shooters in the bed rolled on the ground screaming, his shinbone sticking through his ragged pants leg. Blood black as oil ran in a rivulet into the dirt beneath him.

Jesus... Jesus...

Flash fought his way free of the dream, every muscle still tensed for action. His chest heaved like bellows as he tried to catch his breath. Clammy sweat covered his body and he threw back the covers and shot from the hotel room bed. The pale glow of the early morning sun pierced a narrow crack in the curtains and reflected off the far wall, cutting across the muted wallpaper.

Sunrise. He strode to the window and shoved back the curtains. The Nevada desert looked so similar to Iraq, for a moment he thought he'd been transported back to that dry, dusty place with its miserable, burning heat.

He clenched his fists and rested them against the tempered glass windowpane. The air conditioner worked overtime drying the sweat that beaded his skin. No air conditioning in Iraq. Just heat and sand, sparse greenery, and men trying to kill them.

Why couldn't he quit reliving that last mission?

Because he felt as if he'd been left behind.

The guys would be getting up about now to report to the base for more training. An ache of loss settled just beneath his breastbone. It had been almost ten months since they'd returned from Iraq, and he was still stuck in the same place. Reliving the same shit over and over, because he couldn't leave it behind until he'd moved on with his team.

Had Brett fought his way back from his injuries? He hoped so. Were Hawk and Zoe still together? Were Doc and Bowie okay? Had Greenback made a decision about staying or going? He missed hanging with the guys at Chief Langley Marks's house, with the chief's wife Trish and the kids. A wave of homesickness struck him.

Why hadn't he told his teammates at the time about being approached by the FBI? Had they been told anything about his connection to two FBI agents who'd been shot? Had anyone ever reported that? Had the guys he'd shot even been FBI? He'd begun to doubt they were.

The sweat on his torso finally dry, Flash shivered, turned away from the window and pulled the curtains closed. He had to keep hoping that Gilbert would make a mistake soon. But until that happened, he had to keep putting one foot in front of the other and doing whatever it took to stay alive and ahead of anyone looking for him.

He'd made it across the border using identification he already had. He'd updated his drivers license to represent his change in residence to Nevada, though he'd only been here a week. He'd carefully laid in a history, but it had taken him months to build it, and he'd broken some laws while he was at it.

His identity was tied to the corporation he'd built in Mexico, and all the money he earned for his work went through it, so he could fly under the radar. The letters of incorporation were tied to Travis. There'd been no other way to do it. But Flash was simply an employee of the corporation, so if something went down, Travis couldn't be held accountable. Flash had made certain of that. Javier held the reins of the office in Baja now. So it was just a family organization that had hired him to open a branch office in Nevada.

It would allow Flash to hide in plain sight until he could gather more proof against Gilbert. And he was slowly building a case. He'd hacked into the man's phone, his computer, and his life so deeply he couldn't make a move without Flash knowing about it.

He and Travis had decided on Nevada because taking up a physical residence in California would have been too close and too risky. He just had to follow the plan and hope things came together. And the first step was for him to go about business as usual and create a work history.

He glanced at the clock. He had several hours free before he was supposed to check out the apartment he'd arranged to rent. And though he had a couple of business appointments to keep before that, he'd still have time to use the exercise equipment downstairs. He'd kept up his training, ran every day, swam when he could. There were days discouragement made it hard for him to keep going. But what else could he do? He wanted his life back. And he'd get it one day soon. He had to believe that.

He quickly shed his pajama bottoms and changed into swimming trunks, pulled sweatpants on over them, and slipped on a plain white t-shirt. In the bathroom he threw water on his face and brushed his teeth.

He was finally getting used to the close-cropped beard that darkened the lower half of his face. But the medium brown hair that curled against his head still looked strange. It had been years since he'd allowed his hair and beard to grow. Even when he'd been downrange, he'd scraped away the beard for the sake of staying cool. And he'd certainly never colored his hair. But he'd spent a good deal of time in Vegas before, and couldn't afford to be recognized right now. And as big as the world was, you never knew when you'd run into someone you knew. With that in mind, he shoved the irritating glasses he'd bought as part of his disguise onto his face, grabbed his keycard and MP3 player and left the room.

The hallways were empty as he strolled down to the elevators and rode to the first floor, then followed the arrows to the exercise room. Three other men were already hard at work on the machines, so he did some stretching and chose a treadmill. Inserting the ear buds, he turned on some heavy rock and started running. He started slow and every two minutes increased the speed until he was running a six-minute mile, burning off some of his frustration with the physical activity. Thirty minutes later he eased the machine back to a slower pace every two or three minutes to cool himself down.

"Are you training for something?" a wiry-looking guy with curly hair asked as he stepped up on the treadmill next to him.

Flash shook his head. "Just staying in shape. Going to hit the pool." He threw up a hand in farewell and went through the glass doors to the pool. The smell of chlorine hung strong in the air. Though there were lounges all around the area, it was satisfyingly empty. He shucked his sweatpants and t-shirt and dove into the deep end.

Twenty laps later he stopped, hiked himself out of the pool, and sat on the side to catch his breath. Why was he pushing himself like this? Why couldn't he just let it go? He ran his hand over his hair, slicking it back out of his face.

Because he didn't have anything else. And he didn't know how to stop.

When he found something that meant as much to him, maybe he'd be able to let it go.

CHAPTER 14

Samantha Cross read the end of the web news article with a sense of satisfaction. Even after seven months, the fallout for Judge Moreland just kept coming. A number of his cases were now being reopened. It was going to cost the state of Nevada a fortune to retry them.

After all the heartache he'd caused her, she wasn't sorry he was going to jail. Nor about how his connection to her in-laws had helped her in court. Because of it, the next judge who dealt with the Cross family had not been so sympathetic to their wife-beating son.

Sam left the website and got back to the research paper she'd been working on, typed in the last bit of information and saved the document.

Joy's conversation with her dolls reached her, and she leaned back in her seat at the kitchen table to catch a glimpse of her daughter playing in front of the living room television, hunched over her favorite Barbie dolls. Joy danced one across the floor as if Barbie was doing a ballet.

Samantha saved her class paper to her flash drive and then sent the file to her Dropbox as well. Pulling the flash drive free, she slipped on the attached lanyard like a necklace, closed the laptop, and rose.

"Where's my Joy?" she called out, as though unable see her daughter sitting in the center of the living room rug.

"Here I am!" Joy swung around, her blonde curls bobbing, her smile free of restraint.

"How about we go out for a treat?"

"Ice cream?" Joy asked.

"Pistachio?" Sam asked.

Joy wrinkled her nose. "No, Mommy, chocolate."

"What ever you want, baby."

"I'm not a baby," Joy said. "Miss Karen says so."

Samantha ignored the painful twinge. Her *baby* was growing up. Joy's preschool teacher's attempt to encourage her students to be independent was a good thing. They'd both thank her one day. She needed to keep telling herself that. "Miss Karen is right. Why don't you go put on your shoes and we'll drive down to the grocery store."

"'Kay." Joy clambered to her feet and ran down the hall to her room.

Samantha checked the doors and windows, making sure they were secure. She took the time to turn on a small digital video recorder hidden within a plant atop one of the built-in bookcases on either side of the fireplace. The recorder had cost her fifty dollars at a pawnshop. The money would be well worth it if she could catch Will up to his old tricks. She knew he was coming into her house, touching her things, going through her computer files. He'd destroyed her desktop the last time, wiping out all her schoolwork. Thank God she'd backed up everything.

Scooping up her backpack, she hustled into the kitchen, disconnected her laptop from the power cord and stuffed it inside the bag, then added her small billfold. She carried the backpack into the living room.

Will had done everything he could to pressure or intimidate her into coming back to him. How could he even think his continued abusive behavior was going to accomplish that? *She'd live in a ditch first. Never again would a man raise his hand to her.*

She was learning to protect herself, but she couldn't protect Joy when she went to him on the court-mandated two-hour visits. Those two hours seemed like a month. Every time, she paced the floor, sick with worry. What if he lost patience with Joy and hurt her? It only took a second. And Joy was so small.

What if he punched the supervisor and went on the run with their daughter? She might never see her again.

The only reason he was visiting Joy was to get to Sam. She knew it. And if he ever got unsupervised visitation, he'd really have some leverage to control her.

Then there were times she believed he'd come here and kill her first before he disappeared with Joy. He wouldn't want to leave her behind for fear some other man might take his place.

As though she'd ever let another man close to her. Never again.

Joy was taking too long. She was too quiet. A rush of concern cramped her stomach, spurring her to a near-jog down the hallway. The bedroom door stood open. Samantha peeked inside the room. Dressed in black knit pants, a leopard print top, a pink feather boa and plastic high heel shoes, Joy strutted in front of the mirror. She paused to spread clear lip-gloss over her pursed lips.

Relief and amusement had a smile springing to Samantha's lips. "You about ready to go, girlfriend?"

"I have to get my purse," Joy said and trotted over to pick up a hot pink shoulder bag.

Samantha suppressed a chuckle. "Love the boa. It really makes that outfit."

Joy smiled wide, wrinkling her nose. "I'm ready."

"We'll take a sweater just in case you need it," Samantha grabbed a white sweater hanging on the closet doorknob.

With Joy tottering ahead of her, they returned to the living room. Samantha swung her backpack over her shoulder, snapped up the car keys from a bowl on the coffee table, locked the door as they headed out and, using her house key, secured the dead bolt.

"Hold my hand. You need to practice walking down steps in high heels. Mommy's done it and it's not easy."

"'Kay."

Joy's hand felt sticky as she grasped it. What else besides lip-gloss had she put on? When her daughter nearly pirouetted off the steps, she was grateful she'd held on to her and saved her from a nasty spill.

"Stay on the stepping stones, Joy. High heels and sandy soil don't work very well."

"'Kay, mommy." With her eyes directed downward, she concentrated on doing a tiptoe-hopping maneuver from one steppingstone to the next.

After strapping Joy into the back seat, she got in, and dropped the backpack onto the passenger seat next to her. She backed the car out of the drive and paused for a moment to study the house. The one-story, three bedroom house had seen better days. The outside stucco had cracked in spots, and the eaves had begun to deteriorate, but she loved every inch of the place. It had been home to her from when she was six until she'd married. After that interminable, four-year absence, she'd returned with her heart in pieces and her body battered.

But she was good now, and so was Joy. And it was going to stay that way. *She'd promised Gran.*

"Go, Mommy," Joy demanded, fortunately breaking into Samantha's thoughts before her emotions got the best of her.

Thank God for her daughter. She forced a smile. "We're going." She turned the car east toward South Boulder Highway.

Dry desert, intermittent clumps of grass, sparse trees, and carefully-landscaped desert palms set in business park medians stretched along the road, leaving only a cloudless sky to study. Traffic was light and Sam soon swung left into the shopping center, took another left and pulled into the parking lot in front of the grocery store and parked. "Stay in the car until I come around and get you, Joy." she cautioned as she unbuckled her seat belt. She slid out of the car and hurried around the car. A silver Lexus drove through the lot, and she paused to watch it before opening Joy's door.

Will drove one just like it. Surely it wasn't him she chided herself. But she saw him everywhere she went. The back of a man's head. The way a man walked or stood. A car similar to his. She knew she was paranoid, but experience had taught her she needed to be on her guard. She needed to get a dog. She needed to get a license to carry a gun as well, but thus far she'd been unable to too convince herself to do it. She had two shotguns at the house, loaded, ready and locked up out of Joy's reach. That would have to suffice.

She helped Joy out, grabbed her backpack, and locked the Ford Focus. Joy gripped her hand and they walked across the asphalt to the front entrance. "I think you need a ride around the grocery store, Joy. It will save your feet in your new high heels."

"'Kay."

Sam lifted her into the shopping cart and smiled when Joy flipped her feather boa over her shoulder like a diva. Gran couldn't have bought her anything she enjoyed more. An ache settled at the base of her throat as it tightened, but she swallowed it back. She had to stay strong for Joy.

Sam pushed a happy, chattering Joy down the aisles, picking up a loaf of bread, some bananas, orange juice and the ice cream she'd promised Joy. "Can I borrow that boa for my next date?" the checkout woman, Gloria asked.

Joy looked up and shook her head. "Grandma El bought it for me."

The girl's smile faltered. "Grandma El was the best. You be sure to take good care of it."

"'Kay."

"You knew my grandmother?" Sam asked.

"Yeah, she was always real sweet when she came through. Always had a smile and something friendly to say."

"Thank you for remembering her with a smile. She," Sam swallowed, hard, "She would have appreciated that."

Sam fished inside the backpack for her small purse and handed over the last twenty-dollar bill she had until payday. She'd swallowed her pride and applied for food stamps and any other assistance she could qualify for, but it took time for the paperwork to go through the system and she wouldn't hear anything back for another several weeks. The girl handed her back four dollars and some change.

Sam thanked her and wheeled the cart out the door. As she crossed the drive in front of the store, she frowned. Something wasn't quite right with the car. Her heart plunged and her stomach cramped. All four tires were flat, and the car sat on the ground like a turtle hiding in its shell.

Fear jetted through her and she whipped the cart around and headed back into the store. "Aren't we going home, Mommy?"

"Not just yet, baby."

She was shaking and her breathing came in a labored pants. She fumbled in her purse for the prepaid cell phone she kept for emergencies, and, finding it, dialed nine-one-one.

"Is there a problem, ma'am?" one of the checkers asked.

"Someone's slashed my tires." They'd have to be slashed to deflate so quickly. Fear burned her skin and her face prickled as her chest labored to draw enough oxygen into her lungs. Adrenaline flooded her system.

"Oh my God. I'll get the manager." The woman rushed away.

A thin man with bushy hair and glasses approached just as the dispatcher came on the line. Sam gave her the details of where she was and what had happened. "You have to send someone to my house. While I'm here dealing with this, he'll be going through my house and destroying the place."

"Who is *he*, ma'am?"

Sam stepped away from the buggy to keep Joy from hearing the conversation. "My ex-husband, William Cross."

"Did you see him there?"

"I thought I saw his car earlier. I don't have to see him. I know it was him. I haven't got any other enemies. He's just been released for defying the restraining order I have on him. And now my tires have been slashed."

"I'm dispatching a unit to your location. What is your home address?"

Sam rattled off the address on Warm Springs Road.

"I'm sending a unit there as well."

Relief brought a tremor to her limbs. "Thank you."

"Stay on the phone with me until the officers arrive."

"I'm not going anywhere."

When the automatic door opened and she caught a glimpse of a husky man with dark hair entering the store, she turned and ran toward her daughter. She glanced over her shoulder, her throat contracting, heart beating so harshly against her ribs it hurt.

The man turned his head. It wasn't Will.

CHAPTER 15

Flash slowed his Triumph Sprint to fifteen miles an hour. He passed row after row of cookie-cutter houses, all with tile roofs and sparse landscaping. He glanced at the house numbers. After he reached the 2000s, the houses spread out a little more, leaving long stretches of desert dotted with clumps of grass and Joshua trees.

Finally he came to a mailbox with the number he was looking for pasted on the side. A large detached garage came into view. And a police car sat in a semi-circular driveway.

He started to mosey on down the highway, then at the last minute decided to loop around and keep his appointment. If there was a problem with the place he had arranged to rent, he needed to know about it. And it was better to be straight up and get to know the local cops so they wouldn't be suspicious.

He brought his bike to a stop, pushed it up on the kickstand, and cut the engine.

Two police officers wandered from the back of the house. Both rested their hands on their sidearms as they approached him.

Flash removed his helmet and then his gloves. "Is this the Andrews' residence?"

One of the police officers answered. "Yeah. Can I see some identification?"

Flash shrugged, dug into the back pocket of his jeans, removed his wallet and tugged free his driver's license. He'd changed his license to reflect his change of residency to the state of Nevada, with a slight mis-spelling in his name. The current photo showed a man with a well-trimmed beard, darker hair, and glasses. He had no warrants or tickets here or anywhere that he was aware of—yet. Though the military was still looking for him.

The police officer studied the license. "What's your business here, Mr. Carnes?" He passed off the license to his partner, who took it with him to the squad car.

"I'm supposed to be renting the apartment above the garage and setting up an internet business from here. I have a signed copy of the lease and I've already paid a deposit and gotten the permits." Flash opened the storage compartment on the bike, removed the letter and his paperwork and handed it to the cop.

"What sort of business?" the policeman asked. His partner returned and offered him his license back.

"I custom design security systems and install them."

The two men looked at each other. "You've arrived just in time," the one who had asked him for identification said. The other handed him back the lease agreement.

Flash raised a brow.

"The lady who lives here is having some trouble and could use a system."

"What kind of trouble?" Flash asked.

"We can't really say," his partner said. "But maybe you could give her a good deal on a security system in place of rent. I'd mention that when you get a chance to talk with her."

Flash nodded and replaced his license in his billfold. This didn't really sound like a situation he wanted to get involved in. But he'd already paid a deposit on the room over the garage with a guarantee he'd be able to use the garage if he needed it. "Should I stick around and speak to her while you guys are still here? Or should I come back later?"

"While we're here would be good. She'll know you have legitimate business with her and aren't someone hired to cause a problem."

Things were sounding less and less inviting. *Shit!*

Another police car pulled into the drive and came to a stop behind Flash's bike. The officer behind the wheel got out, moved to the back door, and opened it. He reached in to offer a hand to one of the passengers and smiled at the child who wiggled free of the back seat. Gaining her feet, she tossed her feather boa over her shoulder and strutted across the gravel drive on her plastic high heels like a mini runway model.

The woman who followed was dressed in mid-thigh length shorts and a blue, short-sleeved pullover top with a scooped neckline. Her legs looked long and smooth. Her strawberry-blonde hair, a shade just a bit darker than the child's, was pulled back into a ponytail, baring her face. Her wide-spaced eyes focused on him sitting on the Triumph and she frowned. She reached back into the police car and hiked a backpack over her shoulder. The slender bow of her body as she did that caught Flash's interest and his mouth went dry.

Was he staring? He scanned the cops' expressions and saw their attention fixed on her, too.

One of the policemen approached her and she shifted her attention to the officer. She followed him to the porch and unlocked the door. He went inside ahead of her.

"Who are you?"

The words spoken in a demanding tone drew his attention. He smiled at the little girl who stood, hands on hips, eyeing him with a frown.

"My name is Tim." Using his middle name still felt awkward even after months of doing so. "And you are?"

"Joy." She narrowed her eyes as she studied his bike. "That's a motorcycle."

"Yes, it is."

"Can I ride it?"

Flash grinned. "It's a little too big for you, sweetheart."

"Can I ride with you?"

"If your mom says it's okay."

Her bottom lip jutted out.

Flash grinned. Was that frown a sign of a strong will or disappointment? Or both?

"Joy!" The woman's sharp voice jerked both his and the little girl's heads around. The woman's slim legs ate up the distance and made her seem taller until she'd come to a halt next to them.

"Are you with the police?" she asked.

One of the police approached them. "This fellow says he has a lease on an apartment with you, Ms. Cross. He has paperwork, and it appears legitimate."

Flash frowned at the name Cross. "I signed the lease with a Mrs. Andrews."

"That's my grandmother." She looked away. "She died six weeks ago."

Shock froze his features for a moment. Damn! The woman he'd spoken to had seemed so feisty and full of life. What the hell had happened? An accident? A heart attack? He shoved the glasses he didn't really need up on his nose. "I'm real sorry to hear that. I enjoyed speaking with her and was looking forward to meeting her."

"Thank you."

"We're moving out, Mrs. Cross. Officer Harris set your groceries on the porch. Don't hesitate to call if you need us again."

She moved away to thank all three men for their help. And watched as they got into their vehicles and pulled away.

Flash swung free of the bike and stood to stretch his legs.

She turned to face him, a frown much like her daughter's drawing her brows together. She studied him for a long moment, her pale greenish-gray gaze sharp. She kept a good four feet of space between them and asked, "Do you have a copy of the lease?"

"Sure." Flash again pulled the paperwork from the bike's storage compartment and handed it to her. "I can give you my boss's number and my references, and you can call them and check me out again. I'm staying at the Hampton, but I already have appointments in the area, so I'll have to give you my cell so you can contact me."

"Why have you waited so long to move in?" She scanned the document.

"It took a couple of months to reorganize the other office. We've been based in Baja and doing work in Mexico, but now want to move a satellite office here. We have a lot of clients on both sides of the border."

She nodded. "It says here you made an eight hundred dollar deposit."

"Yes. In March."

She studied his face again. The wariness in her gaze triggered a responsive concern. Based on the police visit and her suspicion, there was something going on here he didn't really need to be a part of.

But finding another out-of-the-way apartment was going to be a bitch. "Look, if there's a problem with this, I'll work out of the van until I find someplace else. Just write me a check for my deposit and I'm gone."

"I can't do that, Mr. Carnes." Her cheeks grew flushed. "The money has already been spent. I wish my grandmother had told me about this—before." She handed him back the lease and stood a moment, studying the toe of her canvas sneaker. "I'll get the keys to the apartment." She held her hand out to the little girl. "Joy, come into the house and I'll make you a snack."

"Ice cream?"

"No, honey. Remember we had to put the ice cream back so it wouldn't melt. We can make some popsicles with the orange juice later."

"'Kay."

Mrs. Cross heaved the backpack over her shoulder, picked up the groceries and went into the house.

Flash wandered around the outside of the garage, looking over the property. The exterior of the building wasn't much to look at, but structurally it appeared sound. Two large flowerpots positioned on either side of the wooden stairs leading up to the door of the apartment spilled over with blossoms, a nice woman's touch. They reminded him of Juanita and her garden.

He heard steps on the gravel drive before she appeared around the edge of the garage.

"I'm sorry it took me so long. I had to get Joy settled in front of the television with a snack." She sounded breathless.

"No problem."

She offered him the keys.

Flash mounted the stairs then looked over his shoulder to find her still standing at the bottom. "Are you going to do a walk-through?"

She bit her lip and glanced toward the house. "I don't feel comfortable leaving Joy unattended. I'll come up in a few minutes, after she's finished her snack."

"Okay." The dead bolt turned with a soft click and he pushed open the door. The room stretched the length of the four-car garage. Mrs. Andrews had told him it had once been her husband's workshop.

Flash wandered around the space. Solid wood floors polished to a shine stretched across the entire length of the room. A small galley-style kitchen spread across opposite corners just inside the door. The solid wood cabinets stained a light oak gleamed with care, and a round table and four chairs separated the kitchen area from the rest of the space. The living room boasted both couch and recliner, with an end table between, and a small entertainment center housing a twenty-seven inch television. A colorful area rug of dark maroon and gold covered the empty floor between.

After seeing the plain exterior of the building, Flash was pleasantly surprised by the quality of the interior.

He pushed open the bedroom door. A sand and blue comforter covered the double bed, a runner in the same colors stretched along the floor on one side. A nightstand with a lamp, a dresser and a chest of drawers made up the furnishings. A pocket-sized closet took up one corner.

The bathroom appeared more utilitarian than the rest of the apartment, tiled in white, with a sink, commode, a shower stall and a stacked washer-dryer unit.

The place would be perfect for his needs. And he'd certainly lived in much worse.

He heard the rattle of the exterior storm door opening in the other room and strode back into the living room to join Mrs. Cross. He'd never introduced himself, nor had she.

"My name is Tim Carnes by the way," Flash said. Every time he introduced himself by the fictitious name his stomach cramped, even though his days of being Harold Timothy Carney had been over for the last six months.

She stayed close to the open door. "Samantha Cross."

"Maybe you'd better tell me why the police were here."

Her gaze settled on his black t-shirt. Her throat worked as she swallowed. "My ex-husband spent five months in jail for assaulting me and a nurse at the hospital where I was admitted. Then two months more for stalking and attempted assault when our divorce went through and for ignoring the restraining order I filed against him. He got out two days ago and today, while we were at the grocery store, he slashed my tires."

Son of a bitch!

He studied her bent head, taking in the curve of her high cheekbones, her smooth skin, the scattering of freckles across her nose. She stood five foot four and wouldn't weigh much more than a hundred and ten pounds. What kind of guy raised a hand against a woman like this? He noticed a scar that marred the delicate skin of her cheek. Had the bastard done that? Anger built, thrusting heat into his face.

The cop's comment about a security system made sense now.

She raised her head, and for a moment met his gaze. "I'll understand if you don't want the apartment."

Flash wandered to the kitchen window and scanned the open land to the east and the mountains in the distance. He didn't need anything that would draw uninvited attention to his presence here. He'd chosen the area for that exact reason. But what suited him worked against her.

The house was too isolated, the nearest neighbor possibly a quarter of a mile away. The ex could break in here and do anything he wanted. She and her daughter would be totally at his mercy. Joy's delicate face flashed through his thoughts. Had he laid hands on her too?

Memories of another place and time tumbled through his mind like a kaleidoscope. Every protective instinct he had leapt to full life.

Fuck!

Frustration tightened his stomach and shoulders. He mentally flipped through his alternatives. A wry smile twisted his lips. He thrust his hands into the back pocket of his jeans and turned to face her. Who was he kidding? It would take a full company of Afghan terrorists to get him out of this apartment. "I think the apartment will work just fine, Samantha."

Will Cross focused his binoculars on the kitchen window of the garage apartment. The late afternoon sun beat against his back and the top of his head, burning all the way through his thin t-shirt. What the hell was she doing with that guy? The man's figure, a silhouette in the window, took up the entire frame. Why was she in there with him?

Will swore. At least while the guy was standing at the window, he knew he wasn't fucking her. He'd kill him if he so much as laid hands on his wife.

Sam appeared at the door and she spoke to the guy over her shoulder as she held the door open. When she descended the stairs, the tension in Will's body dissipated.

He'd been on the brink of breaking into the house when the cops had shown. How had they gotten here so quickly? It had been a close call.

If they caught him again, the judge had promised him two years. After the last seven months in jail, he wasn't going back. No damn way. He'd die first.

His dad wouldn't even attempt to bail him out again. He'd told him to forget about her. He couldn't do that. It drove him crazy not knowing what she was doing. Who she might be with.

She was his wife! *His* wife. But she wouldn't talk to him. Wouldn't read his letters. Wouldn't accept his gifts. And wouldn't speak to him, even in the presence of her attorney or the police.

He knew he'd had a problem with anger. Knew he'd been hard on her. The moment his thoughts started to stray to the baby he cut them off. He couldn't go there. If she'd kept her mouth shut none of this would have happened. She was just as responsible for what had gone down as he was, no matter what his court-appointed psychologist said.

A smile quirked his lips. He had the doctor totally snowed. He followed every instruction the guy gave him. Wrote all sorts of bullshit in his journal. Made all the right apologetic noises. Said all the things the guy wanted to hear. And acted repentant whenever they discussed the times he'd hit her.

He did regret that. Every time he saw her smile now, it drove home how unhappy she had been with him. But they could change that now. She was better. He was more in control.

He just needed her to talk to him.

And eventually she'd cave. Now that she didn't have a car...

He peered through the binoculars. She'd raised two of the garage doors. The guy had come down the stairs and they disappeared inside together. A few minutes later she appeared driving a tractor. *A tractor?*

What the hell? Did she intend to drive that to and from town?

His mouth hung open as she put the machine in gear and pulled around the side of the garage and out of sight. There was a small wooden carport-like structure behind the garage. Just posts stuck in the ground with the roof. He'd seen it when he'd visited before, but also when he'd scoped the place out after he'd gotten out of jail. That had to be where she was taking the tractor.

She appeared again and the guy came out. He was smiling at her, amused, and said something. *She smiled back.*

Jealousy ripped through Will's system and the heat was suddenly unbearable. The *prick* had damn well better keep his distance. He'd fucking rip that guy's head off... The man offered her a piece of paper from his pocket. She stood looking down at it for a moment, then offered him her hand.

They shook and it looked more like a business deal than a seduction. Will's tension eased. "Just business, baby. You'd better keep it that way," he murmured.

CHAPTER 16

San Diego, California

Captain James Jackson studied the row of diplomas on the wall just above the doctor's head. His attention swept down to the man's face. He appreciated Dr. Dawson's professionalism. His calm in the face of disaster. But the pity he sensed behind the man's demeanor did nothing to alleviate his anxiety. He'd felt less fear crouched in a foxhole with live rounds flying overhead. There was a hole in their son's heart and it wasn't getting any better.

The doctor's office looked similar to all the ones they'd visited since Alex's birth. Similar to all the others they'd visited since they'd been attacked and held hostage at gunpoint by terrorists for three days in their home.

James absently touched the scar that ran along his eye socket. His face and body had been pulverized, and he'd been in the hospital for nearly two weeks. Marsha and the baby had been in for a few days. But the physical reminders were nothing compared to the psychological issues he and his wife were dealing with now. She still had nightmares. She still had all the symptoms of PTSD. He saw them in himself, too.

Surgeons, psychologists, pediatricians, cardiologists, neurologists, internists, plastic surgeons. They'd seen them all as a family. One right after another. It was the only thing they did as a family lately.

He scanned the bookcases full of an arrangement of textbooks, medical related knick-knacks and keepsakes from patients against one wall. Two patient chairs sat before a paper-strewn desk. Did all these guys hire the same decorator?

Were they all trained to face life and death with that same calm, purposeful focus? That at least was something he could understand.

That first visit with the pediatrician had been the worst.

Just remembering the doctor saying, "Alex has Aarskog Syndrome. It's a very rare genetic disorder that can affect several parts of the body. You've already noticed the webbing of his fingers and the wide spacing of his eyes. And of course his reproductive organs have been affected to a small degree, but that is a cosmetic thing and can be corrected later."

He'd gone on to list extensive orthodontic treatment, and the possibility that Alex's cognitive function might be completely normal or he might have some learning disabilities. They couldn't judge that yet.

All they wanted to do was test and test.

What had that doctor known of their hopes, their dreams for their son? What did it matter to him or any of the others they'd been to in the last ten months?

James maintained an even expression for Marsha's benefit, though the fear roiled through him.

Dawson continued. "Our main concern right now is the size of the hole. I hear a pronounced murmur with the stethoscope. And the echocardiogram I ordered in the hospital showed an abnormality. We had hoped the medication we prescribed would help the hole close. It might yet."

Marsha's features blanked as she fought back tears and reached for James's hand. He clasped it automatically. She had gone through the entire pregnancy alone. His platoon had been called up before she'd even been aware she was pregnant. He'd arrived home a couple of weeks before she delivered. And as soon as their son was born they'd been slapped with the news that there were genetic problems.

His son could be...retarded. He flinched from the word. Alex had a heart problem on top of that. The news had hit him like a solid punch to his the solar plexus. He hadn't breathed freely since.

He and Marsha didn't drink. And they didn't have any health issues. What had caused this? He dragged his thoughts back to the present.

"How big a hole?" he managed around a throat tight with fear.

Dr. Dawson turned his attention to him. "A number of babies are born with abnormal openings in the wall that divides the atria or the two chambers at the top of the heart. It's called an atrial septal defect. I know you've heard that term from your pediatrician and from our first evaluation."

Marsha nodded.

"For the most part those holes close on their own within a few weeks of birth. And some people have them their whole lives without any symptoms. But Alex's appears larger than normal. And it hasn't responded to the medication. But there is a procedure we can use to repair it."

Alex whimpered and struggled to sit up in the stroller. Marsha pulled her hand free from James's grasp and lifted Alex from the seat to hold him in her lap. Tears shimmered in her eyes before she silently wiped them away.

How many tears had to fall before their son was well? Would he ever be? The frustration and pain built inside James's chest until he wanted to yell. There was nothing he could do for his boy and there seemed to be nothing he could do for his wife, either.

The doctor rose and took up a pad of paper. He leaned back against his desk and drew something on it, then turned it so they could see the image. "This is a normal heart. It's divided into four chambers. This is where Alex's hole is, and the relative size of the hole." He colored in a section opening the two chambers to each other. "Oxygen-poor blood flows into the right side of the heart, down into the right ventricle, then is pumped into the lungs, where it picks up oxygen. In the left side of the heart, arterial blood rich in oxygen flows from the lungs into the atrium, then down into the ventricle, where it's pumped out into the body. Because of the hole between the chambers of his heart, the oxygen-rich blood is mixing with the oxygen-poor blood and Alex's heart has to work overtime to pump all that blood out. What it does eventually is cause one side of the heart to grow larger, and left untreated, can eventually, after several years, damage the vessels in the lungs. That's several years down the road for Alex. Luckily children seem to tolerate the condition very well."

"Are you going to do some kind of surgery to repair it?" James asked.

"Eventually. If he does as well in the next six months we'll wait. He'll have to stay on the medications he's been taking for the last four months."

"And if he doesn't?" Marsha asked.

"The tests we've just done have given us a more thorough picture of the issue. If he should have some distress, we can do the surgery right away. I'd prefer to wait until he's eighteen months to two years of age, though."

"Why did this happen?" James asked.

Dr. Dawson returned to his chair, leaned forward, and folded his hands on the desk. At five foot six inches tall and probably just a hundred and forty-five pounds, the doctor seemed too small, too frail, yet James had seen men that same size leave bigger men in the dust in battle. But at the moment, with his child's future dependent on his actions, James felt he needed to know if they were putting their child in the right hands. His gaze brushed over the diplomas again.

The doctor answered his question. "This occurs once in fifteen hundred births. Because of your son's other genetic issues he ran a greater risk."

"What caused these other genetic problems?" James tried asking his question another way.

"It was caused by a gene mutation on the X chromosome."

"It's my fault, James," Marsha said, her voice just above a whisper. "It's passed from mother to son."

Her soft-spoken admission stole his breath. "You've never said you were aware of any problems, Marsha."

"I didn't know until six months into the pregnancy. And by then it was too late to do anything about it. I just hoped and prayed. Even if I'd found out earlier, I wouldn't have done anything differently. This is our child, James. I carried him inside me for nine months. I loved him from the moment I found out I was pregnant. Whatever issues he may have, I'll continue to love him."

He attempted to keep his voice even while maintaining control of his temper. A sense of betrayal banded his chest. "You could have discussed this with me."

"A good SEAL's wife doesn't bother her husband with problems while he's out of the country." Her eyes held such deep-seated pain, he had no choice but to beat back his anger though an inner voice screamed, '*Problems. Problems? This is more than a problem. This is—life altering.*' But then, what would he have wanted her to do? He ran a hand over his face.

And to be honest, he hadn't asked about the cause before, because with all the chemicals he'd been exposed to during combat, he might have had to hear the words, *'It's your fault'.*

Who the fuck cared whose fault it was? It wouldn't change anything. Alex would still have to go through the surgery. And they'd still be struggling through all the shit that went with those three days of hell they'd endured.

And after everything he'd brought to their door, how could he blame her for anything? It was a miracle she was still with him. He didn't know how much longer she would stay.

"I can suggest some support groups that might help, Captain Jackson. Or a psychologist. Seeing one might help you and your wife deal with the emotional issues that come with having a child with difficulties."

"We're already doing all that," Marsha said. She turned Alex so he could stand up on her lap. At ten months he was sitting up but hadn't yet begun to crawl. But he liked to stand up with help.

"Is the heart condition the reason he tires so quickly?" James asked.

"Yes. It is." Dr. Dawson leaned back in his chair. "He may have moments when his heart will feel like it's beating really hard. And moments when his breathing is very rapid. The medications we've given you will help his heart work more easily and keep fluid from building up in his extremities."

When faced with something that scared the shit out of you, James had learned it was best to face it down. But until they did surgery, how was he to do that?

Marsha placed Alex back in the stroller and strapped him in. As James continued to process everything the doctor had said, he watched his son. Alex represented everything they had ever wanted. Grief swelled in his chest until he wanted to howl from the pain. He locked it away and concentrated on putting one foot in front of the other.

Marsha's hands clenched at her sides as she clamped down on the fear, anger and guilt that threatened to overwhelm her. James pushed the stroller just ahead of her as they crossed the medical office parking lot. The scent of the cream she'd put on Alex's diaper rash lingered on her hands though she'd washed them in the ladies restroom. A whisper of James's cologne reached her on the breeze to blend with the smell. His premature gray hair shone in the afternoon sun. His skin, dark with a tan, contrasting with his pale hair.

Her fault. All of this was her fault. Her son's health problems, his disfigurements were her fault. And now James knew.

Would this be the last straw in their relationship? Would he leave?

How would she feel if he did?

Relieved. Relieved she'd no longer have to live up to his expectations and Alex wouldn't have to live up to them, either. They'd both be free. Or would they?

"I'll put him in his car seat," said James. He punched keys on the electronic keypad to unlock the Equinox. Marsha got into the car but turned to watch over her shoulder. James unstrapped Alex from the umbrella stroller and lifted him free. He held the baby close for a moment, his hand cradling Alex's head. Pain flickered across James's face. He said something to Alex that triggered a toothless smile and James smiled in return, but pain remained in his eyes, in the way his brows creased.

Was that self-contained façade finally cracking? It had been five months since they'd been attacked in their home. And in all that time he'd fought against showing one moment of weakness. Even while lying in a hospital bed after the surgery to repair his fractured eye socket, cheekbone, and arm, he'd maintained a kind of stalwart distance and dignity. The nurses had loved him because he never complained.

What did he talk about with the psychologist? Why couldn't he share some of those things with her? Why didn't they ever talk about what had happened in those three days?

After he had strapped the baby in, put the stroller in the back, and was behind the wheel Marsha laid a hand on his arm. "What did you say to him to make him smile?"

"I told him what a good boy he'd been at the doctor's office."

"He loves the sound of your voice. He always smiles when he hears it." Her son's love for his father was the only thing keeping her from walking away from the marriage. She swallowed. "Are you ever afraid, James?"

He rested his hands on the wheel and focused on something in the distance. "I've had moments. Everyone does."

"Will you tell me about one of those moments?"

"We can talk about this after we get home." He put the key in the ignition.

She grabbed his arm. "I want to hear it now."

"Why?"

"So, I'll know you're human enough to be as afraid as I am."

"Is this about Alex, or is it about the break-in?"

They'd called it the break-in for the last five months, but those two words did nothing to encompass everything that had happened in the three days they'd been held prisoner in their own home, threatened, terrorized, and beaten.

Rage shot through her system. "Open your damn mouth and say something, or I'm packing my bags and Alex and I are leaving."

His look of surprise was followed by a laugh that held no humor. "I've been expecting this for months. Waiting for it to happen." He shook his head. "This is what I've been afraid of."

"Why would you be afraid of something you've worked so hard to make happen for the last five months?" She hated the strident, high-pitched tone of her own voice, but there was no way she could control the wave of resentment and pain that rolled through her.

"What do you mean *I've* worked for it?"

"It's what you've wanted ever since Alex was born. Your life would be simple, wouldn't it? Walk away from your imperfect son, your imperfect wife and go back to the perfect world of your men, your career, your dangerous toys and forget about us."

"I'm not walking away from anything, Marsha. You're pushing me away. You've been doing it since before the baby was born. I came home eager to be a part of Alex's birth, and everything that went with that, and you shut me down. You could have told me about your suspicions. Instead you watched it blindside me in the hospital after the birth and again in the pediatrician's office."

He was right. She'd closed down after three months of fear and dread. Guilt gave her voice an edge. "It's my fault. I've told you it is."

"Well, I thought it was mine. All the crap that we're exposed to when we're downrange—" he shook his head and looked away.

"So now you can relax and know Alex's problems are on me."

"I'm not blaming you!" His voice rose. "Not for this. How were you to know, if your mother never mentioned it?" He gripped the steering wheel hard. "But I do blame you for shutting me out. For not saying anything before that scene in your hospital room after Alex was born. After ten years of marriage and all the stuff we went through to get pregnant, you could have at least given me that."

He was right. She could have told him. But she'd been so devastated herself. So ashamed she'd brought this on them. So hurt she'd brought it on her child.

James twisted the key in the ignition and put the car in gear. "And back to your original complaint about me not being human... Hearing a man talk about cutting into my son's chest and heart scares the shit out of me."

CHAPTER 17

Flash thrust a cordless drill into the leather utility belt around his hips and climbed the ladder to the garage eave. Two more lights and he'd have all the motion-sensor lights in place. The cameras were already installed. Despite the early morning breeze whipping between the garage and the house, sweat ran down between his shoulder blades and dampened the hair around his face.

The sound of wheels spinning on the patio behind the house next door stopped. He glanced over his shoulder to find the little girl, Joy, holding one of the hard plastic tires of the toy Big Wheel she'd been riding. She lifted the rear axil of the toy, and, after several attempts, succeeded in fitting the tire back on. She jumped back on the toy, and pedaled around the patio again. Just as she made another turn the tire came off again. She climbed off the low-riding toy, stood over it for a moment, then put her hands on her hips and glared at it. Her bottom lip thrust out and Flash smiled.

Strong-willed he decided. If she weren't, she'd already be crying and yelling for her mother.

The parallels in her situation and his as a child weren't lost on him. The major difference was her mother wasn't a drug-addicted prostitute and she had stood up for herself and her daughter and broken away from the son of a bitch who had abused them. Or was trying to.

Since moving in he'd kept a close watch on what went on next door. Not out of idle curiosity, but just to get the lay of the land. From his observations, Samantha Cross was caring, loving and afraid. Not sleeping much himself, he'd noticed how many times a night she checked the doors and windows.

Flash climbed down the ladder and moseyed over to the gate leading into Sam's back yard. He thought of her as Sam now, though there wasn't a thing masculine about her. She had a distinctive, feminine sway to her walk and was built like a dancer, her body sleek and streamlined. She made five foot four look like five nine because of her body structure and long, slender legs.

And her daughter, Joy, looked just like her, only in miniature.

"Hey, sweetheart. You having a problem with your Big Wheel?" he asked.

"Uh-huh." She folded her arms and nudged the plastic tire with her toe. "The wheel falled off."

His lips twitched with amusement. "I see that. How 'bout I check it out?"

Her blue eyes lit with a smile. "Can you fix it?"

"I don't know. I'll look and see." He opened the gate, and squatted down to check both back wheels and axles. She'd lost the washers and the lock ring that held the wheel on. He could deal with that. "I'll be right back. You stay in the yard." He picked up the toy and wheel, carried it out of the yard and shut the gate. Inside the garage, he fished through some of the baskets inside his van for the necessary parts. Within five minutes he had the wheel back on and the toy in good working order. He crossed the drive and lifted it over the fence and set it down.

"You fixed it!" Joy bounced up and down in excitement. "Thank you, Mr. Tim."

He smiled at the name she'd called him. "Don't drive too fast, sweetheart."

Joy laughed. "Mommy's wheels were flat, like that." Joy trust her hand palm out and slammed the other one down on top of it. "They'll be all better today."

"They will?"

Joy nodded, her expression solemn "She promised. I don't like that ol' truck."

"You don't?" He eyed the rattle-trap vehicle parked in the driveway.

"It stinks." Joy pinched her nose. "And goes squeak, squeak squeak."

Flash grinned. It did burn some oil. And sounded like things might start flying off at any moment. But it ran and it was only temporary.

"Well maybe today will be the last time you have to ride in it." He waved good-bye and went back to finish the alarm system installation.

A few minutes later, when Sam and Joy came out of the house and got into the truck, he was on the ladder again with both hands occupied. Joy waved good-bye and he smiled at her. Sam had her head turned looking for traffic. Or was she avoiding having to acknowledge him? He'd been doing the same with her. They were both doing the wise thing.

He couldn't get involved. It would be dangerous to get too close—for them both.

Samantha sat at the dining room table and attempted to focus on the assignment for her online class. She was not going to look out the window. She was not going to spy on Tim Carnes. He was just her tenant.

But her head kept turning of its own volition. She glanced out the window toward the garage. Tim's forearm muscles bunched as he carried two large stacked boxes up the steps to the apartment. His legs looked tanned and firm in black shorts that hugged his thighs. Try as she might, she couldn't drag her attention away from him. With one part of her mind she dispassionately recognized he was gorgeous. Thick brown hair with a hint of wave, straight, even teeth, strong, masculine features, just enough beard to be fashionable, and despite how the geeky dark-rimmed glasses he wore partially hid them, eyes so pale a blue... She slammed the breaks on her thoughts, bringing them to a screeching halt. Being attracted to a man was way, way down the road. If it ever happened again.

The nightmare she'd woken from at four this morning emphasized how remote the possibility was. She ran her hands over her face, trying to scrub away the tired ache behind her eyes. It had taken her nearly an hour to calm down. She'd rushed from window to window, checking to make sure the house was secure.

And now Tim had moved in. She wasn't sure how she felt about having him just across the drive. He'd given her his cell phone number and told her to call if she had any problems. When he'd said it, the serious frown he'd given her had been clear enough.

But Tim didn't know Will, or how violent he could be. She couldn't put him in the middle. She had to solve her own problems.

She glanced at the clock. Almost time to pick up Joy. She forced her attention back to the screen, reread the question, deleted the answer she'd been in the process of writing and tried to formulate a better one. She'd have to spend some time studying when she got back.

And tomorrow was her first day as a receptionist-secretary at a lawyer's office. Nerves danced the rumba in her stomach. She'd learn everything she needed to. She had the basic skills, and they'd seemed to like her at the interview.

The check Tim Carnes had given her for his first and last month's rent had covered the cost of new tires and given her a couple of month's breathing room on her utilities. The money couldn't have come at a better time. But his presence here…

A knock sounded at the door. She rose from the computer and paused to look through the peephole. If thinking about Tim Carnes had drawn him to the house, she was going to have to control her wayward thoughts.

His shoulders stretched the fabric of his shirt and defined the musculature of his chest.

Will was strong but not as fit. The thirty extra pounds he carried had settled in his chest and stomach. There was no extra fat on Tim's frame. Her mouth grew dry just looking at him. He could probably hit just as hard as Will. She flinched from the thought.

He tapped again. Her hands shook as she turned the dead bolt and opened the door.

"I have to make one last run to the office to load my bike. I thought if you needed me to, I could drop you at the garage to pick up your car."

She stared at him, suspicious. "How did you know about the car?"

He grinned. "Joy."

When had he spoken to Joy? More than likely it was the other way around. Sam shook her head in exasperation. "She has a tendency to tell everything she knows."

"There's an upside to that. You won't ever have to worry about her becoming a super spy," he quipped.

Sam's laugh slipped free. "But she may dress like one." She'd wondered how she was going to manage Gran's old truck and her car. His giving her a ride would solve that issue. Could she trust him? She studied his even features and bit her lip. "I have to go by to get Joy first and speak to her teacher for a few minutes before I pick up the car. I don't want to inconvenience you."

"It won't be an inconvenience. And you'll have to have a ride to retrieve that old truck if you drive it to the shop to pick up the car." He nodded toward the rust-scarred pickup.

She'd been surprised it still ran, but at least it got them to and from Joy's preschool. She studied Tim's expression.

"It's really not as bad as it looks."

"Uh-huh." His deadpan expression tempted another smile.

Were men really this protective? She'd never known them to be. But then, Will was the only man she'd been around for an extended time. She'd mistaken his possessiveness for protectiveness. Something she wouldn't do again.

She searched Tim's expression. The police had checked him out. They knew he was living here. If something happened it would come right back on him. He'd be stupid to hurt her. And he didn't strike her as unintelligent.

She did need the ride. "You're sure you don't mind?"

"No, I don't mind."

"I'll get my purse. I just have to save something on the computer."

"I'll wait here. Take your time." He sat down in one of the rockers on the porch.

Had he sensed she was anxious about letting him in the house? She hadn't invited him in and had kept the screen door locked between them. Though he hadn't done anything to awaken her fears, trust wasn't something they had established yet. Probably never would.

Sam rushed to save her work to her Drop Box, and then shut the computer down. She unplugged it and stuffed it in her backpack.

How did she know she could trust him to just give her a ride? What did she know about him, even after calling every one of the references he'd given her?

She knew he was patient with Joy. And Joy was fascinated with him. But that was probably because she'd had so little exposure to any men besides Will, and Chaney, her grandfather.

Sam knew Tim was organized, professional, and an expert on security systems. She'd seen how he'd systematized a vanload of equipment on the shelving unit he'd set up in the garage. He'd also installed a security system in the apartment and garage. He'd deemed it a business expense and said it wouldn't do for his customers to know he didn't have one installed in his own place when he wanted them to buy one.

By renting the apartment from her, despite the issues she'd had in the past with Will, she'd discovered he wasn't put off by the possibility of trouble.

There was definitely more to Tim Carnes than his tall, well-built body and sexy smile.

She shouldered her backpack and grabbed her keys. Tim stood up when she came out the door and secured the lock, then gestured for her to precede him down the steps to his van.

He opened the door for her and offered her a hand up into the passenger seat. After a momentary hesitation, she placed her hand in his. His old-school manners and warm grip triggered a tiny blossom of feminine awareness she hadn't felt in years.

To keep from watching his every move as he walked around to the driver's door, she looked around the cramped space inside the van. "How on earth did you get all the equipment in the garage in here *plus* your motorcycle?" she asked, when he settled behind the wheel.

"The equipment I've organized in the garage is stuff I ordered and had shipped to the post office downtown. The system that alerts the police to a security breach is all computerized. And we only have to have two people answering calls if an alarm goes off, which is someone else's responsibility. So I only have to deal with assessments and installations." He buckled his seatbelt, started the engine, and pulled out.

"You're going to be very busy."

"I hope so. I did two assessments the day I arrived. I'm due to install those systems this week."

"How long have you been in town?"

"Before moving into the apartment, four days."

Sam shook her head. "You don't let the grass grow under your feet, do you?"

"Can't afford to with all the other systems out there competing against us."

"How did you get into this business?" she asked.

Tim shoved his dark-rimmed glasses up his nose. "I was between jobs, which gave me some time to take stock of all the skills I had to offer. I decided this would be the perfect fit. I have a friend who thinks I'm a good risk, so we went into business together."

Someone trusted him, depended on him to run this business. That meant he had to be dependable. "It never hurts to have someone who believes in you."

"No, it doesn't."

Sam lapsed into silence, her throat tightening with grief.

"I'm sorry about your grandmother."

How had he guessed? She studied his expression until he glanced in her direction. "I am, too." The words hurt her throat.

"It must have happened very fast. When I talked to her, she sounded fine."

"She put the house in my name. Just in case. She had two more chemo treatments. I tried to talk her out of taking them. She seemed—There was something not quite right. They insisted she go ahead with them. Gave her the spiel that they couldn't be responsible for her health if she didn't take the treatments. She died half an hour after they gave her the last one."

"Jesus!" His throat worked as he swallowed. "Are you going to file a suit?"

"It wouldn't do any good. Ultimately it was her decision to take the medication. She'd signed consent forms saying they'd gone over the risks and she accepted them." She ran a hand through her hair and beat back the rage that threatened to consume her again. "I didn't know until later that cancer patients have a one in ten chance of the drugs killing them before the disease. They tell them, take this or you'll die. And they want to live, so they do."

"There has to be something...someone needs to be held accountable."

His outrage mirrored her own and gave her some comfort. "It wouldn't bring Gran back. And she wasn't about lawsuits and blame. She was all about living." The chance she'd get any money from a suit that would probably drag out for years was very slim. The hospital would blame the chemo company and the chemo company would blame the person administering the drug. It was a cycle that would go on and on and take up time she didn't have.

She had to keep going, to support her child and herself. But she'd live with this soul-deep ache of loss for the rest of her life.

Her only family was gone. She was alone, except for Joy. Every time she thought about it panic threatened to overwhelm her. But she'd made a promise she'd keep putting one foot in front of the other and move on.

A warm hand on her arm tugged her back from her thoughts. And she gazed up into Tim's pale blue eyes as his thumb ran over her skin in a small show of comfort. His eyes had an uneven area of gray around the pupil, and a darker ring of blue around the outside edge of the iris. Being able to look directly into man's eyes without feeling fear was an accomplishment. Her stomach tumbled. The hot rush of need that accompanied it was amazing.

And terrifying.

Flash swallowed against the breathless feeling of arousal that zipped straight to his groin. Her gray-green eyes homed in on his face and pulled him in. His attention dropped to her mouth. Would she taste like the home-baked cookies he'd smelled when he knocked on her door?

He released her arm and put his hand back on the steering wheel. He should never have touched her. But she just seemed so alone. A feeling he identified with more each day.

He had to stow that shit and move on. He couldn't afford to get close to anyone. "Where to from here?" he managed, his Boston accent thick with reaction.

"Turn right, and go seven blocks."

He turned the van. The noisy shift of the components stored in basket shelves along each side of the vehicle sounded loud in the silence between them.

How long since he'd gotten laid? He'd had a brief encounter with an ex-girlfriend after returning from Iraq. But after that he'd been swallowed up by the FBI crap, and though Javier and Josh had tried to fix him up while he was in Baja, he'd avoided anything but casual meetings.

It had been almost eleven months since he'd been with a woman.

He was just horny.

Who'd have thought a woman who smelled like honeysuckle and crayons would set him off? He usually went for the free-spirited kind who didn't expect hearts and flowers. The kind just out to have a good time. Being a SEAL, he had little time for anything other than temporary hook up.

But the female sitting next to him wasn't temporary. She had *permanent, hearts and flowers, forever and ever* emblazoned across her freckle-dusted nose in letters visible to him a mile away.

He'd done some research on Sam since their first meeting. And the story behind her divorce wasn't pretty. Life, and her stalker ex-husband, seemed determined to knock her down. She just kept getting back up and moving forward.

But she was emotionally bruised. Her distrust was right there, staring him in the face every time he spoke to her. Her SOB ex had really done a number on her.

And she certainly didn't need a Navy SEAL on the run from a crooked FBI guy and a drug cartel to add to her worries. He had to remember that. If shit hit the fan and he was arrested, he might put Sam and Joy in the crosshairs. Sam didn't deserve that after everything else she'd been through.

But he couldn't walk away, either. Not with her sneaky, abusive ex making things as difficult for her as possible. And he was going to have to talk her into allowing him to put a security system in her house. He'd sleep better if she had one.

He'd sleep better if she were in his bed.

Shit, he had to get his mind on something else. Because that wasn't happening. No matter how hot she was.

He spotted the kids on a fenced-in playground and pulled to a stop. Joy broke away from a cluster of kids, ran to the fence and waved to him. He smiled and waved back.

"I'll only be a few minutes," Sam said, opening the door.

Sam was a mom, for God's sake. He didn't sleep with moms.

"Take your time." *Please.* So maybe he'd have his head on straight by the time she came back.

CHAPTER 18

James stalked through the outer office and paused beside Seaman Crouch's desk to pick up his mail.

"What is all this, Crouch?" he asked when his aide handed him a stack of forms as thick as a dictionary.

"Requisition forms, sir. It would seem quite a few requests have been denied lately, and the team commanders wanted to draw your attention to the problem."

James bit back an expletive, carried the tome into his office, shut the door and slammed the stack of papers onto the desk. After returning to light duty following the attack at his home, he'd caught up the unit's paperwork while he waited for the bones in his face to knit. And now all those orders were coming back at once. It was the habit of team administrators to request their dream list of equipment, then later settle for what they could get. But this barrage of paperwork was ridiculous.

He jerked up the phone and pushed the button. "Crouch, get Chief Stewart in here."

"Yes, sir."

Twenty minutes later Chief Stewart left James's office, the bundle of requisitions under his arm. His sole purpose would be to check through each one and discover why it had been denied. Every order for a new weapon or safety equipment would be returned to James to deal with personally. Chief Stewart would handle the rest.

James turned on his computer and brought up his email. He answered the first two messages, then noticed a subject heading reminiscent of the last mission one of his teams had participated in, in Iraq. He opened the message and the attachment. His stomach dropped.

Flash had surfaced. He was alive.

James read the short note then clicked on the link. It took him to a private message board where several service men discussed being approached by the FBI to smuggle artifacts from Iraq. Each man used a call sign to protect his identity. But the scenario followed was the same in each instance.

The next seven links were videos of a man named Gilbert. The first one involved an altercation between Flash and the man. The next, two thugs came in, beat Gilbert up and cut him loose. James's pulse drummed in his ears at the blatant way the man set Flash up to take the fall for the beating. *What the fuck?*

The next four clips were phone conversations taped from a camera partially obscured by a mesh screen of some kind. They were meets being arranged between Gilbert and a man named Caesar. The last one was time-stamped in the corner a month ago. All the videos appeared to have been taped in the same location.

James clicked on the next link and another video loaded. It was Flash. He looked healthy but thinner, his features more chiseled, his hair longer. "I hope you receive this. I tried to contact NCIS when this mission first went to hell, but all they were interested in was arresting me for being AWOL. Knowing my history, sir, you know why I couldn't come in." He swallowed and looked away from the camera, then back. "I am not a quitter. I never wanted to leave my team. I am innocent of everything but believing the bullshit I was fed by Special Agent Eric Gilbert. He used me, just as he used the other men whose messages you've just read.

"I've sent you the same evidence I've been feeding NCIS since I've been missing. Our unit worked with Special Agent Rick Dobson several times in the past. I don't believe he was involved in this. I think that's why they took him out. I also believe that Gilbert has gotten looped in by the drug cartel and is in too deep to get out. I believe the Caesar he's speaking to is Caesar Vargas, one of the most notorious drug lords in Mexico. Once you get hung up with those guys the only way you get out is in a body bag."

James watched Flash swallow hard before continuing. "NCIS has the artifacts I smuggled for Dobson and Gilbert. I mailed the carvings to them months ago with a full report. I've attached said report to this email. I kept the money as a bargaining chip, just in case everything goes to shit later and I need it. But it's in a safe place ready to be turned in when this is settled.

"I need your help, sir. I want to get back to my unit—to my team." He looked away from the screen, his jaw tense as he struggled with the strong emotion that worked across his features. When he looked back his face was tense, his eyes like tempered steel. "That's all I've wanted for the last seven months. I've been stuck in limbo waiting for someone to get off their ass and arrest Gilbert." Color flushed his cheeks and his mouth settled into grim lines. "But as you can tell from the videos, he's conducting business as usual. There may be a warrant out for me for the break-in at his apartment and the assault he's accused me of, so I'm lying low. But something has to give, sir.

"I'm reaching out to you, sir. I'm hoping you can light a fire under someone and get them to do something so I can come in. I'll be in touch soon with instructions for how you can contact me. This address is only a temporary thing. I'm sure you understand why, sir."

The video closed out.

"Son of a bitch!" James slammed back his desk chair and lunged to his feet. He circled the desk until some of the anger leached away. Had NCIS been sitting on this and leaving Flash hanging in the wind? That's what it sounded like. Or was Flash shining him on and doing some kind of con to get back in after being AWOL for so long? He paced the floor. No. Not possible. Those videos were legit. He'd bet his left nut on it.

He pushed the button on his phone and asked Crouch to pull Flash's file. The seaman brought it in and left.

Though he'd reviewed it several times since he'd chosen Lieutenant Junior Grade Carney as a member of one of his teams, he went back over the info. He reviewed Flash's juvy record. Though it had been sealed, when a man applied to become a SEAL every part of his life was looked at under a microscope. Flash had come up hard. Abandoned by his mother, never knowing his father, settled into the foster system at the age of seven.

He'd spent time in a juvenile detention facility for dealing dope at twelve, but that charge had been expunged when one of his foster brothers came forward and admitted the drugs were his. He'd never been tagged for drug use.

But he'd had a record of cons and scams. *How could a twelve-year-old be a con artist? Who taught him that shit?* He'd been released from the facility at fourteen and run away from the foster home where he'd been placed that time.

Then somehow he'd ended up in California, where he'd finished high school. *How the hell had he done that?* Though he'd been two years behind for his age, he'd graduated with honors and enrolled in college with a SAT score of twenty-one hundred. He'd excelled in computer skills and had an IQ of one-sixty. The guy was a genius, but he'd chosen to go into the military and become a SEAL.

His military record was exemplary. As a SEAL he'd excelled at everything he'd taken on, had wanted to be a sniper, and became the best.

For the last eleven years, from high school through his SEAL career, he'd toed the line and done everything right. Until he'd hooked up with Gilbert.

Despite the challenges in his early history, the file didn't read like a man falling off the rails.

But James wanted to speak to Hawk first before making a move. He got back on the computer, looked up the SAT phone number for the Afghani base, and dialed it. After identifying himself he asked, "Can you get a message to Lieutenant Yazzie?" The voice on the other end of the line said, "They've just come in off a patrol. Hold a minute and I'll get him."

Five long minutes later Hawk's voice came over the line. "Lieutenant Yazzie."

"Hawk, Captain Jackson. There's been some news about Lieutenant Carney."

After a brief pause, Hawk asked. "Is he dead?"

"No. As of two weeks ago, he was alive and well."

"I knew it." His elation came across the line. "What the hell happened to him? Is it something to do with those fucking guys who came to see him at the end of our last deployment?"

"What do you mean?"

"Greenback saw two guys call Flash out for a powwow. They were dressed in fatigues with no insignias on their uniforms. Greenback didn't recognize either of them, but he got the feeling they were official, maybe FBI. Then when we got home, Flash made himself scarce. He was tied up with something. I assumed he might be spending his R and R in Vegas, then Bowie said he was staying close to home, but had something else going on. Something he wouldn't talk about. Then I found out about the artifacts Zoe, my girlfriend, found in Brett's sea bag, and I thought I'd figured it out. That's when I came to you."

That conversation had happened months ago and he'd submitted the report. But now that Hawk had jogged his memory he remembered most of it. He'd pull it and go back over it. "For now I need you to keep Flash's status to yourself. I need an opportunity to dig into this."

"Roger that, Captain. I'm just glad to know he's alive. Where the hell has he been?"

"I don't know. But he's supposed to contact me again. I'll keep you updated."

"Appreciate it. Will you be joining us in the sandbox?"

Jackson hesitated. His men were in Iraq and Afghanistan without him. Every time he dwelled on that, guilt shoved tension into every muscle, despite the fact he'd been on medical leave until recently. "Not at this time. We just learned my son will have to have heart surgery sometime down the road. I want to be certain he's stable before I leave."

"Understood, sir. Sorry to hear the little guy is ill. If it was my kid, I'd want to do the same."

James had heard about Zoe Weaver's pregnancy through the grapevine. Keeping national secrets came easy to the guys, but any important personal news spread like wildfire. "Thanks, Lieutenant. I'll keep you posted on Flash's status."

He hung up the phone and settled back behind his computer.

If he'd shipped out with his men, he and Marsha might have avoided the trauma of being attacked in their home. If he'd shipped out with his men, he'd have come home to an empty house with no wife and child. With Alex's issues hanging over their heads, and the stress they'd been under after his last deployment, Marsha would have left him. He didn't doubt that.

At least being laid up waiting for his bones to knit, he'd had time to get to know Alex and come to terms with his son's difficulties. Or at least partially come to terms with them.

But would these feelings of grief and anger ever pass?

He'd distanced himself from Marsha and Alex because of guilt for not being there for her during her pregnancy, for possibly being responsible for his son's condition. If nothing else had come from the attack, he'd been forced to accept things. But the damage to his marriage was already done.

Would his wife ever forgive him for those first few months? Would she forgive him for not being able to protect her from the men who'd forced their way into their home?

Marsha paced the floor as Alex's cries escalated into a screaming fit. She had checked his diaper, tried giving him a bottle, and taken him outside into the front yard to distract him, but nothing seemed to help. If only he could tell her what the hell was wrong.

Alex bowed his back and threw open his mouth. For the first time she saw his top gum was red and swollen. She could see where the buds of two teeth pressed against the skin waiting to push through. *Poor baby.* Why hadn't she seen that? And why were these two causing such an issue when the first two hadn't?

She carried him into the kitchen and got the teething ring out of the freezer. She pressed the cold ring against his swollen gums. He started, and the sound of his distress cut off in mid-cry. He reached for it, but when the cold device came into contact with his hands, he jerked them back.

Marsha smiled. "Too cold, huh? But it feels good where those mean ol' teeth are coming through."

After a few minutes, Alex's lips closed around the teething ring and he began to gnaw at it. With the emergency averted, she returned to her bedroom, settled him in his walker, happily gumming the ring where he could see her. She stared hard at her overstuffed closet.

Why did they keep buying stuff when they'd just have to get rid of it when they moved? And now they had a baby, it would mean more to deal with.

She grabbed a hanger and jerked a pale blue maternity dress out. She'd never wear it again. An ache of grief so deep tears couldn't alleviate it settled in her chest. She pulled the hanger free of the garment and tossed the dress onto the floor, then hung the empty hanger back up. With each item she pulled out, her anger and pain grew until she wanted to scream. She stomped on the pile of helpless garments. A sob built in her throat and pushed its way free. She crumpled to the carpet and buried her face against her knees.

When she could finally breathe again, she found Alex watching from his walker, his eyes round with fascination. *What would she do if she didn't have him*? He was her reason for getting up in the morning. For hanging on to her sanity.

She drew a deep breath and forced herself to relax. She focused on the slippers lying at the bottom of the closet. She'd bought them because her feet had swollen badly toward the end of her pregnancy and now they were stretched too big for her to wear. She would never again experience that particular uncomfortable side-effect of having a baby. Or the joy of carrying another child.

What if she packed up what she wanted to keep and walked away? She could leave everything else for James to give away. It would serve him right. How many times had she PCS'd without *him?* She'd been left behind to move their entire house while he was having fun being a SEAL, blowing things up and jumping out of airplanes. He could call it *his job* all he wanted. He loved all of it.

"Permanent change of station my ass," she mumbled beneath her breath. She crawled forward and tossed the shoes onto the crumpled collection, now scattered into a wide circle on the carpet. She sat back on her heels next to Alex's walker.

Drool ran down his chin. She used a discarded blouse to wipe his slobbery mouth and neck and set it aside to launder before boxing it up with the rest of the things.

James loved his job more than he did her. She'd always known he did. Accepted it. Now the break-in had driven a wedge between them, the relationship they had wasn't enough anymore. Life was too short to settle for what had turned out to be precious little.

James was struggling, as badly as she. She'd seen it in the car after Alex's doctor's appointment. Everything they'd experienced in the last months had finally chipped away at the smooth, unbreachable façade he showed the world. Showed to her. She wanted to pick away at those chips until the surface fell away and she could finally meet the real man beneath. Had they ever really known one another? Had they lived as husband and wife for the last ten years, yet remained total strangers? Or had it happened gradually because of too many deployments?

Alex banged the teething ring against the walker tray. She ran a hand over his head, smoothing his blond hair. It bounced back up, haloing his head like dandelion fluff. She smiled and earned an answering smile from him. "You're a good boy." He was loving and sweet.

And his shirt was saturated with slobber.

She grimaced and rose to go get him a dry shirt and a bib.

After his cleanup, she snapped a bib around his neck and lifted him out of the walker. Resting him on her hip, she wandered down the hall, through the kitchen to the side door leading into the garage. She gripped the doorknob and hesitated. Every room in the house held a memory of the break-in she wanted to leave behind. But the garage was where it began. She hadn't been in the room since.

The smell of motor oil leached through the door and triggered the memory of how the scent mingled with the flowers blooming in the drive and the kabobs James was grilling out by the pool. In the next moment, though she hadn't moved or opened the door, she was there inside the garage. Even with one of the doors raised it had been stuffy. Sweat was beading between her breasts and along the inside of her arms. She gripped the plastic container of pool chemicals James had asked her to fetch. A step behind her drew her attention, and she turned and looked into the dark hole of a gun barrel.

She couldn't go there. Marsha shook free of the memory.

Tabarek Moussa and his men were dead. Killed by Brett Weaver in a one-man rescue. If only he had come three days earlier.

She looked around the kitchen. This room and the nursery were the only two rooms in the house untainted by the violence. The only two rooms where she hadn't been touched, hit, or threatened with rape or assault. The only room she hadn't had to watch her husband being beaten and her child threatened with a gun. Her legs felt shaky and her heart raced so she couldn't breathe. She pulled a chair out from the kitchen table and sat down.

James could get the empty boxes for her when he got home.

CHAPTER 19

Sam listened to Joy's chatter. "And Nancy Jane and me—"

"Nancy Jane and I," Sam corrected her.

"No mommy, Nancy Jane and me. You weren't there."

Sam laughed.

"And Ms. Tom-sun said we done good."

"Mrs. Thompson said you did good."

"Yeah, she did."

Sam smiled and shook her head. She'd try to explain later.

If her week had been half as exciting as her daughter's, she'd be raring to go again tomorrow. Luckily she didn't have to. Thank God it was Friday.

Answering telephones, typing letters, copying papers and filing were boring, but at least she got paid. The money had been direct deposited into her checking account, so she hadn't gotten to *see* her first paycheck. But she had experienced the feeling of accomplishment that went along with working and making her own way.

Having a job—making her own money, being independent—was a greater accomplishment than anything she'd ever done…except for Joy. A thought struck her. "How 'bout we go out for ice cream tonight after dinner, Tumblebug?"

"Hot dogs first, black," Joy said.

"The grill's broken, honey. I haven't figured out how to fix it yet."

"Mr. Tim can fix it."

Joy had decided Mr. Tim could make the sun shine and the clouds smile about it. She hadn't been able to figure out why. But because of Joy's fascination with him, Sam had avoided him as much as possible. She couldn't afford to let her daughter grow attached to some random man who would be moving on. And besides, she didn't know enough about him. She didn't think he was a pervert or anything, but a mom couldn't be too careful. And after her reaction when he'd looked into her eyes…it was too soon for her to trust those feelings. "Mr. Tim works a lot and he doesn't have time to fix the grill. I'll get it fixed as soon as I can. We can bake the hot dogs under the broiler and they'll taste just as good."

Joy remained silent a moment. "'Kay."

No argument? Sam breathed a sigh. She was so lucky. Joy was so easygoing. But sometimes Sam worried she was too obedient. Was it because she'd learned to be tractable to please her father and keep him from losing his temper? And if she had, how would it affect her later in life?

Would she stand up to a man if he abused her? Had Sam waited too long to leave Will, and thus set a precedent in her daughter's life?

When she pulled into the driveway ten minutes later she was still wrestling with those questions. She shoved open the car door and the aroma of hot charcoal wafted to her. She glanced at Joy. Her daughter's lip thrust out. Smoke meandered from around the back side of the garage. Joy jumped out of the car and ran around the side of the building. Sam hissed a word of impatience beneath her breath.

Grabbing her small purse and Joy's backpack, Sam exited the car and followed the path her daughter had taken around the garage.

Cut off jeans shorts bared Tim's long, muscular legs. A tank-style t-shirt hugged his torso, outlining firm pectoral muscles and six-pack abs. Stained tennis shoes without socks hugged his feet. Dark sunglasses shielded his eyes and prevented her from judging his expression, but when he saw her, an amused smile spread across the lower half of his face.

The fluttering heat of attraction feathered along her nerve endings and her heartbeat quickened. She tried to ignore the response. His physical attractiveness wasn't the only reason she found him so appealing. His easygoing, patient attitude had a great deal to do with it, too.

"Joy says she likes her dogs burnt black on the outside. How do you like your steak?"

Sam eyed Joy with her sternest mom look. "I'd already told her we'd broil her hot dogs because our grill is torn up."

"Mine's working fine." He motioned to the old-school charcoal grill. The coals are hot and I'm about to throw on a couple of steaks. It's no trouble to put some dogs on, too."

She didn't want to impose. "I don't want our being neighbors to become a disruption for you."

"It's no big deal, Sam. I'd like for the two of you to join me."

Her attention swung back to Joy and she studied her daughter's hopeful expression. Darn the little imp. "Thank you. I appreciate the offer. I'll go get the hot dogs." She held out the backpack to Joy. "We're going to have a talk before dinner."

Joy grabbed the pack and head-down dawdled toward the house.

"Is there anything I can fix to go with the steak?" Sam asked.

"I have potatoes baking and asparagus in butter on the grill. Does Joy like asparagus?"

"Wow. I didn't think guys liked vegetables."

He grinned. "I have to have some carbs in my diet. I run every day."

"I've seen you." Did her admission sound like she'd been watching him? Her face flushed hot. "Joy likes anything green, but I don't think she's ever tried asparagus." Joy'd reached the front porch and was waiting on her. "I'll herd her this way in a few minutes."

"You didn't tell me how you like your steak."

"Just a little pink when you cut into it."

He grinned. "Roger that. Bring the hot dogs."

Roger that? She'd heard the expression before. Where? TV possibly. Wasn't it military lingo? She studied him for a moment. Getting up every morning at five to run, the precision he used to organize his tools and materials, knowing how to fix and install electronic things could be ingrained by military training. And explained his unflappable calm about moving in next door to a woman with a violent ex-husband.

"Be back in a few minutes." She crossed the yard to the front porch, unlocked the front door and held it open for Joy.

"Are you mad, Mommy?"

At the anxious expression on Joy's face, tension curled around the back of Sam's neck. "No, I'm not mad."

Sam set her purse on the small table next to the front door and, taking Joy's backpack, dropped it beneath it. She took Joy's hand, led her to the couch, and pulled her onto her lap. Joy smelled of baby shampoo, the playground, and kid. For a moment she wished for the tiny baby back. Things had been so much simpler when she'd just needed a diaper change and a bottle.

"I know you like Mr. Tim."

"He fixed my Big Wheel."

"He did?" Well that explained how Mr. Tim could fix *everything.* "I'll have to thank him for doing that."

She monitored Joy almost constantly when she played in the back yard. But she had to pee now and then, and fix food for them. "You know you're not allowed to go outside the fence in the backyard, or ride your Big Wheel anywhere but the patio out back."

"I didn't, Mommy."

"How did he know it was torn up?"

"It wouldn't go."

Trying to get information from a five year old was like pulling hen's teeth.

"How did he fix it?"

"He said stay in the yard. He took it for a *long* time."

A *long* time could be anywhere between five minutes to half an hour.

"It goed good again then."

Sam smiled. "I'm glad it goes now."

It had to have been the day he'd been on the ladder putting up the lights. Joy'd been playing out in the yard and watched from the fence. She'd obviously been waiting for him to bring back the Big Wheel. Why hadn't Sam seen him?

Because she'd been getting ready to take Joy to school, making her breakfast and studying for an exam. She'd learned to take multi-tasking to a whole new level since she'd started the college classes.

"It's good that Mr. Tim fixed your Big Wheel. I'll be sure to thank him. But we don't want to bother him too much."

"I don't bother him. He likes me."

"How do you know?"

"He smiles at me and calls me sweet tart."

Sam bit her lip to keep from laughing. She gave Joy a squeeze.

Joy's stomach growled. "My tummy's mad. It's hungry."

"I heard it. How many hot dogs do you want?"

"A ho, ho bunch."

That usually meant two, one on a bun plain and an extra cut up on a plate. The second one she might or might not eat. She'd urge her to try the asparagus and half a potato. But she'd slice her up an apple too, just in case.

"Take your backpack to your room and I'll change."

Joy wiggled free, grabbed her backpack and ran down the hall.

Sam followed at a more sedate pace and went into her bedroom. She changed into shorts, a scoop-necked top and rubber flip-flops. It felt good to get out of the pantyhose and dress she'd worn for work. She padded down the hall to the kitchen. Joy was in the refrigerator and turned with the package of hot dogs in her hand. "I got them, Mommy."

"Thank you. You can carry those for me. We'll take the whole package. Mr. Tim might want a dog, too." Sam put some of the pear salad she'd made the night before in a plastic container for desert, sliced up a couple of apples and put them in another.

Joy wiggled impatiently. "Come on, Mommy."

"Almost done." Sam gathered hot dog buns, paper plates, plastic forks, cups, napkins, bottles of water, and a plastic table cloth to cover the dilapidated picnic table behind the garage, and packed them all into a basket.

"All right, go ahead. I'm right behind you." Joy ran out the back door while Sam paused to flip on the switch to activate the porch light.

By the time she'd made it across the yard and around to the back of the garage, she could hear Joy chatting away to Tim.

My friend Nancy Jane paints real good."

"I bet you do, too," Tim said.

"I try real hard."

Tim chuckled. "The next time you paint a picture will you do one for me? I need something to hang on the wall in the living room."

Joy's whole face lit up when she smiled. "All right."

Sam's heart turned over. He was so good with her.

But he'd never had a steady diet of five-year-old chatter and the hundred questions she asked a day. Joy wanted—needed—a positive male influence in her life. Was hungry for it. And Tim seemed to have won her daughter's heart just by fixing her Big Wheel. That thought brought an ache of tears to her throat.

Tim Carnes would only be around until he got his business established. When the money came rolling in, he'd leave. And she didn't know enough about him to say if he would be a good influence. Or even that she wanted him to be one. She'd made some horrible mistakes in the past and Joy was still paying for them, just as she was. She couldn't afford to make another by trusting a stranger.

The beat-up picnic table sat behind the garage on the concrete slab that stretched the length of the building. She still remembered the truck coming to pour the concrete for the garage floor and this patio they'd used for barbecuing. The distance from the house was only the width of the drive. She set the basket down on one of the benches and spread the plastic cloth over the tabletop.

"Do you want to help me set the table, Joy?"

"I'll do it, Mommy."

Sam stood close by as Joy climbed up on the seat and knelt to delve into the basket. She set the plastic container of pears and apples out, then set out the plastic plates. She positioned them one next to the other on one side of the table.

"Would you like some apple slices until your hot dog is ready?" Sam asked.

"Uh-huh."

Sam pulled the top from the container and shook some apple slices onto one of the plates. Joy settled onto the bench and nibbled at one. She pulled three little people out of her shorts pocket and lined them up next to her plate.

"Don't feed Sarah, Dewey, and Fudi any of your food. They make a terrible mess," Sam said.

Joy giggled.

"Looks as though you've done that a time or two," Tim welded long tongs as he flipped the steaks. He had opened the hot dogs and put some on the grill.

"A few times. Joy and I have picnics out here pretty often."

"There are drinks in the cooler." Using the tongs, he pointed toward a small red cooler sitting next to the grill. "There's a beer or two, but mostly soft drinks."

"I brought water too."

"Can I have a Coke, Mommy?" Joy asked.

Sam looked from Tim to Joy and back again. Darn it, she didn't want to deprive Joy of the treat all the time, but she did try to limit the amount of sugar and caffeine she allowed her, especially later in the day.

Tim's grin was rueful. "Next time I'll know to check it out with you beforehand."

"It's okay." She turned to Joy. "You can have a little." She retrieved the soft drink from the cooler, found a plastic cup in the basket, poured a third of the can into it and set it next to Joy's plate, setting the can at her own place and sliding one of the plates to the other side of the table.

"Do you have children?" she asked.

"No." His look of surprise made her smile. "I've never been married. Why do you ask?"

"You just seem to know how it works."

His expression evened out. "I have good friends who have kids. I've baby-sat for them several times. But I'm no expert."

"You seem to do okay."

"It's easy when all the hard stuff is already done. You're doing a good job with Joy. She's a real sweetheart." He slid the steaks onto a platter and turned the hot dogs.

Sam laughed. "Thank you. She says you call her sweet tart."

Tim laughed. The sound was so masculine, she caught her breath. Will had stopped laughing about a year into the marriage. What had caused him to change so drastically? Had it been something inside him, or was it her?

"I'll have to make a point to call her Sweet Tart from now on." He looked toward the table. Using the tongs he grabbed one of the hot dogs. "Joy, is this black enough to suit you?" he asked holding it up for her to see.

Joy broke away from her pretend conversation with her little people to look up. "Yes."

Tim smiled at her and dished up the hot dogs with the steaks. He turned his attention to Sam. "How'd the new job go this week?"

"It was okay. I'm doing secretarial work and answering the phone. It'll pay the bills until I finish my college degree."

"What kind of degree are you working toward?" He moved a foil-wrapped package off the grill onto a glass plate and set it on the cooler.

"Right now, I'm trying to get my general education requirements. Eventually I want to practice family law."

His brows rose. "Couldn't find anything any more challenging?"

Sam laughed at his dry tone. Her gaze strayed to Joy. "I had a really good lawyer. He helped me a lot. I'd like to pay it forward."

"Any more trouble since the tire incident?" he asked.

Was it kindness or curiosity that pushed him to ask? "No. It's been quiet." But it wouldn't last. It never did.

"Good."

"How long were you in the military?" she asked.

The question reverberated through Flash's brain. Shit! He'd hoped she hadn't noticed his slip. "Seven years." He checked the potatoes with a fork and, finding them tender, took them off the grill and put them with the steaks and dogs.

"What branch?" she asked.

"Navy." What had he been thinking asking them to eat with him? But when Joy had come around the corner with her more than cute smile and asked if he was fixing hot dogs, he just couldn't say no.

"It must have been good training for what you do now."

"Yeah, it was. Chow's on." He could hear the short staccato answers he was giving her. He slipped past her with the meat platter and placed it in the center of the table. "It wasn't so different from what I do now. I just get to sleep more." Yeah, right. It had been constant training, sometimes dangerous stuff, and, when in combat, sometimes moments of pure terror, but he'd loved every minute of it. And he'd never been bored.

Sam smiled. "But you still work seven days a week."

"New businesses require more work at the beginning. It's hard to plan ahead for anything but the next job. But it pays the bills."

"What would you do differently if you could?" she asked, opening the hot dog buns and pulling one out. She stabbed a dog with a fork and put it on the bun and placed it on Joy's plate.

Never agree to do anything for the FBI. "What makes you think I would do something different?" He sat down and used the tongs to put a steak on her plate.

"Nothing. I just wondered. Everybody has a dream."

She sat down next to Joy, divided a potato between her and her daughter and started mashing up the half on Joy's plate.

Sam's blonde hair tumbled over her shoulder. Sunlight filtered through it, setting to light the corn silk like golden strands. She looked up right into his eyes. He grew hard. Why couldn't she be ugly? Why couldn't her eyes be less green? Why couldn't her lips be less inviting? Why did she have to smell so good? He'd caught a hint of her perfume despite the grill smoke. Honeysuckle again.

"I forgot the butter and sour cream. I'll be right back." Flash slid off the wooden bench and jogged around the garage, dashing up the stairs like he was running for cover. He needed a moment to get his head on straight.

He couldn't get involved with Sam. He was living a lie, and she deserved better. He was living a lie, and getting too close could be dangerous for her and her daughter. But he wanted her. *Bad.* And the way she was with her daughter, the loving, gentle nature she had, was something he'd never experienced, which just made him want her even more.

It was perverse human nature, wanting something he couldn't have. He could control this.

He grabbed up the sour cream and the tub of margarine and returned to the impromptu picnic at a slower pace.

"Joy!" Sam's voice was high-pitched with a note in it he'd never heard before. He broke into a jog.

Panic was written all over her features as she stood over her daughter. Joy's face was mottled and red, her mouth wide open in a soundless scream. She clutched the neck of her pink and white shirt.

Flash dropped the containers. Sour cream splattered across the concrete and over his feet as the plastic tub hit bottom first and exploded. He broke into a run. His foot hit the butter bowl and it spun across the concrete like a Frisbee.

Flash jerked Joy to a standing position on the seat, supporting her with his arm, and with the heel of his hand, struck her between her shoulder blades. She felt so fragile, so tiny, if he hurt her—His heart hammered in his ears. He looped his arm around her and, bunching his fist, pushed up against her diaphragm, once, then twice.

A small disk-shaped piece of hot dog popped out of her mouth onto the table and she gasped in air, then started coughing.

"Jesus!" He sucked in a breath. He eased the child down on the seat and knelt to brush her pale blonde hair back from her face. The deep red color infusing her cheeks eased a bit, but she still gasped for air.

Sam sat down next to her, her movements jerky and uncoordinated. Tears streamed down her face. She shook as though electricity danced along her skin. She put her arms around Joy and rested her cheek against her hair.

"Mommy?"

Flash caught his breath. Hearing Joy speak was like manna from heaven.

Sam offered him a shaky smile despite the tears that streamed down her cheeks. "I'm here, baby. You're okay."

"He squeezed me really hard." Joy's voice sounded a bit froggy.

"Yes, he did. He squeezed that piece of hot dog right out so you could breathe."

Joy leaned forward to put her arms around Flash's neck, and she clung to him. Not knowing what else to do, he rose and tucked a forearm under her bottom to hold her close. His hand shook as he rubbed her small back. Jesus, what if he'd really squeezed her too hard? "Maybe we should go to the ER and have her checked out."

"That would be good." Sam reached for a paper towel to wipe her face. She pressed close against him and buried her face against his chest. Her voice was hoarse and muffled. "Thank you, Thank God for you." Her shoulders shook.

It was the most natural thing in the world for him to put his arm around her and hold her.

He felt the pressure of her body all the way down his side. A knot the size of a softball lodged in his throat. His voice husky, he murmured, "We're okay. We're all okay."

Will glared through the binoculars as rage pulsed through his veins and shot heat into his face. He'd kill that son of a bitch for touching her, for touching them. And he'd kill her for letting him. She was *his wife. His* wife. And Joy was *his kid.* No, glorified security guard was going to come in and take what was his. The guy transferred Joy to Sam's arms and started piling food on a platter and disappeared around the garage.

Sam wandered toward the house carrying Joy. The guy jogged around the garage, paused to do something to the grill, then ran toward the house. A few seconds later the car pulled out of the drive and away.

One minute they'd been getting ready to eat and the next they got up and left. Something must have happened.

Now that the guy had the garage wired with alarms, Will couldn't approach the building without setting something off or being videoed. Damn shame. He'd discovered how to jimmy the downstairs garage door lock and had often sat up in the apartment in comfort and watched Sam and Joy. Sam had been a good little wife, keeping to herself, taking care of Joy and that fucking busybody Ellen. Now that the old bitch was dead, he'd planned to edge right back into Sam's life.

And now this fucker had come along. But not for long. He'd burn him out if he had to.

CHAPTER 20

Flash fidgeted in the hard plastic chair, trying to get comfortable. He'd thrown on a shirt and slid his feet into deck shoes, but the smell of grill smoke still clung to him. His knee bobbed in a nervous jig, and he stretched his leg out to stop it.

He glanced at his watch again. Five minutes later than the last time he'd checked. Sam and Joy had disappeared behind the emergency room doors at least an hour ago.

A nurse came to the double doors leading back into the examining rooms and called a name. A man with his hand wrapped in a bloody towel rose and hustled to her.

He scanned the other four people left sitting close by. He'd read somewhere that the average emergency room visit lasted four hours. They'd sat in the waiting room for forty minutes before someone had come to take Joy back, and they'd been in an examining room for over an hour.

Two orderlies with a gurney wheeled by and got on the elevator. Jeez, the staff around here moved at a snail's pace. The florescent lights glared overhead, reflecting off the chrome on the plastic chairs and the wax job on the tile floors. His head throbbed dully.

Maybe he could take a quick power nap. Negative.

He'd never be able to sleep. Not until he found out how she was doing. He'd been up since five, and without dinner his energy level was in a tailspin. Maybe he could find a drive-through somewhere on the way home and get them each a burger.

Shit. He was thinking of anything to keep from freaking out. What if he'd hurt her? What if that was why it was taking so long? When it involved a kid as small as Joy, they'd get right on things, wouldn't they?

If he had to sit here two more hours without knowing something he'd be going alpha on someone.

And he wouldn't have a leg to stand on because she wasn't his kid.

Shit!

Sam appeared at the double doors leading back into the examination room.

He lunged to his feet so quickly he startled one of the nurses strolling past. He murmured an apology and made tracks to Sam.

"They've taken x-rays to make certain she doesn't have any further obstruction in her throat. We're just waiting for them to be read. I'm sorry it's taking so long."

He ran his fingers down the back of her bare arm to sooth her. "No problem. As long as she's okay."

She offered him a tired smile. "The doctor thinks she's fine. Very lucky. You can come on back if you'd like."

Anything was better than sitting on that hard plastic chair and waiting alone. Flash followed Sam down the wide hall. The nurses' duty station spread in a large semi-circle backed against the wall. The examination rooms fanned out around the counter, and Sam stepped inside one. Joy lay on a hospital bed, her bottom lip stuck out and her face, crimped in a frown, a miniature of her mother's. The moment she saw him, her expression cleared and she sat up.

"Mr. Tim's here. We're going home."

"In just a few minutes, honey," Sam said.

"Mommy…" Joy's tone morphed into a huffy whine. She flopped back on the bed.

How many times had Sam heard that in the last hour?

Based on her expression, quite a few.

"You must be feeling better," he said to Joy as he took the only chair in the room, one with arms and actual cushions.

"My tummy's mad," Joy complained.

"What about?"

"It's hungry."

This kid got to him every time she opened her mouth. "If the doc says it's okay, we'll get something to eat on the way home."

Joy's bottom lip popped back out.

Flash looked around the room for something to entertain her with. The place was buttoned up tight. Not a tongue depressor or cotton ball in sight. Just more chrome and squeaky-clean floors. He glanced at Sam. "How long has it been since they x-rayed her?"

"Forever!" Joy exclaimed.

Flash laughed, and Sam did too. Man, Sam was going to have her hands full when this kid got older.

Flash dug in his pocket for his work phone. He surfed the web until he found what he was looking for, a Disney film. He paid for it with the business account and waited for the video to download, then rose and handed the device to Joy. He pushed the arrow to play the video. When the music for *Dumbo* started, her expression cleared.

"Joy, please be careful with that phone. Don't drop it."

"I won't, mommy."

"When Dumbo's mom starts singing the song while she rocks him to sleep, I'll have to leave. It always makes me cry like a baby," Flash said.

Sam's laugh made him smile again. The stress was draining from her features and body. The smile that lingered on her lips, the way she looked at him, had a foreign warmth spreading through his chest. He wanted to hold her again. Caress her. Ease her troubles.

What was it about this woman?

"Thank you," she said.

"You're welcome."

"It's amazing how good you are with her."

"Moms have to worry about all the tough stuff. Guys just worry about having fun."

Her smile widened then slipped away. "One day you'll make a good father."

Having kids had never been one of his goals. He hadn't stayed long enough with one woman to think about it. "How can you tell?"

"You have nerves of steel and the patience of Job. Trust me, you'll be a natural."

So all his SEAL training was still good for something. "Thanks."

Sam shifted her attention away from Tim. Why couldn't she have met someone like him first? Instead of a controlling, abusive, bastard? But then, Will had been all hearts and flowers at first, too. He'd totally snowed her. Was Tim doing that?

Why was he so nice to them, protective almost?

His comment about Dumbo brought another smile to her lips. He had the most disarming sense of humor. Will had none at all.

Would she ever stop comparing every man she met to her ex? Probably not.

She'd learned the hard way when something seemed too good to be true, it usually was. She had to keep her guard up. Hard to do, when Joy insisted on being crazy about him.

She was bound to be crazy about anyone who treated her with kindness. One more thing she had to protect her child against. Joy had no defenses against con men, and anyone else who would take advantage. Why couldn't she be wary of everyone like her mother? Instead she was the opposite.

She looked up to find Tim's attention focused on her. Something in his expression triggered a trembling heat low in her belly.

"Joy seems fine. How are you doing now?"

"I really thought I was going to lose her."

"Scared me, too."

"I'd have never guessed."

"When you're in the military, you learn to keep your head and save the emotional fallout for later."

"Then what?"

He remained silent for a moment, his expression serious. He leaned forward in his chair, and resting his elbows on his knees, laced his fingers. “You just keep pushing on, putting one foot in front of the other and try and leave it behind.”

“And if you can't?”

“You pour it into everything else you do.”

That made sense. And she was doing that. But as long as Will was still out there making her life hell, there would always be a never-ending supply of *more* to deal with.

But then Tim probably had a never-ending supply of his own to work through, and he still seemed pretty well-adjusted.

The doctor came in a few minutes later. “No obstruction and no signs of any lasting trauma to her throat. Next time, really chew those hot dog slices up before you swallow, Joy,” he said in parting.

Joy was more interested in watching the movie than listening to the doctor. She had almost choked to death and was already over it, while Sam would probably have nightmares for weeks.

As soon as the doctor was gone Joy's attention shifted to Tim. “Time to go home,” she announced. Clutching the cell phone, she wiggled to the side of the bed.

Sam grabbed her arm to keep her from pitching headfirst off the side. She kept her stable until she'd gained her feet. “We have to wait for your release paperwork, honey.”

“Mommy…” Joy's impatient whine was back.

“She's not normally this whiney,” Sam said.

He shrugged. “She's a kid. And it's been…” He glanced at his watch. “Three hours. I think she's doing great.”

Joy proceeded to climb into his lap. Sam started to tell her to get down, then bit back the comment when he wedged her in the bend of his arm against his side and offered to hold the phone for her.

Five minutes later, when a nurse appeared with the release paperwork, Joy lay boneless against him, sound asleep.

“Should we wake her?” Tim asked.

“She'll be cranky. But she'll be crankier if she doesn't eat something before she goes to bed. All she's had are some apple slices since her snack at four.”

Sam leaned over her and gave Joy a small shake. “Joy, wake up baby.”

Joy stirred. And curled closer to Tim.

"We're going to get something to eat before we go home," Sam said.

"Nuggets?" Joy asked sleepily.

"As long as you chew them up good."

"'Kay."

Tim leaned forward and holding her close, rose. He shifted her weight onto his arm. Her arms went around his neck and she rested her head on his shoulder.

"Come on, sweet tart. Mommy and Mr. Tim need some chow, too."

"What's chow?" Joy asked.

"Nuggets."

CHAPTER 21

Marsha lay in bed listening to the shower. She studied a fan-shaped shadow that flickered and waved against the pale gold wall of her bedroom. She'd decorated the room in soothing tropical colors and made it a restful, romantic haven.

How long had it been since they'd made love? Or even reached for each other in sleep? Since before the break-in.

James came out of the bathroom, a towel wrapped around his hips. His damp hair shone like pewter. He'd started going gray at twenty, and now, at thirty-five, his hair looked white when dry. His brows and beard had remained dark, and lent his features an attractive, sensual masculinity. He went to the dresser to dig out his underclothes and socks, then moved on to the closet for his uniform.

He might sit behind a desk a great deal of his time, but he made it a priority to stay in shape. Had he not been in excellent condition, he'd have never survived the many beatings he'd sustained. He'd had a severe concussion, a broken nose, a shattered cheekbone and eye socket, broken ribs, a couple of broken teeth and numerous contusions. It had taken weeks for the swelling and bruising to subside.

The terrorists had used her to control him. Tormented him by touching her, threatening rape and worse.

Their efforts had driven underground any desire she'd had to be touched by a man. Was it like that for him too? Had seeing them put their hands on her killed his passion for her? Had the monsters managed to destroy that part of their marriage, too?

"James?"

He looked up from inspecting the khaki uniform he'd taken out of the closet.

"Do you miss making love?"

He studied her features, his eyes dark, then hung the uniform on the closet doorknob. He crossed the teal-colored bedroom carpet to sit on the bed next to her.

"Yeah, I miss making love with you." He cleared his throat. "I miss you wanting to make love with me."

Marsha laid her hand on the bed close to his muscular thigh but didn't touch him. She didn't know if she was ready yet. "They didn't rape me. I've told you before. In spite of everything else he did, Moussa wouldn't let them. He said I was unclean." She studied his reaction, hoping for a clue to his feelings. "Isn't that ironic? It was okay for him to torture us, brutalize you, and try to drown our son, but he drew the line at rape."

"He was a religious zealot bent on revenge. A terrorist. A brute. A coward." He swallowed as though his throat hurt. "I don't give a fuck what his reasons were, I'm just glad he couldn't bring himself to be a rapist, too."

"I know you tried to protect us, put yourself between us and them, as much as you could."

"It wasn't enough." He clenched and unclenched his hands in a show of tension she'd never seen from him before. "All those years of training and I couldn't do a damn thing to keep them off of you."

The bitterness in his tone surprised her. "There were three of them. They had guns. I know you didn't take chances because of Alex and me." She raised a hand to touch his bare back then withdrew it without touching him.

He rose and reached for his t-shirt. He thrust his arms into the sleeves and tugged it over his head. "I know you think I'm a cold blooded son of a bitch. I know you think I put you and Alex last." He jerked the towel free and stepped into his boxer briefs. "But there's never been anyone but you since we got married. Some of the other guys may fuck around on their wives and make excuses, and say they have needs, they're just scratching the itch, that it doesn't mean anything, but I haven't. I won't until you tell me you don't want me anymore, and I'm not sure I could even then. Do you know what it does to me to know you can't bring yourself to touch me?"

Marsha sat up and ran a hand through her bed-tousled hair. She felt emotionally exhausted. As though all the hurt had cauterized her sexual desires. "It isn't because of anything you've done or didn't do, James. It's because I don't want to start something I'm not ready to finish."

He studied her face. "I'm not some over-enthusiastic teenager without any control. I'm not going to rush you into doing anything you don't want. But you started off by asking me if I miss you, miss us, and then you can't even touch me. What do you want from me, Marsha?"

"I wanted to know if their putting their hands on me had killed your feelings for me. It's killed something inside me, James. I want to feel the way I did before, but I just feel numb. How do I make the numbness go away?"

He swallowed and the anger faded from his features. "How do you know you'd feel numb if I held you? If I touched you? You haven't let me since it happened."

The thought had her heart drumming in her ears. What if he broke through the numbness? What if it hurt too much? As long as she was sexually numb she didn't have to face the fear and humiliation. "What if I lose it?"

"Then we'll lose it together. Anything is better than this, Marsha."

Was it?

"I have a meeting I can't miss," he said, glancing at his watch.

She nodded, rested her chin on her knees and watched him dress.

He'd picked himself up and moved on. Why couldn't she?

Alex's cry came just as he finished putting his captain's insignia on the collar of his shirt. She rose from the bed and reached for the robe she'd tossed across the brightly flowered lounge in the corner.

When she moved past James he caught her arm and drew her close. He held her against his tall frame for a moment. She waited for her heartbeat to race, as it always had in the past. She felt nothing until he ran his fingertips along the back of her neck in a soft caress. Her nerve endings tingled and she shivered.

Alex's cry grew louder.

"I'll be home at five. Maybe we can grill out or something."

They hadn't grilled anything since the day of the attack.

She nodded and stepped away then paused at the door. "There hasn't been anyone but you—*ever*, James."

"I know."

Would she have responded to the men's attacks differently if she'd had more than one lover? Probably not. Because it hadn't been about sex, it had been about control, pain, punishment and humiliation.

Did James really love her? He'd remained faithful through all the separations...Ten years of faithfulness had to count for something. Maybe they'd both find out what, if they made it through to the other side.

James dwelled on the conversation all the way into the base. He was at a loss about how to reach Marsha. She'd talked with her counselor, just as he had, about the lack of sex. But she'd never admitted her feelings, until this morning. Was that a good thing?

When he arrived at his office, he was met by the two NCIS agents assigned to Flash's case. He had no choice but to shove his thoughts of Marsha and their problems to the back of his mind and escort the agents to his office.

During and after showing the two agents the videos Flash had sent him, he studied their reactions. Barnett, five foot ten inches tall, about thirty, with dark brown hair and olive complexion, probably had some Italian ancestry, with his heavy features and hooded eyes. He was built like a linebacker, heavy through the chest and shoulders, muscular and fit.

His partner, Agent Cooper, couldn't have been more opposite. She was taller than her partner, model thin, with long, lush, black hair tied back in a ponytail at the base of her neck. Her slacks and plain white shirt could have been sackcloth on her long, lean frame and still look like she'd just come off the runway in a fashion show. Her features were dramatically feminine.

"We'd like a copy of this latest recording. We may be able to figure out his exact location," Barnett said.

Jackson raised a brow. "From a blank white wall and a temporary email address?" How stupid did they think Flash was?

Barnett looked away.

"I've been in touch with Lieutenant Carney's teammates. They back up his story about the FBI visit. As does the base commander we worked under in Iraq when this went down. He's sent me a report on his conversation with the two agents when they arrived at the base as have the men who witnessed their visit."

"We'd like a copy of those reports too, Captain," Barnett said.

James's features tightened in outrage. "You should have generated your own reports by now, Agent Barnett. You have access to as much of Lieutenant Carney's file as I do. And to all the information he's been sharing with you. Why are you sitting on your hands and leaving my guy twisting in the wind?"

Barnett's heavy brows crashed together and his jaw tensed. "Your guy is AWOL, sir. That's our main concern."

Anger heated James's face. He'd watched the videos Flash had sent numerous times. Studied his file over and over. If Harold Timothy Carney had crossed over to the other side, he'd eat his SEAL trident. His man had been fucked by the FBI, and now NCIS lined up to have a go at him, too.

"Has the FBI issued a warrant for him on the bogus assault charge?"

"Yes, they have, sir."

James eyed the man until he looked away.

Agent Cooper spoke for the first time, her voice deeper than he'd expected. "If he contacts you again, Captain, you should let us know right away."

"I'll jump right on that, agent." *As fast as you two seemed to have jumped on my JG's situation.* He rose, went to the door and opened it. "Thank you for your time, agents."

"We'd like a copy of this latest video and the reports you mentioned, Captain," Barnett said.

"And I'd like world peace and my guy back. I guess neither one of us is going to get what we want."

"We can get a warrant, sir."

"I suggest you do that."

Barnett and Cooper rose and marched to the door.

"You aren't helping him with this refusal to cooperate, sir," Agent Cooper said.

"You aren't helping him whether I cooperate or not, agents. Your superiors will hear from me. I'll be reporting to mine about this, too." *Assholes.*

Barnett's facial muscles tightened.

"Just what do you think would happen if he decides to go public with all this?" James asked.

Cooper jumped into the silence. "It would be in his best interest to hold off on that, Captain."

"He isn't bound by any vow of secrecy to the FBI, and, especially now that they've tried to kill him, it would be in his best interests to call attention to his innocence in any way he can. If you aren't going to give him any cover, he has every right to seek it wherever he can find it."

"Can we sit down for a moment longer, sir?" Cooper suggested.

"Only if I hear more than BS from you and your partner," James said.

Cooper bit her lip and studied the floor with great concentration. Barnett found his seat again and she followed his lead, but settled on the edge of her chair.

"Just because we aren't giving him backup doesn't mean we, and others, aren't interested in what he's uncovered, sir," she said.

"The fact that you aren't giving him backup is what's keeping him out there, Cooper."

"We went to Mexico to bring him home," Barnett argued.

"You went to Mexico to arrest him. My operator reached out to you for help, and you reciprocated with a threat."

"We didn't know everything we do now," Cooper said.

"Which is?"

Barnett leaned forward in his seat. "The FBI had a legitimate operation going on until your man got involved."

"Until Agent Gilbert got involved with the ring leader of a drug cartel," James countered. "You haven't given me one ounce of evidence that says my man knew what the hell was going down. And from what I've seen, he's given you plenty to prove Gilbert is in a cartel leader's hip pocket."

Barnett backed off with a scowl. "You can't know for certain Carney wasn't involved."

"And you can't know for certain he was." He'd made a mistake when he hadn't fought for Brett Weaver. When he hadn't supported a wounded man trying to fight his way back. And Brett Weaver had single-handedly taken out the bad guys who had damn near beat him to death. Brett had saved him, Marsha, and Alex. He wasn't going to make the same mistake again. Carney had been a loyal operator. Had risked his life for the men in his team on numerous occasions. He'd provided cover for the Marines he'd been stationed with. Had saved lives with his skill. And he deserved the benefit of a doubt.

"Did Carney seem to know what was going on when he interrogated Gilbert? You heard Gilbert admit that Carney followed orders. And you heard his cover story for what had gone down. Who do you think pulled the con, Agent Barnett?"

Barnett remained sullen and silent.

James leaned forward against the desk. "Lieutenant Carney came up hard. Probably had the worst home life growing up of any of my men, but he still finished high school on his own, went to college, and has become one of the best SEAL snipers in the teams. He's saved more lives than you or I ever will. He's spent seven years fighting bad guys or training to do it. He has an exemplary record with the SEALs. And I think he deserves the benefit of the doubt."

He drew a deep breath. "Now if you want to continue along the path you're traveling with this thing, then do it. But as of right now," James thumped the top of his desk with his index finger for emphasis, "I'm going to make it my calling to bring this man home, back to his team, and get this traitorous son of bitch Gilbert."

"We don't need you interfering in an ongoing investigation," Barnett growled.

“That’s too fucking bad, because I’m already involved. And I already have as much information on this thing as you do *and* the backing of my command. And from what little you’ve shared with me today, I’d say you haven’t got much of an investigation.”

“There’s more going on than we’re at liberty to share with you, Captain,” Cooper said, her tone halfway apologetic.

James leaned back in his chair. He studied the agents through narrowed eyes. He turned his focus on Barnett. “You’re supposed to follow the evidence, be objective, I don’t see that happening here.” He rose and moved around the desk, then leaned back against it and crossed his arms. “Not too long ago, another of my men was investigated by your department for murder. The supposed victim was still alive. That investigative team had the same attitude, the same tunnel vision. The two agents have since had to issue an official apology to that individual. Not a comfortable situation to be in. I don’t think your command would be too thrilled should that happen again.”

Barnett’s face flushed, and his jaw grew taut.

James straightened and moved back around the desk. “Has an arrest warrant been filed charging Lieutenant Carney for the shootings that took place during the operation?”

After a short pause, Cooper said, “No.”

Surprised, James stopped in mid stride and swiveled to face her.

“Gunfire was reported in the area, but no bodies were recovered. We don’t know who he shot. But there’s been no record of any shooting filed by the FBI. Not even his.”

“Then whose credentials did he send you?”

“The credentials were bogus,” Barnet said. “We don’t know who those guys were.”

“And the men who were supposed to pick up the stones and the money?”

“There was blood at the scene, but no sign of them. Because of the bullet holes in his car, Carney’s wanted for questioning. The San Diego PD are saying it was a gang-related shooting.”

What kind of fucked-up con was Gilbert running?

“Well, he couldn’t have cleaned up the scene and fled it at the same time. So without all the info Carney sent you, you wouldn’t have a clue about what went down.”

The two remained silent.

"So the only thing you want him for is AWOL."

"Officially," Cooper said.

James sat back down.

"And the FBI wants him for assaulting Agent Gilbert," Barnett added.

And Gilbert would want him dead because he knows too much. Had he not escaped, the two hit men would have taken him out and they'd never have known what happened.

"There's the stones he smuggled in and the money he's confiscated. We'd like to know how he managed that before we charge him." Barnett smirked.

James's jaw tightened. This guy just wouldn't give it up. "He'd worked with Rick Dobson before. He'd have trusted him. And now Dobson is dead. You going to try and pin that on Carney, too?"

Barnett shifted in his seat and looked away.

"If he should contact you again, Captain, we'd appreciate you alerting us." Agent Cooper rose and placed her card on the desk.

He could see where this was going. *So you can wave your arms around and make him bait. I don't think so.*

"And we'd like copies of the reports you've compiled. They might clear Lieutenant Carney of the smuggling charge should it be filed later," she said, her features impassive.

James rose to see them out. "We've run missions against the cartels before, agents. Being SEALs, our anonymity is of the highest importance. If my man's name is released to these guys, he'll be as good as dead. So, if you're planning on using him as a witness—"

"We're well aware of all this, Captain. We'll protect his identity, but there are variables out of our control," Cooper said.

The biggest one was Gilbert. Should the man offer up Carney's name, the cartel would sick the dogs on him, and he'd be as good as dead. If they could find him. And so far not even the FBI had been able to do that.

And that meant all he could do was wait for Flash to make the first move.

CHAPTER 22

Flash's eyes narrowed against the midmorning glare. The sky hung a cloudless pale blue over the distant hills. Joy wore a sweater against the early morning spring chill as she pedaled her Big Wheel around the concrete patio at the back of the house. She rounded the edge of the slab, then disappeared out of sight as she made the circle. It was good she was up racing away on her bike like normal. Hopefully she'd forget the choking experience quicker than he and Sam would. While Sam had still been shaken as they'd waited to see a doctor at the ER, Joy had fallen asleep against his chest. Kids were so resilient. They could be at the brink one minute and taking a nap the next.

He'd seen it with Langley Marks's kids. A wave of homesickness hit him like a punch. What he'd give to see Lang, Trish and their crew. He'd needed them. They'd been a second family. Travis and 'Nita had been his first.

He had to get back to his team. *Back to his life.*

He turned away from the window to sit down at the cheap prefab computer desk he'd bought to hold his equipment. Flash keyed in the password he needed to access Gilbert's cell phone information. Since Gilbert hadn't turned off the GPS function of his smartphone, Flash tracked him to a southeast area of San Diego close to his apartment.

Flash accessed the list of phone numbers Gilbert had dialed. Why didn't he use a burner phone? Was the man nuts? Or just arrogant? Probably both.

There were no surprises. Filtering through the numbers, he recognized one. There were three calls to Kekoa Velazquez, the man who acted as the go-between for Caesar Vargas. He had no way of listening to the calls. But he could keep a record of when they had gone through. Flash jotted down a couple of unfamiliar phone numbers to trace their user identity.

Next he checked the activity on Gilbert's home computer. It took nearly an hour to go through the emails and web searches the man had done, as every keystroke was recorded. Flash saved a few of the messages, then closed the spyware program that nestled in the coding of one of the major programs on his computer.

He accessed the video files from the computer he'd set up in the crawlspace above the apartment, used a remote site to save them, then wiped them from the crawlspace computer's hard drive. After bouncing the feed through several remote sites so it couldn't be traced, he downloaded them into his computer and fast-forwarded through the boring everyday movements.

At twenty-one hundred hours the day before Gilbert entered his apartment with a woman. Blonde, dressed in dark slacks and blazer and a white blouse with an open-necked collar, she stood surveying the room for a long moment with her hands on her hips, the bulge of her service revolver visible in the shoulder holster beneath her jacket because of her stance. "Damn, Eric. Think you could get anymore electronics in here?"

"I like my creature comforts when I'm home." Gilbert approached her with a cocky walk that telegraphed his moves before he ever reached her. He cupped the back of her neck and dragged her mouth to his.

Feeling like a voyeur, Flash fast-forwarded the images, while they took each other's clothes off and grappled.

Why would he put this woman at risk when he was screwing around with a drug cartel?

"Why am I putting Sam and Joy at risk doing the same thing?" he murmured aloud.

Flash rubbed a hand over his face. Should Gilbert and his pals find him…

When he'd signed the lease with Mrs. Andrews he hadn't known about Sam and Joy. And now he did. He needed to find some place far, far away from them to rent. But with Sam's ex-husband hanging like a threat over the two of them, he couldn't walk away. He had to talk Sam into allowing him to put in an alarm system for her. Then he could at least feel she and Joy were a little safer.

The couple on the screen had progressed to the getting naked phase. Flash placed the cursor on the bar at the bottom of the screen and dragged it forward skipping the sex act. Once the woman was dressed again, he studied her. She stood almost as tall as Gilbert, her body slender and athletic. Since she carried a gun in a shoulder holster, she was probably on the job. Maybe they were just fuck-buddies and not emotionally involved. But since she was involved with Gilbert, she might know what he was up to. He saved the section of video to send to both Captain Jackson and NCIS.

A noise outside drew his attention. He closed the program and went to the window. Sam stood beside her car. She stared at the passenger side of the vehicle with her hand over her mouth. Then she pivoted and bolted back into the house. A few minutes later she returned to the porch, phone in hand.

She sat down on the steps and with her knees curled up against her chest, talking on the phone. When she hung up she laid the phone on the porch next to her and rested her head in her hands.

Her defensive posture screamed *there's a problem.* "It's none of your business, Flash. Stay in the apartment," he murmured to himself. He was getting too involved with Sam and Joy. He needed to distance himself.

He went back to the computer, but the pull of curiosity and concern for Sam kept him returning to the window every few minutes. A police car pulled up the drive and his disquiet kicked up a notch.

He closed the video program, left the apartment and wandered down the stairs. Sam was nowhere in sight and he no longer heard the sound of Joy riding her bike. He meandered up to the car where one of the policemen stood. He recognized Officer Davis as one of the guys who'd responded to her call last time.

His attention swung to the passenger side of the vehicle where the cop stared. Shock held him still for a moment. Gouged into the dark blue paint in big letters stretching across the side of the car was the word 'whore'.

"Fuck!" The word exploded from him.

"Is there anything you can tell us about this?" Davis's solemn expression fed Flash's building rage. "No, but I have the apartment and the garage wired with an alarm, motion sensor lights and cameras. Maybe one of the cameras caught something."

Davis's brows rose with interest. "Let's go see." He keyed his radio and told his partner where he was going.

Flash led the way up the stairs to the apartment. He sat down at the corner computer desk and called up the video from the cameras on each side of the garage. With a few keystrokes he opened the image from the west side and the video file popped up on his screen. He dragged the bar at the bottom to a time just after they'd returned home. He eased the cursor forward in tiny increments. "Mrs. Cross had to take her daughter to the emergency room last night. She choked on a hot dog and they did x-rays to make sure she didn't have any remaining obstruction. I drove them to the hospital in her car. She was a little upset."

"That's probably an understatement," the officer said. "She seems very protective of the little girl."

"Yeah. She was pretty shaken. Her car was in the hospital parking lot until about ten thirty, when the doctor released Joy. I didn't see any damage then. We drove back and I watched to make sure they got into the house okay, then came on up to my apartment."

Reaching zero two hundred, movement out of the corner of the screen drew his attention and he allowed the video to play in real time. A shadow crossed in front of the screen followed by a large figure dressed in dark clothing. The motion-activated lights on that side of the house kicked on and the man broke into a run.

Flash ground his teeth. Jesus, he'd walked right onto the property. He must be losing his edge. There was a time when all it would have taken to wake him was the lights coming on. He was going to have to set an alarm to go off when they lit up.

The guy was bundled in a sweatshirt with a hood, wore gloves so even his skin color remained concealed. He ducked to the passenger side of the car and after a few minutes the lights went out. The weak streetlight at the corner of the lot was still on, but the light too dim to catch anything but the man's occasional movements. When he next appeared from behind the car his face was in shadow and he avoided the drive.

"Shit!" The officer breathed behind his shoulder.

"I'm not done yet," Flash said.

He took a series of stills of the video and put them up on the screen. Using photo software he infused more light into the image and enlarged it. "He's wearing a ski mask. Damn it. But he's got some kind of logo on his hoodie." He kept tweaking the image over and over until the logo grew more detailed, but remained blurry.

"That's the Cross Construction logo," the officer said behind him.

Fuck! "But it isn't enough to make an arrest."

"No. But if you give us a copy of the video and these stills, I'll take them in and see if our lab can do anything else. You can email them to me."

"I don't have a thumb drive to give you but I'll burn them, just incase." Flash transferred the video and stills to a CD and handed it to him, then sent the images to the officer's email address. "I'll save it in case you need anything else."

"Thanks. If you could talk Mrs. Cross into a security system like yours, it might help."

"I tried when I first moved in. She was concerned about the financial aspect. Maybe now she'll change her mind. I'll give it another shot. And I'll urge her to keep her car in the garage at night."

"That would probably be a good idea."

He'd be more watchful, too. What the fuck was wrong with him, letting his guard slip so badly? With Gilbert out there and Sam's ex, he needed to be at DEFCON 1 all the time.

If he could get her ex on tape, then Cross would go back to jail for stalking and would be one less problem for Flash to deal with. "Let's look at the footage from the south side of the garage facing the road. Just in case."

He pulled up the video and scanned it just as he had the other. The figure, already dressed in hoodie and mask, approached the house on foot from the street. Despite Flash's efforts he couldn't do anything more with the images. "I'll email this, too."

"He's a big guy. Broad through the chest and shoulders. It has to be her ex. But without a clear shot of his face we can't arrest him. He's a real piece of work."

"I looked him up when I first moved in."

"You've read about Judge Moreland?"

"Yeah, I have."

"The lady got a raw deal. We're trying to set it right. You hear or see anything, give us a call." Davis offered his hand.

"Will do." Flash shook his hand and rose to walk him out.

Flash followed him down the steps. He'd grown slack. He should have been more vigilant than this. Angry with himself, his shoulders and jaw tightened. Seeing her standing in the drive with the other officer, he stuffed his hands into his pockets to keep her from seeing them clenched into fists. A sign of aggression was the last thing she needed right now. But, damn it, he wanted to pound on something—hard. Like her ex-husband's face.

Sam's expression held weariness, but no fear. "I'm sorry they bothered you," she said as they watched Davis and his partner drive away.

"It's okay. I'd like for you to allow me to put in a security system. It isn't the entire answer to your problem, Sam. If someone wants to get in, they will. But it would give you enough time to lock yourself into the bathroom until the police arrive. I'll help you reinforce the bathroom door and facing."

She studied the word written on the car. "Why do you think he did this?"

"It's about control. You're outside the realm of his control and he wants it back."

"And calling me a whore is going to make that happen?"

Flash flinched from hearing her say the word. It was the last word he'd ever think of in terms of her.

"Every time he does something like this it just makes me more and more grateful I'm away from him. And it makes me...tired. Tired of dealing with him. Tired I ever knew him. I wish I'd never met him!" She closed her eyes and her throat worked as she swallowed. Her breasts heaved up and down as she tried to catch her breath.

What could he say to offer her comfort? Nothing. "He's trying to wear you down. Exhaust you and your resources. Once you're at your most vulnerable he'll start sending gifts, and offering apologies. And start telling you how much you need him. And that he'll never raise his hand to you again." He'd heard it all when he was seven. Watched his drug-addicted mother beaten, then wooed over and over again. He'd watched Derrick Armstrong, his teammate, make the same moves with Valerie, his girlfriend. He'd threatened to turn Derrick in should he find out he was beating her again.

"How do you know what he'll do?" Sam asked drawing his attention back from the past.

He wasn't talking about his mother. He couldn't go there. "I had a buddy who had issues. I watched his behavior escalate out of control."

"What happened to him?"

"He had a meltdown. He's in jail. Been in for a while. I read about his arrest in the papers. But I saw what he did firsthand and called him on it. I even offered to help his girlfriend move out, but she wouldn't do it."

"He didn't—" Her voice faltered.

"No. He didn't kill her." He shook his head. But he'd threatened to kill his own teammates and been taken down by his own team. *And he should have been there.* "He was arrested before that could happen. Now it's going to be a long time before he gets out."

"Maybe it will give her time to rebuild her life. Maybe he'll forget about her...if he's in jail long enough." A wistful note crept into her tone.

Flash studied her expression, so carefully composed. But her body was fraught with tension. He wanted to run his hands over her shoulders, ease the tightness of the muscles there, and work his way down to her feet. And then kiss his way back up. He jerked his attention away from her. She wasn't ready for a relationship with a man. It would probably take her years to recover enough from everything she'd been through to want a man's hands on her again. The thought cramped his stomach.

She was struggling to make a life for herself and her daughter and her *asshole* ex fucking worked against her at every turn. It made him tired to think about it. Sick and tired and fucking angry as hell.

Sam ran a finger over one of the deep gouges carved into the quarter panel over the wheel. "I can get the paint from the dealership and touch this up myself. It won't be hard."

The asshole hadn't been satisfied with just scratching off the paint, he'd dug into the metal, so the word would be etched into the vehicle unless sanded out. She'd have to drive the car with that fucking word etched there for everyone to see. The outraged anger he'd kept a tight rein on ever since he'd seen it tripped over into rage.

He spied the phone she'd left on the porch. *Fuck this shit.* "May I use your phone?"

"Sure."

He strode to the porch and picked up the handset. The son of a bitch had to have called her some time or other. He scanned through the numbers until he saw one listed for Will Cross. He hit the redial button and waited for him to pick up.

"Hey, honey."

From the oily, pandering tone, Cross hadn't expected Sam on the other end, but Joy. "Wrong, *dude*. This is Tim, Sam's neighbor. You know. The guy who rented the apartment next door?"

Sam's head went up. She frowned and shot him a curious look.

"What are you doing talking on Sam's phone?" The first burn of anger came across the line.

"I'm calling to thank you, *dude*."

Cross hesitated. "For what?"

"Every time you pull some asinine shit like puncture her tires or write crap on her car, it gives her a tiny push in my direction. And I really appreciate it. Cuts my seduction time in half."

Sam's eyes widened and she strode toward him.

Will's tone grew cagey. "I don't know what you're talking about."

Flash made the sound of a buzzer going off. "Wrong answer, *dude*. We both know exactly who's responsible for the damage to her car. You don't mind me calling you *dude*, do you? As opposed to *lowlife cocksucker*."

"Put Sam on the phone."

"Isn't that against the terms of your restraining order? I wouldn't want to have to report to the police that you've been talking to her when you shouldn't. But I really do appreciate all you've done to smooth the way for me, *dude*. Because I'm a good guy. Unlike you. And after hanging out with a *motherfucker* who punches women, she's all too happy to hang with a *real* man who likes to make love, not war."

Sam's mouth flew open. "Oh my God!" She clapped both hands over it and shook her head adamantly.

"Keep your goddamn hands off my wife!" The possessiveness in Cross's tone was manic, and his voice climbed to a high-pitched shout.

Flash held the phone away from his ear. His temper tripped over into nuclear mode. "*Ex*-wife, *dude*. *Ex*. As in *divorced*. *No-longer-married*. Separated *permanently*. But I'm just calling to offer you a suggestion. Just keep doing all the *fucked up shit* you've been doing. I love reaping the rewards of your stupidity. And in case you're thinking about doing anything *even more stupid*, I'm putting in a state-of-the-art security system at her house this afternoon with cameras and motion lights. You can show up in your Cross Construction hoodie and ski mask again. We'll take some more video footage of you doing some other *chicken shit* thing to try and make her life miserable. And I'll be here to make her feel *all better*. Catch you later, *dude*." He pushed the off button cutting the call.

Flash's rage-ridden haze lifted and he focused on Sam's stark white face. She held her hand clasped over her mouth, as if she didn't she might scream.

Well, shit! He'd just let his rage rule him and fucked up big time.

CHAPTER 23

"*Oh, my God! Oh, my God!*" Her mouth and brain seemed stuck in a loop where that was all she was capable of saying. Oh, my God! Tim had just put himself between her and Will in a way no one else ever had. He had just painted a bulls-eye on his own back and made himself as much a target as she was.

"Will he be able to call you back and harass you?" Tim asked, the frown darkening his brow, giving his features a harsh masculinity that shot her pulse into the stratosphere. The calmness of his tone leached some of the screaming panic surging through her system.

"No. His number is blocked. Joy can call him, but he can't call her."

"Good." He nodded, his expression mirroring satisfaction. "I'll have to do the same with my private and business numbers."

"You shouldn't have done that. You don't know what he's like. What he's capable of."

"Sure I do." His jaw flexed. "Anything he thinks he can fucking get away with."

Sam's head jerked up at his tone. This was more than just witnessing the meltdown of a buddy who had a problem. The burning rage she'd read in his face as he spoke to Will on the phone had been as explosive as anything she'd seen in Will's, but while Will's was hot, Tim's was cold with control. The masculine planes of his face were razor-sharp with tension, and his voice had cut like a knife. Will Cross had never been spoken to like that. She was certain of it. And every time Tim had called him, *dude*, his tone had said *something else*. Will would kill him if they ever came face to face.

Or was punching reserved for women who couldn't defend themselves?

Tim paced back and forth in front of the car, cooling down. She took in the balanced, deliberate way he placed his feet, the controlled movement of his body and the bulge of his biceps.

On second thought, Will wouldn't face off with Tim, but he might hire someone else to do it. Several someones. She couldn't be responsible for that.

"Tim. You'll have to move. You'll have to leave Henderson. He'll put out the word to all his business contacts and blackball your business. He'll stalk you like he's stalked me. He'll do whatever it takes to make your life a misery."

Tim swiveled to face her and grasped her arms. "It's going to be okay. Just breathe a minute." His cerulean blue eyes gazed down into hers, steady and calm. The bottom seemed to drop out of her stomach and a swift ache of physical arousal shot through her. It had been so satisfying to hear him chew Will up and spit him out with just words. And it was so wonderful to be able to look into a man's face and know he wanted to protect you instead of hurt you. But he didn't realize what he'd done.

He ran the back of his fingers against her cheek. "I want him to come after *me*, Sam. For once he'll have a target he can't intimidate."

"There's no way you can be devious enough, ruthless enough, to best him." Will was going to kill him. He'd kill any man who came close to her.

"I don't want to best him. I want him to hang himself. But first I have to draw him out and make him slip up."

She pressed a hand to her stomach where sick knots of anxiety built, and she leaned back against her scratched and scarred car. "You've made him think we're…more than what we are. He'll be out of his head with rage." She swallowed against a sudden wave of nausea. "You made him believe what he was already thinking."

He frowned. "He's just a man, Sam."

"He's unbalanced. You don't know what you've done." She'd thought she could have a life. That she could live in peace. It had all been a cruel joke.

"It's going to be okay."

Why wasn't he listening? "No, it won't!" Her voice rose in a panicked squeak and she shook her head. "He's going to come after us both. And I can't stay here all day, every day, hiding in the bathroom waiting for him to come. You've never been on the receiving end of one of his punches, his kicks. You've never been tormented and tortured and treated like some*thing* rather than some*one*. You've never lived in constant fear for months." She had to sit down before she fell down. It took all her control to get to the steps. Her bones seemed to melt as she slumped down onto the top stair.

"Yes, I have."

Those three words spoken with such barren control jerked her panicked thoughts to a standstill.

"I was seven when social services took me from my mother. Her boyfriend was using us both as punching bags and she wouldn't leave him. She let them take me because the drugs he supplied her were more important than me."

His words hit her with the force of a punch. He seemed so rock steady, so controlled, so normal. "I'm sorry," Sam blinked back the instant tears. Tears for him and for herself.

Tim sat down beside her. "I won't let him do anything to hurt you or Joy."

"You can't be here with us twenty-four hours a day. He works for his father and can take off any time he wants to do things to torment you. He's a master manipulator. He doesn't live by the same rules the rest of us do."

"He'll have to if he's back in jail," Tim said. There was a dogged determination in his voice and his expression.

She wanted desperately to believe him. More than anything.

The front door opened. "Mommy," Joy's voice came through the screen on the storm door. "Can I change the channel?"

"I'll do it for you." Sam stood.

"I'll need to come in and check the windows. I'll be putting sensors on them."

"I don't have the money for this."

"It's my fault you need the system. I'll pay for it."

"No you won't!" She drew a deep breath to try and control the anger finally surfacing. At him for putting her and Joy in this position. And at Will for having triggered it. As always, Will was creating heartache and grief and financial hardship in her life. And she still had to drive the car with that word scratched across the side. "Two months free rent ought to pay for it."

"Part of one will be enough."

Now he was being reasonable. *Now that he'd gotten his way.*

Men were all the same. She jerked the storm door open. The house had been a haven since she'd left Will. She wasn't ready to let anyone break the sanctity of her home. Not even Tim. No matter what his reasons. Resentment high, she strode into the living room, leaving the door open but not really inviting him in.

The great room combined with the kitchen stretched across the width of the house. The high cathedral ceilings with intricately woven wooden beams crisscrossing the space always surprised anyone who entered the house. Tim's gaze jerked upward. "This is really something."

"My grandfather. He ripped out the attic above these two rooms, opened up the space, and put a skylight in the kitchen. There are smaller things throughout the house, too, that constantly make me think of him."

"If you ever needed to sell the place, this and the garage apartment would cement the deal."

Just the thought brought emotion surging through her. *Never!* She'd go hungry first. "I'll never sell. This is home. I'll work two jobs before I'll see that happen."

He nodded. "I won't damage anything. The units I'll be putting in are small."

"Mommy!" Joy used what Sam called her universal kid voice. All children used it to remind their parents of their presence and their needs.

She turned aside without comment to change the channel for her.

"Want to watch cartoons with me?" Joy asked Tim with a smile.

He grinned back. "I haven't watched cartoons since…Dumbo." He paused. "Maybe I can do that another time. I'm going to do a special job for your mommy."

"'Kay."

Sam's hands clenched. What had happened to him after they'd taken him from his mother? Had he been able to have a normal childhood?

"We don't have any sliding glass doors leading out of the house, but we do have double doors that lead out of the master suite onto the patio out back."

"I'll check the locks and reinforce them if they need it. It's part of the package."

She nodded. She'd hoped she'd never have to make the house a fortress. In doing so, it felt like Will had won yet another battle to make a mess of her life. But if it ensured she and Joy were safe, maybe it would be worth it.

"I'll show you the rest of the house." She walked him through the two smaller bedrooms and the master suite. The two bathrooms had small windows she or Joy might be able to wiggle through, but not anyone larger. When she commented about that, Tim shook his head.

"I've slid through something as small as that by popping out the top pane."

She studied him for a moment and waited for him to further clarify what he meant. "When you were in the service?"

"Yeah."

Guys in the Navy stayed on board aircraft carriers, submarines and vessels like that didn't they? *Didn't they?*

"Were you in Iraq and Afghanistan?"

"Yeah." His gaze, so clear and blue, remained steady on her face.

"Were you Naval Intelligence?"

"I can't tell you what I did, Sam."

The anxious knot in her stomach tightened again. He wasn't regular Navy. Special forces? Or something like that. She bit her lip. "Okay." Her voice came out a little strangled. Should she be afraid of him?

"It isn't because I want to come off all mysterious. We just don't talk about what we did or where we did it."

"O-Okay. I need to start lunch for Joy. I'll leave you to it."

"Wait." Tim grasped her upper arm, his touch careful, light. But the pads of his fingertips warmed her skin. Tiny jets of awareness raced through her breast where the backs of his fingers rested so close. If she shifted even an inch, the contact would become a reality.

"For the last seven years, I've been putting myself between innocent people and the assholes trying to hurt them, Sam. You don't have to be afraid of me."

With her long-dormant sensuality stretching toward him *yes, she did.* She cleared her throat. "I'm not afraid of you." Her voice came out soft and breathy. She swallowed and tried for a stronger tone. "But I have to be wary of everyone. And I can't depend on you or anyone else to protect me. Once your business takes off, you'll move on. Joy and I will still be here, on our own."

His jaw tensed. "Then I'll teach you how to defend yourself." His fingertips ran down her arm to her elbow before he released her.

She leaned back against the wall, her legs feeling weak from the release of tension. She fought the urge to rub the spot where his hand had rested. "You can do that?"

"Hand-to-hand. Weapons. Yeah, I can teach you."

The idea of being able to fight back… She felt stronger just thinking about it. "Truly?"

"Yeah." He tipped his head. "Truly."

"When can we start?"

He smiled and his teeth flashed white in the dim light of the hall. And her heartbeat soared.

"I'll be a little busy today taking care of the hole I dug by shooting my mouth off. And tomorrow I have a job to do. But I'm free on Tuesday."

His admission that he'd done the wrong thing went a long way to soothing her resentment, but not her anxiety. As much as she had enjoyed hearing Will laid flat verbally, she was too aware of the possible repercussions to forget or forgive. But maybe learning some self-defense would help alleviate her PTSD symptoms. "It's a date."

Realizing what she'd said, she bit her lip and hazarded a glance at him.

Tim shifted closer to her, his movements slow and measured. "I won't read more into that than you meant." He paused. "Not this time."

Her mouth grew dry as desert sand beneath the intentness of his regard. Her gaze dropped to his lips, then to the pulse that beat in his strong, tanned throat.

"You're a beautiful woman." His deep voice grew husky. "I'd have to be made of wood not to notice. But I'm not your ex. And I don't force myself on women." His throat worked as he swallowed. "I'll go organize my stuff and get started on the system." He brushed past her, so close she felt the warmth of his body. His steps quiet, he walked on down the hall to the living room.

Sam took several deep breaths to steady herself. He'd fired up her rusty sexuality with just the brush of his fingertips. And he'd even gotten close enough to kiss her and she hadn't felt one moment of fear. She allowed herself to bask in the experience.

But his parting words, *I'm not your ex. And I don't force myself on women*, played through her head. Her stomach plunged and a writhing humiliation killed those wonderful sensations. Was he making a statement about himself? Or had he guessed that Will had forced her?

CHAPTER 24

Marsha breathed in the scent of grilling meat and nausea rolled over her in a rush. It would pass. They said that smell was the strongest sense tied to memory. If that was true, maybe if she just immersed herself in it, this would stop.

She focused on tearing the lettuce into bite-sized pieces in two salad bowls, then added sliced cucumbers, shredded carrots and wedges of tomato. She sprinkled the croutons James liked on his.

Tucking the baby monitor under her arm, she carried the bowls to the door that led out into the back yard. The front door and sliding glass door in the living room had been replaced after the break-in. While they'd all been in the hospital, a team of SEALS had pitched in and done the work. The wonderful perks of being a member of a close-knit community.

The house looked just as it had before the incident.

Except for the memories.

She had to put this behind her. She was fine. Alex was fine. James was fine. This was just a place.

It had been a happy place for the last five years.

Could she lay all that had happened aside and get those feelings back? She studied the late afternoon sunlight as it reflected off the pool. James swam in it every day. How could he bear it? How could he walk the same steps he'd walked that day? He hadn't walked, he'd staggered. She didn't know how he'd survived the beatings.

For the first time she acknowledged her husband's incredible courage He just kept putting one foot in front of the other and *would not give up.* She needed to follow his lead and quit being such a wuss.

She unlatched the door, slid it open, and stepped out onto the patio. She avoided the pool and carried the salads to the glass-topped table under a bright red umbrella. James had already set the table.

"I've opened a bottle of the red wine you like," he said, motioning toward the sideboard next to the grill.

"Thank you." Maybe if she drank enough… No, she couldn't do that. Alex might need her.

"Would you like a glass?" She moved to the sideboard.

"Sure."

He preferred beer and was just trying to be…pleasant. James was never pleasant for conformity's sake. He usually just said what he thought, but rarely how he felt. A side-effect of being in charge of a platoon of SEALs. In the last two weeks he'd shared more of his feelings with her than he had in the previous ten years. He was trying. She could see that. It was time to make up her mind whether she was going to meet him halfway.

She poured two glasses of the wine, walked over to where he stood, and set his glass next to him on the wooden platform attached to the grill.

"Thanks."

Marsha buried her nose in her glass and took a large swallow. Irish courage? Or did that have to be Irish whiskey?

This was her husband! Why did she suddenly feel nervous? He'd never touched her with anything but gentleness. Even in his passion he took care. And, as he'd said, he'd never rush her into anything. But he'd planned this evening to ease her back into them being together. Earlier he'd even suggested a date night once a week so they could have time for just the two of them.

James flipped the steaks with long-handled tongs, then closed the lid on the grill.

"One of my men is in trouble," he said.

Marsha stared at him. In ten years, he had never talked to her about any of the men, except to pass on scuttlebutt about marriages, engagements, breakups, and babies. "What kind of trouble?"

He took a sip of his wine and looked down into his glass. "Before we transferred home he hooked up with the FBI to do some undercover work for them in Iraq, and followed through when he got home. There were other personnel who were approached who did the same." He shifted his weight and raised the lid of the grill to check the meat. "Just a few more minutes." He took another sip of his wine.

She'd never seen him vacillate about anything before. She studied his expression.

"You can't say anything to anyone about this," he said, his expression grave.

He was actually confiding in her. "I understand."

"Because it wasn't a military-sanctioned mission, I've not been ordered to keep it top secret, but since it may affect you down the line, I feel I need to give you a heads up."

She nodded. "How would it affect us?"

He looked toward the pool. "I made a mistake with Brett Weaver, Marsha. He was fighting his way back to his team and I just kept piling shit in his way. I tried to run him out of the teams. I looked at his medical report and decided he was no longer fit to be a SEAL."

"He saved our lives," she said.

"Yeah. When shit hit the fan, he did what he was trained to do." He cleared his throat and set aside his glass. He opened the grill and took the steaks off to put them on individual plates with the baked potatoes he'd already fixed. "You get the wine, I'll get these."

With both glasses in one hand and the bottle in the other, she joined him at the table. Her thoughts raced as she tried to figure out who he was talking about from the scuttlebutt she'd heard. They sat and he reached for the wine to top off their glasses.

He'd never tell her who the team member was unless she guessed. And now he'd started, her interest was piqued. "It's J.G. Carney, isn't it?"

His gaze leaped to her face. "I can't tell you who."

She nodded, but she could tell from his reaction her guess was correct. She placed a napkin in her lap and picked up her knife and fork.

"Things went south during a drop he was doing for the FBI, and the men he was dealing with tried to kill him. He's been AWOL ever since, and he's just recently surfaced."

More interested in what he was saying than her food, she laid aside her knife and reached for her glass again. "Was he injured?"

"Yeah. He was pretty banged up, but he's recovered now." He chewed a bite of steak and swallowed. "He's reached out to me for help, Marsha."

Concern revved through her. "What kind of help?"

"He's been listed as AWOL for seven months. But he's been on the run from some very bad guys. I believe that NCIS is using him as bait to draw a rouge FBI agent out, and the FBI is using him as bait for some very dangerous people."

Her mouth went so dry she couldn't swallow and had to take another healthy swig of wine to wash down the bite of salad. "Is it al Qaeda?"

"No. It's a Mexican drug cartel."

Her face felt numb. Wasn't that just as bad? "What does he expect you to do?"

"To stay on NCIS's ass and try to get them involved in the investigation he's running on the man responsible for the attack on him. I had a meeting with the agents this morning. All they're interested in is arresting him for AWOL—if they can find him. But what they were really saying was that they were waiting for shit to hit the fan so they could ride in on his coattails and catch the man who double-crossed him."

"And what about the FBI?"

"I got the feeling they're running their own investigation."

"So, that leaves Flash on his own. What's to keep him from being killed before they can run to the rescue?"

"Exactly." He set aside his knife and fork and leaned his elbows on the table. "I want to try and bring him home, Marsha."

"How do you propose to do it?" An uneasiness took up residence along the back of her neck, as though someone had blown against the fine hairs there.

"When he contacts me again, I'm going to try to talk him into coming in. I'll speak to the commander about working something out about the AWOL charge. Since he was working for the FBI when all this went down, we can cut him orders to reflect that and rescind the charges."

"Can you do that?"

"I hope so. A ten-month unsanctioned absence could end his career."

"How can they blame him for something he had no control over? He's been injured, and his life has been in danger."

James ran a hand over his close-cropped hair, and, propping his elbow on the table, rested his head in his hand for a moment. "The reasons don't matter. The only thing that will matter to HQ is that he's been gone for ten months."

The injustice of that sparked her outrage. "That isn't reasonable."

"Everything is cut and dried in the military, Marsha. You're either there to do a job or you're not. The reasons behind your absence don't matter."

She shook her head. "Even though he's done his job for years and put his life on the line?"

"Even though."

"But it isn't fair. They expect you to be loyal to them, but where is their loyalty to you?"

He laid his hand over hers and gave it a squeeze. "No it isn't fair, and it has nothing to do with loyalty, sweetheart, just duty. He's been derelict in his duty."

"You have to do something."

"I'm going to try." He picked up his fork. "But if I take a firm stand, things could get rocky for me, for us." His brown eyes looked dark, his jaw set in lines of determination she'd seen numerous times before. "That's why I'm telling you all this."

Would it be so bad for him not to be a SEAL anymore? Or for him not to have to play the politics that went with command and promotion?

To reach for his hand seemed natural for the first time in months. When they'd first met she'd been drawn to his strong, masculine looks, his imposing bearing. His eyes, so deep a brown, looked like dark, rich chocolate. His already-graying hair gave him a distinguished appearance. His hands were wide across his palm, his fingers, long and nimble, were strong and manly.

"I made a mistake with Brett Weaver. I don't want to do the same with this man. From his reports, the evidence he's sent me, I really do believe he was set up and only his training saved him from being murdered."

"Could the FBI intercede on his behalf?"

"They could weigh in, but it probably wouldn't make much difference. It falls under military jurisdiction since he's signed a contract with the Navy."

"If he can prove the FBI hired him to do this, with his commanding officer's backing, would it smooth the way?"

"I never spoke with the FBI, but they did talk with Captain Morrow, the base commander."

"But he truly believed it had gone through channels?" she asked.

"Yes, he did. Flash received an email saying his orders had been changed."

"But they hadn't."

He shook his head. "I never put in the paperwork because I knew nothing about it."

It sounded like Flash was SOL no matter what he did. The thought sent blood rushing to her face. How long had it been since she was seriously upset on another person's behalf? She'd been so caught up in her own cares that it had left little room for anyone else. What kind of person had she become? "How do you think he's been living?"

"I don't know, but he has serious skills, and he adapts. If he'd used his name anywhere the FBI would have been able to find him instantly. That means he's either going by an alias or he's flying under the radar."

"Poor fellow. Everything he's depended on, everyone he's depended on is out of reach." What would she have done had she not had a support network after Alex's birth? After the attack? The other wives had rallied around her, just as the men had reached out in support of James. The SEALs and their families were an extended family.

"Do whatever you have to do to get him home safe. Then we'll deal with the rest after."

"I'll clean up. You go ahead and finish your wine," James said as they rose to stack the dishes.

"I need to check on Alex."

"I'll do it. He seems to be sleeping well. And you have the monitor." They needed to concentrate on them for a while. Alex was doing fine for the present. Much better than seven months ago. But he didn't have to be told their relationship had been getting worse every day.

He made short work of scraping the dishes and putting them in the dishwasher, then scrubbed the grill utensils and left them in the drainer to dry.

He crept down the hall and into his son's room. Standing over the crib, he watched the rise and fall of Alex's chest. After the first six months, he'd begun to sleep more soundly at night and usually woke at five when James was up to give him a fresh diaper and a bottle.

He was getting more and more personality every day, and they were getting to know him better. He smiled often. Cried less. And was content to lie in his crib and play with his toes before and after sleep.

But there were more issues than just his heart. He wasn't reaching the milestones a normal baby did. He was at least three months behind with his physical development. It had taken him longer to hold up his head and at ten months he was just learning to sit up.

Marsha was doing exercises doctor had suggested with Alex every day to help strengthen his muscles and encourage his development. She had devoted her every waking moment to him since his birth, but that had to end if they were going to make it as a couple.

They had to have time for them.

He'd thought she'd withdrawn from him because of his failure to protect her. After her admission earlier this morning he understood it wasn't that simple. But she still loved him didn't she? Otherwise she wouldn't still be here. Armed with that knowledge, he was determined to find a way to woo her back to their life and their physical relationship.

James left the baby's room. Though he'd done it earlier, he checked the front door to make certain it was locked, and then the door that led into the garage. She had her issues and he had his. He often rose at night to check the windows and doors to make sure the house was secure. They'd put in an alarm system as well, but he couldn't arm it until they settled in for the night.

He gathered his CD player and a few disks from his office and took them outside. He set the player on the sideboard, plugged it in, popped in the disk, and pushed play. The smoky voice of Nina Simone floated around the pool. The scent of chlorine blended with the sweet smell of the clematis blooming on a trellis against the privacy fence that surrounded the pool.

Marsha sat at the foot of one of the lounges, cradling her wine glass between her hands. The sun had gone down and the lights had kicked on around the pool.

"He's sleeping well and his breathing is regular," he announced as he stretched out on one of the bright red lounges.

"I put your wine on the table there." She pointed to the small table between their lounges.

She seemed so far away. So withdrawn from him. How could he chip away the distance she'd placed between them?

"How can you bear to swim in the pool?" she asked.

He had to think for a minute before he realized what she meant. "It wasn't the pool that tried to kill us, Marsha. It was Tabarek Moussa."

She remained silent for a moment. "Is that how you get through deployments in those Godforsaken places? Focus on the people instead of the location?"

She had never spoken about his job like this. "Yeah. Most people are just trying to live their lives, *just live*, honey. It's a small percentage who are trying to harm anyone."

"It doesn't feel that way."

"I know." He drew a deep breath. "Will you come over here so we can lie together?" *Like we used to.*

She rose and set aside her wine glass. James eased the back of the lounge down a notch and spread his legs. Marsha crawled between and turned on her hip to lie against him. He draped his arm around her and cuddled her close.

Her weight resting against him felt right. The tension knotting his stomach and shoulder muscles relaxed a bit. "I've missed this," he said, smoothing her hair. He studied the tension in the hand she rested on the arm of the lounge. "Remember that bed and breakfast where we spent a week near Snow Mountain?"

"I remember we were supposed to hike a lot and instead spent the week in our room."

"I'd been to a twelve-week training. It was the first time we'd been apart since the wedding."

"You didn't hear me complaining, did you?"

He smiled. "No. I wouldn't say the sounds you made were complaints."

She slapped his arm. A moment of silence fell between them and she broke it. "I know I've changed since then. I used to be fearless."

His arm tightened around her. "We've both changed since then. It's been ten years. No one remains static." But she'd been doing fine until Alex's birth and—

"I don't suppose so."

"Maybe once Alex has his surgery and is on the mend you can go back to work…if you want to. You're really good with the therapy you do with him each morning. Maybe you could go back to school and do something like that if you don't want to do the CPA gig anymore."

"Maybe."

Well, at least she didn't dismiss either suggestion out of hand.

"When I watch you exercise his joints and get him to laugh, I'm amazed at how patient you are."

"James—" She gripped his shirt and turned her face against him. He couldn't tell if she was laughing or crying. "I know you're trying to be supportive, but you're about as subtle as an elephant's rump."

He laughed. "Subtle isn't my strong suit." He kissed the top of her head and breathed in the apple scent of her shampoo. "I just know that if I didn't have a goal to focus on, I wouldn't get out of bed in the morning. Getting up and going to work has helped me."

"I need to focus on Alex right now. Maybe when he's older and doing more, I'll think about going back to school or work. Right now, he needs me."

"I know." He swallowed. Sharing his feelings didn't come naturally. In all his SEAL training he'd never received one instruction on how to say mushy stuff and have it come out sounding right. "I need you, too, Marsha."

He knew she was crying when he felt her tears wet his chest.

"I know I was a shit when Alex was first born, but I'm trying to make up for that now. If you'll just tell me how."

She covered his lips with her fingers. "You're doing just fi-ne."

At least she was finally letting him hold her. But it hurt like hell to witness her struggling so. If he wasn't such a badass Navy SEAL, he'd do some bawling himself.

Alex's cry came over the baby monitor a few minutes later. It seemed the entire family was venting their unhappiness tonight.

While Marsha slipped away to check on the baby, taking the monitor with her, James gathered the remaining debris from their meal and returned the wine, glasses, CD player and CDs to the house.

Marsha came into the kitchen to fix Alex a bottle while he was washing the crystal wine glasses. "Is he okay?" he asked.

"Yes, just wants a bottle."

"After I'm through here, I'm going to set the alarm," he warned.

"Okay."

She looked washed out, as though those few moments of heart-to-heart discussion had drained her. She'd grown thinner, her face bordering on gaunt. She was a shadow of herself. But what could he do to help her?

They had both been prescribed anti-depressants and therapy after the attack. He hadn't taken the pills, but he'd gone to the sessions alone and with her. If he'd taken the meds, would she have taken hers? Had he made her feel he'd think her weak if she did?

He checked the doors and windows and set the alarm. Pausing outside the nursery on his way to their bedroom he watched Marsha as she gently propelled the rocker back and forth while she cuddled Alex close and fed him the bottle. The baby's fingers caught in her hair and she pulled it free and flipped it over her shoulder. She had always highlighted her blonde hair with pale streaks to give it more color. It had been months since she'd been to the beauty parlor and had it done. It had been months since she'd done anything but see to his and the baby's needs.

He wandered into the bedroom, his thoughts on her. He picked up his cell phone, then checked the time. It was just ten. Surely not too late to call. He keyed down until he found the number.

A woman's voice came across the line.

"Hello, Trish. This is Captain Jackson. I was wondering if you'd have some time tomorrow to meet with me?"

A hollow silence met his words. "This isn't about Langley, is it?" she asked, a husky tone in her voice.

Realizing he may have scared her, calling out of the blue, he rushed to set her mind at ease. "No. Lang and the other team members are fine. It's about Marsha. I want your advice about something. And I know most of the ladies in the team look to you as the go-to person about family issues and just about everything else."

"Oh..." She drew a deep breath. "Sure, Captain."

"What time would be convenient, and where would you like to meet?"

"I can come to the base tomorrow around lunch time, say eleven thirty."

"Thanks, that would be good. I'll arrange my schedule and leave word at the gate about your appointment. I'll provide lunch. Would that be okay?"

"Sure," Trish said. A child's voice sounded in the background.

He rushed to end the conversation. "Sorry to have interrupted your evening. I didn't mean to wake the kids. I'll see you tomorrow."

"Goodnight, sir."

James stripped, put on his pajama pants and t-shirt, and jerked down the covers. He stretched out on the bed and held the television control in his hand but didn't bother to turn it on.

He'd never been a particularly romantic guy. He felt clumsy and inept when trying to plan something he thought Marsha would like. But if it was going to help get their marriage back on track and maybe make Marsha feel better about him and herself, he'd do it.

He loved his wife. And he was going to do whatever it took to make sure she knew it.

Marsha wandered in a few minutes later and disappeared into the bathroom with her gown. When she came out, she'd changed into the homely night apparel. Her face was shiny with lotion and the faint smell of toothpaste came with her.

"Are you going to watch television?" she asked.

"No. I'm beat." James laid the remote on the nightstand.

"I am too." She crawled into her side of the bed. "I never realized how exhausting having another human being depend on you twenty-four/seven can be. But every time he smiles at me it's worth it."

"He does have an incredible smile. A bit gummy, but still terrific."

She smiled, the expression more natural than he'd seen in months. "He's working on a couple more teeth. He's chewing everything I give him."

This stress-free talk of Alex relaxed him and seemed to relax her too. She reached for the light on her side of the bed and he did the same.

When she turned away from him, he suppressed a sigh and turned on his side away from her. It was just going to take time. He had to just recognize that, accept it. But they had been so close before, or at least he'd thought they were. He had his work, she had hers. He had his men, she had a group of friends from work and the other wives she'd spent time with.

He'd noticed that she and her mom weren't talking much these days. That had stopped shortly after Alex's birth. Depression, withdrawal from others, fear, flashbacks, all the symptoms that encompassed PTSD. They were going to therapy. What else could he do but encourage her to take her pills?

The mattress compressed behind him and Marsh slipped an arm around his waist. He placed a hand over hers and held it against him.

"I just need to hold onto you for a moment."

His throat tightened with emotion. "As long as you need, honey."

CHAPTER 25

Will paced the ten feet of open floor space in front of his desk. Where the hell was Zusak? He'd used the private detective numerous times before and he'd *never* been late for an appointment. He was an obsequious little prick, but thorough, and Will needed someone who could find out about that asshole, Tim Carnes.

The cops had dropped by to see Will about Sam's car earlier. They knew he'd done it, Will knew he'd done it. But they didn't have enough evidence to arrest him. Their attitudes had been very clear, however. They were tired of dealing with his shit and would be on the lookout for his car anywhere in the vicinity of Sam's house.

He'd have to lay low for a while. Make everyone think he was walking the straight and narrow.

He wanted to kill that son of a bitch, Carnes. Because he'd touched his wife, but even more because he was in her good graces all cuddled up to her while Will couldn't even call her on the fucking telephone.

He wanted to kill Sam, too. It had only been eight months since they'd separated. Most widows waited a freakin' year before taking up with the next guy.

His lawyer had notified him about Joy's emergency room visit and the role the neighbor had played in saving her. *Great!* The fucker had swooped in like Superman and saved his daughter's life.

Now Sam would feel like she owed him or, even worse, see him as some kind of hero. Damn it.

He thrust his fingers through his hair and pulled. Frustration vied with anger, making his head feel like it might explode. He should never have scratched the word into Sam's car. But he got so angry when he thought of her living without him. She shouldn't want to live without him. He should be everything to her, like she was to him.

And now that asshole was right there, Johnny on the spot, ready to leap to the rescue if Will even came near the place. *Damn it!* Heat flared in his face. It was all Carnes's fault.

He stomped behind the large oak desk and threw himself into the over-stuffed office chair. As his weight hit it, the seat puffed air in protest.

Where the hell was Zusak?

A knock sounded. He lunged to his feet, strode to the door, and jerked it open. "Where the hell—" he cut off the words as his father brushed past him into the room.

"The police came to see me," Chaney announced without waiting for him to close the door.

"So?" Will looked down the hall to see who might be standing outside the office. Luckily, no one. He slammed the door.

"For someone so smart, you're a fucking idiot. When are you going to give it up?"

Was it his imagination, or was his father beginning to age a little? The silver at his temples had begun to thread its way through the rest of his thick hair and lines of tension carved deep trenches between his nose and mouth. His tan seemed to be a shade or two lighter than usual as well.

"What are you talking about?" Will asked. "I didn't do anything."

"If you didn't do it, you hired someone to do it. It has your MO written all over it."

"MO? Since when did you suddenly become a police detective?"

"Stop playing dumb. I know it was you who slashed Sam's tires and carved 'whore' into the side of her car. What is it about that bitch that makes you incapable of leaving her alone?" The impatience in Chaney's voice lay so thick it had a texture.

"She's my wife."

"*Ex-wife. Ex.*" His father stuck his face close to his. "Do you really think you're going to get her back doing crazy shit like this? *Leave her the fuck alone.*"

At hearing words nearly identical to what Tim Carnes had said fall from his father's mouth, rage ripped through Will like a blowtorch. "Get out of my face." He suppressed the urge to shove his father across the room by a fingernail-thin margin of control.

"I mean it, Will. The next time the cops show up at my door, I'm cutting you off. No more job, no more money, no more anything. *Am I clear?*"

No, he wasn't. "You're not going to do anything." Will crowded him and Chaney took a step back. He could read the wariness in his father's face. There was some satisfaction in making the man who'd run his life for so long fear him. "You forget, *Dad,* I know all about this business and how you've conducted it. I know about every bribe and payoff you've made. You cut me off, I'll start making phone calls."

Chaney reared back and raised a hand to strike Will. His arm shook as he fought for control, balled his fist instead, and dropped it to his side. "You ungrateful piss ant. Your mother and I have given you everything, and you dare to threaten *me*?" He narrowed his eyes and his jaw bulged as he ground his teeth. "You've already cost us our granddaughter. You won't cost us anything else. I'll pick up the phone and make a few calls myself, and you'll find yourself back in jail so fast it'll make your head spin."

Had he gone too far? He needed the money to keep rolling in for his plan to work. Will threw out the one thing he knew would make his dad back off. "Not if you want to get custody of Joy, you won't."

"What are you talking about? They're not going to give you or even us custody. Not since Moreland ran his mouth. They know your mother and I turned a blind eye to your obsessive behavior, and your violence toward Sam. They won't give us Joy."

"They will if Sam isn't able to keep a roof over her head and provide for her. I have a plan."

Chaney shook his head. "Why do you hate this woman so much? Why do you keep going after her?"

"I don't hate her, I love her. And I'm going to get her back, no matter what I have to do to accomplish it. If I have custody of Joy, I'll have Sam. They're a package deal. Because the two things Sam loves the most are Joy and that fucking house she lives in. I'll get them both, and I'll get *her*." He grinned. "In fact, I've already put something in motion that almost guarantees I'll get the house, and I'm halfway there."

Chaney stared at him, his face stiff with control. "I'm done, Will. If you get into trouble, don't call me to come bail you out. I won't do it. Leave your mother and me out of this. Besides, they pick you up for stalking her or defying the restraining order she has against you, you'll go away for a lot longer than seven months. Get on with your life. Find someone else."

"You'll be singing a different tune when I get Joy back."

Chaney shook his head and stalked to the door. He rested his hand on the doorknob and glared over his shoulder at Will. "I never completely understood what she went through with you. But now I do—" he jerked open the door. "God help her." He strode down the hall, leaving the door standing open.

In the hall stood the man who'd kept him waiting for the last hour. "Get in here, Zusak, and shut the door. I have a job for you."

Sam read the letter over again for the fourth time. The bank was requesting she come in to discuss her mortgage. She had to refinance because the deed was now in her name instead of her grandmother's. Why hadn't she gone to the bank right away and done this?

Because she was caring for Gran and at the time she just couldn't deal with anything else.

A nauseous fear took up residence in the pit of her stomach. Would she ever know what it was to not be afraid?

She should call her lawyer to find out what needed to be done, but Ben had already helped so much.

She couldn't lose the house. She had to prove she could provide for Joy or the court would revisit the custody agreement.

She wasn't sharing custody with Will. The court wouldn't give him custody because of his history of domestic violence but they might Chaney and Grace.

"Mommy—" Joy's universal kid's voice came from the living room, where she was playing Barbie.

Sam rose from the kitchen table and went to the living room doorway. "Yes, baby."

"I want dogs for supper."

Why did she like hot dogs so much? It was the last thing Sam wanted her to have after her choking incident, so of course it was the first thing Joy wanted. "Pizza?"

Joy's bottom lip popped out, then her eyebrows went up. "Pasghetti."

She had some sauce frozen in the freezer. All she'd have to do would be get it out and heat it up. "Okay. Spaghetti."

"Can Mr. Tim eat with us?"

Sam hesitated. They had ruined the last meal they'd shared with him. But those few minutes when he'd held her after saving Joy had been the first true moments of comfort she'd experienced in a long, long time. She'd avoided him for the last few days, since his meltdown on the phone with Will and he'd installed the alarm system.

Will had been ominously silent.

He was planning something horrible. She could feel it. He never let a slight of any kind go. Tim had called him some pretty colorful names.

And it had felt *good*—until she realized there would be consequences.

"Mommy?" Joy's voice brought her back to the present.

"Yes."

"I want to call him." Joy slid off the couch and ran to get the cordless phone.

Oh, shit!

Joy lifted the receiver off the base and stood with her fingers poised over the keypad. "What's the number, Mommy?"

"Uh." Her mind went blank. "I think it might be in the memory of the phone. Let me find it for you." If she couldn't find the number would that qualify as an excuse not to invite him? She thought of the extra bolts on the double doors at the back side of the house. The reinforcement he'd done to the bathroom doorframe, and the bolts he'd installed to make it into a panic room, including a button above the light switch. Sensors on every window and door. He'd worked for two days on the alarm system and done it all to protect them.

The memory of how he'd smelled up close after Joy's crisis, like grill smoke and laundry detergent. She wanted—she needed—to feel safe again. When she was with him she felt protected. Or was that just a delusion? She could use a delusion of safety right now, with the anxiety still cramping her stomach.

Before she allowed herself to think more about it, she found Tim's number, pushed the button so it would automatically redial and handed the phone to Joy.

"Hello, Mr. Tim." Joy's voice when she spoke with him held a note of confidence it lacked when speaking with her father. She jabbered away about her day at school and her friend Nancy Jane. Then paused when Tim said something. "Uh-huh. Mommy says you can come eat pasghetti with us."

Sam bit her lip to keep from laughing.

"She's right here." Joy shoved the phone at her. "He wants you."

Heat climbed into her face at her daughter's words. Sam pressed the receiver to her ear. "Hello."

"Was that invitation from you both?" he asked, his deep voice holding a note of amusement.

Her heart leapt at the sound of his voice. She had missed it, missed him. "Yes, it was."

"I appreciate it. And I really like pasghetti."

Sam chuckled. "It was either that or hot dogs, and I wasn't ready for those yet."

"I hear you." He paused. "Does this mean I'm forgiven for screwing up?"

"I guess so." She didn't want to talk about Will or even think about him. He had dominated her world long enough. She needed to learn to block him from her mind. It was time she moved on. "Dinner will be ready in about an hour, but you can come whenever you like."

"I have to finish loading the van with some electronics for a job for tomorrow, but I can walk over in about twenty minutes."

"That would be fine. We'll see you then."

She placed the receiver back on the base. She had to get the sauce in the microwave to thaw and make a salad, and if there wasn't any garlic bread in the freezer, there might be some rolls. She hustled into the kitchen and got things going. She'd just put the salad into the refrigerator and poured the defrosted sauce into a pot to heat when the doorbell rang.

Joy leapt from the couch and ran to the door. "Do what we practiced, Joy," Sam said from the kitchen.

Joy looked through the window next to the door.

"It's Mr. Tim." She grinned.

"He's a friend and we're expecting him. You can unlock the door and let him in."

Joy fumbled at the deadbolt and finally got it unlocked. She opened the door. "Come in, Mr. Tim."

"Hey, sweet tart." Swinging open the storm door he flashed Sam a smile that set her heart racing. He knelt before Joy, whipped a rectangular box out from behind his back, and held it up for her to see. "I brought dessert."

"Chocolate ice cream!" Joy bounced with excitement.

"Not just chocolate. Rocky Road. It has nuts and marshmallows in it too."

"I eat marshmallows in my cereal."

"I haven't tried that. But I bet it's pretty good." He rose to his feet. "We better put the ice cream in the freezer until we're ready for it."

"'Kay. It's in here." Joy grabbed his hand and tugged him in the direction of the kitchen.

His gaze fastened on Sam as he sauntered toward her. "Hey."

How could such an innocuous word sound so sexy? He offered her the ice cream.

"Thanks for bringing desert."

"I didn't have any wine. And beer doesn't go well with pasta."

She smiled. "I don't drink anyway."

Joy opened the freezer door. Sam took the half-gallon carton and put it in the freezer. "Joy why don't you go clean up all your Barbie doll mess, while we finish fixing supper."

Joy's bottom lip popped out. "Mommy—"

"If I get up in the middle of the night and step on one of those little plastic high heels, they're going in the trash," Sam warned.

Joy shot her a grumpy frown but went into the living room to do as she asked.

"Plastic high heels?" Tim asked.

"Barbie has spiked heels about a quarter inch long, and they're lethal. I stepped on one and drove it into the bottom of my foot and limped for a week."

"Ouch." He grimaced.

"How's your week been?" she asked while she filled a pot with water.

"It's been okay. Quiet."

"When he's quiet that means he's plotting something. Stay on your guard."

His expression grew solemn. "Understood." He looked about the kitchen. "Can I do something to help?"

"I think I've got everything under control. The sauce is hot and the oven's heating up for the bread."

"I can set the table."

"Thanks." Sam pointed to the oak cabinet above the sink. "Plates are there and the silverware is in the cabinet drawer below.

She stirred the sauce again. Salted the water for the pasta and checked the oven temp.

"A watched pot never boils," Tim said, placing a napkin beside the last plate and arranging the silverware next to it. He pulled out a chair from the kitchen table and sat down. He looked around the room. "Were the cabinets built by hand?" he asked.

"Yeah. My grandfather loved working with his hands. He had plans for every room in the house." She sat down in the chair diagonal to him and scanned the room. The floor was terracotta tile. The hand-built oak cabinets gleamed with care. Tiled countertops framed in with a decorative motif added an artistic flair to the decor.

"He did good work. I can do a few things, but nothing like this."

"Don't say that too loudly. Joy thinks there's nothing you can't do," she teased.

"I wish she didn't. It's too hard to live up to perfection." He grew serious. "She's very trusting."

"I know. On the one hand, I'm grateful I was able to protect her from things that would make her fearful of everyone. But on the other, I worry that she's not wary at all. I can't teach her to be. I've tried. So, I'm trying to teach her to be safe. This week we're practicing how she should answer the door. She looks out, and if it's someone she recognizes and knows we're expecting, she lets me know, then she's allowed to open the door, but only after I've said it's okay. If it's someone she doesn't know, she comes straight to me." She glanced toward the living room. Joy sat on the floor doing more playing than cleaning up.

Sam bobbed up to stir the sauce and turn it off. She put the pasta in the water, stirred it, then slid the bread in the oven and set the timer. She smiled at him as she sat back down. "Next week we're going to work on what she should do if a stranger approaches her outside the house."

"I don't know how you do it all." He rested his fingertips on her wrist and ran them back and forth over a small patch of skin there. His eyes fastened on her face, a look in their depths that made her heart beat in her throat and stole her breath away.

The light brushing movement of his touch set to life a million sensations in that one spot on her arm and spread outward. *Please tell me you really are a good guy. Please be a good guy.* She wanted to trust him so much.

"I talked to a guy who does body work today about your car. He said he could do the work and repaint the side at cost, and he'd be willing to let you pay him in installments."

"How did you manage that?"

"He called me for an estimate on a system and I just asked about it. I can run the car over to him tomorrow after you get home from work."

"Why do you want to help me, Tim?"

He remained silent for a moment, his features thoughtful, solemn. "I keep thinking, if someone had tried to help my mom, maybe things would have been different for us."

Her throat tightened with emotion.

"I stayed away this week, because...I know I shot my mouth off and said some things I shouldn't have. I thought if your ex thought what he was doing was pushing you in my direction, he'd stop."

"I understood the psychology behind it."

"I don't want what he does to affect whether or not you take a step toward trusting me, Sam. I'm trying to earn your trust for myself."

She swallowed. What could she say? The timer on the stove went off and she went to check the pasta and take out the bread.

Tim followed her and leaned back against the cabinet next to the stove.

"I do trust you," she said her voice softening to a whisper. She cleared her throat. "But I'm not sure about...anything else."

He stepped forward, cupped her face in his hands and kissed her. Time stopped and so did her breath. Her hands came to rest on his taut muscular waist. He tasted like cinnamon. His lips covered hers, withdrew, then came back again, the pressure gentle but firm. The brush of his closely-trimmed beard was a sensual texture against her face. The urge to rest against him, to draw him closer, nearly overwhelmed her. It had been so long since she'd been kissed or held. And never with such care. When he raised his head, it took a moment for her to open her eyes. She drew in a breath.

He smiled and enveloped her in his arms, holding her close. She rested against him and found a spot for her head against his chest. And for a moment she knew contentment, and then more when he ran his hand down her back and drew her close enough to feel his reaction to the kiss.

"Mommy, my tummy is growling," Joy called from the living room.

Sam laughed, happiness bubbling up inside her. She patted his chest and looked up at him. "You are a brave man."

His intent expression softened to tenderness, and his lips quirked up. "A hungry one, too."

His double entendre brought heat to her cheeks and she eased out of his arms. "The pasta."

She drained the pasta and with his help dished everything up. "Joy, dinner's ready. Come to the table," she called.

Joy brought Barbie along and climbed up in one of the chairs. Tim pushed it in.

As they sat down together to eat, the normalcy of it all struck her. No rage. No tension so thick you could cut it with a knife. No fear. She drew a deep breath and a smile curved her lips.

Until Joy dropped Barbie into her plate, face-first.

CHAPTER 26

Flash jumped to his feet and grabbed Joy's plate. "I've got it. Go ahead and start eating." He carried the plate to the sink, fished out the doll, rinsed her off and placed her on the window ledge to dry. He dumped the spaghetti in the trash, wiped the plate clean, dried it with a napkin and dished up some more spaghetti and sauce.

Sam and Joy's uncommon stillness at the table struck him as he placed Joy's plate in front of her. His gaze leaped to Sam's face. The small scattering of freckles across her nose stood out against the paleness of her skin.

"Mr. Tim doesn't yell, Mommy," Joy said, her voice just above a whisper.

Sam swallowed and her shoulders dropped as she relaxed. "No, he doesn't." She drew a full breath, color flowed back into her face, and she smiled. "It was just an accident, and people don't yell when you do something without meaning to."

Flash swallowed against the knot in his throat. Their reaction triggered memories he thought had been buried a thousand fathoms deep. But it had been over twenty years ago, and he wasn't going there. He sat down, put a paper napkin in his lap, and picked up his fork. "This smells great."

His words seemed to help dissolve the remaining tension, and Sam and Joy picked up their forks, too.

Twenty minutes later, with dinner over and Joy nibbling at a scoop of Rocky Road, he stretched his legs out under the table. "I can't eat another bite."

"Not even ice cream?" Joy asked.

He grinned at the spaghetti sauce and chocolate that circled her mouth "Not even ice cream."

"I'm done, Mommy," she said after one last bite.

"Wipe your mouth, then say, 'may I be excused,' and you can watch television until bath time."

Joy grabbed a napkin and scrubbed her mouth. "May I be excused?" she parroted.

"Yes, you may." As Joy disappeared into the living room, Sam smiled at him. "Sure you don't want ice cream?"

"No, thanks. Too much pasghetti in there." He patted his stomach.

"Some coffee then?"

"No. I only drink a couple of cups in the morning to wake up."

"I'll get Joy settled then and clear the table." She went into the living room and the sound of the channel changing to a cartoon network reached him. The basic, homey comfort of having dinner with them, breaking bread and sharing the everyday stuff, acted as balm to his homesickness. In the few weeks he'd been here he'd been alone. Except for Sam and Joy.

Some of the women he'd worked for had come on to him. And he'd had more than his share of opportunities for feminine companionship. But it was hard to be interested when you'd already found what you wanted. His gaze strayed to Sam when she returned. Now that she was relaxed again, soft color had bloomed in her cheeks. The lean line of her body as she removed the breadbasket from the center of the table drew his eye to her narrow waist. He remembered the first day they'd met, as she'd stepped out of the police car, how every one of the men's eyes had been on her legs, including his.

He shouldn't allow himself to feel for her. Shouldn't get any more involved than he was. It was only going to hurt them in the long run. But he couldn't seem to control it.

Flash rose and began to clear the table. He scraped the plates and stacked them in the sink.

"You don't have to do that," she said, returning to the table.

"If we work as a team it takes half the time."

"Is that how you do things in the military?" she asked.

"Yeah." He should never have told her he was military. She knew too much already. "Though none of us had to do KP duty other than to hand out K-rations, which pretty much suck. They have the calories to keep you going, but they taste like…" He looked down at her as she ran water in the sink, his gaze tracing the curve of her cheek, then dropping to her breasts, small but firm beneath her blouse. He lost his train of thought.

"You don't have to finish, I get the picture." She chuckled. While she rinsed the dishes and loaded the dishwasher, he finished clearing the table.

He reached for Barbie on the windowsill to distract himself. Though the spaghetti sauce had washed off, her hair was now an orange-blonde mix, and the dress was stained. He grimaced as he held her up. "I hope this wasn't a favorite."

"Periodic favorite." She took the doll and dunked her in the soapy water, clothes and all. "The dress is probably ruined, but I'll let Joy use her markers on the hair so she can turn her into Rocker Barbie." She rinsed the toy, set her on a dishtowel to dry, and smoothed the doll's hair.

He leaned against the counter while she finished up. "I thought maybe I could show you some of the self-defense moves tonight since we didn't do it this week."

She hesitated for a moment. "Okay."

"How about I take off and do some things at my place, and when you get Joy to bed, you can call me and I'll come back over. That will give our food time to settle, too."

"That's a good idea. She might not understand why Mommy's trying to learn how to kick butt."

Flash studied her slender frame. Again. And though she suited him just fine, she'd need to bulk up and gain weight if that was what she was aiming for. He offered her a smile. "If you seriously want to kick butt, you'll have to start lifting weights and gain some upper body strength. But if you want to fight somebody off and disable them long enough for you to escape, I can show you how to do that right away."

"I'm more interested in just being able to fight them off. I don't know if I have the aggressive tendencies needed to try and do more."

"I guess that depends on how angry you are. But to fight when you're angry clouds your judgment, too. Give me a call when you want me to come back over." Though he wanted more, he brushed her cheek with his lips and smiled when soft color rushed into her cheeks. "Thanks for dinner."

"You're welcome." She followed him to the living room.

He said good-bye to Joy on the way out and paused as she ran to him for a hug. He knelt, and her delicate arms went around his neck.

"Rocky road is *good*," she said.

"Yeah it is, sweet tart." He patted her fragile back, and released her when she pulled back. "It's supposed to give you sweet dreams, too."

"Visions of sugar pumpkins, like in the Christmas story?" she asked.

He chuckled. "I think that's sugar plums."

"What's a sugar plum?"

"I have no idea. Maybe you better ask your mom."

He left while Sam was busy explaining. The sun had gone down, leaving behind the sickly yellow haze. The streetlights hadn't kicked on, nor the exterior lights on the garage.

He had reached the steps leading up to his apartment when a man stepped out from behind the edge of the garage. Every nerve went on high alert, and he froze and scanned the area, expecting to see more.

"Stay away from my family," Will Cross said as he walked along the exterior wall to stand six or seven feet away. Dark brown hair lay thick against his skull, and his eyes were the same pale blue as Joy's. He had a strong, angular jaw and wide, flat cheekbones.

He was easily thirty pounds heavier than Flash, and at two-twenty, more than a hundred pounds heavier than Sam. Jesus, how had she survived a blow from this guy?

Flash studied him, trying to see what the pull for Sam might have been. He was just as the cop had described him, wide through the chest and shoulders, a big guy, but he was carrying at least thirty pounds of fat.

"You don't have any say in who Sam associates with any longer. You're divorced."

"Not for long."

"I think Sam might have something different to say about that. She's not going to go back to someone who beats her."

Cross's jaw tensed. "We'll see about that. But in the meantime, I thought I'd introduce myself. I'm the guy who's going to ruin your business and run you out of town."

Flash studied him as he leaned against the railing leading up the apartment stairs. "You can try."

"It will happen."

Flash made a show of looking behind him. "What no backup?"

Cross came to a standstill, his jaw tensing. "I don't need anyone to fight my battles for me."

"No, you just do chicken shit, cowardly stuff like carve names into cars and slice tires."

Flash crossed his arms and let his gaze drift over the sparsely vegetated desert scenery behind Cross, and beyond that to the haze and the distant mountains. "Have you ever been lost out in the desert, Cross? Unless you know the stars and can navigate your way by them, it's easy to get turned around and disoriented. Especially if you don't have enough water, and you get dehydrated. And then there are the snakes and scorpions." He stared at the man. "What do you say we take a trip out there together?"

Cross laughed. "You're a funny man. I don't think so."

"I didn't think you'd be up for a face-to-face, man-to-man confrontation. After all, you only like to smack women around, right?"

"Not anymore," he said, his features stiff.

"Sure," Flash said, a sneer in his voice.

Cross narrowed his eyes and his hands clenched into fists.

Was that how he'd looked when he went after Sam? Anger and adrenaline surged through Flash's system, and he fought his urge to charge the fucker, aware that was exactly what the man was waiting for. "It's time for you to leave."

"What are you going to do? Call the police?"

"No, I won't call the police. I don't want to upset Sam or Joy. Something you're obviously not concerned about."

A sullen look settled over Cross's face and he started forward. When he got close to Flash, his body language grew noticeably tense.

Flash remained relaxed but alert. "As much as I'd like to, I'm not going to punch your fucking face in and get arrested for assault. But the next time you come around, I will call the cops."

Cross shot him a look of controlled violence, and his cheeks turned red. He stomped across the yard and cut across the property diagonally to the street. Flash watched until he was out of sight before he climbed the steps to his apartment.

Though the alarm was still on, he checked the apartment to make sure nothing had been disturbed. He paced the floor, still amped from the adrenaline rush. How had Sam stood against Cross? He was built like a bull. Jesus, no wonder she'd ended up in the hospital. He clenched and unclenched his fists.

He had to get what the son of a bitch had done off his mind or he'd get on his bike and go after him. He couldn't afford to be arrested for beating the shit out of him. The police thought Tim Carnes was a good guy. He had to keep that impression going. If they checked into his background too closely, they might find holes in his history.

That's the first thing Cross would do. Get someone to check him out. He'd done the best he could to cover his tracks. But there wasn't a damn thing he could do if they discovered something. If they somehow came up with the name Harold Timothy Carney, Gilbert might get wind of it and loose the cartel dogs. They'd be coming for him. He'd known it might happen. Had planned for it. But that was before Sam and Joy came into the picture.

He opened his laptop, keyed into the temporary email address he'd created this week and scanned it for any messages from Travis or the boys. He needed cover and there was no one who could provide it. He had to warn Travis. He sent a brief message to Travis's temporary email address. At the end of the week they'd both change to a different one.

He rose and paced again. He had to calm down. Sam would call soon, and he needed to focus on her.

He should be bugging out right now. The chance of causing her more trouble was almost guaranteed. But he couldn't leave her unprotected, either.

What was it about her that drew him? He thought about the look on her face after he'd kissed her. How breathless and amazed she'd been, from a simple kiss.

That look was what it boiled down to?

She was more than just a hookup.

She was what he'd been searching for his whole life.

Sam picked up the phone for the third time, then laid it back down. With Joy asleep, she could now follow through with the self-defense moves Tim promised to show her. But every muscle in her body seemed to have tightened into one big knot. She knew with certainty Tim wasn't going to hurt her. But what if her post-traumatic stress decided to kick in? *Like it wasn't already?* She ran her hands over her face.

As a soldier, he'd understand and help her handle it. She repeated those few things over and over like a mantra until her anxiety level lowered a notch.

She took up the phone again and dialed the number. "I have Joy down for the night, if you still want to come over."

"I'll be right there."

At his tap at the door, she looked through the window. Nervous tremors shook her arms and legs. Her breathing came in ragged gasps. She opened the door to let him in, then backed away as he stepped inside.

Tim didn't offer to come any further into the room, but remained just inside the door.

"We don't have to do this, Sam. We can just sit on the couch and watch television and talk."

She grappled to regain her composure and forced her breathing to a slower pace. "I need this. The more control I take, the more control I have." She fisted her hands at her sides, her fingernails digging into her palms. The little flashes of pain gave her something else to focus on. "I'm not going to freak out."

Tim's handsome, even features settled into grave lines, his eyes darkened to gray-blue. "I'd rather cut off my arm than make you afraid of me."

She swallowed back the surge of anxiety that threatened to close her throat and wreaked havoc with her heart. "You're not." She focused on him instead of the suffocating sensation, taking in the blueness of his eyes, the strong, angular shape of his jaw, the tense line of his lips. She'd tried so hard to be strong around him so he wouldn't see her as a victim. And now she was undoing all of that by being a weak ninny.

Tim offered his hand and she grasped it, her palm gliding over his slightly callused skin. His touch seemed to ground her. She drew her first un-constricted breath.

Though the smile she offered him was shaky, it relaxed the watchful control in his features. "Do you have any slow dance music in the house?" he asked.

"I think Gran has some Patsy Cline CDs around."

"Go get them."

Reluctantly, she released his hand and wandered over to the entertainment center, opening the cabinet doors. She withdrew a stack of CDs and carried them back to him. He chose one and handed it back to her with a smile. "Number three is one of my favorites."

She smiled as she read the title. "What does self-defense have to do with music?"

"Go put it on and I'll show you."

She crossed the area rug to the CD player and put the disk in. The mellow tones of Patsy Cline's voice filled the room singing her hit song 'Crazy'.

"Turn your back to me," Tim instructed.

To hesitate would only make him think she didn't trust him. She turned. The heat from his tall frame caressed her back, though he didn't crowd too close.

He rested his hands on her shoulders, his touch light. "Just listen to the music for a minute, focus on the beat. Part of fending off an opponent is being centered and balanced. It's not much different from dancing. So what I want you to do is brace your feet apart and sway back and forth until you get a feel for when you're at your steadiest."

Sam closed her eyes and did as he said. The music soothed her. The remainder of her anxiety slipped away. She felt steady inside. She shifted her stance until she was just as certain of her balance.

Tim moved around to face her, his gaze searching.

"I'm good now."

He nodded, the movement brief. "Several parts of your body can be used as a weapon. Head, hands, elbows, knees, and feet. And several parts of your attacker's body can be your target. Eyes, ears, mouth, nose, throat, stomach, groin, knees, ankles, and toes. The key is not to be afraid to go after them with everything you have."

Could she do that? Go after someone with no holds barred? Her non-aggressiveness might be what allowed Will to target her in the first place.

Sam shifted her weight, and nodded. "I can learn to be aggressive. I'm not going to be a victim ever again."

"Good." Tim smiled. "This won't come easy to you. You'll have to practice after you get the hang of it."

He demonstrated how to use her hands like weapons, using her fingers, thumbs and palm to do damage to the face, ears, and throat. Next he showed her how to use her hand like a hammer instead of a fist.

"Once you have your opponent disabled you run like hell to safety. Don't allow the adrenaline in your system to make you too bold. You'll be tempted to stick around and exact some payback, but when you're facing someone bigger than you, it's better to live to fight another day. Just get the hell out of there."

"Is that what you did?" she asked.

"Not always, and there were times I regretted it. Especially when I was younger and on the street."

She caught her breath. "Tim—"

He shook his head and looked away. "A lifetime ago. I was lucky. I picked the pocket of the wrong guy, and after he shook me so hard he damn near made my teeth rattle, he and his wife took me in. I'll tell you about it sometime. Right now we're concentrating on you."

But she didn't want to concentrate on herself. She wanted to know as much about him as he'd guessed about her.

When he moved around behind her again, she remained relaxed. "I'm going to put my arm around your neck," he warned. His chest brushed her back as he stepped close. "See the way this muscle is divided in my forearm?" He raised his arm, his other encircling her as he pointed out the division in the well-developed muscle. "There's a nerve there that's particularly open to pain. Especially if you shove your beautiful, sharp chin down into it. To be certain you inflict enough pain to get the attacker to release you, loop your hands behind your head and force your chin down into that groove."

With his arms encircling her, Sam couldn't break away from the sense of safety and caring surrounding her. But she wanted more. She gripped his arm with both hands and leaned back to rest her head against his shoulder.

The CD clicked off.

For a beat, then two, Tim remained still. He shifted his weight and aligned his body with hers. He lowered his arm to encircle her upper shoulders and hold her. His other went around her waist, and his hand splayed against her abdomen. He caught his breath and rested his chin against her hair, the warmth of his breath caressing her ear. She shivered.

"You're losing focus." His voice held a husky note it hadn't had a moment before.

With his body pressed so firm and masculine up against her from behind, and his hand resting so familiarly on her belly, tantalizing tremors worked their way through her lower limbs. A wonderful, empty ache settled between her legs. She fought against the urge to push her hips back against him.

Swallowing to relieve the sudden dryness of her throat, she said. "I think I need some time to digest everything you've shown me so far." She turned to look up at him. Her gaze snagged at the masculine angle of his beard-darkened jaw, then his lips, no longer tightened in concentration but parted. When her gaze finally rose to meet his, his hand curved around her hip, his thumb resting along her pelvic bone, sending jets of sensation downward to tempt her.

A flush rode the crest of his cheekbones. His eyes darkened, his pupils expanded, leaving a rim of cerulean blue electric with emotion. The hot, slumberous desire she read on his face stole her breath. Her body clamored for her to turn against him, guide him between her legs and let nature take its course.

But those fierce moments of anxiety she'd experienced earlier lay too fresh in her mind. When they made love she didn't want fear to have a part in it. "How about some ice cream?" she managed, her voice dwindling to a whisper.

Tim's throat worked as he swallowed. He drew a deep breath. The tension in his body relaxed by degrees, and a wry smile tilted his lips. "Sure. I could use something to cool me down."

Will breathed in the scent of perfume and smoke that lingered on the woman beneath him. How many times had he told Carla to shower before he came over? He'd remind her with a belt or two after he got his rocks off. He pumped away like a piston, and Carla panted his name and wiggled beneath him. With one final thrust, and grunt, he climaxed and found a small outlet for some of the rage still smoldering inside him. It was either sex or beat the crap out of something. Carla was handy and willing. She was always willing—for him.

He rolled off her and lay on his back to catch his breath. Carla curled against his side and once again he smelled the cigarette smoke in her bleached blonde hair.

"Why haven't you showered yet?" he demanded.

"I just got home before you showed up. And you didn't call to let me know you were coming." She rubbed a hand across his chest. "We can take a shower together if you like." She pressed her breasts against him and rubbed.

"Maybe in a few minutes. I have something for you." He pulled his arm from beneath her and reached for his wallet on the nightstand. He extracted a credit card and handed it to her.

"What's this for?" she asked, a frown puckering her brow. "This has your ex-wife's name on it."

"Yes, it's her credit card. I never canceled it after the divorce. He shrugged. "The bills still come to me. I want you to go out and have a good time with it. I want you to get your hair done, professionally, not that home, bottled crap." He gave a strand of her long hair a tug, careful not to be too rough, and smiled. "And get some new clothes and shoes. Now that I'm rid of her, you're the only woman in my life, and I want to take care of you in style."

"But if I sign her name it'll be like I'm pretending to be her, won't it?"

"As long as I pay the bill, honey, the credit card company doesn't give a shit. Just sign her name and get what you want. Spend a couple thousand on clothes, shoes, all the crap women like, and whatever it takes at the salon. You can start first thing in the morning."

Carla studied him for a moment her lips pursed.

In a way she was as pretty as Sam, though her hair wasn't naturally blonde, and she always seemed to have roots showing. Her lips were full, and she could do things with her mouth, Sam never enjoyed doing for him. Her blue eyes could pass for green in a certain light. Where Sam's body was slender and sleek, Carla's breasts were much larger. Thanks to the plastic surgery he'd paid for. While Sam had been in the hospital giving birth to Joy, Carla had been just a floor below going under the knife to have her girls, as she called them, enhanced. He'd visited her right after Joy was born. Every time he thought about it, he wanted to laugh at the irony.

"I really am the only woman you're with now? You've finally given her up?"

"Yeah. I spent seven months behind bars because of that bitch. I'm tired of all the legal crap. I'm over her." Never. But payback would be so satisfying.

"Oh, Will!" She wiggled on top of him and showered his face with kisses. "We're going to be so happy."

He laughed as if he agreed and ran his hands down her back and over her ass. Carla's ass was one of her best features. It was tight and narrow. With the boob job, her body was a little top-heavy, but her figure gave her an edge over the other attendants at the casino where she worked. Men looked at her and thought big tits and a tight snatch. What more could any man want?

"There's just one thing you have to do for me." He cupped the underside of her breast and gave it a squeeze.

"What? Anything."

"I want you to give up sucking on those cancer sticks."

"I've tried to quit smoking. You know I have." A whine crept into her tone. "It's really hard for me."

"Yeah, I know. But if you love me, you'll do it. It's the one thing I can't stand. I want to be able to smell you and your perfume when I hold you." And if he noticed cigarette smoke on her clothes, other people would. Sam didn't smoke.

Her mouth settled into a pout. "Okay. I promise."

"You can go to the doctor and get some of that medication they're always advertising to help you quit. I'll even pay for it."

"Okay." She bent her head and kissed him. "How about that shower now." She nibbled his ear, and slid a hand down between them to stroke him. He grew hard. "If you'll wash my back, I'll make it worth your while," she breathed.

He grinned. "I'm up for it."

CHAPTER 27

James read through the list of suggestions he and Trish were working on. He looked up when she spoke.

"If you take her to San Francisco, you'll have to spend the night, and it will give you more uninterrupted time together," she said. She leaned forward over the paper plate that rested on the corner of his desk and took a bite of her submarine sandwich.

Her sandy red hair, cut in a sleek cap, lay against her head. Freckles covered every inch of her skin, but didn't detract at all from the wholesome prettiness of her features. She was a driving force behind the wives of the SEAL team members. If she ever wanted to give up her job as a social worker, she could easily run the White House. Hell, if they allowed women in the SEALs, she could probably do his job. James had never seen anyone in touch with so many people.

"She's not very eager to leave Alex for any length of time. She even worries when I'm watching him. If I can get her out of the house to go to the beauty shop and have her hair done, a facial, a manicure and pedicure, then take her out to dinner..." James fell silent when she shook her head.

"You need to pry her out of San Diego. If we get someone really dependable to babysit, someone she can't argue isn't qualified to care for Alex, she won't have an excuse not to go."

"Who would that be?" he asked.

"Angela Melzoni. She's a registered nurse. And she works at the Balboa Med Center. She cared for Brett Weaver when he was in a coma." She rattled off the woman's number. "She'd be perfect. She was also dating one of the team for a while, but I don't think they're together any longer. Some of the wives will wander over and visit and play with Alex too, to give Angela a break."

He wrote down the number. "Then there's no guarantee she'll do it."

"You'll have to give her a couple of weeks' notice, but I'm sure she will. I'd surprise Marsha with the makeover a week or so before, so she's feeling all feminine and pampered. Then make arrangements to go somewhere out of town with her the following week. And on the off chance Angela can't do it, give me a call. I'll work with all the other wives, and we'll figure something out."

"Roger that." He nodded. "I appreciate it."

Trish laid her napkin atop the remnants of her meal, picked up her soft drink, and sipped it through the straw. "I think it's great you're doing this for her, by the way."

Did he need to confess it was an act of desperation? "Marsha needs to decompress. I do too, and she can't do it at home. Alex is doing much better. We just have to monitor him closely. But she rarely leaves the house. Rarely talks to the friends she used to speak to every day. It was an adjustment with the baby. She hadn't really recovered from the birth when the break-in happened."

"You're doing counseling?"

"Yes." Uncomfortable with discussing the personal aspects of their treatment, James motioned to the remnants of her food. "Would you like me to do away with that?"

"Sure." She bundled up what was left of her sandwich and handed it to him. He tossed it in the trash with his own.

"I wish I could say it was only going to take a makeover and a trip to get her back on track, but it won't. She'll have to make a conscious decision that she wants to recover before it can happen," Trish said.

"I know. I understand why she hasn't bounced back. I had my work to come back to. She had more stress with a special needs baby to care for."

Trish leaned forward a frown worrying her brow. "They tried to kill Alex, and they tried to kill you. The two most important people in her world. That alone would be enough to leave her with lasting issues. I know it would me. And all the hormonal issues that go along with trying to have a baby, then delivering one, probably added to it as well."

He hadn't thought of that. Could post and prenatal hormones be affecting her recovery? He'd ask the doctor about that the next time he spoke to him. "I appreciate your taking time to come here and help me with all this." He leaned back in his seat. "I've discovered how much pressure you ladies are under while we're deployed or injured. Marsha stood by me while I healed and cared for Alex, too. I want to do the same for her."

"Family and friends help. Marsha's closed herself off since Alex's birth. I'll put out the word, and some of the ladies can swing by and visit or call to check on her more often."

"I think that would be a good idea. I'd appreciate it if you'd keep this other stuff top secret until I get all the plans cemented."

"Of course, Captain." Trish rose. "I have several stops to make on the way back to the office. I better get started."

James rose, walked her to the door and opened it for her. He could get everything arranged, but how was he going to get Marsha to the appointments? He'd figure it out. Trish had helped enough.

"If you need anything else, Captain, don't hesitate to call," Trish said, offering her hand.

He shook it briefly. "I will. Thank you."

She disappeared down the hall toward the front entrance, her steps purposeful and quick.

Seaman Crouch spoke from his desk. "You have a meeting with Admiral Clarence at two, sir."

"Thanks. Buzz me ten minutes before the meeting. I have some phone calls to make." He couldn't afford to be late. He only had twenty minutes of the Admiral's time.

"Yes, sir."

Back at his desk, James checked his email, answered a couple of messages that couldn't wait and paused to scan the rest before closing the program. He noticed the heading of the mission in Iraq Flash had used before and opened the message. Flash had attached another group of videos and a brief message. James opened each video and scanned them quickly. More fuel for the meeting he was about to attend. His telephone calls were going to have to wait. When he got to the end of the video Flash had made of himself, James pumped the air. "I have no one else I can reach out to, sir. So, I'm trusting you'll do the right thing," Flash said.

Do the right thing. He'd already decided what that would be.

NCIS would step up to the plate if they had Admiral Clarence on their ass. And maybe the admiral would have some ideas about how they could save Flash's career, too.

Thirty minutes later, before Crouch could buzz him, he walked out of his office with a folder of printed reports and a thumb-drive filled with all the info Flash had fed him. He left the building, got into his car and drove the half mile to Admiral Clarence's office.

The two-story complex was structured much like the one he'd just left. The halls were a little wider and the offices a little more spacious, but the complex itself was still military-issue, with thick industrial tile over the concrete slab floor, and serviceable military-issue furniture. The only difference was the soundproofing in the walls between the offices. This place was quiet.

James signed in with Admiral Clarence's administrative assistant, Ensign Winchester, and took a seat. Ten minutes passed, and for the first time in a long while, James found himself growing nervous. When Admiral Clarence opened the door and motioned him in, he rose to attention and walked forward.

Clarence stood about five foot nine, four inches shorter than James's six-one, but his bearing and the sheer force of his commanding personality seemed to fill a room. His shock of iron gray hair fell across his forehead, though the sides were cut short. He focused on James with a slight frown.

The interior of the office, decorated much like his own, contained a heavy desk, a large bookcase, and a couple of extra chairs. A framed copy of the Pledge of Allegiance done in some kind of needlework with a flag design at the top hung on one wall. Next to it was a large Trident with the Teams' slogan 'The

Only Easy Day Was Yesterday.' He paused to admire both pieces.

"My wife does cross-stitch. She made those for me when I was promoted to this position two years ago."

"They're very nice, sir."

"Thank you. Now what can I do for you, Captain?"

James offered him the file and the flash drive. Drawing a deep breath, he explained the situation and the files Flash had sent him.

Admiral Clarence moved around his desk and took a seat. His jaw worked as he listened.

"I've compiled signed affidavits from Captain Morrow and Lieutenant J.G. Carney's teammates about Rick Dobson and Agent Gilbert's visit to the base in Iraq. Captain Morrow spoke to them in his office about their plans. They outlined part of what they needed at that time. They followed through with Lieutenant Carney, but not with me, so his orders were not amended. But Carney says he received a packet of orders and put them in a safety deposit box here in San Diego."

"Damn it," Clarence breathed.

"I've also copied all the video files to the flash drive, and forwarded all the emails he's sent me to you. I've done the same for NCIS."

"And what have they done?"

"I've detailed my conversation with them for you as well. They say they are only interested in the AWOL charge."

Admiral Clarence's brows rose and his jaw hardened. "What do you think that's all about?"

"I think they're waiting for the FBI to do their job. If they have an agent who's gone off the reservation, they're not going to reach out to another federal organization to investigate. But NCIS can't bring Carney in without exposing him to retaliation from Gilbert and the cartel. It's become a Catch-22 situation, sir."

"Leaving your man twisting in the wind."

"Yes, sir. I have spoken in depth with Carney's commanding officer, and his teammates. They all believe that he was acting in good faith with Dobson and Gilbert. They've all said he would not abandon his post. He's had an exemplary record under my command, sir. I don't believe he would, either."

"What do you propose we do, Captain?"

"We need to get the AWOL charge amended if we can. Initiate orders where he is acting in concert with NCIS so they can enter the investigation through the back door he's created."

"But we don't know where he is, and neither does NCIS."

James moistened his lips. He'd spent the ten minutes waiting to see the Admiral, debating whether or not to share Flash's message with anyone. "Flash reached out to me today, saying he wants to meet."

"Tell me you haven't notified NCIS," Admiral Clarence demanded.

"No, sir. I wanted to wait until I'd met with you."

"Good. Where does he want to meet?"

"Las Vegas. In two weeks."

Sam eased up to the bathroom doorway and peeked around the edge to check on Joy. Joy played in the bathtub, her plastic mermaid doll in one hand and Barbie in the other. Instead of being upset about her Barbie's hair change, she'd wanted to turn her into a mermaid with technicolor locks.

Joy shoved Barbie under the water and brought her back up onto the edge of the tub. She spoke for Barbie. "I can dive deeper than you." In her Mermaid voice, Joy disagreed, "No you can't. I'm a real mermaid, you're only a pretend mermaid." Joy bobbed Barbie across the edge of the tub in her leg-hugging pink fins designed from an old bathroom curtain. "I am too a real mermaid. And I can dive deeper than you. All you can do is sit on your rock." In a voice tinged with snippy attitude, Mermaid said. "But I can sit on my rock at the bottom of the ocean. All you can do is dive in the bathtub."

Sam clapped her hand over her mouth to keep from laughing out loud and slipped away from the door. What would she do without her little girl? She was the one thing guaranteed to make her smile. Well, almost the only thing.

She glanced at her watch. Two hours and Tim would be coming over to follow up on the training they'd begun. He'd gone over more of the basics the night before and even made her try and attack him. Something she'd never dreamed she could do. At first she'd been afraid of hurting him, but he'd avoided her kicks and punches with ease. His concentration had given her an insight into how he must have been in the service. All business. Thoroughly professional.

On one hand she'd been grateful he was so focused, and on another she'd wanted to do something to break through all his control and focus his intensity on something else. Each time they practiced they ended with a few brief moments of closeness, but so far her fear had her backing off each time. It had to be as frustrating to him as it was to her.

It had been three years since she'd felt the desire to have a physical relationship with a man. What if she couldn't sustain those feelings if they attempted to make love? It wasn't fair to keep sending out signals to him if she couldn't follow through.

She slipped into the bedroom, where she could still hear Joy playing, pulled a pair of sweatpants and a t-shirt from the dresser, and changed clothes. She studied herself in the dresser mirror. This wasn't exactly a come and get it signal.

Every time Tim touched her, he did it carefully, warning her what he was going to do before he did it. In short, he understood a man's arm around her throat could trigger her PTSD. She'd had a few minutes of anxiety the night before, but she'd overcome them because she hadn't felt threatened. But tonight might be different. Every night they practiced could be the night she lost it. If she dwelled on it, she'd lose her nerve for sure.

What would Tim think if she called this off? Would he think her a coward? She didn't want to disappoint him.

But most of all she didn't want Will Cross to rule her life anymore. This was the fifth step toward taking back everything he'd stolen from her. The first had been when she'd walked away. The second when she'd had Will arrested—not once, but twice—and the police had actually backed her up. The third step, she'd filed for divorce and gotten it. The forth step, she'd signed up for a college class and gotten a job. And now the fifth would be learning to protect herself.

Once she'd accomplished this one…what would be the sixth? She couldn't think about that yet. She had to finish the fifth step first. One step at a time.

"Joy? Time to get out of the tub, honey," she called out as she left the bedroom and went down the hall. Barbie perched on the edge of the tub along with Mermaid.

She took two steps into the room. Joy lay face up beneath the surface of the water. Sam's heart stopped then her pulse surged up into her throat.

"Joy!" She fell to her knees and reached for her. Joy sat up and blew against the drops of water running down her face and splattered her.

"Dear God." Sam braced a hand on the tub and held the other one against her heart, its painful beat drumming in her ears.

"I held my breath, Mommy. Grandma El taught me."

Weak with relief, she collapsed to the rug in front of the tub and dragged in breath after breath. After a few moments, she managed, "That's good, baby." Though her muscles shook like Jell-O, she dragged a towel off the bar and held it up. "Come on out, Joy, and dry off. You can watch a little television while you go to sleep."

"Can we look at the pictures instead?" Joy asked as she wiggled like a seal over the edge of the tub, bringing Barbie and Mermaid with her. With easy practice, Sam grabbed her water-slick body to keep her from tumbling onto the floor and set her on her feet. She wrapped the towel around Joy and began to dry her off. Sam held her close for a moment, until her muscles stopped jerking with reaction from the fright.

"Yeah, we can look at the pictures." She swallowed against the dryness of her throat. "It's good Grandma El taught you to hold your breath under water, but when you want to practice again, why don't you call for Mommy so I can watch while you do it, okay?"

"'Kay." Her wet hair dripped onto Sam's shirt as Joy cuddled against her. "I miss Grandma El."

Tears clouded Sam's eyes and she held her close. "I do too, baby." Survival mode had left little time for either of them to grieve for the woman who had saved them and loved them so well.

She rubbed the towel over Joy's hair, drying it. It stood up in fine white-blonde tufts like cotton candy. "It's time to get your jammers on. Then we'll look at the book."

"'Kay." Joy ran naked from the bathroom down the hall to her room.

Sam shook her head. One more thing to work on, bringing her clothes to the bathroom before she got into the tub. She got to her feet and cleaned up the splattered water, rinsed out the tub, and dried Barbie and Mermaid. By the time she'd finished, Joy stood in the hall in her pajamas with the photo album.

Sam guided her into her bedroom and held the book for her while she climbed up on the bed. Sam combed the tangles from her hair, laid the comb on the nightstand, and piled the pillows against the headboard. Getting into bed with Joy, she cuddled her close against her side and they opened the book.

The pictures were a comfort and a torment. One minute, when loneliness wrapped around her like a straitjacket, she wanted to weep for what they had lost, and the next minute laugh at the funny and tender memories.

Joy had a never-ending supply of questions about the people in the photos, though she'd heard it all before. Twenty minutes later she nodded off and Sam closed the album, eased out from under Joy's weight, repositioned her daughter's head on one of the pillows, and pulled the covers up over her shoulder.

Sam stood by the bed for a moment, watching her sleep. She saw changes in her every day. Her chubby baby cheeks had taken on the slimmer curve of childhood, her stubby legs had grown longer, and Sam saw more and more of herself mirrored in Joy every day. She needed to take some pictures to add to the album. Darn it, there was always more and more to do, and only Sam to do it.

She turned out the light and left the room. She had to finish an essay before Tim came over. She settled her computer at the kitchen table and attempted to focus on the assignment. When the phone rang, she rubbed her eyes, glad for the interruption.

"Hey, I'm on my way over."

Just the sound of his voice set off jittery, sensual-exciting feelings low in her belly. Like she was already primed for something to happen. She wanted him. Just thinking it made it hard for her to catch her breath.

"All right. I'll be waiting." Everything she was feeling was projected in the tone of her voice. Heat raced into her cheeks and she bit her lip as she hung up. Had she sounded as provocative to him as it sounded to her?

She had never known how to flirt or be seductive. She'd spent too much time trying not to draw Will's attention.

She had no time to worry about it further because the soft knock at the door alerted her to his arrival. She glanced out the window, saw it was him, and twisted the dead bolt free.

He brought with him the smell of night air tinged with the desert honeysuckle that bloomed alongside the porch, and him. A clean male scent totally his own. His blue eyes searched her face before he shut the door behind him. He stepped close. Her breath hitched and her heart raced. She wanted to feel the texture of his beard beneath her hands, the texture of his skin. Her mouth grew dry with need and she swallowed. When he bent his head, her arms twined around his neck and her lips parted to drink in the touch and taste of his kiss.

Tim's arms wrapped around her, holding her tight. His tongue tasted the parting of her lips, seeking and finding hers with a hunger that melted away her uncertainty. The kiss went on and on. She pressed herself as close as she could get, and at the feel of his arousal, rose on tiptoe to align her hips to his. She lost herself in the sweet fierceness of his embrace until, breathless, she broke the kiss and turned her face into his shoulder. Had she ever felt this way before? As though every bone and muscle might dissolve with need?

Tim drew in a ragged breath, and his hand ran in restless circles up and down her back, molding her closer.

She drew back and looked up at him, then cupped his face and ran her fingers over his jaw. His beard lay in dark bristles against his skin, wiry but smooth, outlining the lips that had just left hers. He kissed her again, his tenderness and care overwhelming her.

"We'll take it slow," he said as his lips brushed her cheek, her jaw, and the sensitive skin beneath her ear. "I'm not in any rush."

"You're such a gift to me," she murmured. "Every day you give me more and I want—I don't know how much I can give you back."

"This is more than enough, Sam."

His tone brought tears to her eyes. She ran her hand down the back of his head, smoothing his hair and holding him close. "How can it be, Tim?"

He drew back to look down at her. "I've been wandering, rootless for months, putting one foot in front of the other, just surviving. When I look at you…" He shook his head and his throat worked as he swallowed. "When you opened your arms to me just now, I finally felt like I'd found my way home."

How had she missed seeing his loneliness? Tears rolled down her face in a rush.

"I know you're not ready for anything heavy. But I need to—I'll be satisfied living on the periphery of what you have, until we figure out if this is right."

Her heart ached. He felt he couldn't expect more because she had allowed fear to build a wall between her and the rest of the world. How could she continue to allow herself to be that way with him? She tugged him toward the couch and he followed. When he sat down, she slid into his lap, drew his lips to hers, and tasted the saltiness of tears. She drew back to wipe her face with the hem of her t-shirt.

"Don't cry, Sam."

"I'm not…anymore." She nestled close to him and laid her head atop his shoulder. He continued to run his hands up and down her back, the pressure both soothing and sensual. Her breath hitched, then grew unsteady. She wanted more.

She traced the shape of his jaw with her fingertips. "Can we just touch one another for a while?" she asked.

Tim's laugh sounded choked. "Honey, we can do whatever you want." He wasted no time sliding his hands beneath her shirt and continuing his slow caresses up her spine and cross the flat plane of her shoulder blades.

Sam waited for the feelings of panic to start, and when they didn't, leaned back to smile at him. She removed his glasses and folded them closed. "Can you see me without these?"

"I can see you just fine."

His husky tone, as much as his touch, loosened the small knot of anxiety that lay coiled and ready to spring.

She set the glasses on the back of the couch. His eyes, so pale a blue, seemed more vibrant in color without the barrier of the glasses. She traced his brows, then his cheekbones, learning the structure of his face. When she cupped his jaw, and kissed him again, he groaned his encouragement. The eager way his lips and tongue responded to hers triggered a sweet tingle between her legs. She loved the way his beard felt against her face.

His hands continued to move under her t-shirt, sliding down her sides and up over her ribs. His fingers released the catch on her bra and he cupped her breast. She leaned into his touch with a feeling of relief, the nipple beading beneath the careful pressure of his fingers and intensifying the tingle to an empty ache that begged to be filled.

When Tim withdrew his hands from beneath her shirt a few minutes later, she caught back a murmur of protest. His arms tightened around her holding her close. The ragged, uneven sound of his breathing mirrored her own. She held him in return and messaged the back of his neck, finding his skin hot to the touch. He drew back to look up at her, his cheeks still flushed, and smiled. "I thought we'd better save some things for another time."

She'd been so lost in her own response, she hadn't thought how difficult he might find it to temper his own. On the one hand it was wonderful she hadn't felt a moment of fear or anxiety—a miracle, in fact. But on the other, he had to control his every move to make sure she didn't.

"Okay."

A wave of color lit his cheeks, and she smiled.

She knew what her sixth step was going to be. And it definitely included Tim Carnes.

CHAPTER 28

James concentrated on the traffic in front of him, only glancing toward Marsha for brief seconds at a time. "It isn't going to kill you to get out of the house for a couple of hours and relax. Jane Wyatt, the woman I hired to sit, was recommended by Trish Marks. She babysits with almost all the other team members' children. Alex is in good hands, and I'll be on call while you're away from him."

"I just look such a mess. Why didn't you tell me this morning we were going somewhere?"

"You look fine." She didn't. Her shoulder-length hair was pulled back in a sloppy ponytail, and beneath her eyes dark circles penetrated the light makeup she'd put on.

Marsha's hand shook as she brushed her hand over her hair. "Where are we going?"

James shot her a smile in the hope of reassuring her. "It's a surprise."

She plucked at a crease in her linen pants. "How long do you think we'll be gone?"

James covered her hand with his own to still her nervous movements. "It doesn't matter. I have everything covered. I just want you to relax and enjoy the day."

He wove through the downtown traffic, turned onto fifth street, and pulled into a parking space in front of the salon she usually frequented. "I called and made you an appointment with your usual stylist, Kathy, for a trim, highlights, a manicure, and a pedicure. The works. It's all paid for."

"All that will take more than a few hours," she protested.

James put the car into park and leaned across the divider between their seats. "Marsha, when you worked non-stop at your job as a CPA, you took a day off now and then to relax and recharge. Just because you're a full-time mom doesn't mean you're not allowed to take one off now."

Her struggle was visible. She didn't want to disappoint him, but she was still concerned about Alex.

"You promise you'll check on him?"

From the anxiety underlining her expression, he knew he'd done the right thing. "I'll call every hour on the hour, and Jane has my number programmed into her phone. Alex is going to be fine without you for a few hours."

"It will be more than a couple of hours," she warned again.

"You can call me when you're done and I'll pick you up."

She drew a deep breath and raised a hand to touch his cheek. "Okay."

James leaned forward and pressed a kiss to her lips. "Just relax and have a good time. Okay?"

She smiled. "Obviously you've never been inside a beauty salon, James. It's not about having a good time." She gathered her purse.

"Maybe it will be this time."

He waited in the car until she'd disappeared inside the shop before pulling away. He had plenty to do before she was through.

An electronic tone sounded as Marsha entered the shop and the familiar scents of hair spray, shampoo, chemicals and perfume enveloped her.

Kathy, her stylist, stood at the desk and sauntered toward her with a smile. "Marsha, it's so good to see you. It's been a few months." She gave her a brief hug. "Come straight back. I've been waiting for you."

"Your sweet husband called and said you needed a day off and your hair done." Kathy spoke over her shoulder as she led the way. "He's even sent over some goodies for you to snack on while we work on you."

Sweet husband? She'd never heard James described as sweet before. Strong, steady, controlled, passionate, but never sweet. But recently he'd been...different. And that he'd surprised her with a trip to the salon was a first. "Goodies?" Marsha asked.

Kathy's well-rounded hips rolled as she ambled to her station. "Have a seat." She patted the back of the adjustable chair. "I thought we'd do your facial before we do your highlights, trim and styling."

Marsha wiggled back into the seat. Kathy whipped out a cape and fastened it around her neck, covering her from nape to knee. Marsha studied herself beneath the harsh florescent lights. She looked washed out and exhausted. A hag. No wonder James had taken things into his own hands. And no wonder she hadn't had the energy to argue with him. She touched her sunken cheek. When had she developed such hollows beneath her cheekbones?

Kathy folded back the aluminum foil on a metal tray. "Your hubby sent you a tray of strawberries dipped in chocolate and a bottle of champagne." Using tongs, she lifted three of the huge berries onto a plate and handed them to Marsha. "You can drink a glass before we get to work."

Marsha's lips puckered in an oh of surprise. James had never gone in for romantic gestures, though he was always generous with money and what little time he had free. "It's barely past lunch," Marsha protested.

"It's five o'clock somewhere, honey. And you look like you could use a sip or two to relax." Kathy wrapped the bottle in a hand towel, removed the foil from the top, and untwisted the wire. She popped the cork, poured some of the pale blond beverage into a wine glass, and handed it to Marsha.

"Will you join me?" Marsha asked. "I'll feel much too spoiled eating and drinking in front of you."

Kathy laughed. "I'll wait until I've got your highlights and trim done first. You wouldn't want me to get tipsy while I'm doing your hair. But afterwards we'll celebrate how wonderful you look. How's that?"

"Okay." Marsha nodded, her gaze scanning the other four workstations and the women in various degrees of primping and processing. "What about the other customers?"

"We have wedding parties in here, drinking champagne while we do their hair and makeup. They won't think a thing about your enjoying your strawberries and wine."

"Okay." Marsha nibbled at one of the strawberries while Kathy set out the bottles and bowls she'd need.

Kathy kept up a steady stream of conversation. Marsha found the muscles in her shoulders and back unknotting for the first time in days. Was it Kathy, the champagne or just being away from the house? Was she a bad mother to feel this way? She stared in the mirror at the gaunt image looking back at her. It wasn't Alex that had her twisted up inside like a pretzel, or even James.

She didn't like the woman staring back at her from the mirror. She was a coward, wallowing in self-pity. She had to *do* something.

"Do you have any pictures of your sweet baby and your handsome hubby?"

"How do you know he's handsome?" Marsha asked.

"I haven't seen a man yet that doesn't look good in uniform. And I could tell he was military from the no-nonsense way he spoke on the phone."

Marsha laughed. "He does have a tendency to speak as though he's fulfilling an objective."

"Well as long as he doesn't do that at home."

Marsha thought of how he'd held Alex this morning and spoken to him. And how Alex had cooed and squealed back at him. "No, he doesn't speak that way to me or Alex."

She tugged her purse onto her lap and rummaged for her billfold. She flipped it open to a snapshot she'd taken at a barbecue. One of her favorite pictures of James. The next one was one she'd taken of James and Alex together, asleep on the couch, the baby cuddled atop his chest.

"OMG he's McDreamy, only better looking."

Marsha laughed. "I'll tell him you said that, but he won't know who you're talking about. He doesn't watch much television."

"I bet that little fellow has him wrapped around his little finger," Kathy said, studying the picture of James and Alex. She didn't say anything about Alex's wide-spaced eyes or large head.

"Yeah, he does. James has such patience with him."

"You have two handsome guys there." Kathy returned the pictures to her.

"Thank you." Having Kathy comment on James's looks had her pausing to look at the picture again. He was a handsome man. His hair and eyes contrasted dramatically. His olive skin tanned well. Why did it take a total stranger calling attention to those things for her to acknowledge them? Was she still holding on to the resentment and hurt of months ago? Was she holding him responsible for what had happened at the house?

"Ready to get started?" Kathy asked, drawing her back to the present.

She handed her the plate and wine glass as she glanced around the shop. He was trying so hard. Doing everything he could to be supportive. And she was still holding onto the past. She looked up at Kathy and nodded. "I'm ready."

Three hours later she shared a last glass of wine with Kathy and took a seat in the reception area to wait for James. This had been exactly what she needed. She felt and looked more herself than she had in months. Kathy brought in the remainder of the strawberries after the other girls had gotten one or two each. "You and your hubby need to finish these off tonight, once the baby's asleep." Kathy said with a wink.

"Thank you, Kathy."

"Thank your husband. He wanted to be sure you were taken care of. What was the occasion? Your anniversary?"

Marsha shook her head. "I've been going through a rough patch. James is trying to make sure I know how much he loves me."

Kathy's eyes glazed with tears. "How sweet."

He was trying new things. While she was sitting on her ass, not attempting anything. Her guilt about Alex's birth seemed as crippling as her depression. *Do something, Marsha.* "I'll make sure he knows how much I appreciate him," she said more to herself than Kathy.

James shoved the large bag of take-out behind the driver's seat. He'd gotten all of Marsha's favorites. Traffic was heavy, and he was anxious to get there to pick her up. He swore beneath his breath as he came to a halt at yet another light. At last reaching the salon, he had to park a block down the street. He locked the car and jogged up the sidewalk to the shop.

Marsha waited in the reception area and set aside the magazine she was reading when he entered. Her features no longer looked pinched, or stressed. Her hair, cut in a wispy bob, brushed her shoulders, and framed her face, softening the angles of her cheekbones and disguising her weight loss. Her makeup was more dramatic than when he'd delivered her to her appointment. It reminded him of when they'd first met at a party ten years before, just after his first deployment to Iraq. She smiled. He realized he was staring.

"Do you like the cut?"

"Yes. You look great." He bent his head to kiss her.

She rose to gather a large two-handled bag and her purse.

"Do you want me to take that?" he asked.

Four women appeared in the doorway.

"James, these are the ladies who work here. Saundra, Isabelle, Kathy and Denise."

He moved forward to shake each one's hand. "It's nice to meet you, ladies." He offered Kathy a nod, a plump woman of about thirty with an engaging smile. "Marsha looks great."

She grinned. "Thanks."

He turned aside to take the bag from Marsha and caught her smile at something going on behind him. He glanced over his shoulder but all four of the women just smiled. He and Marsha said their good-byes, left the shop, and walked down the street to the car. "What was going on back there?" he asked.

"One of the girls was fanning her face which is the universal signal for you're hot."

James laughed, then shook his head. "I have take-out from the Chinese restaurant you like."

"That sounds good."

She opened the back door for him and he set the bag on the back floorboard.

"The strawberries were wonderful. I shared them with all the ladies in the shop and there were still some left."

"Good. I'm glad you enjoyed them." He opened her door and she tossed her purse on the seat, but didn't get in.

She rested her hand on his chest. "Thank you for spoiling me today." She rose on tip-toe to press a kiss to his lips.

James slipped an arm around her waist and drew her close. "I don't suppose I've done enough of it lately, or ever. With all the shit you've had to put up with because of my career, I should have been on top of things more."

"I should have too, James." She smoothed his shirt collar. "I was so obsessed with having a baby." She leaned into him. "I know there were times I treated you like a sperm donor instead of a husband."

He laughed. "That wasn't all bad, honey." With her body resting against his, he couldn't hide his instant reaction, as he grew hard. Even after ten years, he still wanted her more than any other woman he'd ever met. He brushed her forehead with his lips. "Our boy is waiting for us. I bet he's missed you today." He released her.

She stepped back and slipped into the car. "I've missed him, too, but it felt good being out with adults today."

James got behind the wheel and fastened his seatbelt. "We need to plan some days for ourselves."

"Like a date night each week?" she asked.

"That would be good." They could have an out-of-town date in Vegas next week. He reached for her hand and held it. He'd have to plant the seed later tonight and see what happened.

"When was the last time you called to check on Alex?" she asked.

"A few minutes ago. I told Jane we'd be home in little over an hour. He seemed to do okay today. He wasn't crying or anything." *Thank God.*

She offered him a smile and continued to hold his hand in both of hers. She hadn't done that in a long time.

Thirty minutes later James pulled into the driveway and hit the garage door opener. He glanced at Marsha and tried to read her reaction when he pulled past the sitter's car into the garage.

She sat up straighter, a frown on her face, her eyes roaming the space. "You've cleaned out the garage."

He'd called three buddies a few nights before and explained what he wanted to do, and they'd pitched in to help. Two had gone to pick up the materials he'd bought for the quick renovation project. By the time he'd returned from dropping her at the beauty shop, they'd already begun to dismantle the shelving units running the length of the wall facing the cars. They'd put in two by four studs to frame in a closet, slapped up white paneling with molding at the top and rubberized baseboards at the bottom, and then reassembled the shelving units inside the closet. He still had to run the wiring for a couple of lights and paint the louvered doors, but the garage looked more finished.

Best of all, it no longer resembled the space where she'd been accosted by Tabarek Moussa.

James turned off the car and pushed the button to close the garage doors behind them.

"How did you do all this in four hours?"

"Chiefs Caldwell and Reynolds and Jack Taylor came over, and we just got it done. I have to do some finish work, but it squared away the space."

She remained silent for a moment. "It looks really good."

"Thanks." He released his seat belt. "I'm starving, let's go check on Alex and eat dinner."

She laid a hand on his arm and he turned. "You were right here to monitor Alex the whole time."

"Well, it was his first time being left with a sitter, and I thought just in case he wasn't happy, it wouldn't hurt to stay close. I was too busy to look after him."

Her reluctance to go into the garage had been obvious. And when she did, she rushed to her car and locked herself in as though someone were pursuing her. This was their home, at least until it sold. She couldn't continue to live here if every space carried the memory of a threat. He'd changed the space so it looked different so perhaps it would disrupt the memories.

Marsha didn't say anything, but for the first time she looked around instead of rushing to the kitchen door as though Tabarek Moussa were after her.

When they entered the kitchen and Alex saw them, his face lit up with a gummy smile, his mouth wide. He completely ignored the bubble of strained peas that ran down his chin.

Jane Wyatt, the plump, matronly woman James had hired to babysit, laughed and wiped his face before the food could reach his bib. "He's missed you, but he's been a good boy," she said.

Alex kicked his legs and reached for Marsha, and he hummed his signal for momma, drawing a laugh from her.

"I'll finish feeding him after he's calmed down," she said. She lifted him free of his highchair and cuddled him close. He reached for her hair and she caught his pea-stained fist before he could rub green into it. Jane stepped forward to wipe his hand.

The two women talked about Alex, his pleasure in the baby swing out back, and his slight case of diaper rash, while James unpacked the take-out boxes.

"Would you like to stay for dinner, Mrs. Wyatt?" he asked.

"Thank you for asking, but no. My husband and I are going out for a meal and a movie."

James reached for his wallet, extracted money from it and handed it to her.

"If ever you and your crew decide to take your construction skills on the road, I'll be happy to spread the word. I've never seen anything come together as quickly as your garage."

James smiled. They'd accomplished what they set out to do in record time. He owed the guys. "I had a good crew. Thank you for sitting for us."

"You're welcome. Call me any time." She said good night to them, rested a hand against Alex's cheek in farewell and let herself out.

Marsha slipped her arm around James's waist, and he automatically put his arms around her and Alex.

"Thank you for today, James."

He swallowed against the sudden knot in his throat. He wanted his wife back, his marriage. But he couldn't do it alone. "You're welcome."

She pressed in against him, laying her head in the bowl of his shoulder. "I know I haven't been at my best for the last several months. But I'm going to try and do better."

Though he tried not to read too much into her words, hope lifted the feeling of pressure that lay on his chest. He rested his lips against her forehead. "I love you."

"I don't think I could bear it if you didn't," she said.

His heart skipped a beat and his arms tightened around her. "You're my anchor. It's you I think of, hold on to, when I'm facing things I don't want to have to face. I want to be the same for you, Marsha."

She drew back to look up at him. "For a man who has never talked much about his feelings, you've grown damn eloquent."

At her smile, the panicked beat of his heart settled to a slower rhythm. "The saying, 'you can't teach an old seadog new tricks' doesn't apply to SEALs," he replied.

CHAPTER 29

Sam fought against the rising panic. Twenty-five thousand dollars! "But I don't have a credit card in my name. My ex-husband had them all in his."

The loan officer, Mr. Taylor, a slightly built man of about forty with wire-rimmed glasses and thinning hair, stared at his computer screen. "The card was taken out in your name on March of this year. And thus far has a balance due of twenty-five thousand, four hundred dollars and twenty-seven cents."

Her face felt numb and her breathing was unsteady. "Someone's stolen my identity. I don't have the credit card and don't know anything about it."

"Well, that could certainly be the case." He leaned back in his chair. "As long as the minimum payment is made it won't reflect on your credit history."

"Minimum payment! What minimum payment? Are you crazy? I didn't take out the card and I'm not paying for it. I need you to print whatever information you have on that screen and I'm going to the police station to file a report."

Mr. Taylor cheeks grew flushed. "There's no need to yell at me, Mrs. Cross."

Sam was too busy fighting off a wave of nausea to apologize. Twenty-five thousand dollars. She couldn't wrap her mind around it. What if they made her pay for it?

"There's still the problem of the refinancing of your home. Despite your low credit score, we'd be happy to cover that for you. The property value outweighs the twenty-one thousand you owe on it. But since we've held the mortgage for two months. You will owe back payments of twenty-five hundred dollars."

Twenty-five hundred dollars? It might as well be the twenty-five thousand.

"That would be for a loan of twenty-four months plus closing costs, and we will include your insurance on the property for another two hundred dollars a month. That's a requirement for us to carry the mortgage. Your monthly payments would be twelve hundred dollars a month."

Oh God! She could make maybe half that and still feed Joy. Sam breathed in quick gulps of air to try and stem the dizziness and calm herself. She had to think. Just think. This was no time for her PTSD to kick in. She had to stall until she was calm. She had to think clearly to deal with this. "May I use your restroom?"

Taylor frowned at her sudden change of subject. "Certainly. It's just down the hall to the left."

Grabbing her backpack, Sam rose, though her legs shook so much she could hardly stand. She concentrated on placing one foot in front of the other until she reached a metal door with a *women* tag on it. She locked herself inside, lowered the lid to the toilet, and sat down. The need to cry nearly overwhelmed her, but she pushed it back, and for a few minutes rocked back and forth in an attempt to calm herself. She rifled through the pack until she found her phone. She dialed Tim's number.

"Hey, Sam."

Just the sound of his voice eased some of her anxiety, though tears threatened again. She propped her elbow on her knee and rested her head in her hand. "Hey. Is everything okay there?"

"Yeah. We're good. Joy and I decided we'd do nuggets for dinner. Homemade. We searched for a recipe and it seems pretty straightforward. We'll have dinner ready by the time you get home."

God, he was so good for her and for Joy. "That sounds good." She swallowed hard. "Thank you for picking her up."

"You're welcome."

She drew a deep breath. "I'll be home in just a little while."

"Take your time. We're good."

"Okay. I—" *love you.* She caught the words back and with it her breath. *I love you.* She closed her eyes and captured that moment when he'd said, 'when you opened your arms to me, I finally knew I was home.' *I love you.* "I shouldn't be long," she said instead.

"Uh—we have a small flour issue developing. Gotta go."

She shut the phone and tucked it back in her backpack. Had it been Will on the other end of the phone, she'd have to race home for fear of him hurting Joy. Tim would never raise a hand to hurt either of them. That certainty tamped down her anxiety another notch.

Twenty-five thousand dollars. Dear God.

She had to put the credit card out of her mind and deal with the loan issue first. It involved their home. And no one was going to take it from them. She rose, went to the sink and washed her hands, then dried them. She studied her features in the mirror. "You have to be strong. Stand your ground. This guy is trying to rip you off. You want to be a lawyer one day, you're going to have to grow some balls."

She opened the door and walked back down the hall to Taylor's office. She slowed when she heard the murmur of his voice.

Seeing her in the doorway, he hung up the phone and rose to his feet.

Afraid her nerve might desert her, Sam spoke in a rush, "My grandmother had a thirty-year loan and had almost paid off the house. I don't think twenty-four months to pay off the twenty-one thousand still owed on the property is a reasonable expectation, Mr. Taylor."

"It's a small amount, and we're not going to make that much interest off of it. We want it off our books as quickly as possible."

Small to them. Sam stepped further into the room. "And I have to say this sounds as though you're purposely trying to set up something to ensure I lose my house. I seem to remember there are laws against unfair loan practices. I'd rather take care of this myself without having to call my lawyer into it."

His cheeks took on a ruddy color. "You can't expect to have the same terms on the loan as your grandmother. She had a history of making payments every month."

"Which I've continued since her death. I have the receipts to prove it."

"Once your grandmother signed the house over to you, Mrs. Cross, it's a requirement that you refinance, because the house is in your name, not hers."

"I understand that, but you're purposely setting me up to fail in paying back the loan." He was looking at her two hundred fifty thousand-dollar property as easy pickings and was trying to raise the payments to a level she couldn't manage. Anger shoved the rest of her anxiety aside. "With the equity in the property, I believe I can go elsewhere and get a loan at a reasonable rate and pay you off."

Taylor's gaze sharpened. "Your certainly within your right, Mrs. Cross, but time is passing and we're holding the mortgage."

Her anxiety level spiked again. "As for my being two months behind, I just received notification from the bank about this right after I made a payment to you. I have the dated payment receipt. And I have the letter you sent me two weeks ago asking me to come in and deal with this issue. I called at that time and set up this appointment. I have an email confirmation." She set her backpack down on the chair she'd vacated minutes before and unzipped it, intent on retrieving the documents. "I don't believe I owe you anything, since I haven't signed a contract with you, plus I've come here in a timely manner to address this, and my payments are up to date."

"You don't have to show me the letters, Mrs. Cross." Taylor smiled, his expression more a grimace as the color in his cheeks grew even darker. "While you were in the restroom, I notice a typo in our information. You're correct about the time issue. I'm sorry I got ahead of myself and didn't double-check my information." He fell silent a moment, clasping and unclasping his hands on the desk. "I think we'll be able to accommodate a longer mortgage than the two years."

Sam studied his expression. Why was he caving so easily? Was it the threat of a lawyer getting involved?

"What would you say to five years?" he asked.

Nervous tension brought her heartbeat up a notch. "Five years is little more than a car loan, Mr. Taylor. There's certainly more equity in a house than a car, and it doesn't depreciate like a vehicle. If I'm required to pay two hundred a month in insurance, I'd like a ten-year loan. And if I can pay it off earlier I will."

"Seven years," he countered. He sat down in his desk chair.

Still wary, she eased down on the edge of the straight-backed chair. Did she really want to deal with this shyster? But the bank held the mortgage, and she had no credit history other than the twenty-five thousand dollars *she hadn't spent.* "What would the payments be including insurance and closing costs?"

After nearly an hour of haggling, they settled on seven and a half year loan with fixed interest.

"I'll have my secretary type up the agreement and you can come in on Friday to sign the paperwork."

"I'd like my lawyer to look it over before I sign it. Can you fax or email him a copy of the document when it's ready?" she asked.

"Certainly. Just write down his email address or phone number." He slid a pad over to her. Sam retrieved her billfold, removed a business card and copied down the number and email address.

With a relieved sigh, she rose and gathered her things. She was nearly an hour late, but she felt she'd held her own and achieved something she could live with.

"When you looked at my credit history, were you able to see anything about the credit card that was taken out in my name?"

"No." He shook his head. "Just the balance and that it is a major credit card." He reached for the mouse, typed in a command and pulled up an image on the screen. He printed it and handed her the paper.

The address for the card was a post office box. "I'll file a police report tomorrow. Thank you for printing this off for me."

"You're welcome. I'll see you on Friday."

She said goodbye. Once outside in the car, she gave free rein to the nervous trembling she'd barely managed to suppress throughout the ordeal. She rested her forehead against the steering wheel and took deep, cleansing breaths until she felt steadier. A sense of victory and excitement began to build inside her. She'd dealt with this herself and she'd come out on top. She couldn't wait to get home and spend the rest of the evening celebrating with Tim and Joy.

Twenty-five minutes later she swung into the driveway, parked the car, and shoved open the door. High-pitched squeals came from behind the house. A muggy heat hung in the air, though the sun was setting. The light-weight jacket she wore felt too heavy after only a few moments. Carrying her backpack over her shoulder, she wandered around the corner of the house to the gate.

Joy dodged out from behind the gas grill, her hair and clothes wet, the nozzle on the end of the hose in her hand. "Mommy!"

Water struck Sam in the face.

She jerked her head aside and threw up a hand to shield herself from it. The stream stopped and she wiped her face to clear her eyes to find Tim holding the water hose down with one hand while gripping a water gun in the other.

He and Joy wore identical looks of shock, as water streamed down her face and her hair dripped. She laughed, shucked her pack and jacket, hooked them on the fence, then opened the gate.

"Give me that," she said snatching the nozzle from Joy. She turned the hose on Tim and shot him in the chest.

Joy squealed behind her as they chased him around the yard. He was fast and wily, getting in shots with the water pistol she wouldn't have believed possible. He must have been an amazing marksman in the military.

When they were all soaked, she dropped the nozzle in surrender.

She was breathing hard from all the exertion, as was Joy.

"I'm out of ammunition," he complained as he sauntered toward them, shoving the water gun in the pocket of his shorts as though it were a holster. The wet t-shirt clung to his chest, showing dark swirls of the hair and the muscles beneath.

Her mouth grew dry with need and she slipped an arm around his waist, leaned in close against him, and brushed away the water running off his chin.

He slipped an arm around her in immediate response and smiled.

"How come they never have wet t-shirt contests for guys?" she asked. "You'd win." She rose on tiptoe to press her lips to his.

Joy giggled and they both turned to find her watching them.

"How did your meeting go?" he asked.

"Good. I have to go back on Friday and sign the paperwork." She gave his waist a squeeze. "I know I'm late. Have you two eaten?"

"I went ahead and fed Joy, but I wanted to wait for you."

What had she done to deserve him?

"I'll go dry off and change, then come back over. We sort of made a mess in the kitchen."

"The flour mishap?" she asked with a smile.

"Yeah. I didn't realize how much help a five-year-old could be. I'll pitch in with the cleanup."

Sam laughed.

He dipped his head and kissed her again.

"I'll get Joy ready for bed so we can relax while we eat." She released him with such obvious reluctance, he smiled.

She followed him to the fence and he handed her backpack and jacket to her.

"I'll be right back," he promised.

The words 'I love you' clung to the tip of her tongue. She wanted to say them. But how would he feel about hearing them?

Instead, she went into the house with Joy. She groaned when she caught a glimpse of herself in her dresser mirror. Her hair lay plastered to her head, and her eye makeup was smeared. Her blouse, still damp, lay against her breasts like a second layer of skin, her nipples pushing against the fabric. Her face flushed hot. To his credit, he'd looked her in the eye the whole time they'd talked, but he'd probably seen plenty during their water fight. What had she been thinking?

She'd been on a high after conquering a major problem standing in the way of her and Joy's security. On her own! Despite the lingering disquiet about the credit card issue, she was still flying.

Sam washed her face and changed into jeans and a t-shirt while Joy put on her pajamas. She was drying her hair with a towel as she opened the door to Tim. All he had to do was look at her and every nerve came alive just waiting for him to touch her. How had this happened? How had she fallen in love with him? She'd believed she'd never want to be alone in a room with a man…ever again.

Yet, now she wanted to make love with Tim, more than she'd ever wanted anything in her life.

CHAPTER 30

The chicken was dry, the peas a little overcooked, but the salad and bread were okay. And none of that mattered a damn to Flash as he sat across the table from Sam and wished they could be in the bedroom, alone, getting busy.

The message he'd just read on his computer from Captain Jackson had set off his inner alarm. He was running out of time. He was trusting his commanding officer to do right by him, but if he contacted NCIS, they'd sure as fuck pick him up. The thought of leaving Sam, leaving Joy, was like a kick in the gut.

For the first time in his life he'd found something he wanted as much as getting back to his team. Maybe more.

From the moment Sam had sprayed him in the chest with the water hose, he'd been hard. The condom he'd slipped into his shorts pocket was burning a hole through the fabric against his hip. He hoped to use that condom tonight…if it was the right thing for Sam.

He couldn't push her, not after everything she'd been through. But Jesus—he wanted to. He'd even settle for another petting session.

"I'm going to check on Joy. She's gone quiet. That usually means she's either fallen asleep or she's up to something," Sam said as she rose from the table.

She peeked around the edge of the divider between the kitchen and living room. A smile lingered on her lips as she returned to her seat. "She's nearly down for the count. She actually squealed like a normal kid today. She loved helping you cook."

"I'm not sure how successful that was," he said holding up a small piece of chicken on the end of his fork. "I think we might use these for slingshot ammunition."

Sam grinned "Shhhh…" she pressed her finger to her lips.

His eyes fastened on her mouth and he tried not to fantasize where it might linger on his body. He'd dreamed about that more than once.

"Don't let Joy hear you say that. She thinks they're the greatest nuggets ever."

Flash chuckled. "What we both lacked in cooking expertise, she made up in enthusiasm. She was so covered in flour and other stuff, I thought a water fight might be the only way to get her clean. The shirt she had on may never be the same."

Sam laughed. "It'll be fine. Are you finished?" she asked. At his nod stood and took their plates to the sink. She returned with a bowl and two teaspoons. "Why don't you serve us up a couple of scoops of ice cream for dessert and I'll put her to bed. There's mint chocolate chip."

He wasn't hungry for ice cream. He was hungry for her. But to please her, he dug a couple of scoops of ice cream out of the carton. When she padded back into the room barefoot, he shut the container and shoved it back into the freezer.

"Do you want this?" Sam asked, touching the bowl.

He shook his head.

No. He wanted her more than he wanted his next breath of air.

She grasped his hand, led him through the living room and down the hall to her bedroom.

Flash's heartbeat tripped into overdrive and his breathing became uneven.

When she closed the door and locked it, he smiled. "Does this mean you have designs on my body?" he asked.

Sam laughed. Then stifled the sound with her hand. She leaned back against the door and ran her eyes from his face, down over his chest then paused at the obvious bulge pushing against the zipper of his cargo shorts, a bulge that grew as her attention remained directed there. For a moment concern kicked in to dim his desire. He had to let her maintain control of what happened. Once they got this first time behind them, it would be easier for them both.

When her gray-green gaze rose to his face again, and she smiled, he nearly sighed aloud in relief.

"I think about your hands touching me, all the time," she said, pushing away from the door. "I never thought I'd experience that." She moved to the nightstand, opened the top drawer and set a box of condoms within easy reach.

She approached him, the newfound confidence in her long, slow stride sexy as hell. He swallowed, and moistened his lips. He withdrew the condom from his pocket. "I brought my own, just in case." He tucked it in her hand and sat down on the bed to draw her between his legs.

"Only one?" she asked.

He chuckled, delighted by her humor. "I didn't want to assume too much."

Her eyes swept over his face, the look in their depths causing his breath to hitch. She ran her hands across his shoulders. Flash buried his face between her breasts and breathed in her sweet honeysuckle scent. He looked up and she reached for his glasses and set them on the dresser, then tugged at his shirt. He eagerly shed the t-shirt, kicked free of his deck shoes and slid back up on the bed.

God, he wanted to be inside her, moving, feeling her surround him. Just the thought nearly took him over the edge.

But he had to let her control how fast they got there.

Sam slipped her shorts off, leaving on her panties, shirt and bra. She crawled onto the bed. Instead of cuddling against his side as he expected, she straddled his hips and leaned down to kiss him, her hair falling like silk against the side of his face. Their tongues tangled, and he drank in her passion as her palms moved over his chest.

He ran his hands beneath her t-shirt, unfastened her bra and found her breasts. In the few weeks since they'd touched one another, he'd relived those moments, remembering the texture of her skin, the velvety softness of her nipples, the slender shape of her.

Though he'd held her, kissed her, and tempted her in every way he could, they hadn't repeated the touching. He lifted the t-shirt and she wiggled free of it and allowed her bra to slide down her arms.

He was hungry for the sight of her. He sat up to trace the delicate line of her collarbone, the hollow between her breasts, with his fingertips, then his lips. He was fascinated by the sweet curve where her breasts and ribcage came together, the way her nipples tilted upward begging him to take them into his mouth.

He tasted one then the other, his tongue feathering the underside of the peak while he sucked. A tremor shook her. Sam ran her hand down the back of his head, and murmured his name, her voice breathy and soft.

God, he loved the sound. Loved that he could put that note in her voice.

She nestled her breasts against his chest, aligned her stomach against his, and scraped his shoulder with her teeth, then sucked. He grew so hard it hurt.

His mouth found hers. He slid his hand over her buttocks and then touched her through her panties, tempting her, taking it slow, though he wanted to rip the garment from her. When she rocked against his touch, he groaned beneath the kiss and slid his fingers beneath the fabric. She was hot and wet, ready in every way, but she trembled.

"We don't have to—" he began, his voice hoarse.

She reached for his zipper.

Thank you, Jesus! He lay back to give her access. As soon as she opened his fly, he dragged his shorts and briefs down below his knees. He couldn't hide or control how much he wanted her. With her gaze resting on his erection, his need grew stronger.

She tore open the condom and rolled it down over him, her touch squeezing the breath from his lungs.

Sam removed her panties, giving him a chance to kick free of the shorts and briefs.

She ran a hand down the center of his chest and followed the thin line of hair that bisected his stomach and led to his sex.

He was so masculine, so powerfully built, and so aroused. He took her breath away.

Her throat grew dry and she swallowed. She wanted him covering her, filling her. But what if she panicked?

Tim turned on his side and guided her close. He brushed her hair off her face and ran the back of his fingers along her cheek and jaw. "I want you, but if it isn't right for you yet, I understand."

"It is. So much more right than I ever expected." It was. He was. She loved this man and felt certain he cared for her. Which was much, much more than she'd ever known in her entire married life. Her body ached with wanting him. "Please you finish what we started?" she asked.

"Ahhh...honey. The whole point is to finish together."

His kisses took on a tender, unhurried quality, despite the unsteadiness of his breathing and the feverish way he molded her against him. He tempted her with his body, then ran a hand between them to tempt her with his fingers. When he turned to cover her body with his own, she ran her hands up his back and clung to him, though sudden dread spread tension throughout her body.

"This is me, Sam. You say the word and we stop."

Looking up into his eyes, though his body was ready to possess hers, she knew he'd sacrifice his needs for hers. The momentary fear eased. She worked her hand between their bodies and guided him inside her.

Carefully, he pushed into her, settling himself so deep, there was no space left between them. The moment seemed more intimate than any she had ever experienced. She wanted him to stay poised above her forever, protective, passionate, wanting her, filling her.

He seemed completely content to do just that. Until he moved.

With his slow, gliding withdrawal, and returning thrust, she caught her breath and rolled her hips in response.

His murmured, "Oh, God, Sam," completely ripped away the rest of her restraint.

She captured his rhythm, a fine mist of sweat coating her skin as every muscle in her body tensed and released. She was hovering on the brink of something more, reaching for it.

His thrusts grew shorter, deeper, more intent, as though he couldn't get close enough. With every movement he hit that sweet spot inside her, driving her mad, promising her more.

Release rolled through her so intense she cried out. With one final thrust, she felt the throbbing pressure of his climax, and was overcome by another gentler aftershock of pleasure strong enough for her hips to jerk and her breath to catch. She buried her face against his bare shoulder, clinging to him until her breathing eased.

He raised his head to look down at her. "Are you okay?"

She smiled. "I'm perfect."

He grinned. "Yeah. You are." He lowered his mouth to hers in a long, slow kiss. "I should have gone slower, but I wanted you so much."

"In case you missed it, I wanted you, too."

"I did get that idea a time or two."

His understatement triggered a laugh.

"I don't want to move, but I need to deal with the condom," he said, his voice husky. He eased out of her, then paused to kiss her. "I'll be right back."

Sam smiled as she watched his muscular behind disappear into the bathroom. A feeling of triumph, of rightness built within her. She'd made love with him. And she'd only had that one moment of uncertainty. And he'd understood.

She tugged down the blankets and slipped beneath them. He appeared in the bathroom doorway and paused to stretch. Her heart nearly turned over as she watched the smooth movement of his muscles, the way they worked together. The balanced, measured way he placed his feet as he strolled back to bed. The blatancy of his male nudity, and his confidence with it.

What would it be like if she could wake up to him every morning?

She folded back the blankets and he slipped in beside her and invited her in close to his side. She rested her head upon his shoulder and bent her thigh across his.

He ran a caressing hand up her thigh. "What happened today?" he asked, his lips finding her temple and lingering there.

She didn't try to pretend she didn't understand what he was asking about. She hadn't shared her financial issues for fear he'd offer her money or something, and he'd already done enough. "I had a meeting at the bank this afternoon to refinance the house. The loan officer was trying to intimidate me into a loan I couldn't possibly make the payments on. And I found out someone had stolen my identity and opened a credit card in my name."

"Jesus!" He turned toward her, a scowl darkening his features.

Sam shook her head. "I'm going to file a police report tomorrow. After I found out about all that, and the twelve hundred dollars a month the loan officer was expecting for a two-year loan, I really needed a moment to calm down." She ran her fingertips over the light swirls of hair on his chest. "So, I slipped into the bathroom and called you."

His expression relaxed and his arm tightened around her drawing her against him again. "You should have told me. I could have come to the bank and sat in on the meeting. I can do intimidating without even opening my mouth."

She smiled at the thought of how Mr. Taylor might have dealt with him. Not very well, she'd bet. "It's important I learn how to stand up for myself. After I spoke to you, I went back into his office and kicked butt." She clenched her fist and pumped it in the air.

Flash laughed. "I'm not surprised. You can slay me with just a look."

She ran her fingertips over his beard-covered jaw. "You have a soft spot for me."

"More than that, honey."

She pushed herself up on one elbow to look down at him.

His eyes had never looked a clearer blue. "There's something I need to tell you."

CHAPTER 31

Why wasn't he nervous or freaked out about this love stuff? He studied Sam's features. The freckles across her nose. How her eyes changed from gray to green with emotion. It felt right to love her. For him. But was it okay for her?

Maybe he should have put more thought into this. But he loved her. And making love with her had been everything he'd needed and wanted. He'd tried to make it as good for her as it had been for him. And holding her close now, feeling her skin against his...they deserved this.

But if something happened to him, and she learned about his background later, the sense of betrayal might destroy her feelings for him. He'd kept so many things from her.

"I promised to tell you what happened to me while I lived on the street. And I need to tell you now, so you'll really know me. Know who you're with." He swallowed. "I should have told you weeks ago, but I never expected...so much." He grasped the hand resting on his chest, raised it to his cheek and brushed his lips against it.

"I know you care about me and Joy. That's enough."

Did she think she deserved so little? He held her gaze while he continued. "I'm a mutt. I never knew my father. My mother couldn't even tell me who he might have been."

"Do you really think that would change how I feel about you?"

"No." He didn't. She was too caring to be shallow. "No. But I'm concerned if anyone finds out about my early years they may try to stir up trouble for you and say I'm not a good influence around Joy."

She hesitated for a moment. "What happened to you occurred years ago, didn't it?"

"Between the ages of seven and fourteen."

"When you picked the wrong guy's pocket?"

"Or the right one, as it turned out."

She tugged the pillow up behind her against the headboard, leaned back against it and pulled the sheet up to cover her breasts. "Tell me, but it won't change the way I feel."

God, she looked so—he was tempted just to forget this stuff and ease his way back inside her. He grew hard again just thinking about it. Bending his leg to hide the tented sheet, he ran his fingers through his short hair and folded his hands beneath his head to keep from reaching for her.

"Social services took me from my mom when I was seven and put me in a facility, an orphanage, for a while, until they found someone to take me in. I was a handful. I'd been forced into things to help supply my mom and her boyfriend with drugs." He looked away. "I'm not going to go into detail. I don't know how I came out of it whole. Or how I avoided getting killed." He shook his head.

"I ran through a few of foster families, and when I was eleven eventually ended up with a couple with two boys. Their oldest was sixteen. Michael, a star athlete. He punched on me some, but not enough to throw up any flags. The other one, Xander, was fourteen and sneaky, did some shoplifting and other stuff. He put the loot he stole in my room and made sure his mom found it, so I'd get the blame."

"I realized pretty quick they wanted to get rid of me. So I tried to keep my head down and do what I could to stay out of their way."

Sam's eyes glazed with tears and Flash sat up to draw her close. "This is just the past. It can't hurt me anymore, and I don't want it to hurt you, either."

She wiped her face with the sheet. "You were just a boy."

"I don't think I was ever a normal kid, Sam. Hanging with drug-addicted adults who couldn't even take responsibility for themselves—" He shook his head. "I'd seen too much. And even back then I had some built-in survival instincts that kicked in when shit happened."

"Just because you survived it doesn't make it right."

Flash ran his index finger down her cheek and kissed her softly. "No, but it was the hand I was dealt. I survived it, got past it and left it behind."

He tangled his fingers with hers and waited until she'd regained her composure before continuing. "The short of it was Xander planted drugs in my room and I ended up in juvenile hall for it."

"But—" He watched the struggle in her face.

"With Janice's testimony about all the shoplifting and no other home available to take me—" He shrugged. 'That's the way it worked sometimes."

Sam ran a caressing hand over his chest.

"About ten months in, Xander slipped up and got arrested for breaking and entering...and drugs. One of the cops who'd arrested him showed up at the school asking questions. He told me Xander had admitted to setting me up on the drug thing and they were going to try and get me out."

"After one of the longest months of my life, they transferred me out and placed me with a family who took in troubled teens. The place was worse than reform school, and I'd had enough of putting up with other people's shit, so I figured being on my own had to be easier. I stayed a week, just to lull them into thinking I was okay with things, then took off.

"From Boston, I made my way to California. I don't know what the hell I thought I was doing. I could have been killed. Had a couple of close calls along the way. Eventually I landed in San Diego. I managed to get a job waiting tables and scored a place to crash with a couple of other guys. Money was tight, and to subsidize my income I picked pockets when I had to."

"Until I picked Travis's pocket and ran up against someone who was a real hardass. He scared the shit out of me. Read me the riot act. Then took me to a restaurant and fed me. I don't know what he saw in me, but after the meal, he stuffed his phone number in my pocket and told me when I was tired of being on the street to give him a call and he'd try and help me."

"I made it another month, then we got kicked out of the apartment. The second night on the street, I got jumped, had the crap kicked out of me and all my stuff stolen. I ended up in the hospital. It took the doctor about two seconds to start talking social services, so I split. I made it about a block from the hospital, then called Travis, and he came and picked me up."

"So he moved you in with his family?"

"Yeah. I was too beat-up to be a threat. It took me a month to heal. During that time 'Nita, his wife, worked her magic on me. She fussed over me, scolded me, and showered me with love, just like she did their own two boys." Flash smiled. "She's really something.

"At first I was wary. I mean…it just seemed too good to be true, and I kept waiting for someone to either pound on me or worse. But it never happened. About three months after I moved in, Travis got orders, and we had a meeting of the minds. He was about to be deployed, and he didn't want to leave with any misunderstandings between us. To prove I was worthy of staying there, I had to enroll in school, and I had to attend every day. Plus I had to work weekends and help out around the house. If anything happened that 'Nita wasn't happy about, he'd be the one to pick up the phone and call social services. In his words 'No matter where the fuck I am.'"

"He sounds like a real teddy bear."

Flash laughed.

He couldn't tell her about forging a computerized transcript and a shot record so he could enroll. The very last criminal thing he'd done until recently. And now he'd broken several laws—bugging an FBI agent's apartment, monitoring his calls, following his financials, creating a false identity. Jesus. That alone was enough to get him sent to jail.

The stuff he was sharing now was nothing in comparison. What would happen if he got arrested?

His arm tightened around her, and for a moment he just breathed in the scent of her shampoo and held on until the worry eased. He couldn't think about losing her when they were just discovering one another.

"Travis went into the school before he left and talked to the teachers. They put me into an accelerated program and worked my ass off to get me caught up."

"How long was he gone?"

"Seven months. And I toed the line the whole time. I loved 'Nita, and she had the two younger kids to deal with. Josh and Javier. I may have been a little shit at times, but I wasn't a fool. I knew I'd found a good thing. That and the fact Travis had some of his buddies checking up on me on a regular basis."

"So he's Navy too?" she asked.

"Retired now."

"He's your business partner, isn't he?"

"Yeah he is." She was a quick study.

"Am I going to meet him and his wife?" she asked.

He smiled and gave her a squeeze. "I hoped you'd want to. They're the only family I have. Them and the boys, Javier and Josh."

And what about his SEAL team? After so long would they still feel a sense of loyalty, of kinship to him?

"Travis and 'Nita are in Baja right now, but they have a house in San Diego. If we could take a long weekend some time, we could meet them halfway for a visit."

"I can't take Joy out of the state of Nevada. But they're welcome to come here and stay. I have a guest room."

"How 'bout we start with some phone calls?"

Nita would love Sam. And she'd be thrilled one of her boys was serious about someone.

"That sounds good. Is she going to tell me embarrassing things about you, like all mothers do?"

He grimaced. "Probably."

She laughed.

"You'll need to contact your lawyer and talk to him about all this, Sam. I don't want to cause you any trouble."

"If this is a juvenile record, shouldn't it have been sealed?"

"The drug charge was expunged and the rest of the record sealed, but it can be opened by a judge."

"I'll talk to Ben about it. But it's been how many years?"

"Fifteen."

"I don't think there'll be any problem."

He nodded. "There's just one more thing." For now. He had to come clean to her in layers. Otherwise—

"What is it?"

As soon as he could break away from all the shit hanging over him—them—he'd say the words. As soon as he and Captain Jackson met, he'd know whether that was going to be possible. Two weeks had never seemed as long. He had two weeks to tell her everything.

He brushed his lips against her forehead, the tip of her nose, and found her mouth again. If he said the words, and they dragged him off to jail, it might make it worse for her. *I love you.* The feelings were probably written all over his face. "I'm really grateful you bought that box of condoms. I'd hate to have to run back over to my apartment, buck-assed naked, to get another one."

Sam laughed then breathed, "That would be a sight."

He slid further beneath the blankets and tugged her down with him. Sam pressed close and drew his lips to hers. His body heated to her reaction with a need as fierce as the first time. God, he was crazy about this woman. He proceeded to show her.

Will pushed a hand against the top of his head. Rage built inside him like a helium balloon filling and filling until it threatened to explode. He fought the urge to rip the phone from the wall.

"You fucking wuss. All you had to do was push her, and she'd have crumbled and signed whatever you wanted her to, Taylor."

"You're wrong, Will. She's not the cowed little ninny you made her out to be. She's sharp. And she knew exactly what kind of loan she needed to pay off the house." Taylor cleared his throat. "She had the paperwork for the payments she'd made after her grandmother's death. Had she not done so much research, I might have been able to manipulate her into signing something less advantageous. Besides, she wanted to bring in her lawyer. And she's requested I fax the contract to him before she signs it."

"Fuck!" Will paced the length of the barren living room and back again. He hadn't bothered replacing the busted furniture. When he moved in with Sam, they'd sell this house and buy new stuff together. "I want that house. I want you to put something into the contract allowing for an interest fluctuation so you can run up the payments."

"I can't, Will. Her lawyer will be looking over the document. He won't allow her to sign a document different from the one we agreed on."

"Send him one document and have her sign a different one."

"And risk litigation? If I tried something like that, and it came to light, I'd lose my job. I could go to jail."

"You're going to lose your job anyway. I'm going to pull every loan I have with your bank and I'm going to make sure your boss knows I've done so because of you."

The threat met with silence. *Good. Think about it, you cowardly little prick.*

"And I'll tell my boss exactly what you wanted me to do. Bankers talk, Mr. Cross. You'll pay hell getting another loan anywhere local. I'm done with this."

The phone clicked in Will's ear. For five seconds he was able to control his frustration, then he beat the phone on the desk. Semi-circular impressions gouged into the wood. The cordless receiver broke in two and part of it flew half way across the room to ricochet off the wall onto the floor. The sight of the damage he'd wrought jacked his rage up a notch. This was all Sam's fault, and she'd be sorry.

Will jerked his cell phone from his pocket, thumbed down until he found the number he needed and punched it.

"Zusak."

"Tell me you found something on that son of a bitch sniffing around my wife," he demanded.

"I've hit a wall, but I've put one of my best tech guys on chipping away at it. The info we've uncovered thus far is sketchy. I should be able to tell you something by tomorrow or the next day."

Will nodded to himself. Knowing someone was actually accomplishing something he needed done eased back the impatience burning through him. "Good. I knew I could count on you."

CHAPTER 32

Sam listened to Tim's steady breathing and glanced at the clock. He'd be waking any moment to leave before Joy woke. How did he do that? It was as if he had an alarm clock in his head.

For the last two weeks they'd spent every free moment together. And made love often. She had never known what it was to be hungry for a man's touch. To long for moments of intimacy. And to want to rush Joy to bed so they could be alone.

Sex in the past had been something to avoid or endure. Will's needs and demands had dominated that part of their relationship as much as the rest, leaving her only brief moments of pleasure. Her thoughts skated away from even thinking about the last few months of their marriage, when his drive to have a son had superseded everything else.

She shut down the memories and pressed closer to Tim, soaking in the feeling of security she felt lying next to him. Tim was the complete opposite of Will. Patient and persistent, he seemed to know just where to touch her to make her feel as though every nerve in her body came alive.

Her love for him deepened her responses. Left her as vulnerable to him emotionally as she'd ever been physically to Will. In the last two weeks she'd reveled in their closeness, but there had been moments of fear mixed in. What if something happened to end this? Just the thought squeezed her heart and made it difficult for her to breathe. Joy loved Tim as much as she did. He offered Joy all the affection and attention Will hadn't. She would be just as devastated.

And Tim loved them. She saw it in the tenderness and care he showed Joy, the passion he had for her. She had to set aside this fear and just enjoy being with him. And hope Will continued to stay away.

"What are you thinking about?" His voice, gravely with sleep, broke into her thoughts.

"How I wish you didn't have to sneak away so Joy wouldn't see you in my bed."

She turned her lips against his chest and slid her hand down over his stomach in a slow deliberate quest for what lay beneath the sheets. By the time her fingers closed around him, he was already hard in anticipation of her touch.

Tim's heated gaze tripped her heartbeat into thunder mode. They were so lucky to have found each other. A wave of tenderness and love rolled over her. When she bent her head to place an open mouthed kiss on his chest, she felt his quick, indrawn breath. Encouraged by his response, she found one of his flat nipples and laved it, then sucked. His erection hardened in her hand. She rained kisses down the center of his stomach as she continued to caress him, up and down. His stomach muscles tensed beneath the gentle nip of her teeth.

"Sam," he whispered, his voice a voice husky, his fingers tangling in her hair.

When her mouth closed over him, he made a strangled sound of pleasure that made her hum in satisfaction. There was power in giving him pleasure. Each time she shared herself with him, it made her stronger.

"I'm not going to be a damn bit of use to you, if you don't stop," his voice was rough.

It was so arousing, knowing how she could drive him as quickly over the edge as he did her. She straddled his hips and lowered herself over him.

His hips jerked in reaction, deepening the contact. "Jesus, you feel so perfect, Sam." He ran his hand from her hips and up her back, drawing her down for a long, deep kiss.

She captured a slow, intense rhythm, tilting her hips and taking him deep with each movement. *I love you.* The words lay there between them with every movement of their bodies, every shared caress of their hands and lips. All too quickly fulfillment overtook her with a sweet, sweeping pleasure that left her gasping. Tim's climax followed and triggered a renewed need for more.

The words still lay there between them as they looked into each other's eyes. And when he said them aloud, she stopped breathing for a moment.

"I love you," he said again.

She leaned down to rub her cheek against his beard, then turned her lips against his, "I love you, too."

Flash pulled the car in front of the house. They'd spent the morning at the Springs Preserve, walking through the museum, the exterior displays of flora and fauna, then caught a movie after lunch. It had been a perfect family day. He'd even enjoyed the movie about cartoon cars.

But regret and worry had plagued him all day. The more time he spent with Sam and Joy, the harder it was to tell Sam about the trouble he knew was coming. He could feel it. He'd already begun to look over his shoulder, regularly check the rear view mirror, and check the computer monitor and doors at night. Every day he remained here, he put the two most important people in his life in danger.

For the last week he'd spent every moment he could with them. It was selfish and short-sighted, but the time he had with them would give him something to hold on to when he was either in jail or back on his team.

Those thoughts were more than selfish. Now that he had said the words and she had too, it had made it even more real. What would it do to her when he was gone? What would it do to Joy?

Maybe he could ask Sam to leave with him, but she'd struggled so hard to keep the house. It was home to her. Once he'd told her the truth, she'd want him as far away from her and Joy as he could get.

And it would kill him.

He couldn't just disappear like he'd done before. He couldn't leave her wondering what had happened to him, as he had with nearly everyone else in his life. Like his team. Why hadn't he run to them, instead of away? He believed he'd put his experience in juvie behind him, but he hadn't. The abuse dealt to him by the older boys, the barred windows, and locked doors. He'd die in jail. But he couldn't run again. He couldn't bring himself to leave Sam and Joy. And if there was a single chance he could walk away from this and still have Sam and Joy in his life, he had to take it.

"My legs are all wobbly mommy. I'm tired," Joy whined from the back seat.

"I'll get her," Flash said, exiting the car.

Once he'd released her from her booster seat, Joy slipped her arms around his neck and attached herself to him like a spider monkey. He gave her small body a hug and tucked his arm beneath her bottom.

Sam ran up the three steps to unlock the front door. Joy lay against his shoulder and Flash rested a hand against her back to hold her in place as he side-stepped past Sam into the house.

Joy's arms tightened around his neck and she snuggled close. "Are we going to have chow?"

"What kind of chow do you want, sweet tart?" He rubbed her back and breathed in her kid smell of outdoors and cherry Kool-Aid.

"Nuggets."

"You're going to turn into a nugget. In fact, I think I see a brown crunchy spot right there on your arm. I'll nibble it off." He pretended to gnaw her arm, making noises like Tasmanian Devil.

Joy squealed and wiggled in his arms. He swung her down and laid her on the couch. Joy grinned. "Your beard tickles, Mr. Tim."

"So I've been told." Flash looked up at Sam and grinned. She wagged a finger at him and soft color rushed to her cheeks.

"I'll heat up your nuggets left over from lunch, Joy," she said.

"'Kay. Play Barbie with me, Mr. Tim," she begged.

"Uh..."

Sam disappeared behind the dividing wall between the kitchen and living room, but it did nothing to muffle her laughter.

Joy wiggled off the couch and ran to the large pink Barbie house that sat in its place of honor in front of the fireplace. She jerked a male doll out of one of the rooms and hustled back to him with it.

Unable to think of any way out of it, Flash took a seat on the rug in front of the dollhouse. And for the longest ten minutes of his life he played Ken to Joy's Barbie. He dressed the naked doll in the bathing suit and shirt Joy handed him, and pushed him around in a pink convertible he thought did nothing for the dude's image.

Joy jabbered on about the plastic couple's relationship. "And Ken takes her to the movies like you did me and mommy. And drives her around like you did me and mommy."

Sam appeared from the kitchen and called Joy to the table. He heard chairs being pulled out in the next room while he parked the pink monstrosity in front of the dollhouse.

Sam wandered back into the living room. "I've put a frozen pizza in for us. It'll be done in a few minutes."

"I'm good." He flopped back on the brown, red, and cream-patterned area rug. "I may have to lie here for the rest of the evening to recover."

Sam laughed and stretched out next to him on the rug. Flash extended an arm to act as a pillow and she curled in against his side.

"Out of all the protective, caring things you've done for us, I don't think I've ever seen anything as sweet as you playing Barbie with Joy."

"She pretty much has me right here," he said pointing to his heart. "But that dude Ken has some real body issues."

Sam laughed out loud.

"If the guys in my team ever saw me—" Realizing what he was about to say, he stopped.

She ran her hand back and forth across his t-shirt-covered chest, and despite the mental kicking he was giving himself for the slip, his heart and body responded to her touch with a hunger he didn't try to suppress.

"I know you were special ops. Isn't that what they call it?"

His throat was suddenly dry. "Yes. A Navy SEAL." He was still a Navy SEAL—until they discharged him or arrested him for desertion. The thought had his stomach muscles tightening and an ache settled like he'd been punched in the solar plexus. They'd give him a dishonorable discharge and prison time. He'd been AWOL nearly a year. He threw an arm over his eyes to hide his expression.

"You don't have to talk about it. I know you guys can't talk about things, even with your families."

"No. Not much." He grasped the hand that lay on his chest and held her palm against his cheek. "We'll talk about it later, after Joy's in bed."

"You don't have to."

"Yeah. I think I do." He turned on his side and his mouth found hers. He was hungry for her, for everything she was willing to give. He loved her so much. For a moment, Sam's response was as unfettered as his.

The oven timer went off, and Joy yelled, "Mommy."

Sam continued to press soft kisses to his mouth, then with a sigh drew back. "Later," she promised with one last kiss, rolled to her knees, and stood.

Giving himself a moment to rein in his emotions, Flash lay there and swallowed back the pain. He shoved to his feet and followed her into the kitchen.

"Want a nugget?" Joy asked, holding one up.

"No. Thanks, honey." He wasn't sure he could even stomach the slice of pizza Sam slid onto his plate.

"Mommy's honey. I'm sweet tart, Mr. Tim."

He smiled. "Yes, you are."

Though it felt like a fist lay lodged in his throat, Flash choked down one piece of pizza and a little salad, then cleaned his plates and put them in the dishwasher.

"I have to go over to the apartment to get my laptop. I have some things saved on it I want you to see."

"Okay."

He brushed Sam's cheek with his lips before he headed over to the apartment, then rushed back, his heart pounding in his ears. Using the key she'd given him, he let himself back in and reset the alarm. He heard Sam in the bathroom getting Joy out of the tub. He sat at the kitchen table and pulled up two of the videos and put them on the desktop for her to view, then closed the computer. There was no need for her to watch them all; the less she knew, the safer she would be once he was gone. The video reports he'd sent to Captain Jackson were enough.

He went into the living room and sat down in one of the overstuffed chairs. Images flickered across the television screen, but he couldn't concentrate on the comedy playing on it.

Joy ran in with a rag doll and a book and proceeded to climb up into his lap. She tucked herself in against his side and propped her feet onto his knee, her favorite position. She smelled like baby shampoo and her hair lay in soft wisps against his arm.

"Is that what you want to read before bed?" he asked taking the book from her.

"Uh-huh."

He opened the book. He took his time reading each page and allowing her to point out the characters. Sam came into the room and took a seat on the couch. Eventually Joy grew still and curled in against him, and he set the book aside and just held her until she fell asleep.

Sam rose and started forward, but he shook his head. "I'll carry her." She went ahead of him to Joy's room and pulled back the bedclothes to allow him to lay her down. She pulled the covers up. He paused beside the bed, taking in the long sweep of Joy's lashes resting on her cheeks and the flyaway blonde hair. A wave of tenderness and grief nearly brought him to his knees. He turned and left the room, but paused outside in the hall and leaned back against the wall.

Sam came out of the room and stopped to look up at him, concern in the crease of her brow and the anxious expression in her eyes. "What is it?"

"I wish we'd met six years ago. I wish she were ours. He doesn't know what he's thrown away. But I do."

"Oh, Tim..." Her eyes filled with tears and she put her arms around him, holding him tight. He wrapped his arms around her, buried his face in her hair, breathed in her scent and held on until the pain eased a little.

"I love you. Love you both," he said, his voice hoarse.

"I—we—love you, too." Her fingers caressed the back of his head and neck.

He wanted to forget about everything but how they felt about one another, but he couldn't. If something happened to Sam and Joy he'd never forgive himself.

"I'm in trouble, Sam." He swallowed. He forced himself to release her and took a step back. "My commanding officer, Captain Jackson, will be meeting with me at the Bellagio this Thursday." He shook his head. "You need to watch the video files I've compiled for you so you'll understand."

"What kind of trouble?" she asked, a frown drawing her brows together.

She'd never believe him. She'd think he was pretending to be Rambo or trying to pull a con. Even a military spouse would have trouble believing all this. What was he thinking? He drew a deep breath.

"I'll give you the background info, then you need to watch the videos." He drew her into the living room and they sat down on the couch.

God, he didn't want to do this. If he kept his mouth shut, they could go on like they were. Until Gilbert showed up at his door with his cartel buddies.

But if all this were sprung on her, she'd hate him.

Who was he kidding? He had to leave ASAP. Coming clean had been a bad idea. He should have just broken it off with her and packed his gear. Once he told her everything, she'd break it off. She'd be right in doing so.

But looking into her eyes, seeing the love he'd waited for so long—

"My name is Lieutenant Junior Grade Harold Timothy Carney."

"Carney?"

He removed his military ID from his pocket, handed it to her and removed his glasses.

Her hands trembled as she stared at the picture. She swallowed. "Your hair is lighter here."

"I've been using something to darken it." He swallowed. "Fourteen months ago, while I was in Iraq, I was approached by an FBI agent about a smuggling situation going on within the ranks. The FBI gathered enough intel to lead them back to the middlemen stateside. They needed someone who could act on their behalf and purchase some artifacts in Iraq and smuggle them home. Each artifact would be fitted with a chip, so they could monitor where they were being transported. So I bought the artifacts with the money they gave me, smuggled them home, then followed through with the middlemen. Until the last buy went down and everything went to shit."

"I didn't realize SEALs could act as policemen," Sam said.

"We don't. We're not allowed to take any kind of military action on domestic soil unless mandated by Congress. But in international situations, we work with the feds. We go after drug cartels and terrorists mostly. And always out of the country."

He paused to give her a chance to absorb all that. "I got an email saying orders had been cut loaning me to the feds to do these buys and exchanges. And since I'd worked with the FBI agent who approached me before, and I received orders once I got home certified mail, I thought everything was on the up and up.

"Someone was following me, watching my every move. I was told to make it look like I was a high roller. Travel to and from Vegas. Buy a car. Put on a show so the buyers would think I was hungry for cash to fund my gambling and high-rolling lifestyle so they'd never think I was involved with law enforcement. I think it was all to make me appear truly guilty." He looked into her face for the trust she'd given him. It was still there, but for how long.

"But I've never seen you gamble," Sam protested.

"I haven't since I've been here with you. I used to but after all this—" he shook his head. "I lost my stomach for it."

He swallowed and looked away. "Anyway, the first two buys went down in Mexico just fine. The third one was switched to San Diego at the last minute." He ran his fingers through his hair. "I knew something was wrong. I didn't like the idea of the buy going down near the base, or the fact that it was happening on American soil, but the FBI was in charge, and I was following orders."

"The buy went down as it was supposed to, then out of the blue the middlemen were taken down by snipers. The shooters tried to kill me too, but I got away. I thought until recently I'd actually shot two FBI agents. But they weren't FBI."

Sam sucked in a breath, sounding like she'd been punched, and, her color leached away, causing the freckles across her nose to stand out. "You shot them?"

"They'd murdered the two buyers, Sam, and shot me. Then when they knew I was down, they came in from their sniper positions to make certain I was dead." He raked his hair back to expose the scar along the side of his head. A scar she'd remarked on when her fingers found it while they were making love.

"They were injured, both unconscious, but not dead when I left them. By the time the local police arrived at the scene, they'd disappeared."

The more he'd talked, the tighter Sam had curled into the corner of the couch away from him. Seeing her reaction, his chest tightened and his throat ached. She'd seen too much violence, experienced too much. And now he'd shoved the violent side of what he did in her face. He leaned forward and rested his head in his hands.

"What I do for a living isn't everything I am, Sam. I'm a SEAL, not a murderer. There is a difference."

"You have to give me a minute. The man sitting here with me, and the man you're talking about, seem like two different people."

"Well, they're not. I've been hiding out for the last ten months, sending info to the Naval Criminal Investigative Service about the FBI agent involved in all this. I've been building a case against him. Trying to prove I wasn't involved in anything illegal."

"Why didn't you just turn yourself in, Tim?"

"The Navy was only interested in my being AWOL. The day of the buy I got the call we were being deployed. I was shot, bleeding, had a severe concussion and didn't know who I could trust. I knew Gilbert was hunting for me. The man who'd tried to kill me. He's mixed up with some bad people. People who wouldn't think twice about killing me.

"I wasn't going to walk in to a hospital and have him pick me up and finish the job. Or be arrested by the military police, and possibly transferred into his custody, then murdered. I could see him doing just that, then saying I'd resisted arrest and attempted to escape.

"Captain Jackson is trying to mediate with NCIS and the chain of command so I can go back and deal with all this."

Her voice shook when she asked, "Could you go to jail?"

More than likely he would. The penalty for being AWOL would be at the very least two years, his rank stripped, and a dishonorable discharge. If they charged him with desertion, it could be the death penalty, though those charges had only been carried out once during World War II and never since. He swallowed. "Yes."

She rested her head on her updrawn knees, her blonde hair falling forward like silk. He ached to reach out and touch her, but could see a wall going up between them. He was helpless to stop it.

Her head jerked up. "Are we in danger?"

He shook his head. "They don't know where I am. But eventually they will, and Gilbert will be coming after me. That's why I've reached out to my commander. If NCIS takes me in now that I've supplied them with more info about Gilbert, it will end it all."

The ache in his chest grew unbearable, driving him to his feet. "I love you, Sam. The only other woman I've said that to is Nita. No one else. And I know this is a huge thing to accept. I know what you've been through in the past. And God knows you don't need this. But I love you. And I love Joy."

Her skin looked paper-white with shock. And her features locked into lines of grief. They weren't going to make it through this.

"Watch the videos. You'll know I'm not lying or conning you," he said around the knot in his throat.

"I know you're not lying," Sam managed, though it felt as if every bit of air had been sucked from her lungs. He had no reason to lie. In fact the opposite. She felt dull, as though the trauma of learning her perfect man was not so perfect had slowed her thought processes.

Seeing how upset he was didn't ease her own grief and fear. How could they have gone from making love this morning, telling each other how they felt, then having everything implode tonight? How could this happen?

How could he love her and Joy, and be this *other* person?

But she'd known he was military. Had guessed he was special ops. A Navy SEAL.

And he wasn't a different person. The change of one letter in his name didn't change the person she had fallen in love with. Didn't change the man who had just read to Joy and put her to bed. Had taught her how to defend herself. Had tried to protect them.

Or was she just so desperate to believe in him, she couldn't face the truth? What laws had he broken other than his being AWOL? And what kind of punishment did they have for that?

Prison? How would she bear it? Knowing what he'd gone through as a child—How could he?

"Do you want me to go, Sam?" Though his features were set in lines of careful control, the pain was there in his eyes for her to see. Once again he was paying for another person's crime. And it wasn't fair.

"No. I don't know." She swallowed, though her throat felt raw with the effort. She wanted to rock and wail against the pain but instead held it back and turned her face against the couch. "I have to think." She unfolded from the couch, walked down the hall to her bedroom and shut the door.

For an hour all she could do was cry and vent her emotion. When she'd had enough of the pity party, she rose to go into the kitchen to look at the documents he'd compiled for her.

Her heart dropped when she scanned the living room and found it empty. Tim was gone.

When she read the letter he'd written to his commanding officer, her eyes filled with tears and her heart ached. Why had he written it to Lieutenant Yazzie instead of Travis and 'Nita?

When she saw the note at the end asking Lieutenant Yazzie to visit Travis and 'Nita for him and explain, she understood. They'd need to hear about him first-hand, not just from a piece of paper.

After viewing the videos and other things, she paced the floor. She had to put Joy ahead of everything else. Would social services get involved if they discovered she was involved with a—she couldn't bring herself to say deserter or even think it. Could she be charged for harboring a fugitive?

She had to call Ben and meet with him. Tell him everything. And Tim needed to go with her. There had to be a way they could set this right. There had to be a way.

She had to put her child first, but she also wanted to do what her heart told her. For once she didn't want to be a responsible adult, she just wanted to be a woman in love with a good man.

Flash sat on the porch steps and watched the sun rise over the distant hills. The sky took on a bright yellow glow, then turned a warm peach. He hadn't slept, couldn't sleep. He should be inside the apartment packing, but he couldn't get motivated.

The door behind him opened, and he turned to look over his shoulder. Sam came out of the house and took a seat next to him on the steps. Her hair was a mess and dark circles discolored the skin beneath her eyes. The freckles he found so intriguing stood out across her nose. She looked ill.

He had done this.

"My lawyer is going to meet with us at noon at his office."

"On Sunday?"

"Yes. I told him it was an emergency. When I started talking to him about you—You need to take your laptop."

"Okay."

She bit her lip. "He's bringing an associate with him. An expert in federal cases."

"Thanks."

Because he couldn't bear not to touch her, he rested a hand against her back. "I'm sorry, Sam."

She started to tear up and looked away. "I love you. But I have to think of Joy."

"I know." Her love for Joy was part of what had drawn him to her. He couldn't resent the fact Sam put her first. "I never expected to fall in love, Sam. When I first moved in, I tried to stay away."

"I did too. I wasn't looking for anyone. I never expected to ever want any of this again."

He pressed the heels of his palms against his burning eyes. SEALs don't cry. He'd keep telling himself that until the need to do it passed. He looked out into the distance to keep from looking at her.

"There has to be a way," she said, her voice almost a whisper.

He hoped so.

Her hand reached for his and her fingers tightened around it.

Joy's voice calling from inside drew their attention. Sam rose to go inside and after a moment longer he wandered over to his apartment.

As he did every morning, he checked the video feeds in Gilbert's apartment. Lately there had been very little to watch. The son of a bitch was probably spending all his time covering the cartel's ass. When Gilbert's apartment door opened and he and three other men crowded into the living room, Flash slowed the tape.

Where had he seen that third dude before? Realization hit, his heart rate soared and he pumped his fist in the air. "I got you, you son of a bitch! I've got you all."

But was it worth the price he and Sam would have to pay?

CHAPTER 33

James drove the car beneath the front entrance awning that stretched out and away from the Bellagio Hotel and Casino. Bellhops stood ready with metal trolleys for the baggage. James hit the trunk release button and stepped out of the car.

A bellhop approached. "Welcome to the Bellagio, sir. May I get your bags?"

"Sure, thanks," James said. He went around to open Marsha's door, but she had already shoved it open and stood gazing at the façade and fountains.

"Oh my..." she breathed. "This place is unbelievable.

An arched ceiling decorated by coffered panels stretched toward the entrance. Down the center of the structure, a glass skylight supported by curved, metal struts fashioned in an art Nouveau design, cut a wide swath down the roofline, allowing light to filter beneath. Large lights dangled on each side of the glass in regimented order.

"It is pretty impressive," he agreed.

He caught Marsha's hand and they wandered toward the entrance and paused to study the large Chinese dogs guarding each side of the portico. The bellhop followed close behind as they walked across the patterned flagstone walkway and preceded him through the door.

All golds, whites, and maroons, the lobby's décor projected richness. The hotel had an atmosphere of energy and excitement. Several people checked in, while others wandered through the lobby to the casino or moved in and out of shops off the main thoroughfare. A line of bellhops stood by, waiting with loaded luggage trolleys.

James went to the desk, produced his reservation paperwork and handed over his credit card. He filled out paperwork to have the rental car parked.

"Wonder why we never visited Vegas before?" Marsha asked as they waited for their reservation to be processed.

Though she'd had a couple of moments on the plane, anxiety over Alex mostly, she seemed better, and her appetite had picked up. He'd noticed she'd packed the bottle of antidepressants the doctor had prescribed in her overnight bag. He didn't know how long she'd been taking the meds, but he saw a difference. It was slow, and she still had moments, but the pills were helping.

"I guess we haven't come here because we're both a little conservative about money and we don't gamble."

"Speak for yourself. I used to play a mean hand of bridge and win all the time."

James laughed. "I didn't realize bridge was a betting game.

"Well, it is the way the girls and I play." She grinned.

At seeing the genuine amusement in her expression, he experienced the sensation of having just dropped a forty-pound pack from his shoulders. If they weren't in the middle of a busy lobby, he'd kiss her.

How could he jump out of an airplane into a moonless night sky without reserve and not kiss his wife whenever the hell he wanted to? He looped an arm around her waist to bring her in close against him and pressed a quick kiss to her lips.

She rested her head on his shoulder. "Don't you and the guys play poker to break up the monotony when you're deployed?" she asked, picking up a brochure from the counter.

"Sometimes. There are days things will drag and others when we're busy for several consecutive days and nights at a time. The kind of poker they'd play here would be for high stakes. We might be better off trying the slots, if you want to later."

"Okay."

Collecting their keycards from the reservation clerk, James offered the card to the bellhop and the man led the way through the busy casino to the elevators. The conveyance was a work of art, all brass and richly stained wood, and decorated as extravagantly as the rest of the hotel. A rich gold tone threaded through the decor everywhere he looked, with touches of red, brown, and white.

Faced with the baggage cart and several other guests, each having to use their keycard to access their floor, they fell silent while the elevator took them up. The doors opened to a wide hall tiled in gold, black, and white. "Just this way," the bellhop said and turned to the right. The tile petered out into a red patterned carpet that muffled their steps. He came to a stop before their room, inserted the keycard, pushed the door open and waited for Marsha and James to precede him. After the bags were unloaded, James pushed a five dollar bill into the man's hand and followed him to the door.

The room, decorated in purples and greens, looked clean and comfortable. The large king-sized bed beckoned. How long had it been since they'd made love? Almost eleven months. He'd had long periods while deployed when he'd gone without sex, but in their married life they'd always had an active sexual relationship. Until Alex's birth.

Did she still hold him responsible for Tabarek Moussa's attack? Did she still believe he held her responsible for Alex's issues? Revisiting those questions had just seemed to make matters worse.

Could they break away from the past and build a life together again?

Marsha stood at the window looking out and announced, "They're starting the fountain show." He joined her at the window.

The rise and fall of the synchronized jets of water was entertaining, almost hypnotic. He'd never seen water used as an art form before, but the display was a marvel of engineering. It would be even more impressive at night.

"That was truly amazing."

"It was. I've made reservations at the Eiffel Tower Restaurant for dinner at nine tonight and asked for a window seat. One of my men suggested we see the fountain show from there at night and check out the strip."

"That sounds like fun."

"It's just shy of lunchtime. Let's get something to eat," he suggested. "One of the men said the Café Bellagio downstairs is really good."

"Okay."

They rode the elevator back downstairs, and on the way out paused to stand under the blown glass garden created by Dale Chihuly which hung from the ceiling in the lobby. Marsha took several pictures with her phone. "This would be nice to have over our bed and wake up to every morning."

"I wonder what kind of support structure they had to put in to keep it in place?"

She smiled. "Women admire the art, men think of the engineering problems."

"I can do both," he said. "Let me find out where the Café is." He went to the concierge desk and received directions and a map of the hotel.

"The Café is this way." James rested a hand against her waist and guided her from the lobby to the conservatory. Patterned tile swirled beneath their feet, leading into a fanciful garden that transported them onto the set of the *Wizard of Oz.* They followed the walkway and paused to admire the sculptured snails, butterflies and dragonflies enjoying the constructed habitat, a blend of real plants and artistic artificial displays. In one area, large white cranes stood watch over a nest of eggs. In another, a bed of giant glass poppies mirrored the garden hanging from the lobby ceiling. The blossoms reflected the light entering from the arched Art Nouveau steel roof that had been given a green patina much like the awning they'd driven under when they'd first arrived.

"I wonder how Alex would respond to all this?" Marsha said.

"He loves color. I've noticed he likes red. He'd probably be fascinated."

They circled the entire display before going into the cafe.

The food was as good as he'd been told, and for once Marsha ate nearly everything on her plate. If this increase in appetite was a side-effect of the medication, James was grateful for it.

They decided to walk off their lunch on the strip and left the hotel. They strolled down Flamingo Road and paused to look at

Caesar's Palace across the way. Everything was huge and over the top, but there was something fascinating about it. It was both vulgar and beautiful.

She tugged him to a stop when they reached the strip itself. "I'm glad you made reservations at the restaurant. We have to see all this lit up. If the world came to an end and aliens discovered this place, how do you think they'd react to it?"

"I think they'd shake their heads in bafflement. Just like I'm doing right now."

She smiled. "But it's probably something everyone should see at least once."

"I'd say so. And we can try some of the games in the casino later. Our goal here is just to be together and to see the sights."

They spent the afternoon wandering down the strip and doing just that then returned to the hotel.

"When is your meeting?" Marsha asked as they entered their room.

"Tomorrow at two. You're sure you don't mind doing something on your own while I meet with Flash?"

"Not if you don't mind paying for a massage at the spa," she waved the brochure she'd picked up from the desk.

Was it easier to have a total stranger put hands on her than her husband? He knew it wasn't the same thing, but it still rankled. "Maybe I can give you a warm-up beforehand." For once he couldn't read her expression. "I thought maybe a change of scenery and a little romance might help us ease back into making love."

"So you didn't just bring me along as cover for the meeting or an afterthought?"

Would she ever believe he loved her? Where had this doubt come from?

"The *meeting* was an afterthought, Marsha. I can't just jump on a plane and leave the state when I want to. I have to notify people where I'm going and when I'll be back. It does take the spontaneity out of things, but I was already in the stages of planning a weekend away for us when Flash contacted me. I wanted to take you to San Francisco, but when I got his message—" He motioned toward the window. "I thought why not here instead?" He drew a deep breath to release the angry tension. "I'm spending the weekend with you. At most I'll be spending a couple of hours debriefing him."

Why was he always defending himself to her? He didn't fucking do that with anyone else, not even his commanding officers. *It was stopping now.*

She sat on the bed and ran her hands through her hair.

He hadn't expected things to be easy, but this passive-aggressive bullshit had to end. He sat in one of the green-striped chairs next to the bed and rubbed a hand over his face. The weight was back, pressing down on him physically, emotionally. After an afternoon's respite it felt even heavier than before. They seemed to have to fight for every step they took forward. It had been so effortless for them before. They had been so blessed and he hadn't even realized it. He leaned forward in his seat. "I'm going to ask you a question and I want you to think about it before you answer."

She nodded, though her expression was tense with anxiety. "Okay."

"Do you want us to stay together as a couple?"

She paused in silence for a few seconds as he'd asked her to do. "Yes."

"Then it's time we started being a couple again, instead of two people who live in the same house. I know you're dealing with a lot. But I went through it too. You know I wake up in the middle of the night in a cold sweat and get up to check on Alex and you. There are other things—" he cut himself off and shook his head. "If we can't bring ourselves to cling to each other, what does that say about our relationship?"

"It says it's over."

His heart clenched and for a moment he couldn't breathe.

Her eyes clouded with tears. "But I'm not ready for that. Not yet. I still love you."

His throat ached so his voice sounded hoarse. "Why? Why do you love me?"

"Because you *do* slip out of bed in the night and check to make sure Alex and I are safe." Tears rolled down her cheeks in a stream. "Because you smell so good, even first thing in the morning before you've had your shower. Because, even when you're tired, you come home and do things around the house.

Because you brush your teeth before you kiss me in the morning, and you still kiss me even though I haven't."

James laughed, the sound clogged by emotion. He shoved himself from the chair and joined her on the bed. He held her. They held each other. The only other time in their married life he'd ever cried was after Alex's birth. But he struggled not to bawl like a baby now.

He urged Marsha to stretch out on the bed. He tucked her hair behind her ear and waited for her tears to ease, then kissed her even when they didn't.

"I need a tissue," she complained a few minutes later.

He rose and collected some for her. She wiped her face and blew her nose. For a time she lay still, her eyes closed and he watched her struggle for composure.

"Do you think we could just take off our clothes and lie skin to skin for a while?" she asked. "I want to know what it feels like for us to have no barriers between us. It's been a long time."

"If it's what you want," he said, and felt like crying all over again.

"It's what I want."

He waited for her to make the first move, and when she rolled off the bed to undress, he did the same. He shucked his clothing, tugged the heavy comforter off the bed, and slid beneath the covers. When she turned to him she wore nothing but a pair of bikini briefs. Though he had slept with her every night, seen her come in and out of the bathroom in her bathrobe or nightgown, she hadn't allowed him to see her naked. He hadn't realized how thin she'd become. Her pelvic bones pushed against her skin and her waist seemed only a hand's breadth wide. He held the covers open and she slipped beneath them. He gathered her close.

The emotional issues before held passion at bay, but the brush of her bare skin against his set off an instinctive response, and he grew hard. Instead of pulling away she nestled closer.

"I'm sorry I've been so—unpredictable," she said her breath warm against his chest.

"We're just trying to make it past all the hurt the best way we can, honey." He ran his fingers through her hair and cupped the back of her head. His fingers rubbed the band of muscle at the base of her skull where tension lay. She began to relax.

He brushed her forehead with his lips. "I've missed holding you like this. I've missed feeling how you lean into me like we're two pieces of a puzzle, trying to lock in."

She drew a deep breath and her breasts moved against his chest. She ran her hand down his back so slowly it was like she sought to touch every inch of his skin from the base of his neck to his ass. When she ran her hands beneath the fabric to cup his buttocks, his erection pushed forward against her.

"How can you still want me after all I've put you through?" she asked.

"How can you still love me after all I've put you through?" he countered. His fingertips grazed the hollow of her spine and followed it all the way down. He pushed against her and felt the answering tilt of her hips.

"Remember how we used to finish each other's sentences?" she murmured. Her lips turned against his skin. She slipped her hand between them and her fingers closed around his erection.

The wall between them began to crumble. For a moment he thought he might explode, but he fought back the need, though his breathing became unsteady. "And how we used to read each other's thoughts with a look."

He cupped her breast with his other hand and toyed with her nipple, careful to keep the pressure the way she liked it. "We can get it back, Marsha. All we have to do is want it." He slid downward and caught her mouth with his and their tongues reached for one another in long, slow kisses. He bent his head and took her nipple in his mouth. She drew in a shaky breath.

The doctor had warned Marsha the medication he'd prescribed would reduce her sex drive. But the poignancy and tenderness in James's seduction reached past all that. Using his lips, teeth, and tongue, he worked his way from her breasts to her navel, then the sensitive area along her pelvic bones. It was as though her heart, mind and body had been in a sexual hibernation and he awakened each nerve ending, one kiss at a time. The patience he used to bring her to the point of opening herself to him gripped her heart and tugged. She loved him. She'd fought against it. Tried to suppress it. Out of—resentment? hurt? anger? She didn't know. But she couldn't fight this.

He pulled the bikini panties down her legs and off, then nibbled the inside of her thighs. The tiny love bites sent arrows of sensation to the very heart of her and she writhed beneath the sensation. He found her with his mouth, his tongue laving the tender heat, as though he couldn't get enough. Her hands twisted in the sheets. When she thought she might fly apart at any moment, he withdrew and rose above her.

He tempted her with the head of his penis until she rocked her hips up, trying to guide him where she wanted him to be. When he finally thrust home, she groaned in encouragement and ran her nails down his back. His muscles contracted beneath the pressure and his hips thrust forward, deepening the connection. She bowed her back as the pleasurable contractions swept through her.

"Oh, baby," he breathed. His long, measured thrusts built the sensuous tensions all over again. Emotion gripped her and she became overwhelmed by the sweet feeling of unfettered intimacy as she moved beneath him. He swelled inside her, growing harder, his climax building. "Marsha?" he breathed, her name, a plea, a question.

"Go," she demanded. With one last thrust he found release, his hips jerking. She rolled her hips and rode the sensation until she followed him to completion.

Afterwards she held him close and ran her hands up and down his back while they both caught their breath. Her muscles felt well-used but weak as water.

When James shifted position, she opened her eyes to look up at him and found him grinning.

Color ran up her throat to her cheeks, and his smile widened.

"Shut up," she said.

"I didn't say anything."

"The self-satisfied grin on your face says it all."

He laughed. "We've always been good together."

"Yeah, we have." She drew him down to kiss him. "I'm ready for a nap."

He eased onto his side and she turned her back to him so they could spoon. She drew his hand to her breast and held it there. For the first time in a long, long while she felt in complete balance. "I love you."

His lips moved against her shoulder. "Roger that."

James woke more than an hour later when Marsha slipped out of bed and disappeared into the bathroom. He closed his eyes and waited for her to return. When she slipped back into bed he reached for her. They made love again. Slowly. Enjoying touching one another, being close.

Afterwards they called home to check on Alex, and finding everything under control, showered, dressed, and went downstairs to the casino. They wandered through, pausing just to observe from a distance. Then went into the slot room. A wide range of slot machines lined the length of the room.

"Want to try one?" James asked.

Marsha shook her head. "No. But I'd like to go to the art gallery tomorrow. They're supposed to have an exhibit of landscapes. And let's go to the Fashion Show Mall. I don't really need anything, but I'd like to see it."

"Okay." He glanced at his watch. "We'll catch a cab to take us to the restaurant."

Twenty minutes later their cab dropped them at the Paris hotel. The sun was setting and the lights started to come on as they entered the hotel. The French provincial lobby decor featured panels of creamy white edged in gold, and crystal chandeliers gleamed overhead. From there, they were directed by the concierge to a private elevator in the casino manned by an attendant. Once on the restaurant floor, a hostess led them past an open, spotlessly clean kitchen and seated them at a table for two that looked out at the strip and the Bellagio fountains.

They talked about friends and Alex and lingered over their meal, sampling the food, Beef Wellington and wild salmon, from each other's plates. In the middle of the meal Marsha said, "I've been thinking about getting a job I could do from home. What do you think?"

She looked relaxed, and though the subdued lighting created hollows beneath her cheekbones, the more dramatic eye makeup she'd used made her eyes look smoky blue, and her hair gleamed with highlights. She looked beautiful. She raised her brows, waiting for an answer, and he dragged his thoughts back to her question. "I think you should give yourself another couple of months to get back to full fighting form, then see how you feel about it. You may even want to try something different."

She nodded. "You've always been supportive of me in whatever I've wanted to do."

He laid his hand over hers. "You've always supported me, too. And I know it hasn't always been easy. I know what a sacrifice you've made being married to me. If I'm home, I'm running the unit. If I'm downrange, I'm out of touch." How would she respond to being alone if he had to deploy again?

They enjoyed crème brûlée and a caramel soufflé for dessert, and coffee.

Marsha looped her arm through his to cuddle in the back of the cab as they headed back to the hotel. After they arrived at the Bellagio, they strolled toward the front entrance while taking in the sights.

A man stepped from behind one of the Chinese dogs into their path, and Marsha started. James's arm tightened around her.

"Good evening, Captain, Jackson," Agent Barnett said, coming further into the light. He nodded to Marsha. "Ma'am."

Agent Cooper approached from the other direction and nodded to him. "We need to talk, sir."

CHAPTER 34

James settled on the couch in the sitting area of Agent Barnett's room and stretched his arms out along the back. The room was more spacious than his and Marsha's, with a living room area with a couch and two chairs.

"What are you doing here, Captain?" Barnett asked, his face settled into the same bulldog frown he'd kept the entire time they'd spoken before.

"I'm spending some quality time with my wife."

"This place doesn't come cheap. I bet you dropped a hundred fifty to two hundred dollars on dinner. That's a chunk of change on a captain's salary."

As usual Barnett was coming in low and trying for the cheap shot. "Barnett, have you been stuck in bad cop mode for so long you can't do anything else? Or is it your normal personality to be an asshole?"

Barnett scowled.

"You're welcome to look through my financials. Which you probably already have. We haven't taken a vacation in five years." He bore down on the words, "*I was fucking busy somewhere else.* We eat out a couple of times a week. And the rest of the time we lead a quiet life within our means."

"Except you're a SEAL and are gone on deployment or training nine months out of every year," Agent Cooper said.

He swung his attention back to her. "Which goes without saying. Now get to the point, or I'm leaving."

Cooper flipped her ponytail over her shoulder impatiently. "We know this was Lieutenant Carney's favorite vacation spot,

Captain. It just seemed out of character for you to come here. You don't gamble."

"You mean I haven't gambled since I've been here." He leaned forward and rested his elbows on his knees. "There are other things to do here, agent."

Her deadpan expression almost encouraged a smile.

"Because we have a two-hour window to report to base if something goes down, it has to be someplace we could fly to and from within that time frame. Tomorrow we plan to go through the art gallery here, and visit the mall to purchase a gift for our son. We'll probably eat somewhere nice, not nearly as nice as tonight, but that was a one-time deal. While my wife goes for a massage, I'll probably hang out in the casino and try my luck. Then we'll fly back to San Diego around six."

"You flew down on a private plane." Barnett said, leaning forward in his seat.

"Yeah. With several businessmen."

"That must have cost some cash, too."

This accusatory tone Barnett adopted every time he spoke was wearing thin. "Not as much as you think. Dom is ex-military and a friend. He flew us down with the party he'd booked. He'll fly us back tomorrow with another."

"He used to fly Carney down all the time."

"Yes, he did. He's good about that. He knows the life. Knows the time restraints we have with the job and family." James rose to his feet. "Now, if we've covered everything."

"We know Lieutenant Carney is here in Nevada, Captain," Barnett said.

Shit! James's heartbeat ratcheted up to jogging pace in a nanosecond. "Then why aren't you knocking on his door and talking to him instead of me?"

"Because if we approach him, he'll be in the wind again," Cooper said.

Every muscle in James's body grew tense with the need to take action. But he kept his expression under control. "You can't blame him for not wanting to be thrown in jail over something out of his control, agent. You haven't exactly been supportive of his efforts."

"He has bigger issues than us, Captain." She leaned forward in much the same pose as Barnett. "If we've been able to track him here, other factions probably have, too."

James's tone grew sharp. "Do you know they've located him for certain?"

She shook her head. "But we know someone's been picking away at the persona he built for himself. We've been monitoring it for the last few days."

Jesus! He had no way of contacting Flash to warn him. "How did you find him?"

"He sent us a message, sir, stating he was ready to come in."

Barnett and Cooper glanced toward each other in a silent exchange. "Admiral Clarence has already contacted us...well, actually, our superiors," Cooper said.

"I don't know what he's said to them, but he has some major juice," Barnett added.

James sucked in a quick breath, then stood and fished his cell phone out of his pocket.

Both agents leaped to their feet. "Relax, you two. I'm checking my voice mail for a message from Admiral Clarence." He ran through the messages, and not finding one from Clarence, ran through his contacts and selected the admiral's number. He put it on speakerphone.

Clarence answered identifying himself in a gravelly voice.

"I'm calling from Agent Barnett's hotel room here at the Bellagio, sir. He and his partner Agent Cooper ambushed me on my way back in from dinner."

"Their superiors and I are working on it, Captain. And the FBI has decided to come along for the ride. Stand down until you hear from me."

"Yes, sir."

Clarence's tone was impatient. "And tell those two overeager agents to stand down as well."

James raised a brow at Barnett and the man frowned.

Clarence's tone grew short. "I'll call you back in a few hours."

"Yes, sir."

James looked from Cooper to Barnett. "We have nothing more to discuss until I have my orders and you have yours. Good night."

He felt little satisfaction as he left Barnett's room and made his way to his own. Flash was as good as arrested unless something could be done. All the two NCIS agents had to do was wait for him to show tomorrow.

Though it was nearly one in the morning, Marsha was still awake and waiting for him. She muted the television when he entered the room and slipped free from the covers.

"Can you tell me what's going on?"

"Admiral Clarence is in negotiations with NCIS, trying to negotiate some kind of interdepartmental agreement on Flash's behalf." He shrugged free of his suit coat and tossed it on the foot of the bed.

"If they can't?"

He shook his head. "They'll arrest him when he shows tomorrow, and he'll be transported back to San Diego and thrown in the brig."

"After everything he's done to try to lead them in the right direction?"

James nodded. "The only good thing is he'll be safer in custody with us than he'd be out there with the cartel looking for him. They said someone is investigating his background. It could be them." He loosened his tie.

"Is there anything you can do?" she asked.

"I don't have any way of contacting him, and even if I could, I've been ordered to stand down until I hear from the admiral."

Marsha put her arms around him. "I'm sorry, James.

"Me, too." He held her close. "I really hoped we could find a way to get him back." He knew in his gut Flash was getting a raw deal.

"If there's a way, the admiral will find it."

He rested his chin atop her head. "How can you be so certain?"

"He's a SEAL just like you. You guys never give up."

CHAPTER 35

Flash awoke at first light to a breath-stealing ache in his chest. The recurring dream about the mission he'd struggled with for so long had been replaced with one about Sam. He didn't need a psyche eval to understand why he'd spent the last few nights searching for her in his sleep. Still gripped by the aftermath of the dream, his heartbeat raced like an overworked engine. He tightened his arm around Sam and rested his cheek against her hair, allowing her scent, her closeness to calm him.

She stroked his arm. "What is it?" Her voice sounded drowsy.

"Just a dream. It's okay."

She needed to sleep as long as she could. It would save her some of the dread and worry waking was sure to bring.

He tucked his legs beneath hers to spoon and she reached back to rest her hand on his bare thigh.

Sam looked over her shoulder at him, deep shadows darkening the pale skin beneath her eyes. Proof she'd had as sleepless a night as he.

She turned. "Come inside me," she said softly. "I need to be as close to you as I can get."

Flash turned to cover her body with his own. She reached between them to touch him and he grew hard in an instant.

He didn't want their last time to be painful in any way. "Your not ready—"

"You are," she said with a smile that had to cost her. "Come inside me."

He pushed forward entering her the first small bit and felt her body open to him, accepting him. By slow increments he eased forward until he was as deep and close as he could get.

Sam raised a hand to cup his cheek and look into his eyes. "I love you."

Flash kissed her, hoping the taste of her lips would ease the ache in his chest. "I love you, Sam."

Her arms tightened and her slender legs bowed around him holding him, wrapping him close. He thrust forward and rolled his hips deepening the contact as she tilted her hips in response.

A desperate need to be closer seemed to seize them both and instead of withdrawing, he rocked against her, barely separating their bodies, and each time, she canted against the movement. The slow steady ebb and flow of the motion eased his emotional pain and allowed physical pleasure to sweep in.

The hitch in her breathing mirrored his own, the soft sound of her sighs and breathy groans fed his own need and played on his arousal like nothing had before. The natural grip and release of her response drove him toward climax, though he tried to hold off.

When she breathed his name in a husky, plea, he lost his tenuous control and fell over the edge with her.

Afterwards, Sam turned her lips against his throat. "I love you," she whispered.

Flash realized he had never truly understood what those three words meant until meeting her, loving her. But he did now.

Will had never seen Marc Zusak smile so much. His horsy teeth looked too big for his mouth and his nose hooked downward over it. The sight was nauseating this early in the morning. But Zusak had a note of excitement in his voice he'd never heard before. "We finally cracked it last night around four in the morning. We weren't sure who this guy was at first. We both, that's Herman my tech guy and me, thought he was either an undercover cop or a criminal. His background was layered in like it was the real deal. It was a very professional job. We were able to uncover his real name and a little info about his background, but not much. His real name is Carney. Harold Timothy Carney."

"Real name?" Will scowled.

"Yeah. He's living under an alias, but the real name is Carney. Which was smart as hell. If anyone questioned it he could say it was a typo or something. He's originally from Boston but lived in San Diego. Or at least that was his last known address. And he's a Lieutenant Junior Grade in the Navy."

"If he's in the Navy, what the hell's he doing hanging here in Henderson?" Will asked.

"We don't know yet. There weren't any wants or warrants out for his arrest. But we're still picking away at the info, and I'll have more by this afternoon. I just wanted to be sure to report our findings right away."

A lieutenant in the Navy. *God damn it!* But the fucker had something to hide, otherwise he wouldn't be living under an alias. If he turned out to be a criminal—Will rubbed his hands together gleefully. He could take Sam to court again and file for custody, accusing her of being a negligent mother for exposing Joy to a criminal element. Once he got custody, Sam would follow. She'd be too afraid not to.

"Find me something on this fucker so I can get him out of Sam's life for good." Will said. "You do that, and I'll give you a thousand-dollar bonus."

Zusak's smile stretched across his face, becoming downright scary. "Will do, Mr. Cross."

Working at the law office of Hinton, Hinton, and Chase as a receptionist paid the bills, but Sam wished the pace would pick up, giving her less time to think. As it was, she kept dwelling on how Tim had touched her, held her this morning as they'd made love. There had been a desperation in the way they'd clung to one another. She'd wanted to hold him deep inside her as long as possible, to make him as much a part of her as she could. Was that how military wives felt every time their husbands left for deployment? Was that how military men felt when they left their wives behind? If it was, it sucked.

She'd left early to drop Joy at school and Tim had gone on to work, needing to finish an installment before his meeting at the hotel. How could he just go on with business as usual? She felt as though she might fall apart at any minute. He'd said he wanted to meet all his obligations before he went to the meeting. He'd encouraged her to go on to work. Sitting at the house alone would only give her more time to worry.

They were supposed to meet at the hotel after lunch. She'd already asked for half a day off so she could go with him. Would they arrest him right away and take him into custody? Afterwards, would he be able to call her and let her know he was okay? The scenarios the lawyers had gone over had not given either of them much comfort.

The phone rang again. She welcomed the distraction. "Hinton, Hinton, and Chase."

"May I speak to Mrs. Samantha Cross?"

Surprised to hear someone inquiring about her, she hesitated. "This is she."

"Mrs. Cross. This is Detective Danny Howard of the Henderson Police Department. You filed a police report with us about someone opening a credit card under your name."

"Yes, I did."

"We'd like for you to come down to the station this morning so we can go over our findings with you."

She didn't need this today. She could barely concentrate on answering the phones, let alone this credit card issue.

"I just want to go over a few questions with you beforehand. Who besides yourself would have access to your social security number, Mrs. Cross?"

"The bank, my employer, the online college where I'm enrolled. I haven't really given it out to anyone other than places like that. I don't know of anyone else."

"Your ex-husband would have that information, wouldn't he?

"Yes. During our marriage he had to have it for insurance and things like that."

"Do you have any other credit cards in your name?"

"No. I have a debit card I use with my bank account, but that's the only card I have."

"If you could come in around noon it would be good, Mrs. Cross."

"I have a very important meeting I can't miss at two o'clock today, Detective. If it will take longer than an hour, I'll need to come in tomorrow."

"It shouldn't take any more than an hour."

"Okay I'll be there at noon. Which station?"

"Our main department on Lead Street. One more question before I let you go."

"Yes."

"Were you at home on Saturday?"

"No. My boyfriend and I went to the Springs Preserve in the morning with my daughter. We ate lunch there and went to a movie afterwards."

"May I have his phone number and the name of the movie theater?"

Her heart raced and her anxiety level spiked. She didn't need this today. She told him the name of the theater. "What's all this about, Detective?"

"I'm ruling out some things, Mrs. Cross and tying up loose ends."

"Am I in trouble for something?"

"No. Not at all. But we have activity on the card at that time, and if we can establish where you were, we can prove it wasn't you using it."

"Why would I report a fraudulent credit card if I was the one using it?"

"You'd be surprised the things people do and believe they'll never get caught, Mrs. Cross."

No she wouldn't. Not after the year she'd had. She gave him Tim's number.

Flash finished the programming on the laptop and closed it. He took his work computer and the portable printer, printed out the invoice for the work payable to J and J Security Systems, and loaded up his tools and other things. The business would continue to run itself with the monthly fees coming in for monitoring. Travis would only have to hire someone who could take over maintenance of the units.

He found Mrs. Tracey in the kitchen. Her white hair lay tightly curled against her head, and she wore a bright pink warm-up suit. "I'm going to the gym in just a few minutes," she announced.

"Then I finished just in time," Flash said.

"There was a fellow who came by here about a week ago before you started installing the system. He offered me five hundred dollars to tell you I didn't want the system and gave me a list of other companies who could install one."

Flash's brows rose, then a wry smile sprang to his lips. He'd wondered why he'd had a number of customers drop him recently. Cross must have spent a fortune bribing them. "Big guy with dark hair, built like a football player?" he asked.

"That's him."

"I appreciate you turning him down and hiring me anyway, Mrs. Tracey."

"Oh I didn't turn down the money." She took out her purse and pulled out a wallet. She counted out five one hundred dollar bills and laid them on the table. "That's the five hundred dollar tip I'm going to give you for installing my system so quickly. I figure if he's fool enough to hand out money to cause trouble, the person he's trying to hurt should reap the rewards." She rolled the cash up and tucked it into Flash's shirt pocket.

"You don't have to do that, Mrs. Tracey. You should keep it for a rainy day." He stuck his fingers into his pocket to retrieve the money.

She stopped him. "My children are paying for the system, Mr. Carnes. I knew this guy was no good the minute I saw him. It'll give you a little boost knowing you got something back from him, won't it?"

Flash laughed and nodded. "Thank you, ma'am."

She patted his chest. "I'll give that bill to my son when he comes over this evening."

"Thank you, ma'am. Let me go over how to arm and disarm the alarm one more time, and then I'll leave so you can get to the gym."

After running through the process one more time, he left her a sheet with instructions, then headed for the van.

Worry crowded in on him. He'd hoped to have Will Cross back behind bars so he'd know Sam was safe. Knowing he still being free to stalk her prayed on Flash's mind. He hadn't accomplished what he needed to keep her safe. Filing a report about the bribes Cross was giving customers to keep them from hiring him would do nothing.

He should have grabbed the son of a bitch and dropped his ass as far out into the desert as he could and let nature take its course.

His phone rang and an unfamiliar number popped up on the screen. He'd already had a call from a detective from the local police department. Now what?

A female voice he'd never heard before said, "This is NCIS agent Cara Cooper. You need to come to the Bellagio now, Lieutenant Carney. Your info has been compromised and Gilbert is in the air heading your way as we speak. He's traveling with some interesting and very dangerous company. We need to debrief you and set something up to lure him in. Are you up for that?"

"Yeah, but I need conformation you are who you say you are. Just because you have this number doesn't mean shit."

"Flash," Captain Jackson's voice came over the line. "We don't have much time. You need to double-time it over here."

"Yes, sir. I'm on my way."

The room was small, a little larger than a closet with a video monitor. Would Tim be questioned in a place like this? Would he have to spend hours there? Her stomach cramped at the thought.

"Do you recognize the woman?" Detective Howard asked, yanking her back to the present.

Sam focused on the television monitor and the woman sitting in another room similar to this one. She was crying, and her makeup was smeared. But aside from the size of her bust, she looked enough like Sam to pass for a close cousin. "No, I don't know her."

"Her name is Carla Vickers. She's told us William Cross gave her the credit card, gave her permission to buy whatever she wanted, and instructed her to sign your name to the receipts. She says they've had an on-again-off-again relationship for the last six years."

Sam absorbed the information as she stared at the screen. So, while she'd been pregnant, Will had been having sex with someone else and coming home to her. He'd put her and Joy at risk. He'd said he loved her, needed her, wanted her. Stalked her. Harassed her. And he was sleeping with someone else. Someone who looked a great deal like her. Nausea struck and she placed a hand to her stomach. God, he was sick. He'd found a substitute for her even while they were married.

Once the nausea passed and she could breathe again, she shifted her attention to Detective Howard. She found something comforting in the man's demeanor. His iron gray hair and sharp hazel eyes projected focus and determination.

"Detective Howard—" She shook her head. "She's probably telling you the truth. Will truly believes that rules don't apply to him. That whatever he wants to do is law. Have you spoken to Mr. Logan at the bank?"

"Yes, we have. Logan told us your husband wanted him to encourage you to sign a mortgage agreement that you couldn't live up to so Cross could step in and gain control of your property."

She bet he'd been more than pissed when Logan didn't do it, too.

"He's also opened an account in your name at another bank, where he's been taking cash advances on the credit card and stockpiling them. We're not sure what he had in mind for the money. Miss Vickers said he talked about gaining custody of your daughter all the time."

"He doesn't really want her. He just thinks if he has custody of her, he'll have control over me. Will doesn't think of us as humans, we're just possessions."

"I'm aware of his background. That's why we got on this so quickly. We allowed Ms. Vickers to call him, and he admitted the card was his and he'd given it to her. But when he found out she'd been arrested he ended the call."

Sam's gaze shifted back to the monitor. The woman had regained her composure and now sat slumped in her chair, head down. "She's as much a victim of Will Cross as my daughter and I are. I wonder how many times he beat, bullied, and threatened her."

Howard shook his head. "We've traced the date the card was opened and the IP address. The application was sent from his office three months ago. We have an airtight case for credit card fraud against him. And with Logan's testimony, which he's agreed to, we can charge him with stalking again. He's going back to jail."

"For how long?"

"I can only guess. Because this is his first offense with credit card fraud, he would only get six months and fines. But because he chose a woman who looked like you to use the card, used your name on the purchases, and he's opened a bank account in your name and forged your signature to do so, we can prove it was his intent to implicate you in some kind of illegal activity. And by doing that, he's still stalking you. He may get two to five. We're still looking at alternatives."

Will was never going to stop coming after her until he was in prison or dead. He was truly insane. Obsessed.

"Because of this, we'll have an opening into his financials, Mrs. Cross. If he's done this, he may have done other things as well. If we do find other criminal activity, it may add to the charges and add time to his sentence."

"I hope it does." But there was no guarantee. With money and resources, he might weasel out of all of it. But she couldn't worry about this now. She needed to be at the Bellagio for Tim. "Do you need anything else from me?"

"I'll need you to sign your statement once it's typed. And I want to caution you to be careful. We haven't got an arrest warrant out for him, yet, but with Ms. Vickers' arrest, he has to know it's only a matter of hours and that we'll be looking for him."

"I'll be careful." She offered her hand. "Thank you for everything, Detective."

"You're welcome."

Sam left the police station and walked to the parking lot across the street. Once inside her car, she locked the door and drew a deep breath to try and stave off the emotions battling inside her. What more could happen?

She needed to see Tim. Needed for him to hold her one more time before they faced separation. Why hadn't they both just stayed home together? She would still have had to go to the police station. Still had to deliver Joy to school, but at least their last few hours would have been together. But he'd wanted every I dotted and every T crossed for the business, so Travis could take over as easily as possible.

She started the car and pulled out of the parking lot. She caught the Bruce Woodbury Beltway. Traffic was heavy and she fought her own impatience in an attempt to remain calm. She turned onto the Vegas Freeway, then the Flamingo Road exit and merged into traffic. By the time she turned into the Bellagio she was trembling. She unlocked her door, then reached for her seatbelt. The passenger side door swung open and Will Cross slipped into the seat.

Sam reached for the door handle but the seatbelt, still fastened, tugged her back in place. She fumbled at the catch and shoved at the door at the same time.

Will grabbed her arm and forced her back, his grip hard enough to bruise. He raised a large black pistol and pointed it at her face. The hole at the end of the barrel gaped at her, huge, threatening. Her limbs lost all strength and she couldn't catch her breath. Where had he gotten a gun?

“Close the door, start the car, and pull away,” he growled, his jaw set, his eyes narrowed.

She couldn’t move.

He grabbed her by the back of the neck with his free hand and squeezed so hard she felt the pain all the way down both arms. “Do what I say or I’m going to shoot you now.”

Sam gripped the door handle and shut the door. Though it caught, she hadn’t the strength to slam it completely. She started the car and pulled away.

CHAPTER 36

Flash sank into the cushions of the sitting room couch. He'd expected to be handcuffed and interrogated at the police station. The Bellagio Hotel room proved much more comfortable. And so far no one had whipped out handcuffs. He'd carried his weapon in a taped shoebox, so there would be no misunderstanding that he was surrendering. And now there was just one more thing the FBI wanted him to do before the Navy got his ass.

After nearly half an hour of going over the same ground four times, Flash had had enough. He glanced at his watch. Where was Sam? She was half an hour late.

"Have you got somewhere to be, Lieutenant?" Barnett asked, the snide tone grating.

"Yeah. I have a date with a guy who's already tried to kill me once. And this time he's brought some buddies to try and finish the job." He eyed Barnett. "Want to trade places?"

Barnett looked away.

The only person in the room he trusted was Captain Jackson. The captain had always been a hardass, but he'd proven to be a stand-up guy during this whole deal.

The two FBI guys, Russell and Pitt, were keeping their mouths shut and doing a Blues Brothers impression with their dark suits and dark shades. Russell, the tall one, looked a little like Jeff Goldblum. Pitt, the heavier stocky one, had to have played football. Both appeared fit and alert. "Why are you two guys here?" Flash asked.

Russell spoke for the two of them. "We're here to observe and to make sure the chain of custody remains intact."

"Chain of custody?"

Russell spoke for the two of them. "You, Lieutenant. You'll be our star witness against Gilbert. We can't let anything happen to you."

"How do you plan to keep me safe?" he asked.

The man's face hardened. "By any means possible."

So the FBI was pissed one of their own had switched sides and been operating right under their noses. Or maybe not. "How long have you known about him?"

"Since he filed assault charges against you, and we found your surveillance cameras in the apartment. We've been gathering data right along with you the whole time."

"Good."

"We got to your safety deposit box in San Diego before Gilbert did, and we have the bogus orders he sent you," Pitt said, his voice gravelly, as though he'd suffered some kind of vocal damage.

Flash's pulse skyrocketed and every nerve seemed to fire at once. "I had hoped it was a paperwork snafu." Geez, he was fucked.

Pitt shook his head. "We intend to honor the orders as they stand on our end, so you can relax. As far as the FBI is concerned, you've been acting as an agent since first taking on the assignment in Iraq. As long as we recover the hundred thousand you got for the exchange."

"It's safe, and you'll get it."

Russell nodded.

"And the assault charges?" Flash asked.

"We won't be pursuing those, since you were only indirectly responsible for Gilbert's injuries."

The relief was almost numbing. One federal agency down, two more to go.

As far as he knew the only thing NCIS wanted him for was AWOL.

How long would the military give him? Two years? Ten? He'd played it down to Sam and offered her reassurances he knew weren't true. He didn't expect her to wait for him, but he had expected her to be here. Where the hell was she? Worry burrowed into his gut. Had something happened to Joy? She'd have called. He eyed his phone where it sat across the room on a cabinet.

Agent Cooper spoke, breaking into his thoughts. "Whatever happens Lieutenant, don't let Gilbert or his associates into the house. He'll want to recover the artifacts and the money, and he needs you alive to do that, so we don't believe he'll come out shooting. We want everything to go down out in the open. We can offer you more cover in front of the house. As soon as he asks about the contraband we'll move in."

"I got it the first ten times you outlined the plan, agent. I need my weapon back."

When Cooper hesitated, he shook his head. "You really expect me to go into this thing unarmed? If Gilbert decides to shoot it out instead of surrender, I'll be the first one he'll shoot at. He killed Dobson, his partner. And he believes I've had his merchandise for ten months. Why do you think he's brought along backup?"

"You're still a federal agent, Lieutenant," Cooper reminded him.

"Yeah, I know." Until they took his rank and his freedom. He'd had time to accept it, but it still ate at his gut and his heart. For seven years, he'd given the Navy his all. Trained, sacrificed, ate, slept, and lived the life twenty-four/seven, because it was the SEAL way, and it was what he'd signed on to do. He'd served his country in every way he could. And after everything was said and done, none of it would matter now. He'd known it would probably go down this way.

"Why didn't you pick these guys up at the airport in San Diego?" Flash asked.

"They caught private transport minutes before our agents got there," Pitt said.

Cooper moved to the cabinet and picked up his personal belongings. "With as much firepower as Gilbert is bringing with him, it would be too dangerous to try and take him at the airport here. Too many innocent bystanders. The house is isolated enough to ensure no one gets hurt. And thanks to our FBI friends, we know he's heading there as soon as he touches down."

Barnett's phone rang and every eye turned in his direction. "'Gilbert and his crew just landed," he announced. "We have a fifteen-minute window to get everyone in place. We need to go."

"We have agents on their way to your apartment, Lieutenant." Pitt said. "They should be in place before you get there."

Flash nodded. "Can I have my personal items back now?" Flash asked.

Cooper handed back his wallet and the envelope he'd had in his pocket. He gritted his teeth in irritation. It had been opened.

"I'm sorry I opened it, Lieutenant." Her brown eyes held compassion. "You'll have time to say your good-byes before we leave."

Without answering, he accepted the Sig Saur P226 from her, loaded the magazine, and stuck it in his waistband at the small of his back. He scanned the room for Captain Jackson. Approaching him he said, "A minute of your time, sir?"

Jackson led the way to the bedroom area of the room and turned to face him.

"I appreciate all you've done for me, sir."

"You're welcome. We'll have time to discuss everything later on the trip back to San Diego. We're all going on the same flight."

Flash nodded. "Should something unexpected happen, I'd appreciate it if you'd give this to my girl, sir." He offered Jackson the envelope.

"Girl?" Jackson asked.

"Samantha Cross, the woman who owns the apartment I've been renting." His throat worked as he swallowed.

"Admiral Clarence is working with the FBI and NCIS to try and smooth things out, Flash."

"I appreciate it, sir. But we both know the Navy has its own way of looking at unauthorized absences." He looked away for a moment as he struggled to maintain his composure. "I appreciate you backing me up here, sir. Otherwise I'd already be in handcuffs."

"I'm coming along for the ride, so I'll be there when all this is over," Jackson said.

"Good. You deserve it as much as I do. Is my team okay, sir?"

"They deployed in your absence. They'll be back within the month. You've missed a lot. We'll catch up on the plane."

Flash nodded. And he'd missed their deployment. He'd let his guys down. Regret pooled in his chest.

"We have to go," Barnett said. "Cooper and I will be riding with you. We've already called for your van to be brought around. Gilbert will think something's suspicious if he sees one of our vehicles."

In the elevator on the way down, Flash checked his phone. No calls or messages from Sam. Had she decided she couldn't handle this? He found her number and pushed it.

"No calls, Carney," Barnett said.

What was he going to do in a crowded elevator, wrestle him for his phone? "Bite me, Barnett." The call went directly to voice mail.

Something was wrong. No way Sam would bail. He closed the phone. His breathing hitched and his stomach muscles tightened with anxiety. Something was wrong.

"Where are we going?" Sam asked. Every nerve in her body jittered with fear. Her leg bobbed up and down on the gas pedal, making it difficult for her to control the pressure.

The wind whistled through the crack in the door, annoying and loud.

"To your grandmother's house. You're going to pack a bag for you and Joy, then we'll pick her up from day care. We're taking a little trip."

"Where?"

"You'll find out when we get there. Just keep driving."

They pulled to a stop at a red light.

"Fix the goddamn door before a cop stops us," he demanded. He shoved the gun forward. "Don't try anything. I don't have to shoot you to hurt you with this."

No, he didn't. Her neck ached, as did her arm where he'd wrenched it. Sam pushed the unlock button, swung the door open, and slammed it shut.

She concentrated on the road ahead while she tried to think through the worst of her fear. Tim had shown her how to defend herself. If she could get Will to put down the gun once they were out of the car, she might be able to get away.

"How many times did you fuck Navy boy?" Will asked, a sneer in his voice.

"Probably fewer times than you did Carla Vickers in the last six years," she said, her tone calm and quiet.

Her reply first brought a scowl to his face, then a smile. "Are you jealous, baby?"

"No, not at all, Will. Why don't you bail her out and the two of you can live happily ever after together, with my blessing."

"She isn't you, Sam. Just a cheap imitation. I prefer the real deal."

Why couldn't he just stop? What had triggered this obsession? What mechanism in his psychotic brain had caused him to fixate on her?

"I felt sorry for Carla, sitting in that interrogation room alone. You could have at least gotten her a lawyer."

His brows rose and a curious expression settled on his face. "Why are you worried about her?"

She stopped at another light and signaled a left turn, taking her time, driving extra-carefully. She was already late for the meeting at the Bellagio. Would Tim become concerned and ask someone to check on her? He knew she'd planned to be there. "Why aren't *you* worried about her? You've slept with her for six years, gone out with her, bought her gifts, and spent time with her. Why aren't you the least bit concerned about what's happened to her?"

For the first time Will frowned, as though he found her question a little uncomfortable, and the barrel of the gun drifted away from her to point at the dashboard, giving her a moment's respite. "All I care about is getting the hell out of here before the cops start looking for me. And you and Joy are going with me."

Joy wasn't going anywhere with this psychotic bastard.

He renewed his focus and redirected the pistol at her. "I'm not going back to jail, Sam. You've caused me a lot of trouble. Cost me a lot of money. It's time we were together again and stopped all this."

She remained silent, biting back the words she wanted to say despite the fear. But she agreed this time it would stop. She couldn't live like this anymore, and Joy wasn't going to, either.

Her thoughts strayed to Tim and she tried unsuccessfully to cut them off. He'd given her such a gift. He'd loved her with kindness, respect and passion. He hadn't seen her as a victim, but a fighter, and he had encouraged her to think of herself in those terms.

He was strong. He'd move on. And despite Grace and Chaney's faults, they'd take care of Joy.

Twenty minutes later, when they pulled into the driveway at the house, she parked the car and got out.

"Try anything and I'll shoot," Will warned from the other side of the car.

She looked across the top at him, anger and resolve settling deep and hard inside her. "Fuck you, Will." Leaving her purse in the car, she stalked toward the front porch.

She unlocked the door and stepped into the living room. Will crowded close, shoving her forward. The beep of the alarm waiting to be reset sounded loud in the empty house.

"Take care of it," he demanded, pointing at the console with the gun.

Sam took her time punching in the code, waiting until the last minute before hitting the enter button.

"You've learned some bad habits since we've been apart," Will said. He slapped her, and she staggered back against the wall.

Never again. She'd promised herself. *Never again.* With a screech containing six years of pent-up rage, she came back at Will with her fist, hitting him in the throat as hard as she could.

Will gagged and grabbed his neck, half bending. Sam raised a foot and kicked downward into his knee, hyper-extending it. He went down, catching himself with one hand, the pistol still gripped in the other.

She pivoted and ran. The sound of the gun's report seemed to echo through the house. A hole appeared in the sheetrock inches above her head. She dodged into the hallway. If he caught her now, he'd kill her. She rushed into the bathroom, slammed the door, shot the bolt at the bottom into place, then the top. She hit the panic button above the light switch with her palm. As if by magic, a hole appeared in the solid wood door eye-high, then another, lower. She flinched back and dove into the bathtub and out of the line of fire. Although she was safe for the moment, adrenaline pumped through her system, dulling the ache in her face, neck, and arm. Warmth trickled down her side. She pressed her fingers against it. Pain pinched her and her fingers came away red. She'd been shot.

Will yelled from the other side of the door. "I'm going to kill you, Sam." He lunged against the door. The wall shook.

CHAPTER 37

The car's brakes squealed as Flash turned the van onto the residential drive. Agent Barnett gripped the handle above the door. "What's the rush?"

Flash didn't bother to answer. Adrenaline pumped through him, ramping up the tension in his muscles. He had the edgy feeling he'd experienced during the mission that had started this whole cluster-fuck. And he'd learned to pay attention to it. Something was wrong. Where was Sam?

His cell phone rang. He thumbed the screen and answered it without looking at the number.

Sherry, one of the girls who monitored the system said, "The panic button just went off at Mrs. Cross's house. You told me to call you anytime it happened. The police have been notified."

"I'm on my way." He hung up and spoke over his shoulder. "Better grab onto something, Cooper." He shoved the phone into his shirt pocket and floored the gas pedal.

"What the hell, Carney? Slow the hell down," Barnett barked.

"There's an issue at the house." Sam was over an hour late. It had to be Cross. How long had he had her? If he'd hurt her, he was going to take the son of a bitch apart with his bare hands.

"My girl's psycho ex-husband. I was expecting her at the hotel. I haven't heard from her for the last hour. The panic button at the house has been activated. I installed it for her when I first moved in to the apartment next door. Cross has a history of stalking, beating, and harassing her. Been jailed several times for it. He's a narcissistic personality and completely unstable." He described the floor plan of the house succinctly.

"Jesus, Carney. You're a fucking trouble magnet," Barnett muttered. "You can't go into the house. Cooper and I will handle this."

Like hell. He wasn't standing outside and twiddling his thumbs while Sam needed him.

Barnett's phone rang and he listened for a moment. "Hold your position. We're pulling in now. Cooper and I will deal with this. You need to wave off the local police."

"Gilbert?" Cooper asked.

"Not yet. Agents just arrived to take position and realized someone's in the house. We need them ready in the garage and apartment," Barnett said, pulling his weapon. Flash took the drive on two wheels, slammed on the brakes and slid to a stop. He bailed out of the van, pulled his weapon and ran toward the house. He leaped the steps and was at the door ready to enter when Barnett ran up on the porch to join him. Cooper disappeared around the side of the house to cover the back.

Flash waved Barnett away from the door and pushed it open. He secured his Sig in the two-handed grip that was second nature to him, and rushed into the living room in a crouch, his steps measured and quiet.

A meaty thump sounded in the hall. Flash strode to the hall entrance. Cross was backing up to get another run at the bathroom door.

"Back off, Cross," Flash ordered, sighting him with the pistol. If he pulled the trigger, Sam's worries would end, but he would have killed Joy's father.

Will's head jerked up. He threw up his hand and pointed a Glock 9 mm pistol at him. Instinct kicked in and Flash dove to the side of the hall and flattened himself against the wide wooden support framing the opening.

"Federal officer," Barnett yelled, "Drop your weapon." He took a position on the other side of the hallway, his Sig trained on Cross.

"Fuck you," Cross bellowed his face red from exertion, his breathing heavy. "She's my wife, Navy boy. Mine! You've fucked her for the last time." Spittle flew from his mouth. He pulled the Glock's trigger. The bullet gouged into the wood support Flash had taken cover behind.

Barnett fired, striking Cross in the shoulder. He staggered as blood blossomed at the right side of his chest, but he didn't go down. "Put the fucking gun down," Barnett shouted.

"I'm not going back to jail," Cross said, his voice almost calm. He turned his gun on Barnett and the agent fired again, hitting him in the chest. Cross's knees buckled and he crumpled face-first onto the floor.

Flash moved forward, lending Barnett backup.

Barnett kicked the Glock toward him, then bent to check for a pulse. He shook his head. He pushed his mike and announced what had just taken place as he walked toward the master bedroom. "I'll go let Cooper in through the back."

Flash rushed to the bathroom door and saw the bullet holes in the wood for the first time. God, what if she was hurt? Dead? Dying? "Sam." He couldn't seem to get enough air to project his voice. "Sam, honey? It's Tim. Can you open the door?"

"He's bent the bolts you put in. I don't know if I can pull the bottom one up."

Weak with relief at the sound of her voice, Flash leaned against the door. "We'll get you out. Are you hurt?"

"Only a little."

His anxiety spiked, and his voice rose. "What do you mean a little?"

Pitt and Russell appeared from the master bedroom with Cooper and Barnett. Cooper's face was crimped in a pissed scowl. "Appreciate the added security, Lieutenant. By the time I got the door open, everything was over." She eyed Cross's body.

A squeaking screech sounded from the other side of the bathroom door and a thump. The door swung open, though the bottom dragged against the tile. Her skin, white as cotton, her freckles standing out, Sam trembled visibly. Flash dragged her into his arms and held on. Her blouse clung to his arm, tacky with something wet and he jerked back. "Are you hit?"

"I think it's just a graze." She pulled her blouse up, exposing a gouge in her side. Her gaze fell on Will Cross's body lying in the hall. She froze for a second. "Did you?"

"No. One of the agents."

Pitt put his hand up to his ear mike listening and announced. "Gilbert and two men are pulling into the drive."

Agent Cooper stepped forward and took Sam's arm. "Come with me, Mrs. Cross, and I'll bandage that for you."

Flash nodded. "I have something I have to do, but I'll be right back, Sam."

"We'll have two parabolic mikes on you at all times, Lieutenant. Anything they say will be recorded."

In other words, he wanted him to get Gilbert to admit as much as he could.

Flash drew a deep breath, checked his weapon, then held it close against his leg. He took the first step toward the front of the house. Fifteen minutes and all this would be over. He remembered thinking the same thing the last time. Sweat ran down between his shoulder blades.

The sound of a car door slamming sent a spike of adrenaline through his system and his heartbeat sped. He took a deep breath to offset it, opened the front door and stepped out on the porch. The three men paused in their progress toward the apartment. Flash kept the gun down, but allowed them to see he was armed, as he could see they were.

"Stand down, Lieutenant. We've come to negotiate." Gilbert said, his tone almost congenial. "I think you've met agents Ballard and Harrison."

"So they *are* agents?" Damn the FBI and their misinformation.

"Yes. Ballard got a commendation for being injured during the attack on Agent Dobson."

Dobson lost his life, and one of the men responsible got a fucking medal for it. Jesus. That was wrong on every level.

"He and Harrison want their identification back."

Flash wrestled back his anger and attempted to go along with the program Gilbert was manipulating. "That can be arranged…depending."

"On what?"

"They apologize for trying to kill me."

"Since you shot both of them, I'd say what happened was a draw." Gilbert's amiable expression flattened to become deadly serious. "You know why we're here."

"You want your money and artifacts."

"And I have something you need in return."

Flash raised his brows. “What?”

“Your freedom. The penalty for desertion is pretty steep.”

This was getting way too real. “Yeah, it is.”

“You’ve been AWOL for ten months. That could add up to ten years.”

Every time he thought it, it was like a punch in the gut. Hearing Gilbert say it out loud cut deep. “I might have an interesting story or two to tell for a deal.”

Gilbert tilted his head. “If you lived to tell them.” His gaze turned toward the house. “We know about the woman and little girl who live here. Since her car is here, I assume they’re inside.”

“Leave them out of this, Gilbert.”

Gilbert smiled. “You return the money, the artifacts and Agents Ballard and Harrison’s identification, and I’ll forget where I found you—forever.”

If this were a real deal, would he take it? He couldn’t forget about the scenario Gilbert had outlined for him. Was there a grain of truth in it? Were the artifacts being used as a get-into-bed-with-a-cartel card? If he agreed too quickly, Gilbert might grow suspicious.

“There’s three of us and only one of you, Carney. You might take one of us down, but the other two will kill you, then we’ll move on to the woman and little girl.”

With a resurgence of rage, heat exploded in Flash’s face. The man had truly crossed over to a darker side in the past ten months. “You’ve got a deal.”

Gilbert smiled. “Good.”

Flash nodded toward the apartment. “They’re hidden in the garage.”

Gilbert gestured toward the building. “Lead the way.”

Flash smiled. “Not likely, Gilbert. Your men can go ahead, and you and I will follow.”

Gilbert jerked his head in the direction of the garage. Ballard strode toward the building with Harrison close behind.

Flash stepped down off the porch and fell into step with Gilbert, keeping a yard of space between them. His muscles twitched as he braced for some defensive action.

“So who else have you told about all this?” Gilbert asked.

"I don't have anyone to tell. I have no family. And I couldn't very well contact my team."

"You said you'd left the artifacts with someone you trusted."

Flash grew watchful. Gilbert was working himself up to making a move, telegraphing it loud and clear.

"There wasn't anyone, Gilbert. I was hiding out on a boat waiting for your men to come after me. What did you expect me to say?"

Ballard reached the building, grabbed the handle on the garage door and tugged it open. Armed agents poured out of the doorway, overwhelming the two men and taking them down. Their shouts of 'on the ground' overlapped into gibberish.

Gilbert turned to run while at the same time trying to draw his weapon. Flash grabbed his arm and shoved him backward, taking him down. He jammed his knee into Gilbert's groin and clubbed him in the face with his Sig. The man cried out as his nose broke with a pop. Flash jerked Gilbert's sidearm from his shoulder holster and tossed it out of reach. Gripping his pistol two-handed, he thrust his Sig in Gilbert's face. Four well-armed agents swarmed around them.

Blood from his broken nose poured down Gilbert's face. His eyes widened with panic and pain. "Go ahead and pull the trigger. I'm a dead man anyway."

Flash spoke between gritted teeth. His arms trembled as he suppressed the urge to shoot the bastard. "You've lived ten months longer than Rick Dobson. If you die tomorrow it wouldn't be too soon to suit me. But you deserve to have to look over your shoulder every day for the rest of your life. Just as I've done for the last ten months."

Flash handed the Sig to one of the agents butt first, then staggered to his feet. He looked down at Gilbert one last time. "I've been taping everything going on in your apartment for months. And just guess who I taped sitting in your apartment last week?"

Gilbert's color faded and he stared at him as the agents dragged him, none too gently, to his feet.

The adrenaline had leached away leaving Flash shaky. His emotions uncertain, he turned away.

He needed to see and hold Sam for as long as they'd let him.

As the coroner's van holding Will's body pulled away, Sam pressed close to Tim's side and tightened her grip around his waist. His clothes had a chemical smell like burnt firecrackers. She ignored it and homed in on the natural smell of him beneath it.

Crime scene technicians carried their cases out of the house and loaded them into a van. FBI agents stood watch over the scene. Pitt and Russell sat on the hood of their car waiting for things to wrap up.

"Your Captain seemed like a nice man. He said he'd help." Her arms tightened for a moment. "He called you Flash. Is that what your teammates call you?"

"Yeah. You don't need to know why just now, Sam." He rubbed his cheek against her hair. "Where's Joy?"

Her breath hitched. "She's on her way. Officer Davis and his partner went to pick her up and bring her home." She drew a deep breath. "What does it say about your life when you know officers on the police department by name?"

"Most of the time it means you know the right people." His arms tightened and he brushed her forehead with his lips. "Travis and 'Nita will be here tomorrow. Javier, too. They'll help you put the house back in order and fix the doors."

She nodded.

"You'll need to stay in the apartment. It'll be safer until the back door is fixed."

"Don't." She turned her face against his chest and fought against the tears, but they came anyway. How would she and Joy bear being without him?

"I don't know what's going to happen Sam."

"Nobody ever does. You just take it one day at a time and hold on with both hands. Like we're doing now." Her fists clutched his shirt as she clung to him. "Don't give up on us. We're never going to give up on you."

He shuddered, the tension in his body so taut it felt as if his bones were fighting free of his skin. "I'm not." His voice broke. "I love you so much."

A police car pulled into the drive. Officer Davis got out of the front passenger seat and opened the back door. One of the day-care workers stepped out of the car holding Joy's hand. After a moment's hesitation, Joy tugged free. She darted through the people and ran to them. Sam eased away from Tim to catch her as Joy threw herself into her arms.

"What's wrong, Mommy?"

"Nothing." Sam held her close and fought back tears. "Everything's fine. We just had a little bit of trouble, but it's over now." But it wasn't. How was she to tell her daughter that her father was dead? She lifted Joy onto her lap and held her close.

Tim put his arms around them both.

Agent Pitt approached them. "It's time to go, Lieutenant."

Sam wanted, with all her being, to scream *No! Not yet, please.*

"Where are you going, Mr. Tim?" Joy asked.

"I have to go away for a little while."

Joy's attention shifted from one to the other of them, and her face settled into an anxious frown. "No. I don't want you to go," she protested. She leaned across her mother and reached for him.

Tim took her into his arms and held her small body close. Though he shut his eyes, the pain seemed locked into his features, making them appear gaunt.

"I don't want to leave you either, baby, but I promise I'll call you, as much as I can. Okay?" his voice shook.

"When will you be back?"

"I don't know, sweet tart."

He reached for Sam and she leaned into his side. He bent his head and kissed her lips, her forehead, then turned his lips against Joy's cheek.

"I love you, Mr. Tim. I don't want you to go." Joy began to cry. As hard as Sam fought for composure, she couldn't control her own tears.

"I love you too, sweet tart. I love you and your mommy more than anything. I'll be back as soon as I can."

Sam forced herself to reach for Joy and pulled her from his arms. She clung to her child as tightly as Joy clung to her, both seeking comfort where there was none.

Tim scooped up the duffle he'd packed and strode to the car. Each step tore another strip from his composure and his heart. By the time he reached the vehicle, tears flowed down his face and his breathing hitched. Agent Russell opened the back door. Tim tossed the duffle in and braced a hand on the door, fighting for composure. He blinked to clear his vision and looked back one last time at Sam and Joy, taking in his final glimpse of them, both crying, both raising hands to wave and calling out their love.

"I love you," he called out one more time then slid into the car.

EPILOGUE

Flash folded his hands to keep them from shaking. Every muscle in his body seemed poised for action, though there was nothing he could do. He had never felt more helpless in his life.

He glanced at Frank Luttrell, his Naval JAG lawyer. "What kind of chance do you think I have?"

The man adjusted his wire-rimmed glasses. "I don't like to speculate"

Did that mean he thought they were going to lose?

Every courtroom, whether it was military, federal, or criminal was basically the same. He had seen the inside of more of them than he ever hoped to see again. If they lost, could he appeal?

NCIS had closed the books on their investigation into Flash's disappearance and had never arrested him for AWOL. Instead, he'd turned himself in. While he'd been in FBI custody it been like a vacation compared to the six weeks he'd spent in the brig while charges were filed and the legal wheels turned.

And now it all came down to this moment. He tugged a cloth handkerchief from his back pocket, blotted his forehead, and tucked it neatly back into place.

Desperate for something else to focus on, he turned to look over his shoulder at the gallery. In military courts the only people, allowed to attend trials were those directly related to the case or close family. He'd told Travis he needed him with 'Nita and Sam should the verdict go against him. If he couldn't be there to comfort them himself, he wanted Travis to do it.

NCIS Agents Barnett and Cooper sat two seats back from the defense table. Cooper offered him a smile and Barnett a thumbs up. He nodded back. They had both testified on his behalf, as had FBI Agents Pitt and Russell. Even Captain Jackson had testified to his conduct, skill, and value as a member of his team. And though his team members had volunteered to add their weight to the testimony, his lawyer had deemed it unnecessary. He hoped the man's decision had been the right one.

It was both a blessing and a curse Sam and Joy couldn't attend the proceedings. A blessing they wouldn't have to witness his conviction if they found him guilty. A curse he wouldn't be there to comfort Sam when she got the news. His chest tightened just thinking of the two of them.

The bailiff called the court to attention and everyone rose.

The judge, Colonel Ronald T. Sheraton, USMC, took his seat. The five-man jury filed into the courtroom and sat down.

The bailiff read off the trial number, his name and the charge, then called the room to order.

Sheraton got down to business. "As to the charges of desertion filed against Lieutenant Junior Grade Harold Timothy Carney, have the members of the jury reached a verdict?"

The jury foreman, a Marine Corps Major rose from his seat, a piece of paper in his hand. "Yes, sir, a verdict has been reached."

"The defendant will rise," Sheraton ordered.

Flash rose to his feet, as did his defense attorney. Luttrell had done everything in his power to prove Flash's intent had never been to leave his unit or avoid deployment, but to get back to them as soon as possible. But had he done a good enough job? Flash's heart beat high in his throat, his palms sweated, and he felt as though he were drawing breath through a straw.

"You may read the verdict," Sheraton instructed, his gray brows knit in a frown.

The foreman glanced at Flash, then turned his attention to the paper in his hand. "As to the charge of desertion, we find the defendant…not guilty."

Relief rolled over Flash in a rush, but he kept his spine stiff with an effort. His legs shook with the release of tension. He braced his fingertips on the table to steady himself. His attorney maintained his composure as well, but his grin stretched so wide it looked painful.

"Gentlemen of the jury, the Navy and this court thank you for your service in these proceedings. You are dismissed."

After the jury had filed out, Colonel Sheraton turned his attention to Flash. "Lieutenant Junior Grade Carney, I want to address you before we end these proceedings."

Sheraton couldn't change the not guilty verdict, but he could tear into him, if he had an opposing view. "Yes, sir."

"In my twenty-five years of sitting on the bench, this has been one of the most interesting and legally complicated desertion trials I have ever presided over. You're actions in going into hiding may or may not have been the right thing to do, Lieutenant. That you were badly injured when the first call came in tilted things in your favor. Having no contact with your command when the second deployment call went through wouldn't have carried as much weight had you not been neck-deep in feeding NCIS evidence against a terrorist. That spoke to the jury's sense of duty and justice."

Was the guy working his way up to telling him he should be put back in a cell?

Sheraton continued. "In the course of the trial, the diverse range of skills you brought to the FBI investigation you assisted in were mentioned time and time again. Those skills and your drive to see justice done, despite the dangers and cost to yourself, are qualities the Navy needs to retain. I noticed your enlistment is ending in four weeks. I just wondered what you planned to do now you've been cleared."

Flash smiled as the last of the thousand pound weight lifted from his shoulders. "I haven't decided yet, sir. My circumstances have changed since the last time I re-enlisted. I need to talk to my family."

"I hope you'll make the right decision, Lieutenant. You are free to go."

"Thank you, sir."

Flash pumped Luttrell's hand and even looped an arm around him and pounded him on the back. "I can't thank you enough."

"You caught a break. Had the jury decided to stick to the letter of the law, you would be sitting in a jail cell right now. I'm pleased it worked out."

"Thanks." Flash shook his hand again.

"Stay out of trouble. And good luck with your decision," Luttrell said, picking up his briefcase. "Keep me posted on what you decide."

Agents Cooper and Barnett approached him as Luttrell left. "Congratulations, Lieutenant," Barnett said and offered his hand.

"Thanks. I appreciate your help."

"If you decide not to re-up, NCIS might be interested in you," Barnett said. "You have a month to explore your options."

Riding the wave of relief and victory, Flash grinned. "I'll keep that in mind." He was ready to see his two girls and have some face time with them. Talking on the phone and seeing them twice in four months wasn't nearly enough.

Cooper flipped her ponytail over her shoulder. It was longer than it had been when he'd seen her last. And she had a softer edge to her as well. What was going on there? "We've been designated as your official transport to Master Chief Marks's house. Samantha and Joy are there, along with the rest of your family."

"I'm ready. But I have to take care of some paperwork, first." He grabbed his cover and tucked it under his arm.

Half an hour later, having signed all the forms to finalize his release, Flash climbed into the back of their nondescript sedan. He attempted to lean back and enjoy breathing the air of freedom, but he couldn't keep still. He wanted to see Sam and Joy. Didn't they have lights and sirens on these damn vehicles?

"Did you call ahead to let Sam know the verdict?" he asked.

"Done," Cooper said over her shoulder. "She was…more than elated."

"Are you done with the FBI as well?" Cooper asked.

"Yeah. I suppose it will take the Navy a few weeks to cut orders. I know I've lost my slot on my team. I'll probably be training to get back up to fighting form."

"You look pretty fit," Cooper said.

Though he'd exercised while confined, the rigorous training he'd have to do to get back in fighting form… "Not even close. They'll probably send me back to BUD/S and make me train with the recruits." He was tempted to groan aloud.

"How do you think Sam will feel about you returning to your SEAL career?"

They'd have a lot to talk about. She'd never been around anyone in the military before. And the life was so different than anything she'd experienced. Concern cut its way into his bubble of happiness. This four-month separation had been tougher for him than he'd ever dreamed it could be. He'd missed her and Joy so much. If she asked him to give up his career—"I don't know."

He was almost grateful when Barnett said, "Gilbert was really working his way to becoming a terrorist. Murder, attempted murder, drug trafficking, smuggling, and finally terrorism. What was driving him?"

Flash had thought about this more than he ever wanted to again. "I think he did a few smuggling deals on his own, mixed in with the ones he was doing for the FBI. Maybe he was dumb enough to use the same contacts. Someone in their organization found out about it. Once they got their claws into him, he had no choice. When you have someone on your ass who'll behead you and go after your family—what choice *would* you have? That last day I checked the cameras and saw Caesar Vargas sitting in his living room like he'd come over for a beer, I knew I had him, and I called you. But of course the FBI already knew and had stepped in."

Cooper turned to look over her shoulder at him. "How the hell did you even know who Vargas was? It isn't as though they put their picture up on social media sites."

"I can't tell you the particulars, but we've done work against the cartels in South America and Africa. They're all attached to terrorist organizations one way or another. There's too much money involved for them not to be. I almost felt sorry for Gilbert when I saw him sitting there. He wasn't smart enough to be involved with them. But he did do me a favor. He was afraid they'd find out he'd screwed up and kill him. He never told them about me. Otherwise, I'd probably be dead." And Sam and Joy,

Travis and 'Nita, Josh and Javier…everyone he was attached to. *Jesus!*

To have come out of all this and still have his freedom, his life, and his family—*he was the luckiest man alive.* But what would happen to him and Sam if he went back to the teams?

They'd both broken away from things holding them back, standing in their way. Sam had stood up to a man twice her size. She was strong. They could make this work. He hoped.

James stretched his legs out before him and pretended to be paying attention to the conversation bouncing back and forth among the team members. His gaze strayed to Marsha as she pushed Alex around in the pool in a donut-shaped floatation device. From this angle he could see Alex's legs beneath the water stuck through the support on the bottom of the float, pumping away as if he was walking through the water. He was growing stronger and just plain growing. He laughed out loud at everything.

He studied the contrast of Marsha's lightly tanned skin to her hair and smiled. She had come so far. They had come so far—together. Now they were in the new house, she swam a little each day. And played with Alex in the pool to help him build his muscle coordination. Marsha was toned, fit and gorgeous. Just looking at her—

"Can I get you a beer, Captain?" Trish Marks asked.

James switched his attention to Trish. Saved from getting a boner right in the midst of a group of guys. He had it bad. "Point the way and I'll get it myself, Trish," he said, rising.

She turned and gestured toward the deck. "They're on the right side in the red cooler up against the house in the shade."

"Thanks."

He took his time getting the beer, allowing the residual effects of ogling his wife to subside. He wandered over to join Langley Marks. Langley fancied himself a master at grilling, but Trish wandered by quite often to check on the meat's progress. Langley pointed the tongs he held at her. "Begone, woman! I'm not burning anything."

"You burn those burgers and you'll be making a run through a drive-through to get more," she warned, only half teasing. "Keep an eye on him, Captain."

"I've only burnt a few the last couple of times," Langley called after her. James laughed aloud.

They were discussing some of the marksman training he hoped to put into place in the next month, to train the team with some new night scopes they'd just requisitioned, when Marsha wandered up. The mesh cover up she'd thrown on over her bathing suit masked part of her figure but emphasized the curve of her waist and hip. She pressed in close against his side and he looped his arm around her.

"Five minutes out, guys. Agent Cooper just called," she said. Excitement had added a hint of color across her cheekbones.

He brushed her forehead with his lips. She smiled up at him, her expression relaxed, happy. *Love you,* she mouthed. He gave her waist a squeeze.

A grin spread across Langley's lantern-jawed face. "Burgers are almost done, and we have smoked pork and barbecue sauce. Everything will be finished before Flash walks through the gate. Hooyah!"

Had forty-five minutes ever seemed so long? Surely it had been two hours since agent Cooper had called. Camp Pendleton wasn't that far away, was it?

The wives and girlfriends of the SEALs had been trying to distract her and help pass the time, while they all kept watch over the kids in the pool.

Sam scanned the circle. Zoe Weaver held her three-month old baby boy against her shoulder. His head, covered with a dark cap of hair, bobbed as she rubbed his back. She lowered him to her lap and propped him against her.

Hawk, her tall Native American husband of only a month, had been Tim's team leader when all this had started. He had a calm presence about him and piercing gray eyes that lived up to his call sign. Their baby looked so much like him Zoe joked, had she not gone through such terrifying labor, she'd say Adam Joseph was cloned.

Captain Jackson's wife, Marsha, held their son's fingers as he placed one foot in front of the other, walking, but not yet brave enough to turn loose of his mamma. The baby had strangely wide-spaced eyes, and someone had said he had a heart issue. He had personality plus, though, and even the other children loved playing with him.

Tess Kelly, Brett Weaver's girlfriend, stretched her hands out to Alex and encouraged him to come to her. Her copper-colored hair hung like silk against her shoulder. She was so beautiful with her chocolate brown eyes and pale skin, she could have been a model. But instead she was a journalist at a major paper. She and Brett looked like a power couple, him with his blond hair and blue-eyed good looks, and her with her gorgeous coloring.

Then there was Juanita Gallagher, Tim's unofficial foster mother. She had showered genuine affection on both her and Joy, and she'd helped Sam keep it together when she'd been hit so hard by Tim's absence. 'Nita was funny and cheerful, and she had all her boys, wrapped around her little finger, including her gruff, tough-talking ex-SEAL husband, Travis. Javier was holding down the fort for the business in Henderson and living in the apartment. Josh was doing duty as a police officer in Baja and watching over the house until Travis and 'Nita returned.

Trish Marks had offered to open her home to her and Joy at any time. The amazing woman juggled three kids, a husband who adored her, and a social worker's job. She was blonde with a redhead's freckles, and a girl-next-door kind of beauty. All the other women gravitated toward her as their undeclared leader. Sam felt better, calmer when she was with Trish. The woman just seemed to naturally know what to do to lend support.

These women were each remarkable. They'd taken her under their wing in the last forty-eight hours, offered her comfort and encouragement. Warned her about what she was taking on being the girlfriend of a Navy SEAL. But they also made sure she fully understood the rewards. Their men loved as fiercely as they fought. Were as loyal and generous with themselves when they were home as they were with their jobs. She had seen that in Tim. Fallen in love with him because of it. But could she bear the long separations? This last four months, only seeing him briefly twice, had seemed an eternity.

But her feelings for him hadn't wavered. She still loved him, deeply. She'd survived Will Cross. Stayed with him out of fear. How much easier would it be to stay with Tim out of love?

And now she couldn't bear having to wait a single moment longer to see him.

The group had congregated to lend support, to each other and to her, should the verdict be less than they hoped. With good news, the gathering had quickly morphed into a party.

Doc and Bowie waved over the fence. "Cars coming," Doc yelled. They'd been standing outside the gate keeping watch. Everyone rose to their feet at once.

Sam's heart rate skyrocketed and her stomach did a nervous flip as she waited for her first glimpse of Tim. Joy climbed from the pool and ran to her. But it was 'Nita who grabbed a towel to dry her off.

The moment the gate opened into the side yard, she started to tremble. He was surrounded by his teammates as he passed through the opening. They took turns shaking his hand and pounding him on the back. Travis reached him and grabbed him in for a bear hug and said something that made him laugh.

Sam pushed forward, surrounded by the women. But it was Joy who squeezed through the group and disappeared. Her high-pitched voice carried above the lower timbre of the men's. "Mr. Tim, Mr. Tim." Sam slipped between Captain Jackson and Travis, finally reaching the inner circle just as Joy threw herself against Tim's legs, attempting to hug him. He bent to lift her and hold her close despite her wet bathing suit.

"Mommy and me missed you a ho, ho bunch," she complained, her small face scrunched up as though she might cry.

"I missed you, too, sweet tart." He held her close. "A ho, ho bunch." He kissed her cheek, her forehead.

Over Joy's shoulder his blue eyes focused on Sam. "I want to say hi to your mom, okay?" He kissed Joy's cheek one more time and handed her off to Travis.

Sam swallowed against the rush of tears clogging her throat. And stopped after taking a single step. Without his beard he looked younger, his jaw clean-cut and angular. Wearing a white Naval uniform with all his ribbons, bars, and medals, his SEAL trident prominent, he was a heart-stoppingly handsome sight.

"What is it?" he asked.

"I've never seen you in your uniform. I just wanted to check you out."

He grinned, grasped her arm and tugged her close.

"You look really hot," Sam said as her arms went around his neck.

The men close enough to hear chuckled.

Sam pressed herself as close as she could get and ignored the medals jabbing into her breast. Having his arms around her was everything she needed. And when he kissed her as though he'd never get enough, it was more. She understood what the other women had been talking about. She could do this. She had broken away from her past. He was her future.

"I love you," he murmured. "We'll need to talk later about us, about my career."

She leaned back to look up at him and shook her head. "Whatever you need to do, Joy and I will be there for you. We love you, so much."

"Are you sure?" he asked, searching her face.

She nodded. "There's just one thing." She traced a fingertip over his SEAL insignia.

"What is it?"

"Will you do a Chippendale's thing for me later, when you take the uniform off?" she asked.

He ignored the roar of laughter from the crowd around them. A slow, cocky grin spread across his face "Yeah, I can do that."

OTHER BOOKS BY TERESA REASOR

BREAKING FREE
(Book 1 of the SEAL TEAM Heartbreakers)

BREAKING THROUGH
(Book 2 of the SEAL TEAM Heartbreakers)

BREAKING AWAY
(Book 3 of the SEAL TEAM Heartbreakers)

TIMELESS

HIGHLAND MOONLIGHT

CAPTIVE HEARTS

Short stories

AN AUTOMATED DEATH:
A STEAMPUNK SHORT STORY

TO CAPTURE A HIGHLANDERS HEART:
The Beginning

Novellas

TO CAPTURE A HIGHLANDER'S HEART:
THE COURTSHIP

COMING SOON!

TO CAPTURE A HIGHLANDER'S HEART:
THE WEDDING NIGHT

Children's Books

WILLY C. SPARKS
THE DRAGON WHO LOST HIS FIRE

HAIKU CLUE (COMING SOON)

CONNECT WITH TERESA ON SUBSTANCE B

Substance B is a new platform for independent authors to directly connect with their readers. Please visit Teresa's Substance B page (substance-b.com/TeresaReasor.html) where you can:

- Sign up for Teresa's newsletter
- Send a message to Teresa
- See all platforms where Teresa's books are sold
- Request autographed eBooks from Teresa

Visit Substance B today to learn more about your favorite independent authors.

Printed in Great Britain
by Amazon.co.uk, Ltd.,
Marston Gate.